THE FRUIT OF THE TREE

Prometheus's Literary Classics Series

Henry Adams	*Esther*
Aristophanes	*Assembly of Women (Ecclesiazusae)*
Charles Brockden Brown	*Wieland, or The Transformation*
Samuel Butler	*Erewhon*
Lewis Carroll	*Phantasmagoria*
Willa Cather	*One of Ours*
Anton Chekov	*Stories of Men*
	Stories of Women
Kate Chopin	*The Awakening*
	Bayou Folk
Nigel Collins, compiler	*Seasons of Life*
Stephen Crane	*Maggie, A Girl of the Streets*
George Eliot	*Scenes of Clerical Life*
F. Scott Fitzgerald	*This Side of Paradise*
Harold Frederic	*The Damnation of Theron Ware*
Frank Harris	*My Life and Loves*
Nathaniel Hawthorne	*The Scarlet Letter*
Henry James	*The Turn of the Screw* and *The Lesson of the Master*
James Joyce	*Exiles*
Ring Lardner Jr.	*The Ecstasy of Owen Muir*
Sinclair Lewis	*Babbitt*
	Main Street
Jack London	*The Star Rover*
Herman Melville	*Battle-Pieces and Aspects of the War*
	The Confidence Man
John Neal	*Rachel Dyer*
Edgar Allan Poe	*Eureka: A Prose Poem*
Sappho	*The Love Songs of Sappho*
Upton Sinclair	*The Moneychangers*
Henry David Thoreau	*Civil Disobedience, Solitude,* and *Life without Principle*
Leo Tolstoy	*Classic Tales and Fables for Children*
Mark Twain	*The Diaries of Adam and Eve*
	Extract from Captain Stormfield's Visit to Heaven
	The Man That Corrupted Hadleyburg
	The Mysterious Stranger
Jules Verne	*Journey Through the Impossible*
Edith Wharton	*The Fruit of the Tree*
Walt Whitman	*Leaves of Grass*
Oscar Wilde	*Intentions*
Émile Zola	*Lourdes*
	Truth

EDITH WHARTON

THE FRUIT OF THE TREE

■

LITERARY CLASSICS

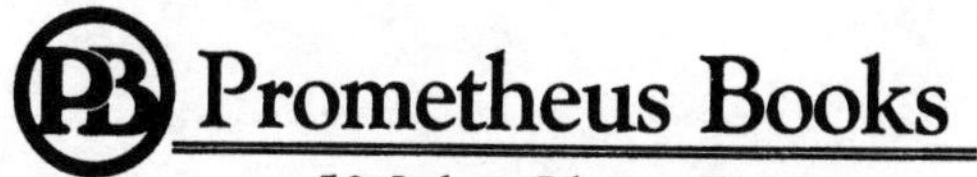

59 John Glenn Drive
Amherst, New York 14228-2197

Published 2004 by Prometheus Books

Inquiries should be addressed to
Prometheus Books
59 John Glenn Drive
Amherst, New York 14228–2197

VOICE: 716–691–0133, EXT. 207; FAX: 716–564–2711.

08 07 06 05 04   5 4 3 2 1

The Fruit of the Tree originally published:
New York: Charles Scribner's Sons, 1907.

Cataloging-in-Publication Data on file at the Library of Congress

ISBN 1–59102–194–4

Printed in the United States of America on acid-free paper.

EDITH NEWBOLD JONES WHARTON was born into an aristocratic, socially prominent family in New York City on January 24, 1862. Her parents, George and Lucretia Jones, were descendants of successful English and Dutch colonists who had made fortunes in shipping, banking, and real estate, which allowed them to live on their inherited wealth. Edith had two older brothers named Frederic and Harry who were twelve and sixteen years when she was born. As a child she was schooled by private tutors and governesses at home in the United States and in Europe, where the family lived for six years after the American Civil War. Returning to New York at the age of ten, young Edith enjoyed the privilege of using her father's extensive library and read extensively. She made up stories that were acted out for her nanny.

After making her debut in society in 1879, Edith married Teddy Wharton, a wealthy Boston banker twelve years older than she, in 1885. With homes in New York, Rhode Island, and Massachusetts, they lived a life of relative ease. Although she had had a book of her own poems published at the age of sixteen, it was not until after she was married that Wharton began to write prolifically. She contributed a few stories and poems to *Harper's*, *Scribner's*, and other magazines throughout the 1890s, and in 1897 she collaborated with architect Ogden Codman Jr. on *The Decoration of Houses*. Her next two books, *The Greater Inclination* (1899) and *Crucial Instances* (1901), were collections of stories.

Wharton's first novel, *The Valley of Decision*, was published in 1902. Her next book, *The House of Mirth* (1905), analyzed the stratified society in which she had been raised and its reaction to social change. The book was critically acclaimed and won her a wide audience. Over the next two decades she wrote such novels as *The Fruit of the Tree* (1907), *The Reef* (1912), *The Custom of the Country* (1913), *Summer* (1917), and *The Age of Innocence* (1920), a depiction of upper-class New York society in the 1870s that won a Pulitzer Prize. Wharton's best-known work is the narrative *Ethan Frome* (1911), which explores the grim realities of the New England farm life she had observed from her comfortable home in Lenox, Massachusetts.

Wharton lived almost exclusively in France after 1907. She divorced her husband in 1912, after discovering that he had taken money from her to support a mistress in Boston. She never remarried. During World War I, Wharton wrote reports for American newspapers. She assisted in organizing the American Hostel for Refugees, and the Children of Flanders Rescue Committee, taking charge of six hundred Belgian children who had to leave their orphanage at the time of the German advance.

Among her later novels are *Twilight Sleep* (1927), *Hudson River Bracketed* (1929), and its sequel, *The Gods Arrive* (1932). An autobiography, *A Backward Glance*, was published in 1934. Edith Wharton continued to write until a stroke took her life on August 11, 1937. She is buried in the American Cemetery at Versailles.

THE FRUIT OF THE TREE

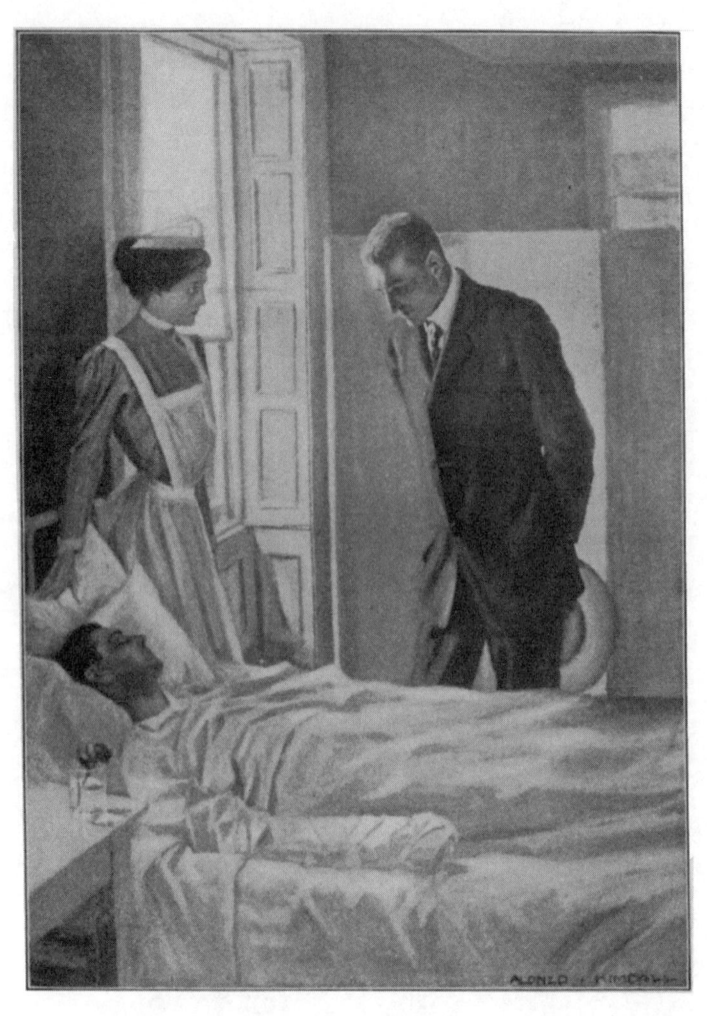

He stood by her in silence, his eyes on the injured man.

ILLUSTRATIONS

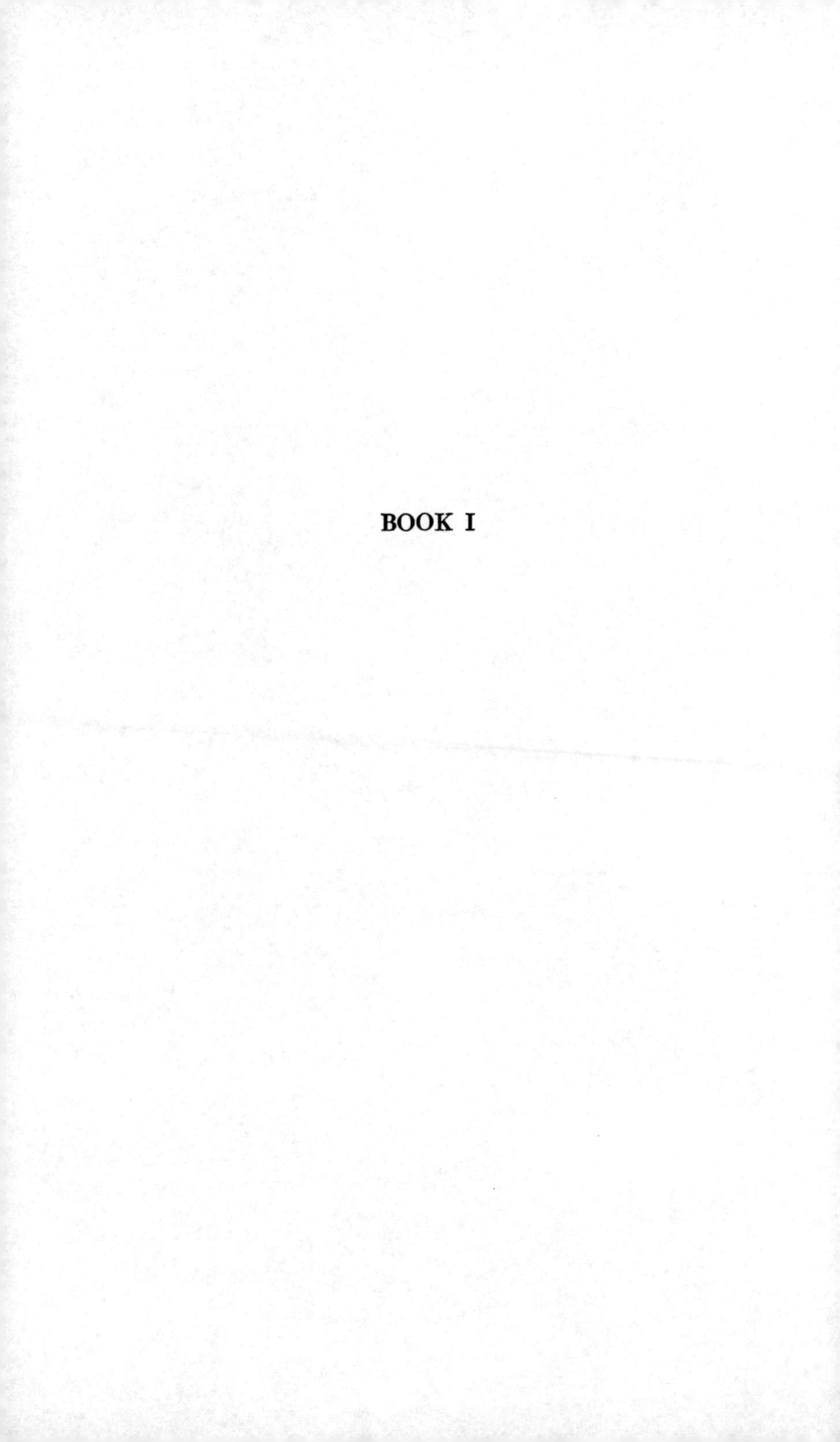

BOOK I

THE

FRUIT OF THE TREE

I

IN the surgical ward of the Hope Hospital at Hanaford, a nurse was bending over a young man whose bandaged right hand and arm lay stretched along the bed.

His head stirred uneasily, and slipping her arm behind him she effected a professional readjustment of the pillows. "Is that better?"

As she leaned over, he lifted his anxious bewildered eyes, deep-sunk under ridges of suffering. "I don't s'pose there's any kind of a show for me, is there?" he asked, pointing with his free hand—the stained seamed hand of the mechanic—to the inert bundle on the quilt.

Her only immediate answer was to wipe the dampness from his forehead; then she said: "We'll talk about that to-morrow."

"Why not now?"

"Because Dr. Disbrow can't tell till the inflammation goes down."

"Will it go down by to-morrow?"

"It will begin to, if you don't excite yourself and keep up the fever."

"Excite myself? I—there's four of 'em at home——"

"Well, then there are four reasons for keeping quiet," she rejoined.

She did not use, in speaking, the soothing inflection of her trade: she seemed to disdain to cajole or trick the sufferer. Her full young voice kept its cool note of authority, her sympathy revealing itself only in the expert touch of her hands and the constant vigilance of her dark steady eyes. This vigilance softened to pity as the patient turned his head away with a groan. His free left hand continued to travel the sheet, clasping and unclasping itself in contortions of feverish unrest. It was as though all the anguish of his mutilation found expression in that lonely hand, left without work in the world now that its mate was useless.

The nurse felt a touch on her shoulder, and rose to face the matron, a sharp-featured woman with a soft intonation.

"This is Mr. Amherst, Miss Brent. The assistant manager from the mills. He wishes to see Dillon."

John Amherst's step was singularly noiseless. The nurse, sensitive by nature and training to all physical characteristics, was struck at once by the contrast between his alert face and figure and the silent way in which he moved. She noticed, too, that the same contrast was repeated in the face itself, its spare energetic outline, with the high nose and compressed lips of the mover of men, being curiously modified by the veiled inward gaze of the grey eyes he turned on her. It was one of the interests of Justine Brent's crowded yet lonely life to attempt a rapid mental classification of the persons she met; but the contradictions in Amherst's face baffled her, and she murmured inwardly "I don't know" as she drew aside to let him approach the bed. He stood by her in silence, his hands clasped behind him, his eyes on the injured man, who lay motionless, as if sunk in a lethargy. The matron, at the call of another nurse, had minced away down the ward, committing Amherst with a glance to Miss Brent; and the two remained alone by the bed.

After a pause, Amherst moved toward the window beyond the empty cot adjoining Dillon's. One of the white screens used to isolate dying patients had been placed against this cot, which was the last at that end of the ward, and the space beyond formed a secluded corner, where a few words could be exchanged out of reach of the eyes in the other beds.

"Is he asleep?" Amherst asked, as Miss Brent joined him.

Miss Brent glanced at him again. His voice betokened not merely education, but something different and deeper—the familiar habit of gentle speech; and his shabby clothes—carefully brushed, but ill-cut and worn along the seams—sat on him easily, and with the same difference.

"The morphine has made him drowsy," she answered. "The wounds were dressed about an hour ago, and the doctor gave him a hypodermic."

"The wounds—how many are there?"

"Besides the hand, his arm is badly torn up to the elbow."

Amherst listened with bent head and frowning brow. "What do you think of the case?"

She hesitated. "Dr. Disbrow hasn't said——"

"And it's not your business to?" He smiled slightly. "I know hospital etiquette. But I have a particular reason for asking." He broke off and looked at her again, his veiled gaze sharpening to a glance of concentrated attention. "You're not one of the regular nurses, are you? Your dress seems to be of a different colour."

She smiled at the "seems to be," which denoted a tardy and imperfect apprehension of the difference between dark-blue linen and white.

"No: I happened to be staying at Hanaford, and hearing that they were in want of a surgical nurse, I offered my help."

Amherst nodded. "So much the better. Is there any place where I can say two words to you?"

"I could hardly leave the ward now, unless Mrs. Ogan comes back."

"I don't care to have you call Mrs. Ogan," he interposed quickly. "When do you go off duty?"

She looked at him in surprise. "If what you want to ask about is—anything connected with the management of things here—you know we're not supposed to talk of our patients outside of the hospital."

"I know. But I am going to ask you to break through the rule—in that poor fellow's behalf."

A protest wavered on her lip, but he held her eyes steadily, with a glint of good-humour behind his determination. "When do you go off duty?"

"At six."

"I'll wait at the corner of South Street and walk a little way with you. Let me put my case, and if you're not convinced you can refuse to answer."

"Very well," she said, without farther hesitation; and Amherst, with a slight nod of farewell, passed through the door near which they had been standing.

II

WHEN Justine Brent emerged from the Hope Hospital the October dusk had fallen and the wide suburban street was almost dark, except when the illuminated bulk of an electric car flashed by under the maples.

She crossed the tracks and approached the narrower

thoroughfare where Amherst awaited her. He hung back a moment, and she was amused to see that he failed to identify the uniformed nurse with the girl in her trim dark dress, soberly complete in all its accessories, who advanced to him, smiling under her little veil.

"Thank you," he said as he turned and walked beside her. "Is this your way?"

"I am staying in Oak Street. But it's just as short to go by Maplewood Avenue."

"Yes; and quieter."

For a few yards they walked on in silence, their long steps falling naturally into time, though Amherst was somewhat taller than his companion.

At length he said: "I suppose you know nothing about the relation between Hope Hospital and the Westmore Mills."

"Only that the hospital was endowed by one of the Westmore family."

"Yes; an old Miss Hope, a great-aunt of Westmore's. But there is more than that between them—all kinds of subterranean passages." He paused, and began again: "For instance, Dr. Disbrow married the sister of our manager's wife."

"Your chief at the mills?"

"Yes," he said with a slight grimace. "So you see, if Truscomb—the manager—thinks one of the mill-hands is only slightly injured, it's natural that his brother-in-law, Dr. Disbrow, should take an optimistic view of the case."

"Natural? I don't know——"

"Don't you think it's natural that a man should be influenced by his wife?"

"Not where his professional honour is concerned."

Amherst smiled. "That sounds very young—if you'll excuse my saying so. Well, I won't go on to insinuate that, Truscomb being high in favour with the Westmores, and the Westmores having a lien on the hospital, Disbrow's position there is also bound up with his taking—more or less—the same view as Truscomb's."

Miss Brent had paused abruptly on the deserted pavement.

"No, don't go on—if you want me to think well of you," she flashed out.

Amherst met the thrust composedly, perceiving, as she turned to face him, that what she resented was not so much his insinuation against his superiors as his allusion to the youthfulness of her sentiments. She was, in fact, as he now noticed, still young enough to dislike being excused for her youth. In her severe uniform of blue linen, her dusky skin darkened by the nurse's cap, and by the pale background of the hospital walls, she had seemed older, more competent and experienced; but he now saw how fresh was the pale curve of her cheek, and how smooth the brow clasped in close waves of hair.

"I began at the wrong end," he acknowledged. "But let me put Dillon's case before you dismiss me."

She softened. "It is only because of my interest in that poor fellow that I am here——"

"Because you think he needs help—and that you can help him?"

But she held back once more. "Please tell me about him first," she said, walking on.

Amherst met the request with another question. "I wonder how much you know about factory life?"

"Oh, next to nothing. Just what I've managed to pick up in these two days at the hospital."

He glanced at her small determined profile under its dark roll of hair, and said, half to himself: "That might be a good deal."

She took no notice of this, and he went on: "Well, I won't try to put the general situation before you, though Dillon's accident is really the result of it. He works in the carding room, and on the day of the accident his 'card' stopped suddenly, and he put his hand behind him to get a tool he needed out of his trouser-pocket. He reached back a little too far, and the card behind him caught his hand in its million of diamond-pointed wires. Truscomb and the overseer of the room maintain that the accident was due to his own carelessness; but the hands say that it was caused by the fact of the cards being too near together, and that just such an accident was bound to happen sooner or later."

Miss Brent drew an eager breath. "And what do *you* say?"

"That they're right: the carding-room is shamefully overcrowded. Dillon hasn't been in it long—he worked his way up at the mills from being a bobbin-boy—and he hadn't yet learned how cautious a man must be in there. The cards are so close to each other that even the old hands run narrow risks, and it takes the cleverest operative some time to learn that he must calculate every movement to a fraction of an inch."

"But why do they crowd the rooms in that way?"

"To get the maximum of profit out of the minimum of floor-space. It costs more to increase the floor-space than to maim an operative now and then."

"I see. Go on," she murmured.

"That's the first point; here is the second. Dr. Disbrow told Truscomb this morning that Dillon's hand would certainly be saved, and that he might get back to work in a couple of months if the company would present him with an artificial finger or two."

Miss Brent faced him with a flush of indignation. "Mr. Amherst—who gave you this version of Dr. Disbrow's report?"

"The manager himself."

"Verbally?"

"No—he showed me Disbrow's letter."

For a moment or two they walked on silently through the quiet street; then she said, in a voice still stirred with feeling: "As I told you this afternoon, Dr. Disbrow has said nothing in my hearing."

"And Mrs. Ogan?"

"Oh, Mrs. Ogan—" Her voice broke in a ripple of irony. "Mrs. Ogan 'feels it to be such a beautiful dispensation, my dear, that, owing to a death that very morning in the surgical ward, we happened to have a bed ready for the poor man within three hours of the accident.'" She had exchanged her deep throat-tones for a high reedy note which perfectly simulated the matron's lady-like inflections.

Amherst, at the change, turned on her with a boyish burst of laughter: she joined in it, and for a moment they were blent in that closest of unions, the discovery of a common fund of humour.

She was the first to grow grave. "That three hours' delay didn't help matters—how is it there is no emergency hospital at the mills?"

Amherst laughed again, but in a different key. "That's part of the larger question, which we haven't time for now." He waited a moment, and then added: "You've not yet given me your own impression of Dillon's case."

"You shall have it, if you saw that letter. Dillon will certainly lose his hand—and probably the whole arm." She spoke with a thrilling of her slight frame that transformed the dispassionate professional into a girl shaken with indignant pity.

Amherst stood still before her. "Good God! Never anything but useless lumber?"

"Never——"

"And he won't die?"

"Alas!"

"He has a consumptive wife and three children. She ruined her health swallowing cotton-dust at the factory," Amherst continued.

"So she told me yesterday."

He turned in surprise. "You've had a talk with her?"

"I went out to Westmore last night. I was haunted by her face when she came to the hospital. She looks forty, but she told me she was only twenty-six." Miss Brent paused to steady her voice. "It's the curse of my trade that it's always tempting me to interfere in cases where I can do no possible good. The fact is, I'm not fit to be a nurse—I shall live and die a wretched sentimentalist!" she ended, with an angry dash at the tears on her veil.

Her companion walked on in silence till she had regained her composure. Then he said: "What did you think of Westmore?"

"I think it's one of the worst places I ever saw—and I am not unused to slums. It looks so dead. The slums of big cities are much more cheerful."

He made no answer, and after a moment she asked: "Does the cotton-dust always affect the lungs?"

"It's likely to, where there is the least phthisical tendency. But of course the harm could be immensely reduced by taking up the old rough floors which hold the dust, and by thorough cleanliness and ventilation."

"What does the company do in such cases? Where an operative breaks down at twenty-five?"

"The company says there was a phthisical tendency."

"And will they give nothing in return for the two lives they have taken?"

"They will probably pay for Dillon's care at the hospital, and they have taken the wife back as a scrubber."

"To clean those uncleanable floors? She's not fit for it!"

"She must work, fit for it or not; and there is less strain in scrubbing than in bending over the looms or cards. The pay is lower, of course, but she's very grateful for being taken back at all, now that he's no longer a first-class worker."

Miss Brent's face glowed with a fine wrath. "She can't possibly stand more than two or three months of it without breaking down!"

"Well, you see they've told her that in less than that time her husband will be at work again."

"And what will the company do for them when the wife is a hopeless invalid, and the husband a cripple?"

Amherst again uttered the dry laugh with which he had met her suggestion of an emergency hospital. "I know what I should do if I could get anywhere near Dillon—give him an overdose of morphine, and let the widow collect his life-insurance, and make a fresh start."

She looked at him curiously. "Should you, I wonder?"

"If I saw the suffering as you see it, and knew the circumstances as I know them, I believe I should feel justified—" He broke off. "In your work, don't you ever feel tempted to set a poor devil free?"

She mused. "One might. . . but perhaps the professional instinct to save would always come first."

"To save—what? When all the good of life is gone?"

"I daresay," she sighed, "poor Dillon would do it himself if he could—when he realizes that all the good *is* gone."

"Yes, but he can't do it himself; and it's the irony of such cases that his employers, after ruining his life, will do all they can to patch up the ruins."

"But that at least ought to count in their favour."

"Perhaps; if—" He paused, as though reluctant

to lay himself open once more to the charge of uncharitableness; and suddenly she exclaimed, looking about her: "I didn't notice we had walked so far down Maplewood Avenue!"

They had turned a few minutes previously into the wide thoroughfare crowning the high ground which is covered by the residential quarter of Hanaford. Here the spacious houses, withdrawn behind shrubberies and lawns, revealed in their silhouettes every form of architectural experiment, from the symmetrical pre-Revolutionary structure, with its classic portico and clipped box-borders, to the latest outbreak in boulders and Moorish tiles.

Amherst followed his companion's glance with surprise. "We *have* gone a block or two out of our way. I always forget where I am when I'm talking about anything that interests me."

Miss Brent looked at her watch. "My friends don't dine till seven, and I can get home in time by taking a Grove Street car," she said.

"If you don't mind walking a little farther you can take a Liberty Street car instead. They run oftener, and you will get home just as soon."

She made a gesture of assent, and as they walked on he continued: "I haven't yet explained why I am so anxious to get an unbiassed opinion of Dillon's case."

She looked at him in surprise. "What you've told

me about Dr. Disbrow and your manager is surely enough."

"Well, hardly, considering that I am Truscomb's subordinate. I shouldn't have committed a breach of professional etiquette, or asked you to do so, if I hadn't a hope of bettering things; but I have, and that is why I've held on at Westmore for the last few months, instead of getting out of it altogether."

"I'm glad of that," she said quickly.

"The owner of the mills—young Richard Westmore—died last winter," he went on, "and my hope—it's no more—is that the new broom may sweep a little cleaner."

"Who is the new broom?"

"Westmore left everything to his widow, and she is coming here to-morrow to look into the management of the mills."

"Coming? She doesn't live here, then?"

"At Hanaford? Heaven forbid! It's an anomaly nowadays for the employer to live near the employed. The Westmores have always lived in New York—and I believe they have a big place on Long Island."

"Well, at any rate she *is* coming, and that ought to be a good sign. Did she never show any interest in the mills during her husband's life?"

"Not as far as I know. I've been at Westmore three years, and she's not been seen there in my time.

She is very young, and Westmore himself didn't care. It was a case of inherited money. He drew the dividends, and Truscomb did the rest."

Miss Brent reflected. "I don't know much about the constitution of companies—but I suppose Mrs. Westmore doesn't unite all the offices in her own person. Is there no one to stand between Truscomb and the operatives?"

"Oh, the company, on paper, shows the usual official hierarchy. Richard Westmore, of course, was president, and since his death the former treasurer—Halford Gaines—has replaced him, and his son, Westmore Gaines, has been appointed treasurer. You can see by the names that it's all in the family. Halford Gaines married a Miss Westmore, and represents the clan at Hanaford—leads society, and keeps up the social credit of the name. As treasurer, Mr. Halford Gaines kept strictly to his special business, and always refused to interfere between Truscomb and the operatives. As president he will probably follow the same policy, the more so as it fits in with his inherited respect for the *status quo*, and his blissful ignorance of economics."

"And the new treasurer—young Gaines? Is there no hope of his breaking away from the family tradition?"

"Westy Gaines has a better head than his father; but he hates Hanaford and the mills, and his chief object in life is to be taken for a New Yorker. So far he hasn't been here much, except for the quarterly meetings, and his routine work is done by another cousin —you perceive that Westmore is a nest of nepotism."

Miss Brent's work among the poor had developed her interest in social problems, and she followed these details attentively.

"Well, the outlook is not encouraging, but perhaps Mrs. Westmore's coming will make a change. I suppose she has more power than any one."

"She might have, if she chose to exert it, for her husband was really the whole company. The official cousins hold only a few shares apiece."

"Perhaps, then, her visit will open her eyes. Who knows but poor Dillon's case may help others—prove a beautiful dispensation, as Mrs. Ogan would say?"

"It does come terribly pat as an illustration of some of the abuses I want to have remedied. The difficulty will be to get the lady's ear. That's her house we're coming to, by the way."

An electric street-lamp irradiated the leafless trees and stone gate-posts of the building before them. Though gardens extended behind it, the house stood so near the pavement that only two short flights of steps intervened between the gate-posts and the portico. Light shone from every window of the pompous rusticated façade—in the turreted "Tuscan villa" style of the 'fifties—and as Miss Brent and Amherst approached, their advance was checked by a group of persons who were just descending from two carriages at the door.

The lamp-light showed every detail of dress and countenance in the party, which consisted of two men, one slightly lame, with a long white moustache and a distinguished nose, the other short, lean and professional, and of two ladies and their laden attendants.

"Why, that must be her party arriving!" Miss Brent exclaimed; and as she spoke the younger of the two ladies, turning back to her maid, exposed to the glare of the electric light a fair pale face shadowed by the projection of her widow's veil.

"Is that Mrs. Westmore?" Miss Brent whispered; and as Amherst muttered: "I suppose so; I've never seen her——" she continued excitedly: "She looks so like—do you know what her name was before she married?"

He drew his brows together in a hopeless effort of remembrance. "I don't know—I must have heard—but I never can recall people's names."

"That's bad, for a leader of men!" she said mockingly, and he answered, as though touched on a sore point: "I mean people who don't count. I never forget an operative's name or face."

"One can never tell who may be going to count," she rejoined sententiously.

He dwelt on this in silence while they walked on

catching as they passed a glimpse of the red-carpeted Westmore hall on which the glass doors were just being closed. At length he roused himself to ask: "Does Mrs. Westmore look like some one you know?"

"I fancied so—a girl who was at the Sacred Heart in Paris with me. But isn't this my corner?" she exclaimed, as they turned into another street, down which a laden car was descending.

Its approach left them time for no more than a hurried hand-clasp, and when Miss Brent had been absorbed into the packed interior her companion, as his habit was, stood for a while where she had left him, gazing at some indefinite point in space; then, waking to a sudden consciousness of his surroundings, he walked off toward the centre of the town.

At the junction of two business streets he met an empty car marked "Westmore," and springing into it, seated himself in a corner and drew out a pocket Shakespeare. He read on, indifferent to his surroundings, till the car left the asphalt streets and illuminated shop-fronts for a grey intermediate region of mud and macadam. Then he pocketed his volume and sat looking out into the gloom.

The houses grew less frequent, with darker gaps of night between; and the rare street-lamps shone on cracked pavements, crooked telegraph-poles, hoardings tapestried with patent-medicine posters, and all the mean desolation of an American industrial suburb. Farther on there came a weed-grown field or two, then a row of operatives' houses, the showy gables of the "Eldorado" road-house—the only building in Westmore on which fresh paint was freely lavished—then the company "store," the machine shops and other out-buildings, the vast forbidding bulk of the factories looming above the river-bend, and the sudden neatness of the manager's turf and privet hedges. The scene was so familiar to Amherst that he had lost the habit of comparison, and his absorption in the moral and material needs of the workers sometimes made him forget the outward setting of their lives. But to-night he recalled the nurse's comment—"it looks so dead"—and the phrase roused him to a fresh perception of the scene. With sudden disgust he saw the sordidness of it all—the poor monotonous houses, the trampled grass-banks, the lean dogs prowling in refuse-heaps, the reflection of a crooked gas-lamp in a stagnant loop of the river; and he asked himself how it was possible to put any sense of moral beauty into lives bounded forever by the low horizon of the factory. There is a fortuitous ugliness that has life and hope in it: the ugliness of overcrowded city streets, of the rush and drive of packed activities; but this out-spread meanness of the suburban working colony, uncircumscribed by any pressure of surrounding life, and sunk into blank acceptance of its isolation, its banishment from beauty and variety and surprise, seemed to Amherst the very negation of hope and life.

"She's right," he mused—"it's dead—stone dead: there isn't a drop of wholesome blood left in it."

The Moosuc River valley, in the hollow of which, for that river's sake, the Westmore mills had been planted, lingered in the memory of pre-industrial Hanaford as the pleasantest suburb of the town. Here, beyond a region of orchards and farm-houses, several "leading citizens" had placed, above the river-bank, their prim wood-cut "residences," with porticoes and terraced lawns; and from the chief of these, Hopewood, brought into the Westmore family by the Miss Hope who had married an earlier Westmore, the grim mill-village had been carved. The pillared "residences" had, after this, inevitably fallen to base uses; but the old house at Hopewood, in its wooded grounds, remained, neglected but intact, beyond the first bend of the river, deserted as a dwelling but "held" in anticipation of rising values, when the inevitable growth of Westmore should increase the demand for small building lots. Whenever Amherst's eyes were refreshed by the hanging foliage above the roofs of Westmore, he longed to convert the abandoned country-seat into a park and playground for the mill-hands; but he knew that the company counted on the gradual sale of Hopewood as a source of profit. No—the mill-town would not grow beautiful as it grew larger—rather, in obedience to the grim law of industrial prosperity, it would soon lose its one lingering grace and spread out in unmitigated ugliness, devouring green fields and shaded slopes like some insect-plague consuming the land. The conditions were familiar enough to Amherst; and their apparent inevitableness mocked the hopes he had based on Mrs. Westmore's arrival.

"Where every stone is piled on another, through the whole stupid structure of selfishness and egotism, how can one be pulled out without making the whole thing topple? And whatever they're blind to, they always see that," he mused, reaching up for the strap of the car.

He walked a few yards beyond the manager's house, and turned down a side street lined with scattered cottages. Approaching one of these by a gravelled path he pushed open the door, and entered a sitting-room where a green-shaded lamp shone pleasantly on bookshelves and a crowded writing-table.

A brisk little woman in black, laying down the evening paper as she rose, lifted her hands to his tall shoulders.

"Well, mother," he said, stooping to her kiss.

"You're late, John," she smiled back at him, not reproachfully, but with affection.

She was a wonderfully compact and active creature, with face so young and hair so white that she looked as unreal as a stage mother till a close view revealed the fine lines that experience had drawn about her mouth and eyes. The eyes themselves, brightly black and glancing, had none of the veiled depths of her son's gaze. Their look was outward, on a world which had dealt her hard blows and few favours, but in which her interest was still fresh, amused and unabated.

Amherst glanced at his watch. "Never mind—Duplain will be later still. I had to go into Hanaford, and he is replacing me at the office."

"So much the better, dear: we can have a minute to ourselves. Sit down and tell me what kept you."

She picked up her knitting as she spoke, having the kind of hands that find repose in ceaseless small activities. Her son could not remember a time when he had not seen those small hands in motion—shaping garments, darning rents, repairing furniture, exploring the inner economy of clocks. "I make a sort of rag-carpet of the odd minutes," she had once explained to a friend who wondered at her turning to her needle-work in the moment's interval between other tasks.

Amherst threw himself wearily into a chair. "I was trying to find out something about Dillon's case," he said.

His mother turned a quick glance toward the door, rose to close it, and reseated herself.

"Well?"

"I managed to have a talk with his nurse when she went off duty this evening."

"The nurse? I wonder you could get her to speak."

"Luckily she's not the regular incumbent, but a volunteer who happened to be here on a visit. As it was, I had some difficulty in making her talk—till I told her of Disbrow's letter."

Mrs. Amherst lifted her bright glance from the needles. "He's very bad, then?"

"Hopelessly maimed!"

She shivered and cast down her eyes. "Do you suppose she really knows?"

"She struck me as quite competent to judge."

"A volunteer, you say, here on a visit? What is her name?"

He raised his head with a vague look. "I never thought of asking her."

Mrs. Amherst laughed. "How like you! Did she say with whom she was staying?"

"I think she said in Oak Street—but she didn't mention any name."

Mrs. Amherst wrinkled her brows thoughtfully. "I wonder if she's not the thin dark girl I saw the other day with Mrs. Harry Dressel. Was she tall and rather handsome?"

"I don't know," murmured Amherst indifferently. As a rule he was humorously resigned to his mother's habit of deserting the general for the particular, and following some irrelevant thread of association in utter disregard of the main issue. But to-night, preoccupied with his subject, and incapable of conceiving how any-one else could be unaffected by it, he resented her in-difference as a sign of incurable frivolity.

"How she can live close to such suffering and forget it!" was his thought; then, with a movement of self-reproach, he remembered that the work flying through her fingers was to take shape as a garment for one of the infant Dillons. "She takes her pity out in action, like that quiet nurse, who was as cool as a drum-major till she took off her uniform—and then!" His face softened at the recollection of the girl's outbreak. Much as he admired, in theory, the woman who kept a calm exterior in emergencies, he had all a man's desire to know that the springs of feeling lay close to the unruffled surface.

Mrs. Amherst had risen and crossed over to his chair. She leaned on it a moment, pushing the tossed brown hair from his forehead.

"John, have you considered what you mean to do next?"

He threw back his head to meet her gaze.

"About this Dillon case," she continued. "How are all these investigations going to help you?"

Their eyes rested on each other for a moment; then he said coldly: "You are afraid I am going to lose my place."

She flushed like a girl and murmured: "It's not the kind of place I ever wanted to see you in!"

"I know it," he returned in a gentler tone, clasping one of the hands on his chair-back. "I ought to have followed a profession, like my grandfather; but my father's blood was too strong in me. I should never have been content as anything but a working-man."

"How can you call your father a working-man? He had a genius for mechanics, and if he had lived he would have been as great in his way as any statesman or lawyer."

Amherst smiled. "Greater, to my thinking; but he gave me his hard-working hands without the genius to create with them. I wish I had inherited more from him, or less; but I must make the best of what I am, rather than try to be somebody else." He laid her hand caressingly against his cheek. "It's hard on you, mother—but you must bear with me."

"I have never complained, John; but now you've chosen your work, it's natural that I should want you to stick to it."

He rose with an impatient gesture. "Never fear; I could easily get another job——"

"What? If Truscomb black-listed you? Do you forget that Scotch overseer who was here when we came?"

"And whom Truscomb hounded out of the trade? I remember him," said Amherst grimly; "but I have an idea I am going to do the hounding this time."

His mother sighed, but her reply was cut short by the noisy opening of the outer door. Amherst seemed to hear the sound with relief. "There's Duplain," he said, going into the passage; but on the threshold he encountered, not the young Alsatian overseer who boarded with them, but a small boy who said breathlessly: "Mr. Truscomb wants you to come down bimeby."

"This evening? To the office?"

"No—he's sick a-bed."

The blood rushed to Amherst's face, and he had to press his lips close to check an exclamation. "Say I'll come as soon as I've had supper," he said.

The boy vanished, and Amherst turned back to the sitting-room. "Truscomb's ill—he has sent for me; and I saw Mrs. Westmore arriving tonight! Have supper, mother—we won't wait for Duplain." His face still glowed with excitement, and his eyes were dark with the concentration of his inward vision.

"Oh, John, John!" Mrs. Amherst sighed, crossing the passage to the kitchen.

III

AT the manager's door Amherst was met by Mrs. Truscomb, a large flushed woman in a soiled wrapper and diamond earrings.

"Mr. Truscomb's very sick. He ought not to see you. The doctor thinks—" she began.

Dr. Disbrow, at this point, emerged from the sitting-room. He was a pale man, with a beard of mixed grey-and-drab, and a voice of the same indeterminate quality.

"Good evening, Mr. Amherst. Truscomb is pretty poorly—on the edge of pneumonia, I'm afraid. As he seems anxious to see you I think you'd better go up for two minutes—not more, please." He paused, and went on with a smile: "You won't excite him, of course—nothing unpleasant——"

"He's worried himself sick over that wretched Dillon," Mrs. Truscomb interposed, draping her wrapper majestically about an indignant bosom.

"That's it—puts too much heart into his work. But we'll have Dillon all right before long," the physician genially declared.

Mrs. Truscomb, with a reluctant gesture, led Amherst up the handsomely carpeted stairs to the room where her husband lay, a prey to the cares of office. She ushered the young man in, and withdrew to the next room, where he heard her coughing at intervals, as if to remind him that he was under observation.

The manager of the Westmore mills was not the type of man that Amherst's comments on his superior suggested. As he sat propped against the pillows, with a brick-red flush on his cheek-bones, he seemed at first glance to belong to the innumerable army of American business men—the sallow, undersized, lack-lustre drudges who have never lifted their heads from the ledger. Even his eye, now bright with fever, was dull and non-committal in daily life; and perhaps only the ramifications of his wrinkles could have revealed what particular ambitions had seamed his soul.

"Good evening, Amherst. I'm down with a confounded cold."

"I'm sorry to hear it," the young man forced himself to say.

"Can't get my breath—that's the trouble." Truscomb paused and gasped. "I've just heard that Mrs. Westmore is here—and I want you to go round—to-morrow morning—" He had to break off once more.

"Yes, sir," said Amherst, his heart leaping.

"Needn't see her—ask for her father, Mr. Langhope. Tell him what the doctor says—I'll be on my legs in a day or two—ask 'em to wait till I can take 'em over the mills."

He shot one of his fugitive glances at his assistant, and held up a bony hand. "Wait a minute. On your way there, stop and notify Mr. Gaines. He was to meet them here. You understand?"

"Yes, sir," said Amherst; and at that moment Mrs. Truscomb appeared on the threshold.

"I must ask you to come now, Mr. Amherst," she began haughtily; but a glance from her husband reduced her to a heaving pink nonentity.

"Hold on, Amherst. I hear you've been in to Hanaford. Did you go to the hospital?"

"Ezra—" his wife murmured: he looked through her.

"Yes," said Amherst.

Truscomb's face seemed to grow smaller and dryer. He transferred his look from his wife to his assistant.

"All right. You'll just bear in mind that it's Disbrow's business to report Dillon's case to Mrs. Westmore? You're to confine yourself to my message. Is that clear?"

"Perfectly clear. Goodnight," Amherst answered, as he turned to follow Mrs. Truscomb.

That same evening, four persons were seated under the bronze chandelier in the red satin drawing-room of the Westmore mansion. One of the four, the young lady in widow's weeds whose face had arrested Miss Brent's attention that afternoon, rose from a massively upholstered sofa and drifted over to the fireplace near which her father sat.

"Didn't I tell you it was awful, father?" she sighed, leaning despondently against the high carved mantelpiece surmounted by a bronze clock in the form of an obelisk.

Mr. Langhope, who sat smoking, with one faultlessly-clad leg crossed on the other, and his ebony stick reposing against the arm of his chair, raised his clear ironical eyes to her face.

"As an archæologist," he said, with a comprehensive wave of his hand, "I find it positively interesting. I should really like to come here and dig."

There were no lamps in the room, and the numerous gas-jets of the chandelier shed their lights impartially on ponderously framed canvases of the Bay of Naples and the Hudson in Autumn, on Carrara busts and bronze Indians on velvet pedestals.

"All this," murmured Mr. Langhope, "is getting to be as rare as the giant sequoias. In another fifty years we shall have collectors fighting for that Bay of Naples."

Bessy Westmore turned from him impatiently. When she felt deeply on any subject her father's flippancy annoyed her.

"*You* can see, Maria," she said, seating herself beside the other lady of the party, "why I couldn't possibly live here."

Mrs. Eustace Ansell, immediately after dinner, had bent her slender back above the velvet-covered writing-table, where an inkstand of Vienna ormolu offered its empty cup to her pen. Being habitually charged with a voluminous correspondence, she had foreseen this contingency and met it by despatching her maid for her own writing-case, which was now outspread before her in all its complex neatness; but at Bessy's appeal she wiped her pen, and turned a sympathetic gaze on her companion.

Mrs. Ansell's face drew all its charm from its adaptability. It was a different face to each speaker: now kindling with irony, now gently maternal, now charged with abstract meditation—and few paused to reflect that, in each case, it was merely the mirror held up to some one else's view of life.

"It needs doing over," she admitted, following the widow's melancholy glance about the room. "But you are a spoilt child to complain. Think of having a house of your own to come to, instead of having to put up at the Hanaford hotel!"

Mrs. Westmore's attention was arrested by the first part of the reply.

"Doing over? Why in the world should I do it over? No one could expect me to come here *now*—could they, Mr. Tredegar?" she exclaimed, transferring her appeal to the fourth member of the party.

Mr. Tredegar, the family lawyer, who had deemed it his duty to accompany the widow on her visit of inspection, was strolling up and down the room with short pompous steps, a cigar between his lips, and his arms behind him. He cocked his sparrow-like head, scanned the offending apartment, and terminated his survey by resting his eyes on Mrs. Westmore's charming petulant face.

"It all depends," he replied axiomatically, "how large an income you require."

Mr. Tredegar uttered this remark with the air of one who pronounces on an important point in law: his lightest observation seemed a decision handed down from the bench to which he had never ascended. He restored the cigar to his lips, and sought approval in Mrs. Ansell's expressive eye.

"Ah, that's it, Bessy. You've that to remember," the older lady murmured, as if struck by the profundity of the remark.

Mrs. Westmore made an impatient gesture. "We've always had money enough—Dick was perfectly satisfied." Her voice trembled a little on her husband's name. "And you don't know what the place is like by daylight—and the people who come to call!"

"Of course you needn't see any one now, dear," Mrs. Ansell reminded her, "except the Halford Gaineses."

"I am sure they're bad enough. Juliana Gaines will say: 'My dear, is that the way widows' veils are worn in New York this autumn?' and Halford will insist on our going to one of those awful family dinners, all Madeira and terrapin."

"It's too early for terrapin," Mrs. Ansell smiled consolingly; but Bessy had reverted to her argument.

"Besides, what difference would my coming here make? I shall never understand anything about business," she declared.

Mr. Tredegar pondered, and once more removed his cigar. "The necessity has never arisen. But now that you find yourself in almost sole control of a large property——"

Mr. Langhope laughed gently. "Apply yourself, Bessy. Bring your masterly intellect to bear on the industrial problem."

Mrs. Ansell restored the innumerable implements to her writing-case, and laid her arm with a caressing gesture on Mrs. Westmore's shoulder. "Don't tease her. She's tired, and she misses the baby."

"I shall get a telegram tomorrow morning," exclaimed the young mother, brightening.

"Of course you will. 'Cicely has just eaten two boiled eggs and a bowl of porridge, and is bearing up wonderfully.'"

She drew Mrs. Westmore persuasively to her feet, but the widow refused to relinquish her hold on her grievance.

"You all think I'm extravagant and careless about money," she broke out, addressing the room in general from the shelter of Mrs. Ansell's embrace; "but I know one thing: If I had my way I should begin to economize by selling this horrible house, instead of leaving it shut up from one year's end to another."

Her father looked up: proposals of retrenchment always struck him as business-like when they did not affect his own expenditure. "What do you think of that, eh, Tredegar?"

The eminent lawyer drew in his thin lips. "From the point of view of policy, I think unfavourably of it," he pronounced.

Bessy's face clouded, and Mrs. Ansell argued gently: "Really, it's too late to look so far into the future. Remember, my dear, that we are due at the mills to-morrow at ten."

The reminder that she must rise early had the effect of hastening Mrs. Westmore's withdrawal, and the two ladies, after an exchange of goodnights, left the men to their cigars.

Mr. Langhope was the first to speak.

"Bessy's as hopelessly vague about business as I am, Tredegar. Why the deuce Westmore left her everything outright—but he was only a heedless boy himself."

"Yes. The way he allowed things to go, it's a wonder there was anything to leave. This Truscomb must be an able fellow."

"Devoted to Dick's interests, I've always understood."

"He makes the mills pay well, at any rate, and that's not so easy nowadays. But on general principles it's as well he should see that we mean to look into everything thoroughly. Of course Halford Gaines will never be more than a good figure-head, but Truscomb must be made to understand that Mrs. Westmore intends to interest herself personally in the business."

"Oh, by all means—of course—" Mr. Langhope assented, his light smile stiffening into a yawn at the mere suggestion.

He rose with an effort, supporting himself on his stick. "I think I'll turn in myself. There's not a readable book in that God-forsaken library, and I believe Maria Ansell has gone off with my volume of Loti."

The next morning, when Amherst presented himself at the Westmore door, he had decided to follow his chief's instructions to the letter, and ask for Mr. Langhope only. The decision had cost him a struggle, for his heart was big with its purpose; but though he knew that he must soon place himself in open opposition to Truscomb, he recognized the prudence of deferring the declaration of war as long as possible

On his round of the mills, that morning, he had paused in the room where Mrs. Dillon knelt beside her mop and pail, and had found her, to his surprise, comparatively reassured and cheerful. Dr. Disbrow, she told him, had been in the previous evening, and had told her to take heart about Jim, and left her enough money to get along for a week—and a wonderful new cough-mixture that he'd put up for her special. Amherst found it difficult to listen calmly, with the nurse's words still in his ears, and the sight before him of Mrs. Dillon's lean shoulder-blades travelling painfully up and down with the sweep of the mop.

"I don't suppose that cost Truscomb ten dollars," he said to himself, as the lift lowered him to the factory door; but another voice argued that he had no right to accuse Disbrow of acting as his brother-in-law's agent, when the gift to Mrs. Dillon might have been prompted by his own kindness of heart.

"And what prompted the lie about her husband? Well, perhaps he's an incurable optimist," he summed up, springing into the Hanaford car.

By the time he reached Mrs. Westmore's door his wrath had subsided, and he felt that he had himself well in hand. He had taken unusual pains with his appearance that morning—or rather his mother, learning of the errand on which Truscomb had sent him, had laid out his carefully-brushed Sunday clothes, and adjusted his tie with skilful fingers. "You'd really be handsome, Johnny, if you were only a little vainer," she said, pushing him away to survey the result; and when he stared at her, repeating: "I never heard that vanity made a man better-looking," she responded gaily: "Oh, up to a certain point, because it teaches him how to use what he's got. So remember," she charged him, as he smiled and took up his hat, "that you're going to see a pretty young woman, and that you're not a hundred years old yourself."

"I'll try to," he answered, humouring her, "but as I've been forbidden to ask for her, I am afraid your efforts will be wasted."

The servant to whom he gave his message showed him into the library, with a request that he should wait; and there, to his surprise, he found, not the white-moustached gentleman whom he had guessed the night before to be Mr. Langhope, but a young lady in deep black, who turned on him a look of not unfriendly enquiry.

It was not Bessy's habit to anticipate the clock; but her distaste for her surroundings, and the impatience to have done with the tedious duties awaiting her, had sent her downstairs before the rest of the party. Her life had been so free from tiresome obligations that she had but a small stock of patience to meet them with; and already, after a night at Hanaford, she was pining to get back to the comforts of her own country-house, the soft rut of her daily habits, the funny chatter of her little girl, the long stride of her Irish hunter across the Hempstead plains—to everything, in short, that made it conceivably worth while to get up in the morning.

The servant who ushered in Amherst, thinking the room empty, had not mentioned his name; and for a moment he and his hostess examined each other in silence, Bessy puzzled at the unannounced appearance of a good-looking young man who might have been some one she had met and forgotten, while Amherst felt his self-possession slipping away into the depths of a pair of eyes so dark-lashed and deeply blue that his only thought was one of wonder at his previous indifference to women's eyes.

"Mrs. Westmore?" he asked, restored to self-command by the perception that his longed-for opportunity was at hand; and Bessy, his voice confirming the inference she had drawn from his appearance, replied with a smile: "I am Mrs. Westmore. But if you have come to see me, I ought to tell you that in a moment I shall be obliged to go out to our mills. I have a business appointment with our manager, but if——"

She broke off, gracefully waiting for him to insert his explanation.

"I have come from the manager; I am John Amherst—your assistant manager," he added, as the mention of his name apparently conveyed no enlightenment.

Mrs. Westmore's face changed, and she let slip a

murmur of surprise that would certainly have flattered Amherst's mother if she could have heard it; but it had an opposite effect on the young man, who inwardly accused himself of having tried to disguise his trade by not putting on his everyday clothes.

"How stupid of me! I took you for—I had no idea; I didn't expect Mr. Truscomb here," his employer faltered in embarrassment; then their eyes met and both smiled.

"Mr. Truscomb sent me to tell you that he is ill, and will not be able to show you the mills today. I didn't mean to ask for you—I was told to give the message to Mr. Langhope," Amherst scrupulously explained, trying to repress the sudden note of joy in his voice.

He was subject to the unobservant man's acute flashes of vision, and Mrs. Westmore's beauty was like a blinding light abruptly turned on eyes subdued to obscurity. As he spoke, his glance passed from her face to her hair, and remained caught in its meshes. He had never seen such hair—it did not seem to grow in the usual orderly way, but bubbled up all over her head in independent clusters of brightness, breaking, about the brow, the temples, the nape, into little irrelevant waves and eddies of light, with dusky hollows of softness where the hand might plunge. It takes but the throb of a nerve to carry such a complex impression from the eye to the mind, but the object of the throb had perhaps felt the electric flash of its passage; for her colour rose while Amherst spoke.

"Ah, here is my father now," she said with a vague accent of relief, as Mr. Langhope's stick was heard tapping its way across the hall.

When he entered, accompanied by Mrs. Ansell, his sharp glance of surprise at her visitor told her that he was as much misled as herself, and gave her a sense of being agreeably justified in her blunder. "If *father* thinks you're a gentleman——" her shining eyes seemed to say, as she explained: "This is Mr. Amherst, father: Mr. Truscomb has sent him."

"Mr. Amherst?" Langhope, with extended hand, echoed affably but vaguely; and it became clear that neither Mrs. Westmore nor her father had ever before heard the name of their assistant manager.

The discovery stung Amherst to a somewhat unreasoning resentment; and while he was trying to subordinate this sentiment to the larger feelings with which he had entered the house, Mrs. Ansell, turning her eyes on him, said gently: "Your name is unusual. I had a friend named Lucy Warne who married a very clever man—a mechanical genius——"

Amherst's face cleared. "My father *was* a genius; and my mother is Lucy Warne," he said, won by the soft look and the persuasive voice.

"What a delightful coincidence! We were girls together at Albany. You must remember Judge Warne?" she said, turning to Mr. Langhope, who, twirling his white moustache, murmured, a shade less cordially: "Of course—of course—delightful—most interesting."

Amherst did not notice the difference. His perceptions were already enveloped in the caress that emanated from Mrs. Ansell's voice and smile; and he only asked himself vaguely if it were possible that this graceful woman, with her sunny autumnal air, could really be his mother's contemporary. But the question brought an instant reaction of bitterness.

"Poverty is the only thing that makes people old nowadays," he reflected, painfully conscious of his own share in the hardships his mother had endured; and when Mrs. Ansell went on: "I must go and see her—you must let me take her by surprise," he said stiffly: "We live out at the mills, a long way from here."

"Oh, we're going there this morning," she rejoined, unrebuffed by what she probably took for a mere social awkwardness, while Mrs. Westmore interposed: "But, Maria, Mr. Truscomb is ill, and has sent Mr. Amherst to say that we are not to come."

"Yes: so Gaines has just telephoned. It's most unfortunate," Mr. Langhope grumbled. He too was already beginning to chafe at the uncongenial exile of Hanaford, and he shared his daughter's desire to despatch the tiresome business before them.

Mr. Tredegar had meanwhile appeared, and when Amherst had been named to him, and had received his Olympian nod, Bessy anxiously imparted her difficulty.

"But how ill is Mr. Truscomb? Do you think he can take us over the mills tomorrow?" she appealed to Amherst.

"I'm afraid not; I am sure he can't. He has a touch of bronchitis."

This announcement was met by a general outcry, in which sympathy for the manager was not the predominating note. Mrs. Ansell saved the situation by breathing feelingly: "Poor man!" and after a decent echo of the phrase, and a doubtful glance at her father, Mrs. Westmore said: "If it's bronchitis he may be ill for days, and what in the world are we to do?"

"Pack up and come back later," suggested Mr. Langhope briskly; but while Bessy sighed "Oh, that dreadful journey!" Mr. Tredegar interposed with authority: "One moment, Langhope, please. Mr. Amherst, is Mrs. Westmore expected at the mills?"

"Yes, I believe they know she is coming."

"Then I think, my dear, that to go back to New York without showing yourself would, under the circumstances, be—er—an error in judgment."

"Good Lord, Tredegar, you don't expect to keep us kicking our heels here for days?" her father ejaculated.

"I can certainly not afford to employ mine in that manner for even a fraction of a day," rejoined the lawyer, always acutely resentful of the suggestion that he had a disengaged moment; "but meanwhile——"

"Father," Bessy interposed, with an eagerly flushing cheek, "don't you see that the only thing for us to do is to go over the mills now—at once—with Mr. Amherst?"

Mr. Langhope stared: he was always adventurously ready to unmake plans, but it flustered him to be called on to remake them. "Eh—what? Now—at once? But Gaines was to have gone with us, and how on earth are we to get at him? He telephoned me that, as the visit was given up, he should ride out to his farm."

"Oh, never mind—or, at least, all the better!" his daughter urged. "We can see the mills just as well without him; and we shall get on so much more quickly."

"Well—well—what do you say, Tredegar?" murmured Mr. Langhope, allured by her last argument; and Bessy, clasping her hands, summed up enthusiastically: "And I shall understand so much better without a lot of people trying to explain to me at once!"

Her sudden enthusiasm surprised no one, for even Mrs. Ansell, expert as she was in the interpreting of tones, set it down to the natural desire to have done as quickly as might be with Hanaford.

"Mrs. Westmore has left her little girl at home,"

she said to Amherst, with a smile intended to counteract the possible ill-effect of the impression.

But Amherst suspected no slight in his employer's eagerness to visit Westmore. His overmastering thought was one of joy as the fulness of his opportunity broke on him. To show her the mills himself—to bring her face to face with her people, unhampered by Truscomb's jealous vigilance, and Truscomb's false explanations; to see the angel of pity stir the depths of those unfathomable eyes, when they rested, perhaps for the first time, on suffering that it was in their power to smile away as easily as they had smiled away his own distrust—all this the wonderful moment had brought him, and thoughts and arguments thronged so hot on his lips that he kept silence, fearing lest he should say too much.

IV

JOHN AMHERST was no one-sided idealist. He felt keenly the growing complexity of the relation between employer and worker, the seeming hopelessness of permanently harmonizing their claims, the recurring necessity of fresh compromises and adjustments. He hated rant, demagogy, the rash formulating of emotional theories; and his contempt for bad logic and subjective judgments led him to regard with distrust the panaceas offered for the cure of economic evils. But his heart ached for the bitter throes with which the human machine moves on. He felt the menace of industrial conditions when viewed collectively, their poignancy when studied in the individual lives of the toilers among whom his lot was cast; and clearly as he saw the need of a philosophic survey of the question, he was sure that only through sympathy with its personal, human side could a solution be reached. The disappearance of the old familiar contact between master and man seemed to him one of the great wrongs of the new industrial situation. That the breach must be farther widened by the ultimate substitution of the stock-company for the individual employer—a fact obvious to any student of economic tendencies—presented to Amherst's mind one of the most painful problems in the scheme of social readjustment. But it was characteristic of him to dwell rather on the removal of immediate difficulties than in the contemplation of those to come, and while the individual employer was still to be reckoned with, the main thing was to bring him closer to his workers. Till he entered personally into their hardships and aspirations—till he learned what they wanted and why they wanted it—Amherst believed that no mere law-making, however enlightened, could create a wholesome relation between the two.

This feeling was uppermost as he sat with Mrs.

Westmore in the carriage which was carrying them to the mills. He had meant to take the trolley back to Westmore, but at a murmured word from Mr. Tredegar Bessy had offered him a seat at her side, leaving others to follow. This culmination of his hopes—the unlooked-for chance of a half-hour alone with her—left Amherst oppressed with the swiftness of the minutes. He had so much to say—so much to prepare her for—yet how begin, while he was in utter ignorance of her character and her point of view, and while her lovely nearness left him so little chance of perceiving anything except itself?

But he was not often the victim of his sensations, and presently there emerged, out of the very consciousness of her grace and her completeness, a clearer sense of the conditions which, in a measure, had gone to produce them. Her dress could not have hung in such subtle folds, her white chin have nestled in such rich depths of fur, the pearls in her ears have given back the light from such pure curves, if thin shoulders in shapeless gingham had not bent, day in, day out, above the bobbins and carders, and weary ears throbbed even at night with the tumult of the looms. Amherst, however, felt no sensational resentment at the contrast. He had lived too much with ugliness and want not to believe in human nature's abiding need of their opposite. He was glad there was room for such beauty in the world, and sure that its purpose was an ameliorating one, if only it could be used as a beautiful spirit would use it.

The carriage had turned into one of the nondescript thoroughfares, half incipient street, half decaying lane, which dismally linked the mill-village to Hanaford. Bessy looked out on the ruts, the hoardings, the starved trees dangling their palsied leaves in the radiant October light; then she sighed: "What a good day for a gallop!"

Amherst felt a momentary chill, but the naturalness of the exclamation disarmed him, and the words called up thrilling memories of his own college days, when he had ridden his grandfather's horses in the famous hunting valley not a hundred miles from Hanaford.

Bessy met his smile with a glow of understanding. "You like riding too, I'm sure?"

"I used to; but I haven't been in the saddle for years. Factory managers don't keep hunters," he said laughing.

Her murmur of embarrassment showed that she took this as an apologetic allusion to his reduced condition, and in his haste to correct this impression he added: "If I regretted anything in my other life, it would certainly be a gallop on a day like this; but I chose my trade deliberately, and I've never been sorry for my choice."

He had hardly spoken when he felt the inappropriateness of this avowal; but her prompt response showed him, a moment later, that it was, after all, the straightest way to his end.

"You find the work interesting? I'm sure it must be. You'll think me very ignorant—my husband and I came here so seldom. . . I feel as if I ought to know so much more about it," she explained.

At last the note for which he waited had been struck. "Won't you try to—now you're here? There's so much worth knowing," he broke out impetuously.

Mrs. Westmore coloured, but rather with surprise than displeasure. "I'm very stupid—I've no head for business—but I will try to," she said.

"It's not business that I mean; it's the personal relation—just the thing the business point of view leaves out. Financially, I don't suppose your mills could be better run; but there are over seven hundred women working in them, and there's so much to be done, just for them and their children."

He caught a faint hint of withdrawal in her tone. "I have always understood that Mr. Truscomb did everything——"

Amherst flushed; but he was beyond caring for the personal rebuff. "Do you leave it to your little girl's nurses to do everything for her?" he asked.

Her surprise seemed about to verge on annoyance:

he saw the preliminary ruffling of the woman who is put to the trouble of defending her dignity. "Really, I don't see—" she began with distant politeness; then her face changed and melted, and again her blood spoke for her before her lips.

"I am glad you told me that, Mr. Amherst. Of course I want to do whatever I can. I should like you to point out everything——"

Amherst's resolve had been taken while she spoke. He *would* point out everything, would stretch his opportunity to its limit. All thoughts of personal prudence were flung to the winds—her blush and tone had routed the waiting policy. He would declare war on Truscomb at once, and take the chance of dismissal. At least, before he went he would have brought this exquisite creature face to face with the wrongs from which her luxuries were drawn, and set in motion the regenerating impulses of indignation and pity. He did not stop to weigh the permanent advantage of this course. His only feeling was that the chance would never again be given him—that if he let her go away, back to her usual life, with eyes unopened and heart untouched, there would be no hope of her ever returning. It was far better that he should leave for good, and that she should come back, as come back she must, more and more often, if once she could be made to feel the crying need of her presence.

But where was he to begin? How give her even a glimpse of the packed and intricate situation?

"Mrs. Westmore," he said, "there's no time to say much now, but before we get to the mills I want to ask you a favour. If, as you go through them, you see anything that seems to need explaining, will you let me come and tell you about it tonight? I say to-night," he added, meeting her look of enquiry, "because later—tomorrow even—I might not have the chance. There are some things—a good many—in the management of the mills that Mr. Truscomb doesn't see as I do. I don't mean business questions: wages and dividends and so on—those are out of my province. I speak merely in the line of my own work—my care of the hands, and what I believe they need and don't get under the present system. Naturally, if Mr. Truscomb were well, I shouldn't have had this chance of putting the case to you; but since it's come my way, I must seize it and take the consequences."

Even as he spoke, by a swift reaction of thought, those consequences rose before him in all their seriousness. It was not only, or chiefly, that he feared to lose his place; though he knew his mother had not spoken lightly in instancing the case of the foreman whom Truscomb, to gratify a personal spite, had for months kept out of a job in his trade. And there were special reasons why Amherst should heed her warning. In adopting a manual trade, instead of one of the gentlemanly professions which the men of her family had always followed, he had not only disappointed her hopes, and to a great extent thrown away the benefits of the education she had pinched herself to give him, but had disturbed all the habits of her life by removing her from her normal surroundings to the depressing exile of a factory-settlement. However much he blamed himself for exacting this sacrifice, it had been made so cheerfully that the consciousness of it never clouded his life with his mother; but her self-effacement made him the more alive to his own obligations, and having placed her in a difficult situation he had always been careful not to increase its difficulties by any imprudence in his conduct toward his employers. Yet, grave as these considerations were, they were really less potent than his personal desire to remain at Westmore. Lightly as he had just resolved to risk the chance of dismissal, all his future was bound up in the hope of retaining his place. His heart was in the work at Westmore, and the fear of not being able to get other employment was a small factor in his intense desire to keep his post. What he really wanted was to speak out, and yet escape the consequences: by some miraculous reversal of probability to retain his position and yet effect Truscomb's removal. The idea was so fantastic that he felt it merely as a quickening of all his activities, a tremendous pressure of will along undetermined lines. He had no wish to take the manager's place; but his dream was to see Truscomb superseded by a man of the new school, in sympathy with the awakening social movement—a man sufficiently practical to "run" the mills successfully, yet imaginative enough to regard that task as the least of his duties. He saw the promise of such a man in Louis Duplain, the overseer who boarded with Mrs. Amherst: a young fellow of Alsatian extraction, a mill-hand from childhood, who had worked at his trade in Europe as well as in America, and who united with more manual skill, and a greater nearness to the workman's standpoint, all Amherst's enthusiasm for the experiments in social betterment that were making in some of the English and continental factories. His strongest wish was to see such a man as Duplain in control at Westmore before he himself turned to the larger work which he had begun to see before him as the sequel to his factory-training.

All these thoughts swept through him in the instant's pause before Mrs. Westmore, responding to his last appeal, said with a graceful eagerness: "Yes, you must come tonight. I want to hear all you can tell me—and if there is anything wrong you must show me how I can make it better."

"I'll show her, and Truscomb shan't turn me out

for it," was the vow he passionately registered as the carriage drew up at the office-door of the main building.

How this impossible result was to be achieved he had no farther time to consider, for in another moment the rest of the party had entered the factory with them, and speech was followed up in the roar of the machinery.

Amherst's zeal for his cause was always quickened by the sight of the mills in action. He loved the work itself as much as he hated the conditions under which it was done; and he longed to see on the operatives' faces something of the ardour that lit up his own when he entered the work-rooms. It was this passion for machinery that at school had turned him from his books, at college had drawn him to the courses least in the line of his destined profession; and it always seized on him afresh when he was face to face with the monstrous energies of the mills. It was not only the sense of power that thrilled him—he felt a beauty in the ordered activity of the whole intricate organism, in the rhythm of dancing bobbins and revolving cards, the swift continuous outpour of doublers and ribbon-laps, the steady ripple of the long ply-frames, the terrible gnashing play of the looms—all these varying subordinate motions, gathered up into the throb of the great engines which fed the giant's arteries, and were in turn ruled by the invisible action of quick thought and obedient hands, always produced in Amherst a responsive rush of life.

He knew this sensation was too specialized to affect his companions; but he expected Mrs. Westmore to be all the more alive to the other side—the dark side of monotonous human toil, of the banquet of flesh and blood and brain perpetually served up to the monster whose insatiable jaws the looms so grimly typified. Truscomb, as he had told her, was a good manager from the profit-taking standpoint. Since it was profitable to keep the machinery in order, he maintained throughout the factory a high standard of mechanical supervision, except where one or two favoured overseers—for Truscomb was given to favoritism—shirked the duties of their departments. But it was of the essence of Truscomb's policy—and not the least of the qualities which made him a "paying" manager—that he saved money scrupulously where its outlay would not have resulted in larger earnings. To keep the floors scrubbed, the cotton-dust swept up, the rooms freshly whitewashed and well-ventilated, far from adding the smallest fraction to the quarterly dividends, would have deducted from them the slight cost of this additional labour; and Truscomb therefore economized on scrubbers, sweepers and window-washers, and on all expenses connected with improved ventilation and other hygienic precautions. Though the whole factory was over-crowded, the newest buildings were more carefully planned, and had the usual sanitary improvements; but the old mills had been left in their original state, and even those most recently built were fast lapsing into squalor. It was no wonder, therefore, that workers imprisoned within such walls should reflect their long hours of deadening toil in dull eyes and anæmic skins, and in the dreary lassitude with which they bent to their tasks.

Surely, Amherst argued, Mrs. Westmore must feel this; must feel it all the more keenly, coming from an atmosphere so different, from a life where, as he instinctively divined, all was in harmony with her own graceful person. But a deep disappointment awaited him. He was still under the spell of their last moments in the carriage, when her face and voice had promised so much, when she had seemed so deeply, if vaguely, stirred by his appeal. But as they passed from one resounding room to the other—from the dull throb of the carding-room, the groan of the ply-frames, the long steady pound of the slashers, back to the angry shriek of the fierce unappeasable looms—the light faded from her eyes and she looked merely bewildered and stunned.

Amherst, hardened to the din of the factory, could not measure its effect on nerves accustomed to the subdued sounds and spacious stillnesses which are the last refinement of luxury. Habit had made him unconscious of that malicious multiplication and subdivision of noise that kept every point of consciousness vibrating to a different note, so that while one set of nerves was torn as with pincers by the dominant scream of the looms, others were thrilled with a separate pain by the ceaseless accompaniment of drumming, hissing, grating and crashing that shook the great building. Amherst felt this tumult only as part of the atmosphere of the mills; and to ears trained like his own he could make his voice heard without difficulty. But his attempts at speech were unintelligible to Mrs. Westmore and her companions, and after vainly trying to communicate with him by signs they hurried on as if to escape as quickly as possible from the pursuing whirlwind.

Amherst could not allow for the depressing effect of this enforced silence. He did not see that if Bessy could have questioned him the currents of sympathy might have remained open between them, whereas, compelled to walk in silence through interminable ranks of meaningless machines, to which the human workers seemed mere automatic appendages, she lost all perception of what the scene meant. He had forgotten, too, that the swift apprehension of suffering in others is as much the result of training as the immediate perception of beauty. Both perceptions may be inborn, but if they are not they can be developed only through the discipline of experience.

"That girl in the hospital would have seen it all," he reflected, as the vision of Miss Brent's small incisive profile rose before him; but the next moment he caught the light on Mrs. Westmore's hair, as she bent above a card, and the paler image faded like a late moon in the sunrise.

Meanwhile Mrs. Ansell, seeing that the detailed inspection of the buildings was as trying to Mr. Langhope's lameness as to his daughter's nerves, had proposed to turn back with him and drive to Mrs. Amherst's, where he might leave her to call while the others were completing their rounds. It was one of Mrs. Ansell's gifts to detect the first symptoms of *ennui* in her companions, and produce a remedy as patly as old ladies whisk out a scent-bottle or a cough-lozenge; and Mr. Langhope's look of relief showed the timeliness of her suggestion.

Amherst was too preoccupied to wonder how his mother would take this visit; but he welcomed Mr. Langhope's departure, hoping that the withdrawal of his ironic smile would leave his daughter open to gentler influences. Mr. Tredegar, meanwhile, was projecting his dry glance over the scene, trying to converse by signs with the overseers of the different rooms, and pausing now and then to contemplate, not so much the workers themselves as the special tasks which engaged them.

How these spectators of the party's progress were affected by Mrs. Westmore's appearance, even Amherst, for all his sympathy with their views, could not detect. They knew that she was the new owner, that a disproportionate amount of the result of their toil would in future pass through her hands, spread carpets for her steps, and hang a setting of beauty about her eyes; but the knowledge seemed to produce no special interest in her personality. A change of employer was not likely to make any change in their lot: their welfare would probably continue to depend on Truscomb's favour. The men hardly raised their heads as Mrs. Westmore passed; the women stared, but with curiosity rather than interest; and Amherst could not tell whether their sullenness reacted on Mrs. Westmore, or whether they were unconsciously chilled by her indifference. The result was the same: the distance between them seemed to increase instead of diminishing; and he smiled ironically to think of the form his appeal had taken—"If you see anything that seems to need explaining." Why, she saw nothing—nothing but the greasy floor under her feet, the cotton-dust in her eyes, the dizzy incomprehensible whirring of innumerable belts and wheels! Once out of it all, she would make haste to forget the dreary scene without pausing to ask for any explanation of its dreariness.

In the intensity of his disappointment he sought a pretext to cut short the tour of the buildings, that he might remove his eyes from the face he had so vainly watched for any sign of awakening. And then, as he despaired of it, the change came.

They had entered the principal carding-room, and were half-way down its long central passage, when Mr. Tredegar, who led the procession, paused before one of the cards.

"What's that?" he asked, pointing to a ragged strip of black cloth tied conspicuously to the frame of the card.

The overseer of the room, a florid young man with dissipated eyes, who, at Amherst's signal, had attached himself to the party, stopped short and turned a furious glance on the surrounding operatives.

"What in hell . . . ? It's the first I seen of it," he exclaimed, making an ineffectual attempt to snatch the mourning emblem from its place.

At the same instant the midday whistle boomed through the building, and at the signal the machinery stopped, and silence fell on the mills. The more distant workers at once left their posts to catch up the hats and coats heaped untidily in the corners; but those nearer by, attracted by the commotion around the card, stood spell-bound, fixing the visitors with a dull stare.

Amherst had reddened to the roots of his hair. He knew in a flash what the token signified, and the sight stirred his pity; but it also jarred on his strong sense of discipline, and he turned sternly to the operatives.

"What does this mean?"

There was a short silence; then one of the hands, a thin bent man with mystic eyes, raised his head and spoke.

"We done that for Dillon," he said.

Amherst's glance swept the crowded faces. "But Dillon was not killed," he exclaimed, while the overseer, drawing out his pen-knife, ripped off the cloth and tossed it contemptuously into a heap of cotton-refuse at his feet.

"Might better ha' been," came from another hand; and a deep "That's so" of corroboration ran through the knot of workers.

Amherst felt a touch on his arm, and met Mrs. Westmore's eyes. "What has happened? What do they mean?" she asked in a startled voice.

"There was an accident here two days ago: a man got caught in the card behind him, and his right hand was badly crushed."

Mr. Tredegar intervened with his dry note of command. "How serious is the accident? How did it happen?" he enquired.

"Through the man's own carelessness—ask the manager," the overseer interposed before Amherst could answer.

A deep murmur of dissent ran through the crowd, but Amherst, without noticing the overseer's reply, said to Mr. Tredegar: "He's at the Hope Hospital. He will lose his hand, and probably the whole arm."

He had not meant to add this last phrase. However strongly his sympathies were aroused, it was against his rule, at such a time, to say anything which might inflame the quick passions of the workers: he had meant to make light of the accident, and dismiss the operatives with a sharp word of reproof. But Mrs. Westmore's face was close to his: he saw the pity in her eyes, and feared, if he checked its expression, that he might never again have the chance of calling it forth.

"His right arm? How terrible! But then he will never be able to work again!" she exclaimed, in all the horror of a first confrontation with the inexorable fate of the poor.

Her eyes turned from Amherst and rested on the faces pressing about her. There were many women's faces among them—the faces of fagged middle-age, and of sallow sedentary girlhood. For the first time Mrs. Westmore seemed to feel the bond of blood between herself and these dim creatures of the underworld: as Amherst watched her the lovely miracle was wrought.

Her pallour gave way to a quick rush of colour, her eyes widened like a frightened child's, and two tears rose and rolled slowly down her face.

"Oh, why wasn't I told? Is he married? Has he children? What does it matter whose fault it was?" she cried, her questions pouring out disconnectedly on a wave of anger and compassion.

"It warn't his fault. . . . The cards are too close . . . . It'll happen again. . . . He's got three kids at home," broke from the operatives; and suddenly a voice exclaimed "Here's his wife now," and the crowd divided to make way for Mrs. Dillon, who, passing through the farther end of the room, had been waylaid and dragged toward the group.

She hung back, shrinking from the murderous machine, which she beheld for the first time since her husband's accident; then she saw Amherst, guessed the identity of the lady at his side, and flushed up to her haggard forehead. Mrs. Dillon had been good-looking in her earlier youth, and sufficient prettiness lingered in her hollow-cheeked face to show how much more had been sacrificed to sickness and unwholesome toil.

"Oh, ma'am, ma'am, it warn't Jim's fault—there ain't a steadier man living. The cards is too crowded," she sobbed out.

Some of the other women began to cry: a wave of

sympathy ran through the circle, and Mrs. Westmore moved forward with an answering exclamation. "You poor creature. . . you poor creature. . . ." She opened her arms to Mrs. Dillon, and the scrubber's sobs were buried on her employer's breast.

"I will go to the hospital—I will come and see you—I will see that everything is done," Bessy reiterated. "But why are you here? How is it that you have had to leave your children?" She freed herself to turn a reproachful glance on Amherst. "You don't mean to tell me that, at such a time, you keep the poor woman at work?"

"Mrs. Dillon has not been working here lately," Amherst answered. "The manager took her back to-day at her own request, that she might earn something while her husband was in hospital."

Mrs. Westmore's eyes shone indignantly. "Earn something? But surely——"

She met a silencing look from Mr. Tredegar, who had stepped between Mrs. Dillon and herself.

"My dear child, no one doubts—none of these good people doubt—that you will look into the case, and do all you can to alleviate it; but let me suggest that this is hardly the place——"

She turned from him with an appealing glance at Amherst.

"I think," the latter said, as their eyes met, "that

you had better let me dismiss the hands: they have only an hour at midday."

She signed her assent, and he turned to the operatives and said quietly: "You have heard Mrs. Westmore's promise; now take yourselves off, and give her a clear way to the stairs."

They dropped back, and Mr. Tredegar drew Bessy's arm through his; but as he began to move away she turned and laid her hand on Mrs. Dillon's shoulder.

"You must not stay here—you must go back to the children. I will make it right with Mr. Truscomb," she said in a reassuring whisper; then, through her tears, she smiled a farewell at the lingering knot of operatives, and followed her companions to the door.

In silence they descended the many stairs and crossed the shabby unfenced grass-plot between the mills and the manager's office. It was not till they reached the carriage that Mrs. Westmore spoke.

"But Maria is waiting for us—we must call for her!" she said, rousing herself; and as Amherst opened the carriage-door she added: "You will show us the way? You will drive with us?"

During the drive Bessy remained silent, as if reabsorbed in the distress of the scene she had just witnessed; and Amherst found himself automatically answering Mr. Tredegar's questions, while his own mind had no room for anything but the sense of her tremulous lips and of her eyes enlarged by tears. He had been too much engrossed in the momentous issues of her visit to the mills to remember that she had promised to call at his mother's for Mrs. Ansell; but now that they were on their way thither he found himself wishing that the visit might have been avoided. He was too proud of his mother to feel any doubt of the impression she would produce; but what would Mrs. Westmore think of their way of living, of the cheap jauntiness of the cottage, and the smell of cooking penetrating all its thin partitions? Duplain, too, would be coming in for dinner; and Amherst, in spite of his liking for the young overseer, became conscious of a rather overbearing freedom in his manner, the kind of misplaced ease which the new-made American affects as the readiest sign of equality. All these trifles, usually non-existent or supremely indifferent to Amherst, now assumed a sudden importance, behind which he detected the uneasy desire that Mrs. Westmore should not regard him as less of her own class than his connections and his bringing-up entitled him to be thought. In a flash he saw what he had forfeited by his choice of a calling—equal contact with the little circle of people who gave life its crowning grace and facility; and the next moment he was blushing at this reversal of his standards, and wondering, almost contemptuously, what could be the nature of the woman whose mere presence could produce such a change.

But there was no struggling against her influence; and as, the night before, he had looked at Westmore with the nurse's eyes, so he now found himself seeing his house as it must appear to Mrs. Westmore. He noticed the shabby yellow paint of the palings, the neglected garden of their neighbour, the week's wash flaunting itself indecently through the denuded shrubs about the kitchen porch; and as he admitted his companions to the narrow passage he was assailed by the expected whiff of "boiled dinner," with which the steam of wash-tubs was intimately mingled.

Duplain was in the passage; he had just come out of the kitchen, and the fact that he had been washing his hands in the sink was made evident by his rolled-back shirt-sleeves, and by the shiny redness of the knuckles he was running through his stiff black hair.

"Hallo, John," he said, in his aggressive voice, which rose abruptly at sight of Amherst's companions; and at the same moment the frowsy maid-of-all-work, crimson from stooping over the kitchen stove, thrust her head out to call after him: "See here, Mr. Duplain, don't you leave your cravat laying round in my dough."

V

MRS. WESTMORE stayed just long enough not to break in too abruptly on the flow of her friend's reminiscences, and to impress herself on Mrs. Amherst's delighted eyes as an embodiment of tactfulness and grace—looking sympathetically about the little room, which, with its books, its casts, its photographs of memorable pictures, seemed, after all, a not incongruous setting to her charms; so that when she rose to go, saying, as her hand met Amherst's, "Tonight, then, you must tell me all about those poor Dillons," he had the sense of having penetrated so far into her intimacy that a new Westmore must inevitably result from their next meeting.

"Say, John—the boss is a looker," Duplain commented across the dinner-table, with the slangy grossness he sometimes affected; but Amherst left it to his mother to look a quiet rebuke, feeling himself too aloof from such contacts to resent them.

He had to rouse himself with an effort to take in the overseer's next observation. "There was another lady at the office this morning," Duplain went on, while the two men lit their cigars in the porch. "Asking after you—tried to get me to show her over the mills when I said you were busy."

"Asking after me? What did she look like?"

"Well, her face was kinder white and small, with an awful lot of black hair fitting close to it. Said she came from Hope Hospital."

Amherst looked up. "Did you show her over?" he asked with sudden interest.

Duplain laughed slangily. "What? Me? And have Truscomb get on to it and turn me down? How'd I know she wasn't a yellow reporter?"

Amherst uttered an impatient exclamation. "I wish to heaven a yellow reporter *would* go through these mills, and show them up in head-lines a yard high!"

He regretted not having seen the nurse again: he felt sure she would have been interested in the working of the mills, and quick to notice the signs of discouragement and ill-health in the workers' faces; but a moment later his regret was dispelled by the thought of his visit to Mrs. Westmore. The afternoon hours dragged slowly by in the office, where he was bound to his desk by Truscomb's continued absence; but at length the evening whistle blew, the clerks in the outer room caught their hats from the rack, Duplain presented himself with the day's report, and the two men were free to walk home.

Two hours later Amherst was mounting Mrs. Westmore's steps; and his hand was on the bell when the door opened and Dr. Disbrow came out. The physician drew back, as if surprised and slightly disconcerted; but his smile promptly effaced all signs of vexation, and he held his hand out affably.

"A fine evening, Mr. Amherst. I'm glad to say I have been able to bring Mrs. Westmore an excellent report of both patients—Mr. Truscomb, I mean, and poor Dillon. This mild weather is all in their favour, and I hope my brother-in-law will be about in a day or two." He passed on with a nod.

Amherst was once more shown into the library where he had found Mrs. Westmore that morning; but on this occasion it was Mr. Tredegar who rose to meet him, and curtly waved him to a seat at a respectful distance from his own. Amherst at once felt a change of atmosphere, and it was easy to guess that the lowering of temperature was due to Dr. Disbrow's recent visit. The thought roused the young man's combative instincts, and caused him to say, as Mr. Tredegar continued to survey him in silence from the depths of a capacious easy-chair: "I understood from Mrs. Westmore that she wished to see me this evening."

It was the wrong note, and he knew it; but he had been unable to conceal his sense of the vague current of opposition in the air.

"Quite so: I believe she asked you to come," Mr. Tredegar assented, laying his hands together vertically, and surveying Amherst above the acute angle formed by his parched finger-tips. As he leaned back, small, dry, dictatorial, in the careless finish of his evening dress and pearl-studded shirt-front, his appearance put the finishing touch to Amherst's irritation. He felt the incongruousness of his rough clothes in this atmosphere of after-dinner ease, the mud on his walking-boots, the clinging cotton-dust which seemed to have entered into the very pores of the skin; and again his annoyance escaped in his voice.

"Perhaps I have come too early—" he began; but Mr. Tredegar interposed with glacial amenity: "No, I believe you are exactly on time; but Mrs. Westmore is unexpectedly detained. The fact is, Mr. and Mrs. Halford Gaines are dining with her, and she has delegated to me the duty of hearing what you have to say."

Amherst hesitated. His impulse was to exclaim: "There is no duty about it!" but a moment's thought showed the folly of thus throwing up the game. With the prospect of Truscomb's being about again in a day or two, it might well be that this was his last chance of reaching Mrs. Westmore's ear; and he was bound to put his case while he could, irrespective of personal feeling. But his disappointment was too keen to be denied, and after a pause he said: "Could I not speak with Mrs. Westmore later?"

Mr. Tredegar's cool survey deepened to a frown. The young man's importunity was really out of proportion to what he signified. "Mrs. Westmore has asked me to replace her," he said, putting his previous statement more concisely.

"Then I am not to see her at all?" Amherst exclaimed; and the lawyer replied indifferently: "I am afraid not, as she leaves tomorrow."

Mr. Tredegar was in his element when refusing a favour. Not that he was by nature unkind; he was, indeed, capable of a cold beneficence; but to deny what it was in his power to accord was the readiest way of proclaiming his authority, that power of loosing and binding which made him regard himself as almost consecrated to his office.

Having sacrificed to this principle, he felt free to add as a gratuitous concession to politeness: "You are perhaps not aware that I am Mrs. Westmore's lawyer, and one of the executors under her husband's will."

He dropped this negligently, as though conscious of the absurdity of presenting his credentials to a subordinate; but his manner no longer incensed Amherst: it merely strengthened his resolve to sink all sense of affront in the supreme effort of obtaining a hearing.

"With that stuffed canary to advise her," he reflected, "there's no hope for her unless I can assert myself now"; and the unconscious wording of his thought expressed his inward sense that Bessy Westmore stood in greater need of help than her work-people.

Still he hesitated, hardly knowing how to begin. To Mr. Tredegar he was no more than an underling, without authority to speak in his superior's absence; and the lack of an official warrant, which he could have disregarded in appealing to Mrs. Westmore, made it hard for him to find a good opening in addressing her representative. He saw, too, from Mr. Tredegar's protracted silence, that the latter counted on the effect of this embarrassment, and was resolved not to minimize it by giving him a lead; and this had the effect of increasing his caution.

He looked up and met the lawyer's eye. "Mrs. Westmore," he began, "asked me to let her know something about the condition of the people at the mills——"

Mr. Tredegar raised his hand. "Excuse me," he said. "I understood from Mrs. Westmore that it was you who asked her permission to call this evening and set forth certain grievances on the part of the operatives."

Amherst reddened. "I did ask her—yes. But I don't in any sense represent the operatives. I simply wanted to say a word for them."

Mr. Tredegar folded his hands again, and crossed one lean little leg over the other, bringing into his line of vision the glossy tip of a patent-leather pump, which he studied for a moment in silence.

"Does Mr. Truscomb know of your intention?" he then enquired.

"No, sir," Amherst answered energetically, glad that he had forced the lawyer out of his passive tactics. "I am here on my own responsibility—and in direct opposition to my own interests," he continued with a slight smile. "I know that my proceeding is quite out of order, and that I have, personally, everything to lose by it, and in a larger way probably very little to gain; but I thought Mrs. Westmore's attention ought to be called to certain conditions at the mills, and no one else seemed likely to speak of them."

"May I ask why you assume that Mr. Truscomb will not do so when he has the opportunity?"

Amherst could not repress a smile. "Because it is owing to Mr. Truscomb that they exist."

"The real object of your visit then," said Mr. Tredegar, speaking with deliberation, "is—er—an underhand attack on your manager's methods?"

Amherst's face darkened, but he kept his temper. "I see nothing especially underhand in my course——"

"Except," the other interposed ironically, "that you have waited to speak till Mr. Truscomb was not in a position to defend himself."

"I never had the chance before. It was at Mrs. Westmore's own suggestion that I took her over the mills, and feeling as I do I should have thought it cowardly to shirk the chance of pointing out to her the conditions there."

Mr. Tredegar mused, his eyes still bent on his gently-oscillating foot. Whenever a sufficient pressure from without parted the fog of self-complacency in which he moved, he had a shrewd enough outlook on men and motives; and it may be that the vigorous ring of Amherst's answer had effected this momentary clearing of the air.

At any rate, his next words were spoken in a more accessible tone. "To what conditions do you refer?"

"To the conditions under which the mill-hands work and live—to the whole management of the mills, in fact, in relation to the people employed."

"That is a large question. Pardon my possible ignorance—" Mr. Tredegar paused to make sure that his hearer took in the full irony of this—"but surely in this state there are liability and inspection laws for the protection of the operatives?"

"There are such laws, yes—but most of them are either a dead letter, or else so easily evaded that no employer thinks of conforming to them."

"No employer? Then your specific charge against the Westmore mills is part of a general arraignment of all employers of labour?"

"By no means, sir. I only meant that, where the hands are well treated, it is due rather to the personal good-will of the employer than to any fear of the law."

"And in what respect do you think the Westmore hands unfairly treated?"

Amherst paused to measure his words. "The question, as you say, is a large one," he rejoined. "It has its roots in the way the business is organized—in the traditional attitude of the company toward the operatives. I hoped that Mrs. Westmore might return to the mills—might visit some of the people in their houses. Seeing their way of living, it might have occurred to her to ask a reason for it—and one enquiry would have led to another. She spoke this morning of going to the hospital to see Dillon."

"She did go to the hospital: I went with her. But as Dillon was sleeping, and as the matron told us he was much better—a piece of news which, I am happy to say, Dr. Disbrow has just confirmed—she did not go up to the ward."

Amherst was silent, and Mr. Tredegar pursued: "I gather, from your bringing up Dillon's case, that for some reason you consider it typical of the defects you find in Mr. Truscomb's management. Suppose, therefore, we drop generalizations, and confine ourselves to the particular instance. What wrong, in your view, has been done the Dillons?"

He turned, as he spoke, to extract a cigar from the

box at his elbow. "Let me offer you one, Mr. Amherst: we shall talk more comfortably," he suggested with distant affability; but Amherst, with a gesture of refusal, plunged into his exposition of the Dillon case. He tried to put the facts succinctly, presenting them in their bare ugliness, without emotional drapery; setting forth Dillon's good record for sobriety and skill, dwelling on the fact that his wife's ill-health was the result of perfectly remediable conditions in the work-rooms, and giving his reasons for the belief that the accident had been caused, not by Dillon's carelessness, but by the over-crowding of the carding-room. Mr. Tredegar listened attentively, though the cloud of cigar-smoke between himself and Amherst masked from the latter his possible changes of expression. When he removed his cigar, his face looked smaller than ever, as though desiccated by the fumes of the tobacco.

"Have you ever called Mr. Gaines's attention to these matters?"

"No: that would have been useless. He has always refused to discuss the condition of the mills with any one but the manager."

"H'm—that would seem to prove that Mr. Gaines, who lives here, sees as much reason for trusting Truscomb's judgment as Mr. Westmore, who delegated his authority from a distance."

Amherst did not take this up, and after a pause Mr.

Tredegar went on: "You know, of course, the answers I might make to such an indictment. As a lawyer, I might call your attention to the employé's waiver of risk, to the strong chances of contributory negligence, and so on; but happily in this case such arguments are superfluous. You are apparently not aware that Dillon's injury is much slighter than it ought to be to serve your purpose. Dr. Disbrow has just told us that he will probably get off with the loss of a finger; and I need hardly say that, whatever may have been Dillon's own share in causing the accident—and as to this, as you admit, opinions differ—Mrs. Westmore will assume all the expenses of his nursing, besides making a liberal gift to his wife." Mr. Tredegar laid down his cigar and drew forth a silver-mounted note-case. "Here, in fact," he continued, "is a cheque which she asks you to transmit, and which, as I think you will agree, ought to silence, on your part as well as Mrs. Dillon's, any criticism of Mrs. Westmore's dealings with her operatives."

The blood rose to Amherst's forehead, and he just restrained himself from pushing back the cheque which Mr. Tredegar had laid on the table between them.

"There is no question of criticizing Mrs. Westmore's dealings with her operatives—as far as I know, she has had none as yet," he rejoined, unable to control his voice as completely as his hand. "And the proof of it is the impunity with which her agents deceive her—in this case, for instance, of Dillon's injury. Dr. Disbrow, who is Mr. Truscomb's brother-in-law, and apt to be influenced by his views, assures you that the man will get off with the loss of a finger; but some one equally competent to speak told me last night that he would lose not only his hand but his arm."

Amherst's voice had swelled to a deep note of anger, and with his tossed hair, and eyes darkening under furrowed brows, he presented an image of revolutionary violence which deepened the disdain on Mr. Tredegar's lip.

"Some one equally competent to speak? Are you prepared to name this anonymous authority?"

Amherst hesitated. "No—I shall have to ask you to take my word for it," he returned with a shade of embarrassment.

"Ah—" Mr. Tredegar murmured, giving to the expressive syllable its utmost measure of decent exultation.

Amherst quivered under the thin lash, and broke out: "It is all you have required of Dr. Disbrow—" but at this point Mr. Tredegar rose to his feet.

"My dear sir, your resorting to such arguments convinces me that nothing is to be gained by prolonging our talk. I will not even take up your insinuations against two of the most respected men in the community—such charges reflect only on those who make them."

Amherst, whose flame of anger had subsided with the sudden sense of its futility, received this in silence, and the lawyer, reassured, continued with a touch of condescension: "My only specific charge from Mrs. Westmore was to hand you this cheque; but, in spite of what has passed, I take it upon myself to add, in her behalf, that your conduct of today will not be allowed to weigh against your record at the mills, and that the extraordinary charges you have seen fit to bring against your superiors will—if not repeated—simply be ignored"

When, the next morning at about ten, Mrs. Eustace Ansell joined herself to the two gentlemen who still lingered over a desultory breakfast in Mrs. Westmore's dining-room, she responded to their greeting with less than her usual vivacity.

It was one of Mrs. Ansell's arts to bring to the breakfast-table just the right shade of sprightliness, a warmth subdued by discretion as the early sunlight is tempered by the lingering coolness of night. She was, in short, as fresh, as temperate, as the hour, yet without the concomitant chill which too often marks its human atmosphere: rather her soft effulgence dissipated the morning frosts, opening pinched spirits to a promise of midday warmth. But on this occasion a mist of uncertainty hung on her smile, and veiled the glance which

"No—I shall have to ask you to take my word for it."

she turned on the contents of the heavy silver dishes successively presented to her notice. When, at the conclusion of this ceremony, the servants had withdrawn, she continued for a moment to stir her tea in silence, while her glance travelled from Mr. Tredegar, sunk in his morning mail, to Mr. Langhope, who leaned back resignedly in his chair, trying to solace himself with Hanaford Banner, till midday should bring him a sight of the metropolitan press.

"I suppose you know," she said suddenly, "that Bessy has telegraphed for Cicely, and made her arrangements to stay here another week."

Mr. Langhope's stick slipped to the floor with the sudden displacement of his whole lounging person, and Mr. Tredegar, removing his tortoise-shell reading-glasses, put them hastily into their case, as though to declare for instant departure.

"My dear Maria—" Mr. Langhope gasped, while she rose and restored his stick.

"She considers it, then, her duty to wait and see Truscomb?" the lawyer asked; and Mrs. Ansell, regaining her seat, murmured discreetly: "She puts it so—yes."

"My dear Maria—" Mr. Langhope repeated helplessly, tossing aside his paper and drawing his chair up to the table.

"But it would be perfectly easy to return: it is quite

unnecessary to wait here for his recovery," Mr. Tredegar pursued, as though setting forth a fact which had not hitherto presented itself to the more limited intelligence of his hearers.

Mr. Langhope emitted a short laugh, and Mrs. Ansell answered gently: "She says she detests the long journey."

Mr. Tredegar rose and gathered up his letters with a gesture of annoyance. "In that case—if I had been notified earlier of this decision, I might have caught the morning train," he interrupted himself, glancing resentfully at his watch.

"Oh, don't leave us, Tredegar," Mr. Langhope entreated. "We'll reason with her—we'll persuade her to go back by the three-forty."

Mrs. Ansell smiled. "She telegraphed at seven. Cicely and the governess are already on their way."

"At seven? But, my dear friend, why on earth didn't you tell us?"

"I didn't know till a few minutes ago. Bessy called me in as I was coming down."

"Ah—" Mr. Langhope murmured, meeting her eyes for a fraction of a second. In the encounter, she appeared to communicate something more than she had spoken, for as he stooped to pick up his paper he said, more easily: "My dear Tredegar, if we're in a box there's no reason why we should force you into it too. Ring for Ropes, and we'll look up a train for you."

Mr. Tredegar appeared slightly ruffled at this prompt acquiescence in his threatened departure. "Of course, if I had been notified in advance, I might have arranged to postpone my engagements another day; but in any case, it is quite out of the question that I should return in a week—and quite unnecessary," he added, snapping his lips shut as though he were closing his last portmanteau.

"Oh, quite—quite," Mr. Langhope assented. "It isn't, in fact, in the least necessary for any of us either to stay on now or to return. Truscomb could come to Long Island when he recovers, and answer any questions we may have to put; but if Bessy has sent for the child, we must of course put off going for today—at least I must," he added sighing, "and, though I know it's out of the question to exact such a sacrifice from you, I have a faint hope that our delightful friend here, with the altruistic spirit of her sex——"

"Oh, I shall enjoy it—my maid is unpacking," Mrs. Ansell gaily affirmed; and Mr. Tredegar, shrugging his shoulders, said curtly: "In that case I will ring for the time-table."

When he had withdrawn to consult it in the seclusion of the library, and Mrs. Ansell, affecting a sudden desire for a second cup of tea, had reseated herself to await the replenishment of the kettle, Mr. Langhope exchanged his own chair for a place at her side.

"Now what on earth does this mean?" he asked, lighting a cigarette in response to her slight nod of consent.

Mrs. Ansell's gaze lost itself in the depths of the empty tea-pot.

"A number of things—or any one of them," she said at length, extending her arm toward the tea-caddy.

"For instance—?" he rejoined, following appreciatively the movements of her long slim hands.

She raised her head and met his eyes. "For instance: it may mean—don't resent the suggestion—that you and Mr. Tredegar were not quite well-advised in persuading her not to see Mr. Amherst yesterday evening."

Mr. Langhope uttered an exclamation of surprise. "But, my dear Maria—in the name of reason. . . why, after the doctor's visit—after his coming here last night, at Truscomb's request, to put the actual facts before her—should she have gone over the whole business again with this interfering young fellow? How, in fact, could she have done so," he added, after vainly waiting for her reply, "without putting a sort of slight on Truscomb, who is, after all, the only person entitled to speak with authority?"

Mrs. Ansell received his outburst in silence, and the butler, reappearing with the kettle and fresh toast, gave her the chance to prolong her pause for a full minute. When the door had closed on him, she said: "Judged by reason, your arguments are unanswerable; but when it comes to a question of feeling——"

"Feeling? What kind of feeling? You don't mean to suggest anything so preposterous as that Bessy——?"

She made a gesture of smiling protest. "I confess it is to be regretted that his mother is a lady, and that he looks—you must have noticed it?—so amazingly like the portraits of the young Schiller. But I only meant that Bessy forms all her opinions emotionally; and that she must have been very strongly affected by the scene Mr. Tredegar described to us."

"Ah," Mr. Langhope interjected, replying first to her parenthesis, "how a woman of your good sense stumbled on that idea of hunting up the mother—!" but Mrs. Ansell answered, with a slight grimace: "My dear Henry, if you could see the house they live in you'd think I had been providentially guided there!" and, reverting to the main issue, he went on fretfully: "But why, after hearing the true version of the facts, should Bessy still be influenced by that sensational scene? Even if it was not, as Tredegar suspects, cooked up expressly to take her in, she must see that the hospital doctor is, after all, as likely as any one to know how the accident really happened, and how seriously the fellow is hurt."

"There's the point. Why should Bessy believe Dr. Disbrow rather than Mr. Amherst?"

"For the best of reasons—because Disbrow has nothing to gain by distorting the facts, whereas this young Amherst, as Tredegar pointed out, has the very obvious desire to give Truscomb a bad name and shove himself into his place."

Mrs. Ansell contemplatively turned the rings upon her fingers. "From what I saw of Amherst I'm inclined to think that, if that is his object, he is too clever to have shown his hand so soon. But if you are right, was there not all the more reason for letting Bessy see him and find out as soon as possible what he was aiming at?"

"If one could have trusted her to find out—but you credit my poor child with more penetration than I've ever seen in her."

"Perhaps you've looked for it at the wrong time—and about the wrong things. Bessy has the penetration of the heart."

"The heart! You make mine jump when you use such expressions."

"Oh, I use this one in a general sense. But I want to help you to keep it from acquiring a more restricted significance."

"Restricted—to the young man himself?"

Mrs. Ansell's expressive hands seemed to commit the

question to fate. "All I ask you to consider for the present is that Bessy is quite unoccupied and excessively bored."

"Bored? Why, she has everything on earth she can want!"

"The ideal state for producing boredom—the only atmosphere in which it really thrives. And besides—to be humanly inconsistent—there's just one thing she hasn't got."

"Well?" Mr. Langhope groaned, fortifying himself with a second cigarette.

"An occupation for that rudimentary little organ, the mention of which makes you jump."

"There you go again! Good heavens, Maria, do you want to encourage her to fall in love?"

"Not with a man, just at present, but with a hobby, an interest, by all means. If she doesn't, the man will take the place of the interest—there's a vacuum to be filled, and human nature abhors a vacuum."

Mr. Langhope shrugged his shoulders. "I don't follow you. She adored her husband."

His friend's fine smile was like a magnifying glass silently applied to the gross stupidity of his remark. "Oh, I don't say it was a great passion—but they got on perfectly," he corrected himself.

"So perfectly that you must expect her to want a little storm and stress for a change. The mere fact that you and Mr. Tredegar objected to her seeing Mr. Amherst last night has roused the spirit of opposition in her. A year ago she hadn't any spirit of opposition."

"There was nothing for her to oppose—poor Dick made her life so preposterously easy."

"My ingenuous friend! Do you still think that's any reason? The fact is, Bessy wasn't awake, she wasn't even born, then. . . . She is now, and you know the infant's first conscious joy is to smash things."

"It will be rather an expensive joy if the mills are the first thing she smashes."

"Oh I imagine the mills are pretty substantial. I should, I own," Mrs. Ansell smiled, "not object to seeing her try her teeth on them."

"Which, in terms of practical conduct, means——?"

"That I advise you not to disapprove of her staying on, or of her investigating the young man's charges. You must remember that another peculiarity of the infant mind is to tire soonest of the toy that no one tries to take away from it."

"*Que diable!* But suppose Truscomb turns rusty at this very unusual form of procedure? Perhaps you don't quite know how completely he represents the prosperity of the mills."

"All the more reason," Mrs. Ansell persisted, rising at the sound of Mr. Tredegar's approach. "For don't you perceive, my poor distracted friend, that if Truscomb turns rusty, as he undoubtedly will, the inevitable result will be his manager's dismissal—and that thereafter there will presumably be peace in Warsaw?"

"Ah, you divinely wicked woman!" cried Mr. Langhope, snatching at an appreciative pressure of her hand as the lawyer reappeared in the doorway.

VI

BEFORE daylight that same morning Amherst, dressing by the gas-flame above his cheap washstand, strove to bring some order into his angry thoughts.

It humbled him to feel his purpose tossing rudderless on unruly waves of emotion, yet strive as he would he could not regain a hold on it. The events of the last twenty-four hours had been too rapid and unexpected for him to preserve his usual clear feeling of mastery; and he had, besides, to reckon with the first complete surprise of his senses. His way of life had excluded him from all contact with the subtler feminine influences, and the primitive side of the relation left his imagination untouched. He was therefore the more assailable by those refined forms of the ancient spell that lurk in delicacy of feeling interpreted by loveliness of face. By his own choice he had cut himself off from all possibility of such communion; had accepted complete abstinence for that part of his nature which might have offered a refuge from the stern prose of his daily task. But his personal indifference to his surroundings—deliberately encouraged as a defiance to the attractions of the life he had renounced—proved no defence against this appeal; rather, the meanness of his surroundings combined with his inherited refinement of taste to deepen the effect of Bessy's charm.

As he reviewed the incidents of the past hours, a reaction of self-derision came to his aid. What was this exquisite opportunity from which he had cut himself off? What, to reduce the question to a personal issue, had Mrs. Westmore said or done that, on the part of a plain woman, would have quickened his pulses by the least fraction of a second? Why, it was only the old story of the length of Cleopatra's nose! Because her eyes were a heavenly vehicle for sympathy, because her voice was pitched to thrill the tender chords, he had been deluded into thinking that she understood and responded to his appeal. And her own emotions had been wrought upon by means as cheap: it was only the obvious, theatrical side of the incident that had affected her. If Dillon's wife had been old and ugly, would she have been clasped to her employer's bosom? A more expert knowledge of the sex would have told Amherst that such ready sympathy is likely to be followed by as prompt a reaction of indifference. Luckily Mrs. Westmore's course had served as a corrective for his lack of experience; she had even, as it appeared, been at some pains to hasten the process of disillusionment. This timely discipline left him blushing at his own insincerity; for he now saw that he had risked his future not because of his zeal for the welfare of the mill-hands, but because Mrs. Westmore's look was like sunshine on his frozen senses, and because he was resolved, at any cost, to arrest her attention, to associate himself with her by the only means in his power.

Well, he deserved to fail with such an end in view; and the futility of his scheme was matched by the vanity of his purpose. In the cold light of disenchantment it seemed as though he had tried to build an impregnable fortress out of nursery blocks. How could he have foreseen anything but failure for so preposterous an attempt? His breach of discipline would of course be reported at once to Mr. Gaines and Truscomb; and the manager, already jealous of his assistant's popularity with the hands, which was a tacit criticism of his own methods, would promptly seize the pretext to be rid of him. Amherst was aware that only his technical efficiency, and his knack of getting the maximum of work out of the operatives, had secured him from Truscomb's animosity. From the outset there had been small sympathy between the two; but the scarcity of competent and hard-working assistants had made Truscomb endure him for what he was worth to the mills. Now, however, his own folly had put the match to the manager's smouldering dislike, and he saw himself, in consequence, discharged and black-listed, and perhaps roaming for months in quest of a job. He knew the efficiency of that far-reaching system of defamation whereby the employers of labour pursue and punish the subordinate who incurs their displeasure. In the case of a mere operative this secret persecution often worked complete ruin; and even to a man of Amherst's worth it opened the dispiriting prospect of a long struggle for rehabilitation.

Deep down, he suffered most at the thought that his blow for the operatives had failed; but on the surface it was the manner of his failure that exasperated him. For it seemed to prove him unfit for the very work to which he was drawn: that yearning to help the world forward that, in some natures, sets the measure to which the personal adventure must keep step. Amherst had hitherto felt himself secured by his insight and self-control from the emotional errors besetting the way of the enthusiast; and behold, he had stumbled into the first sentimental trap in his path, and tricked his eyes with a Christmas-chromo vision of lovely woman dispensing coals and blankets! Luckily, though such wounds to his self-confidence cut deep, he could apply to them the antiseptic of an unfailing humour; and before he had finished dressing, the picture of his wide schemes of social reform contracting to a blue-eyed philanthropy of cheques and groceries, had provoked a reaction of laughter. Perhaps the laughter came too soon, and rang too loud, to be true to the core; but at any rate it healed the edges of his hurt, and gave him a sound surface of composure.

But he could not laugh away the thought of the trials to which his intemperance had probably exposed his mother; and when, at the breakfast-table, from which Duplain had already departed, she broke into praise of their visitor, it was like a burning irritant on his wound.

"What a face, John! Of course I don't often see people of that kind now—" the words, falling from her too simply to be reproachful, wrung him, for that, all the more—"but I'm sure that kind of soft loveliness is rare everywhere; like a sweet summer morning with the mist on it. The Gaines girls, now, are my idea of the modern type; very handsome, of course, but you see just *how* handsome the first minute. I like a story that keeps one wondering till the end. It was very kind of Maria Ansell," Mrs. Amherst wandered happily on, "to come and hunt me out yesterday, and I enjoyed our quiet talk about old times. But what I liked best was seeing Mrs. Westmore—and, oh, John, if she came to live here, what a benediction to the mills!"

Amherst was silent, moved most of all by the unimpaired simplicity of heart with which his mother could take up past relations, and open her meagre life to the high visitations of grace and fashion, without a tinge of self-consciousness or apology. "I shall never be as genuine as that," he thought, remembering how he had wished to have Mrs. Westmore know that he was of her own class. How mixed our passions are, and how elastic must be the word that would cover any one of them! Amherst's, at that moment, were all stained with the deep wound to his self-love.

The discolouration he carried in his eye made the mill-village seem more than commonly cheerless and ugly as he walked over to the office after breakfast. Beyond the grim roof-line of the factories a dazzle of rays sent upward from banked white clouds the promise of another brilliant day; and he reflected that Mrs. Westmore would soon be speeding home to the joy of a gallop over the plains.

Far different was the task that awaited him—yet it gave him a pang to think that he might be performing it for the last time. In spite of Mr. Tredegar's assurances, he was certain that the report of his conduct must by this time have reached the President, and been transmitted to Truscomb; the latter was better that morning, and the next day he would doubtless call his rebellious assistant to account. Amherst, meanwhile, took up his routine with a dull heart. Even should his offense be condoned, his occupation presented, in itself, little future to a man without money or powerful connections. Money! He had spurned the thought of it in choosing his work, yet he now saw that, without its aid, he was powerless to accomplish the object to which his personal desires had been sacrificed. His love of his craft had gradually been merged in the larger love for his fellow-workers, and in the resulting desire to lift and widen their lot. He had once fancied that this end might be attained by an internal revolution in the management of the Westmore mills; that he might succeed in creating an industrial object-lesson conspicuous enough to point the way to wiser law-making and juster relations between the classes. But the last hours' experiences had shown him how vain it was to assault single-handed the strong barrier between money and labour, and how his own dash at the breach had only thrust him farther back into the obscure ranks of the strugglers. It was, after all, only through politics that he could return successfully to the attack; and financial independence was the needful preliminary to a political career. If he had stuck to the law he might, by this time, have been nearer to his goal; but then the goal might not have mattered, since it was only by living among the workers that he had learned to care for their fate. And rather than have forfeited that poignant yet mighty vision of the onward groping of the mass, rather than have missed the widening of his own nature that had come through sharing their hopes and pains, he would still have turned from the easier way, have chosen the deeper initiation rather than the readier attainment.

But this philosophic view of the situation was a mere thread of light on the farthest verge of his sky: much nearer were the clouds of immediate care, amid which his own folly, and his mother's possible suffering from it, loomed darkest; and these considerations made him resolve that, if his insubordination were overlooked, he would swallow the affront of a pardon, and continue for the present in the mechanical performance of his duties. He had just brought himself to this leaden state of acquiescence when one of the clerks in the outer office thrust his head in to say: "A lady asking for you—" and looking up, Amherst beheld Bessy Westmore.

She came in alone, with an air of high self-possession in marked contrast to her timidity and indecision of the previous day. Amherst thought she looked taller, more majestic; so readily may the upward slant of a soft chin, the firmer line of yielding brows, add a cubit to the outward woman. Her aspect was so commanding that he fancied she had come to express her disapproval of his conduct, to rebuke him for lack of respect to Mr. Tredegar; but a moment later it became clear, even to his inexperienced perceptions, that it was not to himself that her challenge was directed.

She advanced toward the seat he had moved forward, but in her absorption forgot to seat herself, and stood with her clasped hands resting on the back of the chair.

"I have come back to talk to you," she began, in her sweet voice with its occasional quick lift of appeal. "I knew that, in Mr. Truscomb's absence, it would be hard for you to leave the mills, and there are one or two things I want you to explain before I go away—some of the things, for instance, that you spoke to Mr. Tredegar about last night."

Amherst's feeling of constraint returned. "I'm afraid I expressed myself badly; I may have annoyed him—" he began.

She smiled this away, as though irrelevant to the main issue. "Perhaps you don't quite understand each other—but I am sure you can make it clear to me." She sank into the chair, resting one arm on the edge of the desk behind which he had resumed his place. "That is the reason why I came alone," she continued. "I never can understand when a lot of people are trying to tell me a thing all at once. And I don't suppose I care as much as a man would—a lawyer especially—about the forms that ought to be observed. All I want is to find out what is wrong and how to remedy it."

Her blue eyes met Amherst's in a look that flowed

like warmth about his heart. How should he have doubted that her feelings were as exquisite as her means of expressing them? The iron bands of distrust were loosened from his spirit, and he blushed for his cheap scepticism of the morning. In a woman so evidently nurtured in dependence, whose views had been formed, and her actions directed, by the most conventional influences, the mere fact of coming alone to Westmore, in open defiance of her advisers, bespoke a persistence of purpose that put his doubts to shame.

"It will make a great difference to the people here if you interest yourself in them," he rejoined. "I tried to explain to Mr. Tredegar that I had no wish to criticise the business management of the mills—even if there had been any excuse for my doing so—but that I was sure the condition of the operatives could be very much improved, without permanent harm to the business, by any one who felt a personal sympathy for them; and in the end I believe such sympathy produces better work, and so benefits the employer materially."

She listened with her gentle look of trust, as though committing to him, with the good faith of a child, her ignorance, her credulity, her little rudimentary convictions and her little tentative aspirations, relying on him not to abuse or misdirect them in the boundless supremacy of his masculine understanding.

"That is just what I want you to explain to me,"

she said. "But first I should like to know more about the poor man who was hurt. I meant to see his wife yesterday, but Mr. Gaines told me she would be at work till six, and it would have been difficult to go after that. I *did* go to the hospital; but the man was sleeping—is Dillon his name?—and the matron told us he was much better. Dr. Disbrow came in the evening and said the same thing—told us it was all a false report about his having been so badly hurt, and that Mr. Truscomb was very much annoyed when he heard of your having said, before the operatives, that Dillon would lose his arm."

Amherst smiled. "Ah—Mr. Truscomb heard that? Well, he's right to be annoyed: I ought not to have said it when I did. But unfortunately I am not the only one to be punished. The operative who tied on the black cloth was dismissed this morning."

Mrs. Westmore flamed up. "Dismissed for that? Oh, how unjust—how cruel!"

"You must look at both sides of the case," said Amherst, finding it much easier to remain temperate in the glow he had kindled than if he had had to force his own heat into frozen veins. "Of course any act of insubordination must be reprimanded—but I think a reprimand would have been enough."

It gave him an undeniable throb of pleasure to find that she was not to be checked by such arguments. "But he shall be put back—I won't have any one discharged for such a reason! You must find him for me at once—you must tell him——"

Once more Amherst gently restrained her. "If you'll forgive my saying so, I think it is better to let him go, and take his chance of getting work elsewhere. If he were taken back he might be made to suffer. As things are organized here, the hands are very much at the mercy of the overseers, and the overseer in that room would be likely to make it uncomfortable for a hand who had so openly defied him."

With a heavy sigh she bent her puzzled brows on him. "How complicated it is! I wonder if I shall ever understand it all. *You* don't think Dillon's accident was his own fault, then?"

"Certainly not; there are too many cards in that room. I pointed out the fact to Mr. Truscomb when the new machines were set up three years ago. An operative may be ever so expert with his fingers, and yet not learn to measure his ordinary movements quite as accurately as if he were an automaton; and that is what a man must do to be safe in the carding-room."

She sighed again. "The more you tell me, the more difficult it all seems. Why is the carding-room so overcrowded?"

"To make it pay better," Amherst returned bluntly; and the colour flushed her sensitive skin.

He thought she was about to punish him for his

plain-speaking; but she went on after a pause: "What you say is dreadful. Each thing seems to lead back to another—and I feel so ignorant of it all." She hesitated again, and then said, turning her bluest glance on him: "I am going to be quite frank with you, Mr. Amherst. Mr. Tredegar repeated to me what you said to him last night, and I think he was annoyed that you were unwilling to give any proof of the charges you made."

"Charges? Ah," Amherst exclaimed, with a start of recollection, "he means my refusing to say who told me that Dr. Disbrow was not telling the truth about Dillon?"

"Yes. He said that was a very grave accusation to make, and that no one should have made it without being able to give proof."

"That is quite true, theoretically. But in this case it would be easy for you or Mr. Tredegar to find out whether I was right."

"But Mr. Tredegar said you refused to say who told you."

"I was bound to, as it happened. But I am not bound to prevent your trying to get the same information."

"Ah—" she murmured understandingly; and, a sudden thought striking him, he went on, with a glance at the clock: "If you really wish to judge for yourself, why not go to the hospital now? I shall be free in five minutes, and could go with you if you wish it."

Amherst had remembered the nurse's cry of recognition when she saw Mrs. Westmore's face under the street-lamp; and it immediately occurred to him that, if the two women had really known each other, Mrs. Westmore would have no difficulty in obtaining the information she wanted; while, even if they met as strangers, the dark-eyed girl's perspicacity might still be trusted to come to their aid. It remained only to be seen how Mrs. Westmore would take his suggestion; but some instinct was already telling him that the high-handed method was the one she really preferred.

"To the hospital—now? I should like it of all things," she exclaimed, rising with what seemed an almost childish zest in the adventure. "Of course that is the best way of finding out. I ought to have insisted on seeing Dillon yesterday—but I begin to think the matron didn't want me to."

Amherst left this inference to work itself out in her mind, contenting himself, as they drove back to Hanaford, with answering her questions about Dillon's family, the ages of his children, and his wife's health. Her enquiries, he noticed, did not extend from the particular to the general: her curiosity, as yet, was too purely personal and emotional to lead to any larger consideration of the question. But this larger view might grow out of the investigation of Dillon's case; and meanwhile Amherst's own purposes were momentarily lost in the sweet confusion of feeling her near him—of seeing the exquisite grain of her skin, the way her lashes grew out of a dusky line on the edge of the white lids, the way her hair, stealing in spirals of light from brow to ear, wavered off into a fruity down on the edge of the cheek.

At the hospital they were protestingly admitted by Mrs. Ogan, though the official "visitors' hour" was not till the afternoon; and beside the sufferer's bed, Amherst saw again that sudden flowering of compassion which seemed the key to his companion's beauty: as though her lips had been formed for consolation and her hands for tender offices. It was clear enough that Dillon, still sunk in a torpor broken by feverish tossings, was making no perceptible progress toward recovery; and Mrs. Ogan was reduced to murmuring some technical explanation about the state of the wound while Bessy hung above him with reassuring murmurs as to his wife's fate, and promises that the children should be cared for

Amherst had noticed, on entering, that a new nurse—a gaping young woman instantly lost in the study of Mrs. Westmore's toilet—had replaced the dark-eyed attendant of the day before; and supposing that the latter was temporarily off duty, he asked Mrs. Ogan if she might be seen.

The matron's face was a picture of genteel perplexity. "The other nurse? Our regular surgical nurse, Miss Golden, is ill—Miss Hibbs, here, is replacing her for the present." She indicated the gaping damsel; then, as Amherst persisted: "Ah," she wondered negligently, "do you mean the young lady you saw here yesterday? Certainly—I had forgotten: Miss Brent was merely a—er—temporary substitute. I believe she was recommended to Dr. Disbrow by one of his patients; but we found her quite unsuitable—in fact, unfitted—and the doctor discharged her this morning."

Mrs. Westmore had drawn near, and while the matron delivered her explanation, with an uneasy sorting and shifting of words, a quick signal of intelligence passed between her hearers. "You see?" Amherst's eyes exclaimed; "I see—they have sent her away because she told you," Bessy's flashed back in wrath, and his answering look did not deny her inference.

"Do you know where she has gone?" Amherst enquired; but Mrs. Ogan, permitting her brows a faint lift of surprise, replied that she had no idea of Miss Brent's movements, beyond having heard that she was to leave Hanaford immediately

In the carriage Bessy exclaimed: "It was the nurse, of course—if we could only find her! Brent—did Mrs. Ogan say her name was Brent?"

"Do you know the name?"

"Yes—at least—but it couldn't, of course, be the girl I knew——"

"Miss Brent saw you the night you arrived, and thought she recognized you. She said you and she had been at some school or convent together."

"The Sacred Heart? Then it *is* Justine Brent! I heard they had lost their money—I haven't seen her for years. But how strange that she should be a hospital nurse! And why is she at Hanaford, I wonder?"

"She was here only on a visit; she didn't tell me where she lived. She said she heard that a surgical nurse was wanted at the hospital, and volunteered her services; I'm afraid she got small thanks for them."

"Do you really think they sent her away for talking to you? How do you suppose they found out?"

"I waited for her last night when she left the hospital, and I suppose Mrs. Ogan or one of the doctors saw us. It was thoughtless of me," Amherst exclaimed with compunction.

"I wish I had seen her—poor Justine! We were the greatest friends at the convent. She was the ringleader in all our mischief—I never saw any one so quick and clever. I suppose her fun is all gone now."

For a moment Mrs. Westmore's mind continued to linger among her memories; then she reverted to the question of the Dillons, and of what might best be done for them if Miss Brent's fears should be realized.

As the carriage neared her door she turned to her companion with extended hand. "Thank you so much, Mr. Amherst. I am glad you suggested that Mr. Truscomb should find some work for Dillon about the office. But I must talk to you about this again—can you come in this evening?"

VII

AMHERST could never afterward regain a detailed impression of the weeks that followed. They lived in his memory chiefly as exponents of the unforeseen, nothing he had looked for having come to pass in the way or at the time expected; while the whole movement of life was like the noon-day flow of a river, in which the separate ripples of brightness are all merged in one blinding glitter. His recurring conferences with Mrs. Westmore formed, as it were, the small surprising kernel of fact about which sensations gathered and grew with the swift ripening of a magician's fruit. That she should remain on at Hanaford to look into the condition of the mills did not, in itself, seem surprising to Amherst; for his short phase of doubt had been succeeded by an abundant inflow of faith in her intentions. It satisfied his inner craving for harmony that her face and spirit should, after all, so corroborate and complete each other; that it needed no moral sophistry to adjust her acts to her appearance, her words to the promise of her smile. But her immediate confidence in him, her resolve to support him in his avowed insubordination, to ignore, with the royal license of her sex, all that was irregular and inexpedient in asking his guidance while the whole official strength of the company darkened the background with a gathering storm of disapproval—this sense of being the glove flung by her hand in the face of convention, quickened astonishingly the flow of Amherst's sensations. It was as though a mountain-climber, braced to the strain of a hard ascent, should suddenly see the way break into roses, and level itself in a path for his feet.

On his second visit he found the two ladies together, and Mrs. Ansell's smile of approval seemed to cast a social sanction on the episode, to classify it as comfortably usual and unimportant. He could see that her friend's manner put Bessy at ease, helping her to ask her own questions, and to reflect on his suggestions, with less bewilderment and more self-confidence. Mrs. Ansell had the faculty of restoring to her the belief in her reasoning powers that her father could dissolve in a monosyllable.

The talk, on this occasion, had turned mainly on the future of the Dillon family, on the best means of compensating for the accident, and, incidentally, on the care of the young children of the mill-colony. Though

Amherst did not believe in the extremer forms of industrial paternalism, he was yet of opinion that, where married women were employed, the employer should care for their children. He had been gradually, and somewhat reluctantly, brought to this conviction by the many instances of unavoidable neglect and suffering among the children of the women-workers at Westmore; and Mrs. Westmore took up the scheme with all the ardour of her young motherliness, quivering at the thought of hungry or ailing children while her Cicely, leaning a silken head against her, lifted puzzled eyes to her face.

On the larger problems of the case it was less easy to fix Bessy's attention; but Amherst was far from being one of the extreme theorists who reject temporary remedies lest they defer the day of general renewal, and since he looked on every gain in the material condition of the mill-hands as a step in their moral growth, he was quite willing to hold back his fundamental plans while he discussed the establishment of a nursery, and of a night-school for the boys in the mills.

The third time he called, he found Mr. Langhope and Mr. Halford Gaines of the company. The President of the Westmore mills was a trim middle-sized man, whose high pink varnish of good living would have turned to purple could he have known Mr. Langhope's opinion of his jewelled shirt-front and the padded shoulders of his evening-coat. Happily he had no inkling of these views, and was fortified in his command of the situation by an unimpaired confidence in his own appearance; while Mr. Langhope, discreetly withdrawn behind a veil of cigar-smoke, let his silence play like a fine criticism over the various phases of the discussion.

It was a surprise to Amherst to find himself in Mr. Gaines's presence. The President, secluded in his high office, seldom visited the mills, and when there showed no consciousness of any presence lower than Truscomb's; and Amherst's first thought was that, in the manager's enforced absence, he was to be called to account by the head of the firm. But he was affably welcomed by Mr. Gaines, who made it clear that his ostensible purpose in coming was to hear Amherst's views as to the proposed night-schools and nursery. These were pointedly alluded to as Mrs. Westmore's projects, and the young man was made to feel that he was merely called in as a temporary adviser in Truscomb's absence. This was, in fact, the position Amherst preferred to take, and he scrupulously restricted himself to the answering of questions, letting Mrs. Westmore unfold his plans as though they had been her own. "It is much better," he reflected, "that they should all think so, and she too, for Truscomb will be on his legs again in a day or two, and then my hours will be numbered."

Meanwhile he was surprised to find Mr. Gaines oddly amenable to the proposed innovations, which he appeared to regard as new fashions in mill-management, to be adopted for the same cogent reasons as a new cut in coat-tails.

"Of course we want to be up-to-date—there's no reason why the Westmore mills shouldn't do as well by their people as any mills in the country," he affirmed, in the tone of the entertainer accustomed to say: "I want the thing done handsomely." But he seemed even less conscious than Mrs. Westmore that each particular wrong could be traced back to a radical vice in the system. He appeared to think that every murmur of assent to her proposals passed the sponge, once for all, over the difficulty propounded: as though a problem in algebra should be solved by wiping it off the blackboard.

"My dear Bessy, we all owe you a debt of gratitude for coming here, and bringing, so to speak, a fresh eye to bear on the subject. If I've been, perhaps, a little too exclusively absorbed in making the mills profitable, my friend Langhope will, I believe, not be the first to—er—cast a stone at me." Mr. Gaines, who was the soul of delicacy, stumbled a little over the awkward associations connected with this figure, but, picking himself up, hastened on to affirm: "And in that respect, I think we can challenge comparison with any industry in the state; but I am the first to admit that there may be another side, a side that it takes a woman—a mother—to see. For instance," he threw in jocosely, "I flatter myself that I know how to order a good dinner; but I always leave the flowers to my wife. And if you'll permit me to say so," he went on, encouraged by the felicity of his image, "I believe it will produce a most pleasing effect—not only on the operatives themselves, but on the whole of Hanaford—on our own set of people especially—to have you come here and interest yourself in the—er—philanthropic side of the work."

Bessy coloured a little. She blushed easily, and was perhaps not over-discriminating as to the quality of praise received; but under her ripple of pleasure a stronger feeling stirred, and she said hastily: "I am afraid I never should have thought of these things if Mr. Amherst had not pointed them out to me."

Mr. Gaines met this blandly. "Very gratifying to Mr. Amherst to have you put it in that way; and I am sure we all appreciate his valuable hints. Truscomb himself could not have been more helpful, though his larger experience will no doubt be useful later on, in developing and—er—modifying your plans."

It was difficult to reconcile this large view of the moral issue with the existence of abuses which made the management of the Westmore mills as unpleasantly notorious in one section of the community as it was agreeably notable in another. But Amherst was impartial enough to see that Mr. Gaines was unconscious of the incongruities of the situation. He left the reconciling of incompatibles to Truscomb with the simple faith of the believer committing a like task to his maker: it was in the manager's mind that the dark processes of adjustment took place. Mr. Gaines cultivated the convenient and popular idea that by ignoring wrongs one is not so much condoning as actually denying their existence; and in pursuance of this belief he devoutly abstained from studying the conditions at Westmore.

A farther surprise awaited Amherst when Truscomb reappeared in the office. The manager was always a man of few words; and for the first days his intercourse with his assistant was restricted to asking questions and issuing orders. Soon afterward, it became known that Dillon's arm was to be amputated, and that afternoon Truscomb was summoned to see Mrs. Westmore. When he returned he sent for Amherst; and the young man felt sure that his hour had come.

He was at dinner when the message reached him, and he knew from the tightening of his mother's lips that she too interpreted it in the same way. He was glad that Duplain's presence kept her from speaking her fears; and he thanked her inwardly for the smile with which she watched him go.

That evening, when he returned, the smile was still at its post; but it dropped away wearily as he said, with his hands on her shoulders: "Don't worry, mother; I don't know exactly what's happening, but we're not blacklisted yet."

Mrs. Amherst had immediately taken up her work, letting her nervous tension find its usual escape through her finger-tips. Her needles flagged as she lifted her eyes to his.

"Something *is* happening, then?" she murmured.

"Oh, a number of things, evidently—but though I'm in the heart of them, I can't yet make out how they are going to affect me."

His mother's glance twinkled in time with the flash of her needles. "There's always a safe place in the heart of a storm," she said shrewdly; and Amherst rejoined with a laugh: "Well, if it's Truscomb's heart, I don't know that it's particularly safe for me."

"Tell me just what he said, John," she begged, making no attempt to carry the pleasantry farther, though its possibilities still seemed to flicker about her lip; and Amherst proceeded to recount his talk with the manager.

Truscomb, it appeared, had made no allusion to Dillon; his avowed purpose in summoning his assistant had been to discuss with the latter the question of the proposed nursery and schools. Mrs. Westmore, at

Amherst's suggestion, had presented these projects as her own; but the question of a site having come up, she had mentioned to Truscomb his assistant's proposal that the company should buy for the purpose the notorious Eldorado. The road-house in question had always been one of the most destructive influences in the mill-colony, and Amherst had made one or two indirect attempts to have the building converted to other uses; but the persistent opposition he encountered gave colour to the popular report that the manager took a high toll from the landlord.

It therefore at once occurred to Amherst to suggest the purchase of the property to Mrs. Westmore; and he was not surprised to find that Truscomb's opposition to the scheme centred in the choice of the building. But even at this point the manager betrayed no open resistance; he seemed tacitly to admit Amherst's right to discuss the proposed plans, and even to be consulted concerning the choice of a site. He was ready with a dozen good reasons against the purchase of the road-house; but here also he proceeded with a discretion unexampled in his dealings with his subordinates. He acknowledged the harm done by the dance-hall, but objected that he could not conscientiously advise the company to pay the extortionate price at which it was held, and reminded Amherst that, if that particular source of offense were removed, others would inevitably spring up to replace it; marshalling the usual temporizing arguments of tolerance and expediency, with no marked change from his usual tone, till, just as the interview was ending, he asked, with a sudden drop to conciliation, if the assistant manager had anything to complain of in the treatment he received.

This came as such a surprise to Amherst that before he had collected himself he found Truscomb ambiguously but unmistakably offering him—with the practised indirection of the man accustomed to cover his share in such transactions—a substantial "consideration" for dropping the matter of the road-house. It was incredible, yet it had really happened: the all-powerful Truscomb, who held Westmore in the hollow of his hand, had stooped to bribing his assistant because he was afraid to deal with him in a more summary manner. Amherst's leap of anger at the offer was curbed by the instant perception of its cause. He had no time to search for a reason; he could only rally himself to meet the unintelligible with a composure as abysmal as Truscomb's; and his voice still rang with the wonder of the incident as he retailed it to his mother.

"Think of what it means, mother, for a young woman like Mrs. Westmore, without any experience or any habit of authority, to come here, and at the first glimpse of injustice, to be so revolted that she finds the courage and cleverness to put her little hand to the machine and reverse the engines—for it's nothing less that she's done! Oh, I know there'll be a reaction—the pendulum's sure to swing back: but you'll see it won't swing *as far*. Of course I shall go in the end—but Truscomb may go too: Jove, if I could pull him down on me, like what's-his-name and the pillars of the temple!"

He had risen and was measuring the little sitting-room with his long strides, his head flung back and his eyes dark with the inward look his mother had not always cared to see there. But now her own glance seemed to have caught a ray from his, and the knitting flowed from her hands like the thread of fate, as she sat silent, letting him exhale his hopes and his wonder, and murmuring only, when he dropped again to the chair at her side: "You won't go, Johnny—you won't go."

Mrs. Westmore lingered on for over two weeks, and during that time Amherst was able, in various directions, to develop her interest in the mill-workers. His own schemes involved a complete readjustment of the relation between the company and the hands: the suppression of the obsolete company "store" and tenements, which had so long sapped the thrift and ambition of the workers; the transformation of the Hopewood grounds into a park and athletic field, and the division of its remaining acres into building lots for the mill-hands; the establishing of a library, a dispensary and emergency hospital, and various other centres of humanizing influence; but he refrained from letting her see that his present suggestion was only a part of this larger plan, lest her growing sympathy should be checked. He had in his mother an example of the mind accessible only to concrete impressions: the mind which could die for the particular instance, yet remain serenely indifferent to its causes. To Mrs. Amherst, her son's work had been interesting simply because it *was* his work: remove his presence from Westmore, and the whole industrial problem became to her as non-existent as star-dust to the naked eye. And in Bessy Westmore he divined a nature of the same quality—divined, but no longer criticized it. Was not that concentration on the personal issue just the compensating grace of her sex? Did it not offer a warm tint of human inconsistency to eyes chilled by contemplating life in the mass? It pleased Amherst for the moment to class himself with the impersonal student of social problems, though in truth his interest in them had its source in an imagination as open as Bessy's to the pathos of the personal appeal. But if he had the same sensitiveness, how inferior were his means of expressing it! Again and again, during their talks, he had the feeling which had come to him when she bent over Dillon's bed—that her exquisite lines were, in some mystical sense, the visible flowering of her nature, that they had taken shape in response to the inward motions of the heart.

To a young man ruled by high enthusiasms there can be no more dazzling adventure than to work this miracle in the tender creature who yields her mind to his—to see, as it were, the blossoming of the spiritual seed in forms of heightened loveliness, the bluer beam of the eye, the richer curve of the lip, all the physical currents of life quickening under the breath of a kindled thought. It did not occur to him that any other emotion had effected the change he perceived. Bessy Westmore had in full measure that gift of unconscious hypocrisy which enables a woman to make the man in whom she is interested believe that she enters into all his thoughts. She had—more than this—the gift of self-deception, supreme happiness of the unreflecting nature, whereby she was able to believe herself solely engrossed in the subjects they discussed, to regard him as the mere spokesman of important ideas, thus saving their intercourse from present constraint, and from the awkward contemplation of future contingencies. So, in obedience to the ancient sorcery of life, these two groped for and found each other in regions seemingly so remote from the accredited domain of romance that it would have been as a great surprise to them to learn whither they had strayed as to see the arid streets of Westmore suddenly bursting into leaf.

With Mrs. Westmore's departure Amherst, for the first time, became aware of a certain flatness in his life. His daily task seemed dull and purposeless, and he was galled by Truscomb's studied forbearance, under which he suspected a quickly accumulating store of animosity. He almost longed for some collision which would release the manager's pent-up resentment; yet he dreaded increasingly any accident that might make his stay at Westmore impossible.

It was on Sundays, when he was freed from his weekly task, that he was most at the mercy of these opposing feelings. They drove him forth on long solitary walks beyond the town, walks ending most often in the deserted grounds of Hopewood, beautiful now in the ruined gold of October. As he sat under the beech-limbs above the river, watching its brown current sweep the willow-roots of the banks, he thought how this same current, within its next short reach, passed from wooded seclusion to the noise and pollution of the mills. So his own life seemed to have passed once more from the tranced flow of the last weeks into its old channel of unillumined labour. But other thoughts came to him too: the vision of converting that melancholy pleasure-ground into an outlet for the cramped lives of the mill-workers; and he pictured the weed-grown lawns and paths thronged with holiday-makers, and the slopes nearer the factories dotted with houses and gardens.

An unexpected event revived these hopes. A few days before Christmas it became known to Hanaford that Mrs. Westmore would return for the holidays. Cicely was drooping in town air, and Bessy had persuaded Mr. Langhope that the bracing cold of Hanaford would be better for the child than the milder atmosphere of Long Island. They reappeared, and brought with them a breath of holiday cheerfulness such as Westmore had never known. It had always been the rule at the mills to let the operatives take their pleasure as they saw fit, and the Eldorado and the Hanaford saloons throve on this policy. But Mrs. Westmore arrived full of festal projects. There was to be a giant Christmas tree for the mill-children, a supper on the same scale for the operatives, and a bout of skating and coasting at Hopewood for the older lads—the "band" and "bobbin" boys in whom Amherst had always felt a special interest. The Gaines ladies, resolved to show themselves at home in the latest philanthropic fashions, actively seconded Bessy's endeavours, and for a week Westmore basked under a sudden heat-wave of beneficence.

The time had passed when Amherst might have made light of such efforts. With Bessy Westmore smiling up, holly-laden, from the foot of the ladder on which she kept him perched, how could he question the efficacy of hanging the opening-room with Christmas wreaths, or the ultimate benefit of gorging the operatives with turkey and sheathing their offspring in red mittens? It was just like the end of a story-book with a pretty moral, and Amherst was in the mood to be as much taken by the tinsel as the youngest mill-baby held up to gape at the tree.

At the New Year, when Mrs. Westmore left, the negotiations for the purchase of the Eldorado were well advanced, and it was understood that on their completion she was to return for the opening of the night-school and nursery. Suddenly, however, it became known that the proprietor of the road-house had decided not to sell. Amherst heard of the decision from Duplain, and at once foresaw the inevitable result—that Mrs. Westmore's plan would be given up owing to the difficulty of finding another site. Mr. Gaines and Truscomb had both discountenanced the erection of a special building for what was, after all, only a tentative enterprise. Among the purchasable houses in Westmore no other was suited to the purpose, and they had, therefore, a good excuse for advising Bessy to defer her experiment.

Almost at the same time, however, another piece of news changed the aspect of affairs. A scandalous occurrence at the Eldorado, witnesses to which were unexpectedly forthcoming, put it in Amherst's power to threaten the landlord with exposure unless he should at once accept the company's offer and withdraw from Westmore. Amherst had no long time to consider the best means of putting this threat into effect. He knew it was not only idle to appeal to Truscomb, but essential to keep the facts from him till the deed was done; yet how obtain the authority to act without him? The seemingly insuperable difficulties of the situation whetted Amherst's craving for a struggle. He thought first of writing to Mrs. Westmore; but now that the spell of her presence was withdrawn he felt how hard it would be to make her understand the need of prompt and secret action; and besides, was it likely that, at such short notice, she could command the needful funds? Prudence opposed the attempt, and on reflection he decided to appeal to Mr. Gaines, hoping that the flagrancy of the case would rouse the President from his usual attitude of indifference.

Mr. Gaines was roused to the extent of showing a profound resentment against the cause of his disturbance. He relieved his sense of responsibility by some didactic remarks on the vicious tendencies of the working-classes, and concluded with the reflection that the more you did for them the less thanks you got. But when Amherst showed an unwillingness to let the matter rest on this time-honoured aphorism, the President retrenched himself behind ambiguities, suggestions that they should await Mrs. Westmore's return, and general considerations of a pessimistic nature, tapering off into a gloomy view of the weather.

"By God, I'll write to her!" Amherst exclaimed, as the Gaines portals closed on him; and all the way back to Westmore he was busy marshalling his arguments and entreaties.

He wrote the letter that night, but did not post it. Some unavowed distrust of her restrained him—a distrust not of her heart but of her intelligence. He felt that the whole future of Westmore was at stake, and decided to await the development of the next twenty-four hours. The letter was still in his pocket when, after dinner, he was summoned to the office by Truscomb.

That evening, when he returned home, he entered the little sitting-room without speaking. His mother sat there alone, in her usual place—how many nights he had seen the lamplight slant at that particular angle across her fresh cheek and the fine wrinkles about her eyes! He was going to add another wrinkle to the number now—soon they would creep down and encroach upon the smoothness of the cheek.

She looked up and saw that his glance was turned to the crowded bookshelves behind her.

"There must be nearly a thousand of them," he said as their eyes met.

"Books? Yes—with your father's. Why—were you thinking. . . ?" She started up suddenly and crossed over to him.

"Too many for wanderers," he continued, drawing her hands to his breast; then, as she clung to him, weeping and trembling a little: "It had to be, mother," he said, kissing her penitently where the fine wrinkles died into the cheek.

VIII

AMHERST'S dismissal was not to take effect for a month; and in the interval he addressed himself steadily to his task.

He went through the routine of the work numbly; but his intercourse with the hands tugged at deep fibres of feelings. He had always shared, as far as his duties allowed, in the cares and interests of their few free hours: the hours when the automatic appendages of the giant machine became men and women again, with desires and passions of their own. Under Amherst's influence the mixed elements of the mill-community had begun to crystallize into social groups: his books had served as an improvised lending-library, he had organized a club, a rudimentary orchestra, and various other means of binding together the better spirits of the community. With the older men, the attractions of the

Eldorado, and kindred inducements, often worked against him; but among the younger hands, and especially the boys, he had gained a personal ascendency that it was bitter to relinquish.

It was the severing of this tie that cost him most pain in the final days at Westmore; and after he had done what he could to console his mother, and to put himself in the way of getting work elsewhere, he tried to see what might be saved out of the ruins of the little polity he had built up. He hoped his influence might at least persist in the form of an awakened instinct of fellowship; and he gave every spare hour to strengthening the links he had tried to form. The boys, at any rate, would be honestly sorry to have him go: not, indeed, from the profounder reasons that affected him, but because he had not only stood persistently between the overseers and themselves, but had recognized their right to fun after work-hours as well as their right to protection while they worked.

In the glow of Mrs. Westmore's Christmas visitation an athletic club had been formed, and leave obtained to use the Hopewood grounds for Saturday afternoon sports; and thither Amherst continued to conduct the boys after the mills closed at the week-end. His last Saturday had now come: a shining afternoon of late February, with a red sunset bending above frozen river and slopes of unruffled snow. For an hour or more he had led the usual sports, coasting down the steep descent from the house to the edge of the woods, and skating and playing hockey on the rough river-ice which eager hands kept clear after every snow-storm. He always felt the contagion of these sports: the glow of movement, the tumult of young voices, the sting of the winter air, roused all the boyhood in his blood. But today he had to force himself through his part in the performance. To the very last, as he now saw, he had hoped for a sign in the heavens: not the reversal of his own sentence—for, merely on disciplinary grounds, he perceived that to be impossible—but something pointing to a change in the management of the mills, some proof that Mrs. Westmore's intervention had betokened more than a passing impulse of compassion. Surely she would not accept without question the abandonment of her favourite scheme; and if she came back to put the question, the answer would lay bare the whole situation. . . So Amherst's hopes had persuaded him; but the day before he had heard that she was to sail for Europe. The report, first announced in the papers, had been confirmed by his mother, who brought back from a visit to Hanaford the news that Mrs. Westmore was leaving at once for an indefinite period, and that the Hanaford house was to be closed. Irony would have been the readiest caustic for the wound inflicted; but Amherst, for that very reason, disdained it. He would not taint his disappointment with mockery, but would leave it among the unspoiled sadnesses of life. . .

He flung himself into the boys' sports with his usual energy, meaning that their last Saturday with him should be their merriest; but he went through his part mechanically, and was glad when the sun began to dip toward the rim of the woods.

He was standing on the ice, where the river widened just below the house, when a jingle of bells broke on the still air, and he saw a sleigh driven rapidly up the avenue. Amherst watched it in surprise. Who, at that hour, could be invading the winter solitude of Hopewood? The sleigh halted near the closed house, and a muffled figure, alighting alone, began to move down the snowy slope toward the skaters.

In an instant he had torn off his skates and was bounding up the bank. He would have known the figure anywhere—known that lovely poise of the head, the mixture of hesitancy and quickness in the light tread which even the snow could not impede. Half-way up the slope to the house they met, and Mrs. Westmore held out her hand. Face and lips, as she stood above him, glowed with her swift passage through the evening air, and in the blaze of the sunset she seemed saturated with heavenly fires.

"I drove out to find you—they told me you were here—I arrived this morning, quite suddenly. . ."

She broke off, as though the encounter had checked her ardour instead of kindling it; but he drew no discouragement from her tone.

"I hoped you would come before I left—I knew you would!" he exclaimed; and at his last words her face clouded anxiously.

"I didn't know you were leaving Westmore till yesterday—the day before—I got a letter. . ." Again she wavered, perceptibly trusting her difficulty to him, in the sweet way he had been trying to forget; and he answered with recovered energy: "The great thing is that you should be here."

She shook her head at his optimism. "What can I do if you go?"

"You can give me a chance, before I go, to tell you a little about some of the loose ends I am leaving."

"But why are you leaving them? I don't understand. Is it inevitable?"

"Inevitable," he returned, with an odd glow of satisfaction in the word; and as her eyes besought him, he added, smiling: "I've been dismissed, you see; and from the manager's standpoint I think I deserved it. But the best part of my work needn't go with me—and that is what I should like to speak to you about. As assistant manager I can easily be replaced—have been, I understand, already; but among these boys here I should like to think that a little of me stayed

Half-way up the slope to the house they met.

—and it will, if you'll let me tell you what I've been doing."

She glanced away from him at the busy throng on the ice and at the other black cluster above the coasting-slide.

"How they're enjoying it!" she murmured. "What a pity it was never done before! And who will keep it up when you're gone?"

"You," he answered, meeting her eyes again; and as she coloured a little under his look he went on quickly: "Will you come over and look at the coasting? The time is almost up. One more slide and they'll be packing off to supper."

She nodded "yes," and they walked in silence over the white lawn, criss-crossed with tramplings of happy feet, to the ridge from which the coasters started on their run. Amherst's object in turning the talk had been to gain a moment's respite. He could not bear to waste his perfect hour in futile explanations: he wanted to keep it undisturbed by any thought of the future. And the same feeling seemed to possess his companion, for she did not speak again till they reached the knoll where the boys were gathered.

A sled packed with them hung on the brink: with a last shout it was off, dipping down the incline with the long curved flight of a swallow, flashing across the wide meadow at the base of the hill, and tossed upward again by its own impetus, till it vanished in the dark rim of wood on the opposite height. The lads waiting on the knoll sang out for joy, and Bessy clapped her hands and joined with them.

"What fun! I wish I'd brought Cicely! I've not coasted for years," she laughed out, as the second detachment of boys heaped themselves on another sled and shot down. Amherst looked at her with a smile. He saw that every other feeling had vanished in the exhilaration of watching the flight of the sleds. She had forgotten why she had come—forgotten her distress at his dismissal—forgotten everything but the spell of the long white slope, and the tingle of cold in her veins.

"Shall we go down? Should you like it?" he asked, feeling no resentment under the heightened glow of his pulses.

"Oh, do take me—I shall love it!" Her eyes shone like a child's—she might have been a lovelier embodiment of the shouting boyhood about them.

The first band of coasters, sled at heels, had by this time already covered a third of the homeward stretch; but Amherst was too impatient to wait. Plunging down to the meadow he caught up the sled-rope, and raced back with the pack of rejoicing youth in his wake. The sharp climb up the hill seemed to fill his lungs with flame: his whole body burned with a strange intensity of life. As he reached the top, a distant bell rang across the fields from Westmore, and the boys began to snatch up their coats and mufflers.

"Be off with you—I'll look after the sleds," Amherst called to them as they dispersed; then he turned for a moment to see that the skaters below were also heeding the summons.

A cold pallor lay on the river-banks and on the low meadow beneath the knoll; but the woodland opposite stood black against scarlet vapours that ravelled off in sheer light toward a sky hung with an icy moon.

Amherst drew up the sled and held it steady while Bessy, seating herself, tucked her furs close with little breaks of laughter; then he placed himself in front.

"Ready?" he cried over his shoulder, and "Ready!" she called back.

Their craft quivered under them, hanging an instant over the long stretch of whiteness below; the level sun dazzled their eyes, and the first plunge seemed to dash them down into darkness. Amherst heard a cry of glee behind him; then all sounds were lost in the whistle of air humming by like the flight of a million arrows. They had dropped below the sunset and were tearing through the clear nether twilight of the descent; then, with a bound, the sled met the level, and shot away across the meadow toward the opposite height. It seemed to Amherst as though his body had been left behind, and only the spirit in him rode the wild blue currents of galloping air; but as the sled's rush began to slacken with the strain of the last ascent he was recalled to himself by the touch of the breathing warmth at his back. Bessy had put out a hand to steady herself, and as she leaned forward, gripping his arm, a flying end of her furs swept his face. There was a delicious pang in being thus caught back to life; and as the sled stopped, and he sprang to his feet, he still glowed with the sensation. Bessy too was under the spell. In the dusk of the beech-grove where they had landed, he could barely distinguish her features; but her eyes shone on him, and he heard her quick breathing as he stooped to help her to her feet.

"Oh, how beautiful—it's the only thing better than a good gallop!"

She leaned against a tree-bole, panting a little, and loosening her furs.

"What a pity it's too dark to begin again!" she sighed, looking about her through the dim weaving of leafless boughs.

"It's not so dark in the open—we might have one more," he proposed; but she shook her head, seized by a new whim.

"It's so still and delicious in here—did you hear the snow fall when that squirrel jumped across to the pine?" She tilted her head, narrowing her lids as she peered upward. "There he is! One gets used to the light. . . Look! See his little eyes shining down at us!"

As Amherst looked where she pointed, the squirrel leapt to another tree, and they stole on after him through the hushed wood, guided by his grey flashes in the dimness. Here and there, in a break of the snow, they trod on a bed of wet leaves that gave out a breath of hidden life, or a hemlock twig dashed its spicy scent into their faces. As they grew used to the twilight their eyes began to distinguish countless delicate gradations of tint: cold mottlings of grey-black boles against the snow, wet russets of drifted beech-leaves, a distant network of mauve twigs melting into the woodland haze. And in the silence just such fine gradations of sound became audible: the soft drop of loosened snow-lumps, a stir of startled wings, the creak of a dead branch, somewhere far off in darkness.

They walked on, still in silence, as though they had entered the glade of an enchanted forest and were powerless to turn back or to break the hush with a word. They made no pretense of following the squirrel any longer; he had flashed away to a high tree-top, from which his ironical chatter pattered down on their unheeding ears. Amherst's sensations were not of that highest order of happiness where mind and heart mingle their elements in the strong draught of life: it was a languid fume that stole through him from the cup at his lips. But after the sense of defeat and failure which the last weeks had brought, the reaction was too exquisite to be analyzed. All he asked of the moment was its immediate sweetness. . .

They had reached the brink of a rocky glen where a little brook still sent its thread of sound through mufflings of ice and huddled branches. Bessy stood still a moment, bending her head to the sweet cold tinkle; then she moved away and said slowly: "We must go back."

As they turned to retrace their steps a yellow line of light through the tree-trunks showed them that they had not, after all, gone very deep into the wood. A few minutes' walk would restore them to the lingering daylight, and on the farther side of the meadow stood the sleigh which was to carry Bessy back to Hanaford. A sudden sense of the evanescence of the moment roused Amherst from his absorption. Before the next change in the fading light he would be back again among the ugly realities of life. Did she, too, hate to return to them? Or why else did she walk so slowly—why did she seem as much afraid as himself to break the silence that held them in its magic circle?

A dead pine-branch caught in the edge of her skirt, and she stood still while Amherst bent down to release her. As she turned to help him he looked up with a smile.

"The wood doesn't want to let you go," he said.

She made no reply, and he added, rising: "But you'll come back to it—you'll come back often, I hope."

He could not see her face in the dimness, but her voice trembled a little as she answered: "I will do what you tell me—but I shall be alone—against all the others: they don't understand."

The simplicity, the helplessness, of the avowal, appealed to him not as a weakness but as a grace. He understood what she was really saying: "How can you desert me? How can you put this great responsibility on me, and then leave me to bear it alone?" and in the light of her unuttered appeal his action seemed almost like cruelty. Why had he opened her eyes to wrongs she had no strength to redress without his aid?

He could only answer, as he walked beside her toward the edge of the wood: "You will not be alone—in time you will make the others understand; in time they will be with you."

"Ah, you don't believe that!" she exclaimed, pausing suddenly, and speaking with an intensity of reproach that amazed him.

"I hope it, at any rate," he rejoined, pausing also. "And I'm sure that if you will come here oftener—if you'll really live among your people——"

"How can you say that, when you're deserting them?" she broke in, with a feminine excess of inconsequence that fairly dashed the words from his lips.

"Deserting them? Don't you understand——?"

"I understand that you've made Mr. Gaines and Truscomb angry—yes; but if I should insist on your staying——"

Amherst felt the blood rush to his forehead. "No—no, it's not possible!" he exclaimed, with a vehemence addressed more to himself than to her.

"Then what will happen at the mills?"

"Oh, some one else will be found—the new ideas are stirring everywhere. And if you'll only come back here, and help my successor——"

"Do you think they are likely to choose any one else with your ideas?" she interposed with unexpected acuteness; and after a short silence he answered: "Not immediately, perhaps; but in time—in time there will be improvements."

"As if the poor people could wait! Oh, it's cruel, cruel of you to go!"

Her voice broke in a throb of entreaty that went to his inmost fibres.

"You don't understand. It's impossible in the present state of things that I should do any good by staying."

"Then you refuse? Even if I were to insist on their asking you to stay, you would still refuse?" she persisted.

"Yes—I should still refuse."

She made no answer, but moved a few steps nearer

to the edge of the wood. The meadow was just below them now, and the sleigh in plain sight on the height beyond. Their steps made no sound on the sodden drifts underfoot, and in the silence he thought he heard a catch in her breathing. It was enough to make the brimming moment overflow. He stood still before her and bent his head to hers.

"Bessy!" he said, with sudden vehemence.

She did not speak or move, but in the quickened state of his perceptions he became aware that she was silently weeping. The gathering darkness under the trees enveloped them. It absorbed her outline into the shadowy background of the wood, from which her face emerged in a faint spot of pallor; and the same obscurity seemed to envelop his faculties, merging the hard facts of life in a blur of feeling in which the distinctest impression was the sweet sense of her tears.

"Bessy!" he exclaimed again; and as he drew a step nearer he felt her yield to him, and bury her sobs against his arm.

BOOK II

IX

"BUT, Justine——"

Mrs. Harry Dressel, seated in the June freshness of her Oak Street drawing-room, and harmonizing by her high lights and hard edges with the white-and-gold angularities of the best furniture, cast a rebuking eye on her friend Miss Brent, who stood arranging in a glass bowl the handful of roses she had just brought in from the garden.

Mrs. Dressel's intonation made it clear that the entrance of Miss Brent had been the signal for renewing an argument which the latter had perhaps left the room to escape.

"When you were here three years ago, Justine, I could understand your not wanting to go out, because you were in mourning for your mother—and besides, you'd volunteered for that bad surgical case in the Hope Hospital. But now that you've come back for a rest and a change I can't imagine why you persist in shutting yourself up—unless, of course," she concluded, in a higher key of reproach, "it's because you think so little of Hanaford society——"

Justine Brent, putting the last rose in place, turned from her task with a protesting gesture.

"My dear Effie, who am I to think little of any society, when I belong to none?" She passed a last light touch over the flowers, and crossing the room, brushed her friend's hand with the same caressing gesture.

Mrs. Dressel met it with an unrelenting turn of her plump shoulder, murmuring: "Oh, if you take *that* tone!" And on Miss Brent's gaily rejoining: "Isn't it better than to have other people take it for me?" she replied, with an air of affront that expressed itself in a ruffling of her whole pretty person: "If you'll excuse my saying so, Justine, the fact that you are staying with *me* would be enough to make you welcome anywhere in Hanaford!"

"I'm sure of it, dear; so sure that my horrid pride rather resents being floated in on the high tide of such overwhelming credentials."

Mrs. Dressel glanced up doubtfully at the dark face laughing down on her. Though she was president of the Maplewood Avenue Book-club, and habitually figured in the society column of the "Banner" as one of the intellectual leaders of Hanaford, there were moments when her self-confidence trembled before Justine's light sallies. It was absurd, of course, given the relative situations of the two; and Mrs. Dressel, behind her friend's back, was quickly reassured by the thought that Justine was only a hospital nurse, who had to work for her living, and had really never "been anywhere"; but when Miss Brent's verbal arrows were flying, it seemed somehow of more immediate consequence that she was fairly well-connected, and lived in New York. No one placed a higher value on the abstract qualities of wit and irony than Mrs. Dressel; the difficulty was that she never quite knew when Justine's retorts were loaded, or when her own susceptibilities were the target aimed at; and between her desire to appear to take the joke, and the fear of being ridiculed without knowing it, her pretty face often presented an interesting study in perplexity. As usual, she now took refuge in bringing the talk back to a personal issue.

"I can't imagine," she said, "why you won't go to the Gaines's garden-party. It's always the most brilliant affair of the season; and this year, with the John Amhersts here, and all their party—that fascinating Mrs. Eustace Ansell, and Mrs. Amherst's father, old Mr. Langhope, who is quite as quick and clever as *you* are—you certainly can't accuse us of being dull and provincial!"

Miss Brent smiled. "As far as I can remember, Effie, it is always you who accuse others of bringing that charge against Hanaford. For my part, I know too little of it to have formed any opinion; but whatever it may have to offer me, I am painfully conscious of having, at present, nothing but your kind commendation to give in return."

Mrs. Dressel rose impatiently. "How absurdly you talk! You're a little thinner than usual, and I don't like those dark lines under your eyes; but Westy Gaines told me yesterday that he thought you handsomer than ever, and that it was intensely becoming to some women to look over-tired."

"It's lucky I'm one of that kind," Miss Brent rejoined, between a sigh and a laugh, "and there's every promise of my getting handsomer every day if somebody doesn't soon arrest the geometrical progression of my good looks by giving me the chance to take a year's rest!"

As she spoke, she stretched her arms above her head, with a gesture revealing the suppleness of her slim young frame, but also its tenuity of structure—the frailness of throat and shoulders, and the play of bones in the delicate neck. Justine Brent had one of those imponderable bodies that seem a mere pinch of matter shot through with light and colour. Though she did not flush easily, auroral lights ran under her clear skin, were lost in the shadows of her hair, and broke again in her eyes; and her voice seemed to shoot light too, as though her smile flashed back from her words as they fell—all her features being so fluid and changeful that the one solid thing about her was the massing of dense black hair which clasped her face like the noble metal of some antique bust.

Mrs. Dressel's face softened at the note of weariness in the girl's voice. "Are you very tired, dear?" she asked drawing her down to a seat on the sofa.

"Yes, and no—not so much bodily, perhaps, as in spirit." Justine Brent drew her brows together, and stared moodily at the thin brown hands interwoven between Mrs. Dressel's plump fingers. Seated thus, with hollowed shoulders and brooding head, she might have figured a young sibyl bowed above some mystery of fate; but the next moment her face, inclining toward her friend's, cast off its shadows and resumed the look of a plaintive child.

"The worst of it is that I don't look forward with any interest to taking up the old drudgery again. Of course that loss of interest may be merely physical—I should call it so in a nervous patient, no doubt. But in myself it seems different—it seems to go to the roots of the world. You know it was always the imaginative side of my work that helped me over the ugly details—the pity and beauty that disinfected the physical horror; but now that feeling is lost, and only the mortal disgust remains. Oh, Effie, I don't want to be a ministering angel any more—I want to be uncertain, coy and hard to please. I want something dazzling and unaccountable to happen to me—something new and unlived and indescribable!"

She snatched herself with a laugh from the bewildered Effie, and flinging up her arms again, spun on a light heel across the polished floor.

"Well, then," murmured Mrs. Dressel with gentle obstinacy, "I can't see why in the world you won't go to the Gaines's garden-party!" And caught in the whirlwind of her friend's incomprehensible mirth, she still persisted, as she ducked her blonde head to it: "If you'll only let me lend you my dress with the Irish lace, you'll look smarter than anybody there. . ."

Before her toilet mirror, an hour later, Justine Brent seemed in a way to fulfill Mrs. Dressel's prediction. So mirror-like herself, she could no more help reflecting the happy effect of a bow or a feather than the subtler influence of word and look; and her face and figure were so new to the advantages of dress that, at four-and-twenty, she still produced the effect of a young girl in her first "good" frock. In Mrs. Dressel's festal raiment, which her dark tints subdued to a quiet elegance, she was like the golden core of a pale rose illuminating and scenting its petals.

Three years of solitary life, following on a youth of confidential intimacy with the mother she had lost, had produced in her the quaint habit of half-loud soliloquy. "Fine feathers, Justine!" she laughed back at her laughing image. "You look like a phœnix risen from your ashes. But slip back into your own plumage, and you'll be no more than a little brown bird without a song!"

The luxurious suggestions of her dress, and the way her warm youth became it, drew her back to memories of a childhood nestled in beauty and gentle ways, before her handsome prodigal father had died, and her mother's face had grown pinched in the long struggle with poverty. But those memories were after all less dear to Justine than the grey years following, when, growing up, she had helped to clear a space in the wilderness for their tiny hearth-fire, when her own efforts had fed the flame and roofed it in from the weather. A great heat, kindled at that hearth, had burned in her veins, making her devour her work, lighting and warming the long cold days, and reddening the horizon through dark passages of revolt and failure; and she felt all the more deeply the chill of reaction that set in with her mother's death.

She thought she had chosen her work as a nurse in a spirit of high disinterestedness; but in the first hours of her bereavement it seemed as though only the personal aim had sustained her. For a while, after this, her sick people became to her mere bundles of disintegrating matter, and she shrank from physical pain with a distaste the deeper because, mechanically, she could not help working on to relieve it. Gradually her sound nature passed out of this morbid phase, and she took up her task with deeper pity if less exalted ardour; glad to do her part in the vast impersonal labour of easing the world's misery, but longing with all the warm instincts of youth for a special load to lift, a single hand to clasp.

Ah, it was cruel to be alive, to be young, to bubble with springs of mirth and tenderness and folly, and to live in perpetual contact with decay and pain—to look persistently into the grey face of death without having lifted even a corner of life's veil! Now and then, when she felt her youth flame through the sheath of dullness which was gradually enclosing it, she rebelled at the conditions that tied a spirit like hers to its monotonous task, while others, without a quiver of wings on their dull shoulders, or a note of music in their hearts, had the whole wide world to range through, and saw in it no more than a frightful emptiness to be shut out with tight walls of habit. . .

A tap on the door announced Mrs. Dressel, garbed for conquest, and bestowing on her brilliant person the last anxious touches of the artist reluctant to part from a masterpiece.

"My dear, how well you look! I *knew* that dress would be becoming!" she exclaimed, generously transferring her self-approval to Justine; and adding, as the latter moved toward her: "I wish Westy Gaines could see you now!"

"Well, he will presently," Miss Brent rejoined, ignoring the slight stress on the name.

Mrs. Dressel continued to brood on her maternally. "Justine—I wish you'd tell me! You say you hate the life you're leading now—but isn't there somebody who might——?"

"Give me another, with lace dresses in it?" Justine's slight shrug might have seemed theatrical, had it not been a part of the ceaseless dramatic play of her flexible person. "There might be, perhaps. . . only I'm not sure—" She broke off whimsically.

"Not sure of what?"

"That this kind of dress might not always be a little tight on the shoulders."

"Tight on the shoulders? What do you mean, Justine? My clothes simply *hang* on you!"

"Oh, Effie dear, don't you remember the fable of the wings under the skin, that sprout when one meets a pair of kindred shoulders?" And, as Mrs. Dressel bent on her a brow of unenlightenment—"Well, it doesn't matter: I only meant that I've always been afraid good clothes might keep my wings from sprouting!" She turned back to the glass, giving herself a last light touch such as she had bestowed on the roses.

"And that reminds me," she continued—"how about Mr. Amherst's wings?"

"John Amherst?" Mrs. Dressel brightened into immediate attention. "Why, do you know him?"

"Not as the owner of the Westmore Mills; but I came across him as their assistant manager three years ago, at the Hope Hospital, and he was starting a very promising pair then. I wonder if they're doing as well under his new coat."

"I'm not sure that I understand you when you talk poetry," said Mrs. Dressel with less interest; "but personally I can't say I like John Amherst—and he is certainly not worthy of such a lovely woman as Mrs. Westmore. Of course she would never let any one see that she's not perfectly happy; but I'm told he has given them all a great deal of trouble by interfering in the management of the mills, and his manner is so cold and sarcastic—the truth is, I suppose he's never quite at ease in society. *Her* family have never been really reconciled to the marriage; and Westy Gaines says——"

"Ah, Westy Gaines *would*," Justine interposed lightly. "But if Mrs. Amherst is really the Bessy Langhope I used to know it must be rather a struggle for the wings!"

Mrs. Dressel's flagging interest settled on the one glimpse of fact in this statement. "It's such a coincidence that you should have known her too! Was she always so perfectly fascinating? I wish I knew how she gives that look to her hair!"

Justine gathered up the lace sunshade and long gloves which her friend had lent her. "There was not much more that was genuine about her character—that was her very own, I mean—than there is about my appearance at this moment. She was always the dearest little chameleon in the world, taking everybody's colour in the most flattering way, and giving back, I must say, a most charming reflection—if you'll excuse the mixed metaphor; but when one got her by herself, with no reflections to catch, one found she hadn't any particular colour of her own. One of the girls used to say she ought to wear a tag, because she was so easily mislaid— Now then, I'm ready!"

Justine advanced to the door, and Mrs. Dressel followed her downstairs, reflecting with pardonable complacency that one of the disadvantages of being clever was that it tempted one to say sarcastic things of other women—than which she could imagine no more crying social error.

During the drive to the garden-party, Justine's thoughts, drawn to the past by the mention of Bessy Langhope's name, reverted to the comic inconsequences of her own lot—to that persistent irrelevance of incident that had once made her compare herself to an actor always playing his part before the wrong stage-setting. Was there not, for instance, a mocking incongruity in the fact that a creature so leaping with life should have, for chief outlet, the narrow mental channel of the excellent couple between whom she was now being borne to the Gaines garden-party? All her friendships were the result of propinquity or of early association, and fate had held her imprisoned in a circle of well-to-do mediocrity, peopled by just such figures as those of the kindly and prosperous Dressels. Effie Dressel, the daughter of a cousin of Mrs. Brent's, had obscurely but safely allied herself with the heavy blond young man who was to succeed his father as President of the Union Bank, and who was already regarded by the "solid business interests" of Hanaford as possessing talents likely to carry him far in the development of the paternal fortunes. Harry Dressel's honest countenance gave no evidence of peculiar astuteness, and he was in fact rather the product of special conditions than of an irresistible bent. He had the sound Saxon love of games, and the most interesting game he had ever been taught was "business." He was a simple domestic being, and according to Hanaford standards the most obvious obligation of the husband and father was to make his family richer. If Harry Dressel had ever formulated his aims, he might have said that he wanted to be the man whom Hanaford most respected, and that was only another way of saying, the richest man in Hanaford. Effie embraced his creed with a zeal facilitated by such evidence of its soundness as a growing income and the early prospects of a carriage. Her mother-in-law, a kind old lady with a simple unquestioning love of money, had told her on her wedding day that Harry's one object would always be to make his family proud of him; and the recent purchase of the victoria in which Justine and the Dressels were now seated was regarded by the family as a striking fulfillment of this prophecy.

In the course of her hospital work Justine had of necessity run across far different types; but from the connections thus offered she was often held back by the subtler shades of taste that civilize human intercourse. Her world, in short, had been chiefly peopled by the dull or the crude, and, hemmed in between the two, she had created for herself an inner kingdom where the fastidiousness she had to set aside in her outward relations recovered its full sway. There must be actual beings worthy of admission to this secret precinct, but hitherto they had not come her way; and the sense that they were somewhere just out of reach still gave an edge of youthful curiosity to each encounter with a new group of people.

Certainly, Mrs. Gaines's garden-party seemed an unlikely field for the exercise of such curiosity: Justine's few glimpses of Hanaford society had revealed it as rather a dull thick body, with a surface stimulated only by ill-advised references to the life of larger capitals; and the concentrated essence of social Hanaford was of course to be found at the Gaines entertainments. It presented itself, however, in the rich June afternoon, on the long shadows of the well-kept lawn, and among the paths of the rose-garden, in its most amiable aspect; and to Justine, wearied by habitual contact with ugliness and suffering, there was pure delight in the verdant setting of the picture, and in the light harmonious tints of the figures peopling it. If the company was dull, it was at least decorative; and poverty, misery and dirt were shut out by the placid unconsciousness of the guests as securely as by the leafy barriers of the garden.

X

"AH, Mrs. Dressel, we were on the lookout for you—waiting for the curtain to rise. Your friend Miss Brent? Juliana, Mrs. Dressel's friend Miss Brent——"

Near the brilliantly-striped marquee that formed the axis of the Gaines garden-parties, Mr. Halford Gaines, a few paces from his wife and daughters, stood radiating a royal welcome on the stream of visitors pouring across the lawn. It was only to eyes perverted by a different social perspective that there could be any doubt as to the importance of the Gaines entertainments. To Hanaford itself they were epoch-making; and if any rebellious spirit had cherished a doubt of the fact, it would have been quelled by the official majesty of Mr. Gaines's frock-coat and the comprehensive cordiality of his manner.

There were moments when New York hung like a disquieting cloud on the social horizon of Mrs. Gaines and her daughters; but to Halford Gaines Hanaford was all in all. As an exponent of the popular and patriotic "good-enough-for-me" theory he stood in high favour at the Hanaford Club, where a too-keen consciousness of the metropolis was alternately combated by easy allusion and studied omission, and where the unsettled fancies of youth were chastened and steadied by the reflection that, if Hanaford was good enough for Halford Gaines, it must offer opportunities commensurate with the largest ideas of life.

Never did Mr. Gaines's manner bear richer witness to what could be extracted from Hanaford than when he was in the act of applying to it the powerful pressure of his hospitality. The resultant essence was so bubbling with social exhilaration that, to its producer at any rate, its somewhat mixed ingredients were lost in one highly flavoured draught. Under ordinary circumstances no one discriminated more keenly than Mr. Gaines between different shades of social importance;

but any one who was entertained by him was momentarily ennobled by the fact, and not all the anxious telegraphy of his wife and daughters could, for instance, recall to him that the striking young woman in Mrs. Dressel's wake was only some obscure protégée, whom it was odd of Effie to have brought, and whose presence was quite unnecessary to emphasize.

"Juliana, Miss Brent tells me she has never seen our roses. Oh, there are other roses in Hanaford, Miss Brent; I don't mean to imply that no one else attempts them; but unless you can afford to give *carte blanche* to your man—and mine happens to be something of a specialist. . . well, if you'll come with me, I'll let them speak for themselves. I always say that if people want to know what we can do they must come and see—they'll never find out from *me!*"

A more emphatic signal from his wife arrested Mr. Gaines as he was in the act of leading Miss Brent away.

"Eh?—What? The Amhersts and Mrs. Ansell? You must excuse me then, I'm afraid—but Westy shall take you. Westy, my boy, it's an ill-wind. . . I want you to show this young lady our roses." And Mr. Gaines, with mingled reluctance and satisfaction, turned away to receive the most important guests of the day.

It had not needed his father's summons to draw the expert Westy to Miss Brent: he was already gravitating toward her, with the nonchalance bred of cosmopolitan successes, but with a directness of aim due also to his larger opportunities of comparison.

"The roses will do," he explained, as he guided her through the increasing circle of guests about his mother; and in answer to Justine's glance of enquiry: "To get you away, I mean. They're not much in themselves, you know; but everything of the governor's always begins with a capital letter."

"Oh, but these roses deserve to," Justine exclaimed, as they paused under the evergreen archway at the farther end of the lawn.

"I don't know—not if you've been in England," Westy murmured, watching furtively for the impression produced, on one who had presumably not, by the great blush of colour massed against its dusky background of clipped evergreens.

Justine smiled. "I *have* been—but I've been in the slums since; in horrible places that the least of those flowers would have lighted up like a lamp."

Westy's guarded glance imprudently softened. "It's the beastliest kind of a shame, your ever having had to do such work——"

"Oh, *had* to?" she flashed back at him disconcertingly. "It was my choice, you know: there was a time when I couldn't live without it. Philanthropy is one of the subtlest forms of self-indulgence."

Westy met this with a vague laugh. If a chap who

was as knowing as the devil *did*, once in a way, indulge himself in the luxury of talking recklessly to a girl with exceptional eyes, it was rather upsetting to discover in those eyes no consciousness of the risk he had taken!

"But I *am* rather tired of it now," she continued, and his look grew guarded again. After all, they were all the same—except in that particular matter of the eyes. At the thought, he risked another look, hung on the sharp edge of betrayal, and was snatched back, not by the manly instinct of self-preservation, but by some imp of mockery lurking in the depths that lured him.

He recovered his balance and took refuge in a tone of worldly ease. "I saw a chap the other day who said he knew you when you were at Saint Elizabeth's—wasn't that the name of your hospital?"

Justine assented. "One of the doctors, I suppose. Where did you meet him?"

Ah, *now* she should see! He summoned his utmost carelessness of tone. "Down on Long Island last week—I was spending Sunday with the Amhersts." He held up the glittering fact to her, and watched for the least little blink of awe; but her lids never trembled. It was a confession of social blindness which painfully negatived Mrs. Dressel's hint that she knew the Amhersts; if she had even known *of* them, she could not so fatally have missed his point.

"Long Island?" She drew her brows together in puzzled retrospection. "I wonder if it could have been Stephen Wyant? I heard he had taken over his uncle's practice somewhere near New York."

"Wyant—that's the name. He's the doctor at Clifton, the nearest town to the Amhersts' place. Little Cicely had a cold—Cicely Westmore, you know—a small cousin of mine, by the way—" he switched a rose-branch loftily out of her path, explaining, as she moved on, that Cicely was the daughter of Mrs. Amherst's first marriage to Richard Westmore. "That's the way I happened to see this Dr. Wyant. Bessy—Mrs. Amherst—asked him to stop to luncheon, after he'd seen the kid. He seems rather a discontented sort of a chap—grumbling at not having a New York practice. I should have thought he had rather a snug berth, down there at Lynbrook, with all those swells to dose."

Justine smiled. "Dr. Wyant is ambitious, and swells don't have as interesting diseases as poor people. One gets tired of giving them bread pills for imaginary ailments. But Dr. Wyant is not strong himself and I fancy a country practice is better for him than hard work in town."

"You think him clever though, do you?" Westy enquired absently. He was already bored with the subject of the Long Island doctor, and vexed at the lack of perception that led his companion to show more concern in the fortunes of a country practitioner than in the fact of his own visit to the Amhersts; but the topic was a safe one, and it was agreeable to see how her face kindled when she was interested.

Justine mused on his question. "I think he has very great promise—which he is almost certain not to fulfill," she answered with a sigh which seemed to Westy's anxious ear to betray a more than professional interest in the person referred to.

"Oh, come now—why not? With the Amhersts to give him a start—I heard my cousin recommending him to a lot of people the other day——"

"Oh, he may become a fashionable doctor," Justine assented indifferently; to which her companion rejoined, with a puzzled stare: "That's just what I mean—with Bessy backing him!"

"Has Mrs. Amherst become such a power, then?" Justine asked, taking up the coveted theme just as he despaired of attracting her to it.

"My cousin?" he stretched the two syllables to the cracking-point. "Well, she's awfully rich, you know; and there's nobody smarter. Don't you think so?"

"I don't know; it's so long since I've seen her."

He brightened. "You *did* know her, then?" But the discovery made her obtuseness the more inexplicable!

"Oh, centuries ago: in another world."

"*Centuries*—I like that!" Westy gallantly protested,

his ardour kindling as she swam once more within his social ken. "And Amherst? You know him too, I suppose? By Jove, here he is now——"

He signalled a tall figure strolling slowly toward them with bent head and brooding gaze. Justine's eye had retained a vivid image of the man with whom, scarcely three years earlier, she had lived through a moment of such poignant intimacy, and she recognized at once his lean outline, and the keen spring of his features, still veiled by the same look of inward absorption. She noticed, as he raised his hat in response to Westy Gaines's greeting, that the vertical lines between his brows had deepened; and a moment later she was aware that this change was the visible token of others which went deeper than the fact of his good clothes and his general air of leisure and well-being—changes perceptible to her only in the startled sense of how prosperity had aged him.

"Hallo, Amherst—trying to get under cover?" Westy jovially accosted him, with a significant gesture toward the crowded lawn from which the new-comer had evidently fled. "I was just telling Miss Brent that this is the safest place on these painful occasions—Oh, confound it, it's not as safe as I thought! Here's one of my sisters making for me!"

There ensued a short conflict of words, before his feeble flutter of resistance was borne down by a resolute

Miss Gaines who, as she swept him back to the marquee, cried out to Amherst that her mother was asking for him too; and then Justine had time to observe that her remaining companion had no intention of responding to his hostess's appeal.

Westy, in naming her, had laid just enough stress on the name to let it serve as a reminder or an introduction, as circumstances might decide, and she saw that Amherst, roused from his abstraction by the proffered clue, was holding his hand out doubtfully.

"I think we haven't met for some years," he said.

Justine smiled. "I have a better reason than you for remembering the exact date;" and in response to his look of surprise she added: "You made me commit a professional breach of faith, and I've never known since whether to be glad or sorry."

Amherst still bent on her the gaze which seemed to find in external details an obstacle rather than a help to recognition; but suddenly his face cleared. "It was you who told me the truth about poor Dillon! I couldn't imagine why I seemed to see you in such a different setting. . ."

"Oh, I'm disguised as a lady this afternoon," she said smiling. "But I'm glad you saw through the disguise."

He smiled back at her. "Are you? Why?"

"It seems to make it—if it's so transparent—less of a sham, less of a dishonesty," she began impulsively, and then paused again, a little annoyed at the over-emphasis of her words. Why was she explaining and excusing herself to this stranger? Did she propose to tell him next that she had borrowed her dress from Effie Dressel? To cover her confusion she went on with a slight laugh: "But you haven't told me."

"What was I to tell you?"

"Whether to be glad or sorry that I broke my vow and told the truth about Dillon."

They were standing face to face in the solitude of the garden-walk, forgetful of everything but the sudden surprised sense of intimacy that had marked their former brief communion. Justine had raised her eyes half-laughingly to Amherst, but they dropped before the unexpected seriousness of his.

"Why do you want to know?" he asked.

She made an effort to sustain the note of pleasantry. "Well—it might, for instance, determine my future conduct. You see I'm still a nurse, and such problems are always likely to present themselves."

"Ah, then don't!"

"Don't?"

"I mean—" He hesitated a moment, reaching up to break a rose from the branch that tapped his shoulder. "I was only thinking what risks we run when we scramble into the chariot of the gods and try to do the driving. Be passive—be passive, and you'll be happier!"

"Oh, as to that—!" She swept it aside with one of her airy motions. "But Dillon, for instance—would *he* have been happier if I'd been passive?"

Amherst seemed to ponder. "There again—how can one tell?"

"And the risk's not worth taking?"

"No!"

She paused, and they looked at each other again. "Do you mean that seriously, I wonder? Do you——"

"Act on it myself? God forbid! The gods drive so badly. There's poor Dillon. . . he happened to be in their way. . . as we all are at times." He pulled himself up, and went on in a matter-of-fact tone: "In Dillon's case, however, my axioms don't apply. When my wife heard the truth she was, of course, immensely kind to him; and if it hadn't been for you she might never have known."

Justine smiled. "I think you would have found out —I was only the humble instrument. But now—" she hesitated—"now you must be able to do so much—"

Amherst lifted his head, and she saw the colour rise under his fair skin. "Out at Westmore? You've never been there since? Yes—my wife has made some changes; but it's all so problematic—and one would have to live here. . ."

"You don't, then?"

He answered by an imperceptible shrug. "Of course

I'm here often; and she comes now and then. But the journey's tiresome, and it is not always easy for her to get away." He checked himself, and Justine saw that he, in turn, was suddenly conscious of the incongruity of explaining and extenuating his personal situation to a stranger. "But then we're *not* strangers!" a voice in her exulted, just as he added, with an embarrassed attempt to efface and yet justify his moment of expansion: "That reminds me—I think you know my wife. I heard her asking Mrs. Dressel about you. She wants so much to see you."

The transition had been effected, at the expense of dramatic interest, but to the obvious triumph of social observances; and to Justine, after all, regaining at his side the group about the marquee, the interest was not so much diminished as shifted to the no less suggestive problem of studying the friend of her youth in the unexpected character of John Amherst's wife.

Meanwhile, however, during the brief transit across the Gaines greensward, her thoughts were still busy with Amherst. She had seen at once that the peculiar sense of intimacy reawakened by their meeting had been chilled and deflected by her first allusion to the topic which had previously brought them together: Amherst had drawn back as soon as she named the mills. What could be the cause of his reluctance? When they had last met, the subject burned within him: her being in actual fact a stranger had not, then, been an obstacle to his confidences. Now that he was master at Westmore it was plain that another tone became him—that his situation necessitated a greater reserve; but her enquiry did not imply the least wish to overstep this restriction: it merely showed her remembrance of his frankly-avowed interest in the operatives. Justine was struck by the fact that so natural an allusion should put him on the defensive. She did not for a moment believe that he had lost his interest in the mills; and that his point of view should have shifted with the fact of ownership she rejected as an equally superficial reading of his character. The man with whom she had talked at Dillon's bedside was one in whom the ruling purposes had already shaped themselves, and to whom life, in whatever form it came, must henceforth take their mould. As she reached this point in her analysis, it occurred to her that his shrinking from the subject might well imply not indifference, but a deeper preoccupation: a preoccupation for some reason suppressed and almost disavowed, yet sustaining the more intensely its painful hidden life. From this inference it was but a leap of thought to the next—that the cause of the change must be sought outside of himself, in some external influence strong enough to modify the innate lines of his character. And where could such an influence be more obviously sought than in the marriage which had transformed the assistant manager of the Westmore Mills not, indeed, into their owner—that would rather have tended to simplify the problem—but into the husband of Mrs. Westmore? After all, the mills were Bessy's—and for a farther understanding of the case it remained to find out what manner of person Bessy had become.

Justine's first impression, as her friend's charming arms received her—with an eagerness of welcome not lost on the suspended judgment of feminine Hanaford—the immediate impression was of a gain of emphasis, of individuality, as though the fluid creature she remembered had belied her prediction, and run at last into a definite mould. Yes—Bessy had acquired an outline: a graceful one, as became her early promise, though with, perhaps, a little more sharpness of edge than her youthful texture had promised. But the side she turned to her friend was still all softness—had in it a hint of the old pliancy, the impulse to lean and enlace, that at once woke in Justine the corresponding instinct of guidance and protection, so that their first kiss, before a word was spoken, carried the two back to the precise relation in which their school-days had left them. So easy a reversion to the past left no room for the sense of subsequent changes by which such reunions are sometimes embarrassed. Justine's sympathies had, instinctively, and almost at once, transferred themselves to Bessy's side—passing over at a leap the pained recognition that there *were* sides already—and Bessy had gathered up Justine into the circle of gentle self-absorption which left her very dimly aware of any distinctive characteristic in her friends except that of their affection for herself—since she asked only, as she appealingly put it, that they should all be "dreadfully fond" of her.

"And I've wanted you so often, Justine: you're the only clever person I'm not afraid of, because your cleverness always used to make things clear instead of confusing them. I've asked so many people about you—but I never heard a word till just the other day—wasn't it odd?—when our new doctor at Rushton happened to say that he knew you. I've been rather unwell lately—nervous and tired, and sleeping badly—and he told me I ought to keep perfectly quiet, and be under the care of a nurse who could make me do as she chose: just such a nurse as a wonderful Miss Brent he had known at St. Elizabeth's, whose patients obeyed her as if she'd been the colonel of a regiment. His description made me laugh, it reminded me so much of the way you used to make me do what you wanted at the convent—and then it suddenly occurred to me that I had heard of your having gone in for nursing, and we compared notes, and I found it was really you! Wasn't it odd that we should discover each other in that way?

I daresay we might have passed in the street and never known it—I'm sure I must be horribly changed. . ."

Thus Bessy discoursed, in the semi-isolation to which, under an overarching beech-tree, the discretion of their hostess had allowed the two friends to withdraw for the freer exchange of confidences. There was, at first sight, nothing in her aspect to bear out Mrs. Amherst's plaintive allusion to her health, but Justine, who knew that she had lost a baby a few months previously, assumed that the effect of this shock still lingered, though evidently mitigated by a reviving interest in pretty clothes and the other ornamental accessories of life. Certainly Bessy Amherst had grown into the full loveliness which her childhood promised. She had the kind of finished prettiness that declares itself early, holds its own through the awkward transitions of girlhood, and resists the strain of all later vicissitudes, as though miraculously preserved in some clear medium impenetrable to the wear and tear of living.

"You absurd child! You've not changed a bit except to grow more so!" Justine laughed, paying amused tribute to the childish craving for "a compliment" that still betrayed itself in Bessy's eyes.

"Well, *you* have, then, Justine—you've grown extraordinarily handsome!"

"That *is* extraordinary of me, certainly," the other acknowledged gaily. "But then think what room for improvement there was—and how much time I've had to improve in!"

"It is a long time, isn't it?" Bessy assented. "I feel so intimate, still, with the old Justine of the convent, and I don't know the new one a bit. Just think—I've a great girl of my own, almost as old as we were when we went to the Sacred Heart. But perhaps you don't know anything about me either. You see, I married again two years ago, and my poor baby died last March. . . so I have only Cicely. It was such a disappointment—I wanted a boy dreadfully, and I understand little babies so much better than a big girl like Cicely. . . Oh, dear, here is Juliana Gaines bringing up some more tiresome people! It's such a bore, but John says I must know them all. Well, thank goodness we've only one more day in this dreadful place—and of course I shall see you, dear, before we go. . ."

XI

AFTER conducting Miss Brent to his wife, John Amherst, by the exercise of considerable strategic skill, had once more contrived to detach himself from the throng on the lawn, and, regaining a path in the shrubbery, had taken refuge on the verandah of the house.

Here, under the shade of the awning, two ladies were

seated in a seclusion agreeably tempered by the distant strains of the Hanaford band, and by the shifting prospect of the groups below them.

"Ah, here he is now!" the younger of the two exclaimed, turning on Amherst the smile of intelligence that Mrs. Eustace Ansell was in the habit of substituting for the idle preliminaries of conversation. "We were not talking of you, though," she added as Amherst took the seat to which his mother beckoned him, "but of Bessy—which, I suppose, is almost as indiscreet."

She added the last phrase after an imperceptible pause, and as if in deprecation of the hardly more perceptible frown which, at the mention of his wife's name, had deepened the lines between Amherst's brows.

"Indiscreet of his own mother and his wife's friend?" Mrs. Amherst protested, laying her trimly-gloved hand on her son's arm; while the latter, with his eyes on her companion, said slowly: "Mrs. Ansell knows that indiscretion is the last fault of which her friends are likely to accuse her."

"*Raison de plus*, you mean?" she laughed, meeting squarely the challenge that passed between them under Mrs. Amherst's puzzled gaze. "Well, if I take advantage of my reputation for discretion to meddle a little now and then, at least I do so in a good cause. I was just saying how much I wish that you would take Bessy to Europe; and I am so sure of my cause, in this case, that I am going to leave it to your mother to give you my reasons."

She rose as she spoke, not with any sign of haste or embarrassment, but as if gracefully recognizing the desire of mother and son to be alone together; but Amherst, rising also, made a motion to detain her.

"No one else will be able to put your reasons half so convincingly," he said with a slight smile, "and I am sure my mother would much rather be spared the attempt."

Mrs. Ansell met the smile as freely as she had met the challenge. "My dear Lucy," she rejoined, laying, as she reseated herself, a light caress on Mrs. Amherst's hand, "I'm sorry to be flattered at your expense, but it's not in human nature to resist such an appeal. You see," she added, raising her eyes to Amherst, "how sure I am of myself—and of *you*, when you've heard me."

"Oh, John is always ready to hear one," his mother murmured innocently.

"Well, I don't know that I shall even ask him to do as much as that—I'm so sure, after all, that my suggestion carries its explanation with it."

There was a moment's pause, during which Amherst let his eyes wander absently over the dissolving groups on the lawn.

"The suggestion that I should take Bessy to Europe?" He paused again. "When—next autumn?"

"No: now—at once. On a long honeymoon."

He frowned slightly at the last word, passing it by to revert to the direct answer to his question.

"At once? No—I can't see that the suggestion carries its explanation with it."

Mrs. Ansell looked at him hesitatingly. She was conscious of the ill-chosen word that still reverberated between them, and the unwonted sense of having blundered made her, for the moment, less completely mistress of herself.

"Ah, you'll see farther presently—" She rose again, unfurling her lace sunshade, as if to give a touch of definiteness to her action. "It's not, after all," she added, with a sweet frankness, "a case for argument, and still less for persuasion. My reasons are excellent —I should insist on putting them to you myself if they were not! But they're so good that I can leave you to find them out—and to back them up with your own, which will probably be a great deal better."

She summed up with a light nod, which included both Amherst and his mother, and turning to descend the verandah steps, waved a signal to Mr. Langhope, who was limping disconsolately toward the house.

"What has she been saying to you, mother?" Amherst asked, returning to his seat beside his mother

Mrs. Amherst replied by a shake of her head and a

raised forefinger of reproval. "Now, Johnny, I won't answer a single question till you smooth out those lines between your eyes."

Her son relaxed his frown to smile back at her. "Well, dear, there have to be some wrinkles in every family, and as you absolutely refuse to take your share—" His eyes rested affectionately on the frosty sparkle of her charming old face, which had, in its setting of recovered prosperity, the freshness of a sunny winter morning, when the very snow gives out a suggestion of warmth.

He remembered how, on the evening of his dismissal from the mills, he had paused on the threshold of their sitting-room to watch her a moment in the lamplight, and had thought with bitter compunction of the fresh wrinkle he was about to add to the lines about her eyes. The three years which followed had effaced that wrinkle and veiled the others in a tardy bloom of well-being. From the moment of turning her back on Westmore, and establishing herself in the pretty little house at Hanaford which her son's wife had placed at her disposal, Mrs. Amherst had shed all traces of the difficult years; and the fact that his marriage had enabled him to set free, before it was too late, the pent-up springs of her youthfulness, sometimes seemed to Amherst the clearest gain in his life's confused total of profit and loss. It was, at any rate, the sense of Bessy's share in the change that softened his voice when he spoke of her to his mother.

"Now, then, if I present a sufficiently unruffled surface, let us go back to Mrs. Ansell—for I confess that her mysterious reasons are not yet apparent to me."

Mrs. Amherst looked deprecatingly at her son. "Maria Ansell is devoted to you too, John——"

"Of course she is! It's her *rôle* to be devoted to everybody—especially to her enemies."

"Her enemies?"

"Oh, I didn't intend any personal application. But why does she want me to take Bessy abroad?"

"She and Mr. Langhope think that Bessy is not looking well."

Amherst paused, and the frown showed itself for a moment. "What do *you* think, mother?"

"I hadn't noticed it myself: Bessy seems to me prettier than ever. But perhaps she has less colour—and she complains of not sleeping. Maria thinks she still frets over the baby."

Amherst made an impatient gesture. "Is Europe the only panacea?"

"You should consider, John, that Bessy is used to change and amusement. I think you sometimes forget that other people haven't your faculty of absorbing themselves in a single interest. And Maria says that the new doctor at Clifton, whom they seem to think so clever, is very anxious that Bessy should go to Europe this summer."

"No doubt; and so is every one else: I mean her father and old Tredegar—and your friend Mrs. Ansell not least."

Mrs. Amherst lifted her bright black eyes to his. "Well, then—if they all think she needs it——"

"Good heavens, if travel were what she needed!—Why, we've never stopped travelling since we married. We've been everywhere on the globe except at Hanaford—this is her second visit here in three years!" He rose and took a rapid turn across the deserted verandah. "It's not because her health requires it—it's to get me away from Westmore, to prevent things being done there that ought to be done!" he broke out vehemently, halting again before his mother.

The aged pink faded from Mrs. Amherst's face, but her eyes retained their lively glitter. "To prevent things being done? What a strange thing to say!"

"I shouldn't have said it if I hadn't seen you falling under Mrs. Ansell's spell."

His mother had a gesture which showed from whom he had inherited his impulsive movements. "Really, my son—!" She folded her hands, and added after a pause of self-recovery: "If you mean that I have ever attempted to interfere——"

"No, no: but when they pervert things so damnably——"

"John!"

He dropped into his chair again, and pushed the hair from his forehead with a groan.

"Well, then—put it that they have as much right to their view as I have: I only want you to see what it is. Whenever I try to do anything at Westmore—to give a real start to the work that Bessy and I planned together—some pretext is found to stop it: to pack us off to the ends of the earth, to cry out against reducing her income, to encourage her in some new extravagance to which the work at the mills must be sacrificed!"

Mrs. Amherst, growing pale under this outbreak, assured herself by a nervous backward glance that their privacy was still uninvaded; then her eyes returned to her son's face.

"John—are you sure you're not sacrificing your wife to the mills?"

He grew pale in turn, and they looked at each other for a moment without speaking.

"You see it as they do, then?" he rejoined with a discouraged sigh.

"I see it as any old woman would, who had my experiences to look back to."

"Mother!" he exclaimed.

She smiled composedly. "Do you think I mean

that as a reproach? That's because men will never understand women—least of all, sons their mothers. No real mother wants to come first; she puts her son's career ahead of everything. But it's different with a wife—and a wife as much in love as Bessy."

Amherst looked away. "I should have thought that was a reason——"

"That would reconcile her to being set aside, to counting only second in your plans?"

"They were *her* plans when we married!"

"Ah, my dear—!" She paused on that, letting her shrewd old glance, and all the delicate lines of experience in her face, supply what farther comment the ineptitude of his argument invited.

He took the full measure of her meaning, receiving it in a baffled silence that continued as she rose and gathered her lace mantle about her, as if to signify that their confidences could not, on such an occasion, be farther prolonged without singularity. Then he stood up also and joined her, resting his hand on hers while she leaned on the verandah rail.

"Poor mother! And I've kept you to myself all this time, and spoiled your good afternoon."

"No, dear; I was a little tired, and had slipped away to be quiet." She paused, and then went on, persuasively giving back his pressure: "I know how you feel about doing your duty, John; but now that things are so comfortably settled, isn't it a pity to unsettle them?"

Amherst had intended, on leaving his mother, to rejoin Bessy, whom he could still discern, on the lawn, in absorbed communion with Miss Brent; but after what had passed it seemed impossible, for the moment, to recover the garden-party tone, and he made his escape through the house while a trio of Cuban singers, who formed the crowning number of the entertainment, gathered the company in a denser circle about their guitars.

As he walked on aimlessly under the deep June shadows of Maplewood Avenue his mother's last words formed an ironical accompaniment to his thoughts. "Now that things are comfortably settled—" he knew so well what that elastic epithet covered! Himself, for instance, ensconced in the impenetrable prosperity of his wonderful marriage; herself too (unconsciously, dear soul!), so happily tucked away in a cranny of that new and spacious life, and no more able to conceive why existing conditions should be disturbed than the bird in the eaves understands why the house should be torn down. Well—he had learned at last what his experience with his poor, valiant, puzzled mother might have taught him: that one must never ask from women any view but the personal one, any measure of conduct but that of their own pains and pleasures. She, indeed, had borne undauntedly enough the brunt of their earlier trials; but that was merely because, as she said, the mother's instinct bade her heap all her private hopes on the great devouring altar of her son's ambition; it was not because she had ever, in the very least, understood or sympathized with his aims.

And Bessy—? Perhaps if their little son had lived she might in turn have obeyed the world-old instinct of self-effacement—but now! He remembered with an intenser self-derision that, not even in the first surprise of his passion, had he deluded himself with the idea that Bessy Westmore was an exception to her sex. He had argued rather that, being only a lovelier product of the common mould, she would abound in the adaptabilities and pliancies which the lords of the earth have seen fit to cultivate in their companions. She would care for his aims because they were his. During their precipitate wooing, and through the first brief months of marriage, this profound and original theory had been gratifyingly confirmed; then its perfect surface had begun to show a flaw. Amherst had always conveniently supposed that the poet's line summed up the good woman's rule of ethics: *He for God only, she for God in him.* It was for the god in him, surely, that she had loved him: for that first glimpse of an "ampler ether, a diviner air" that he had brought into her cramped and curtained life. He could never, now, evoke that earlier delusion without feeling on its still-tender surface the keen edge of Mrs. Ansell's smile. She, no doubt, could have told him at any time why Bessy had married him: it was for his *beaux yeux*, as Mrs. Ansell would have put it—because he was young, handsome, persecuted, an ardent lover if not a subtle one—because Bessy had met him at the fatal moment, because her family had opposed the marriage—because, in brief, the gods, that day, may have been a little short of amusement. Well, they were having their laugh out now—there were moments when high heaven seemed to ring with it. . .

With these thoughts at his heels Amherst strode on, overtaken now and again by the wheels of departing guests from the garden-party, and knowing, as they passed him, what was in their minds—envy of his success, admiration of his cleverness in achieving it, and a little half-contemptuous pity for his wife, who, with her wealth and looks, might have done so much better. Certainly, if the case could have been put to Hanaford—the Hanaford of the Gaines garden-party—it would have sided with Bessy to a voice. And how much justice was there in what he felt would have been the unanimous verdict of her class? Was his mother right in hinting that he was sacrificing Bessy to the mills? But the mills *were* Bessy—at least he had thought so when he married her! They were her particular form of contact with life, the expression of her relation to her fellow-men, her pretext, her opportunity—unless they were merely a vast purse in which to plunge for her pin-money! He had fancied it would rest with him to determine from which of these stand-points she should view Westmore; and at the outset she had enthusiastically viewed it from his. In her eager adoption of his ideas she had made a pet of the mills, organizing the Mothers' Club, laying out a recreation-ground on the Hopewood property, and playing with pretty plans in water-colour for the Emergency Hospital and the building which was to contain the night-schools, library and gymnasium; but even these minor projects—which he had urged her to take up as a means of learning their essential dependence on his larger scheme—were soon to be set aside by obstacles of a material order. Bessy always wanted money—not a great deal, but, as she reasonably put it, "enough"—and who was to blame if her father and Mr. Tredegar, each in his different capacity, felt obliged to point out that every philanthropic outlay at Westmore must entail a corresponding reduction in her income? Perhaps if she could have been oftener at Hanaford these arguments would have been counteracted, for she was tender-hearted, and prompt to relieve such suffering as she saw about her; but her imagination was not active, and it was easy for her to forget painful sights when they were not under her eye. This was perhaps—half-consciously—one of the reasons why she avoided Hanaford; why, as Amherst exclaimed, they had been everywhere since their marriage but to the place where their obligations called them. There had, at any rate, always been some good excuse for not returning there, and consequently for postponing the work of improvement which, it was generally felt, her husband could not fitly begin till she *had* returned and gone over the ground with him. After their marriage, and especially in view of the comment excited by that romantic incident, it was impossible not to yield to her wish that they should go abroad for a few months; then, before her confinement, the doctors had exacted that she should be spared all fatigue and worry; and after the baby's death Amherst had felt with her too tenderly to venture an immediate return to unwelcome questions.

For by this time it had become clear to him that such questions were, and always would be, unwelcome to her. As the easiest means of escaping them, she had once more dismissed the whole problem to the vague and tiresome sphere of "business," whence he had succeeded in detaching it for a moment in the early days of their union. Her first husband—poor unappreciated Westmore!—had always spared her the boredom of "business," and Halford Gaines and Mr. Tredegar were ready to show her the same consideration; it was part of the modern code of chivalry that lovely woman should not be bothered about ways and means. But Bessy was too much the wife—and the wife in love—to consent that her husband's views on the management of the mills should be totally disregarded. Precisely because her advisers looked unfavourably on his intervention, she felt bound—if only in defense of her illusions—to maintain and emphasize it. The mills were, in fact, the official "platform" on which she had married: Amherst's devoted *rôle* at Westmore had justified the unconventionality of the step. And so she was committed—the more helplessly for her dense misintelligence of both sides of the question—to the policy of conciliating the opposing influences which had so uncomfortably chosen to fight out their case on the field of her poor little existence: theoretically siding with her husband, but surreptitiously, as he well knew, giving aid and comfort to the enemy, who were really defending her own cause.

All this Amherst saw with that cruel insight which had replaced his former blindness. He was, in truth, more ashamed of the insight than of the blindness: it seemed to him horribly cold-blooded to be thus analyzing, after two years of marriage, the source of his wife's inconsistencies. And, partly for this reason, he had put off from month to month the final question of the future management of the mills, and of the radical changes to be made there if his system were to prevail. But the time had come when, if Bessy had to turn to Westmore for the justification of her marriage, he had even more need of calling upon it for the same service. He had not, assuredly, married her because of Westmore; but he would scarcely have contemplated marriage with a rich woman unless the source of her wealth had offered him some such opportunity as Westmore presented. His special training, and the natural bent of his mind, qualified him, in what had once seemed a predestined manner, to help Bessy to use her power nobly, for her own uplifting as well as for that of Westmore; and so the mills became, incongruously enough, the plank of safety to which both clung in their sense of impending disaster.

It was not that Amherst feared the temptation to idleness if this outlet for his activity were cut off. He had long since found that the luxury with which his wife surrounded him merely quickened his natural bent for hard work and hard fare. He recalled with a touch of bitterness how he had once regretted having separated himself from his mother's class, and how seductive for a moment, to both mind and senses, that other life had appeared. Well—he knew it now, and it had neither charm nor peril for him. Capua must have been a dull place to one who had once drunk the joy of battle. What he dreaded was not that he should learn to love the life of ease, but that he should grow to loathe it uncontrollably, as the symbol of his mental and spiritual bondage. And Westmore was his safety-valve, his refuge—if he were cut off from Westmore what remained to him? It was not only the work he had found to his hand, but the one work for which his hand was fitted. It was his life that he was fighting for in insisting that now at last, before the close of this long-deferred visit to Hanaford, the question of the mills should be faced and settled. He had made that clear to Bessy, in a scene he still shrank from recalling; for it was of the essence of his somewhat unbending integrity that he would not trick her into a confused surrender to the personal influence he still possessed over her, but must seek to convince her by the tedious process of argument and exposition, against which she knew no defense but tears and petulance. But he had, at any rate, gained her consent to his setting forth his views at the meeting of directors the next morning; and meanwhile he had meant to be extraordinarily patient and reasonable with her, till the hint of Mrs. Ansell's stratagem produced in him a fresh reaction of distrust.

XII

THAT evening when dinner ended, Mrs. Ansell, with a glance through the tall dining-room windows, had suggested to Bessy that it would be pleasanter to take coffee on the verandah; but Amherst detained his wife with a glance.

"I should like Bessy to stay," he said.

The dining-room being on the cool side the house, with a refreshing outlook on the garden, the men preferred to smoke there rather than in the stuffily-draped Oriental apartment destined to such rites; and Bessy Amherst, with a faint sigh, sank back into her seat, while Mrs. Ansell drifted out through one of the open windows.

The men surrounding Richard Westmore's table were the same who nearly three years earlier had gathered in his house for the same purpose: the discussion of conditions at the mills. The only perceptible change in the relation to each other of the persons composing this group was that John Amherst was now the host of the other two, instead of being a subordinate called in for cross-examination; but he was so indifferent, or at least so heedless, a host—so forgetful, for instance, of Mr. Tredegar's preference for a "light" cigar, and of Mr. Langhope's feelings on the duty of making the Westmore madeira circulate with the sun—

that the change was manifest only in his evening-dress, and in the fact of his sitting at the foot of the table.

If Amherst was conscious of the contrast thus implied, it was only as a restriction on his freedom. As far as the welfare of Westmore was concerned he would rather have stood before his companions as the assistant manager of the mills than as the husband of their owner; and it seemed to him, as he looked back, that he had done very little with the opportunity which looked so great in the light of his present restrictions. What he *had* done with it—the use to which, as unfriendly critics might insinuate, he had so adroitly put it—had landed him, ironically enough, in the ugly *impasse* of a situation from which no issue seemed possible without some wasteful sacrifice of feeling.

His wife's feelings, for example, were already revealing themselves in an impatient play of her fan that made her father presently lean forward to suggest: "If we men are to talk shop, is it necessary to keep Bessy in this hot room?"

Amherst rose and opened the window behind his wife's chair.

"There's a breeze from the west—the room will be cooler now," he said, returning to his seat.

"Oh, I don't mind—" Bessy murmured, in a tone intended to give her companions the full measure of what she was being called on to endure.

Mr. Tredegar coughed slightly. "May I trouble you for that other box of cigars, Amherst? No, *not* the Cabañas." Bessy rose and handed him the box on which his glance significantly rested. "Ah, thank you, my dear. I was about to ask," he continued, looking about for the cigar-lighter, which flamed unheeded at Amherst's elbow, "what special purpose will be served by a preliminary review of the questions to be discussed tomorrow."

"Ah—exactly," murmured Mr. Langhope. "The madeira, my dear John? No—ah—*please*—to the left!"

Amherst impatiently reversed the direction in which he had set the precious vessel moving, and turned to Mr. Tredegar, who was conspicuously lighting his cigar with a match extracted from his waist-coat pocket.

"The purpose is to define my position in the matter; and I prefer that Bessy should do this with your help rather than with mine."

Mr. Tredegar surveyed his cigar through drooping lids, as though the question propounded by Amherst were perched on its tip.

"Is not your position naturally involved in and defined by hers? You will excuse my saying that—technically speaking, of course—I cannot distinctly conceive of it as having any separate existence."

Mr. Tredegar spoke with the deliberate mildness that was regarded as his most effective weapon at the bar, since it was likely to abash those who were too intelligent to be propitiated by it.

"Certainly it is involved in hers," Amherst agreed; "but how far that defines it is just what I have waited till now to find out."

Bessy at this point recalled her presence by a restless turn of her graceful person, and her father, with an affectionate glance at her, interposed amicably: "But surely—according to old-fashioned ideas—it implies identity of interests?"

"Yes; but whose interests?" Amherst asked.

"Why—your wife's, man! She owns the mills."

Amherst hesitated. "I would rather talk of my wife's interest in the mills than of her interests there; but we'll keep to the plural if you prefer it. Personally, I believe the terms should be interchangeable in the conduct of such a business."

"Ah—I'm glad to hear that," said Mr. Tredegar quickly, "since it's precisely the view we all take."

Amherst's colour rose. "Definitions are ambiguous," he said. "Before you adopt mine, perhaps I had better develop it a little farther. What I mean is, that Bessy's interests in Westmore should be regulated by her interest in it—in its welfare as a social body, aside from its success as a commercial enterprise. If we agree on this definition, we are at one as to the other: namely that my relation to the matter is defined by hers."

He paused a moment, as if to give his wife time to contribute some sign of assent and encouragement; but she maintained a puzzled silence and he went on: "There is nothing new in this. I have tried to make Bessy understand from the beginning what obligations I thought the ownership of Westmore entailed, and how I hoped to help her fulfill them; but ever since our marriage all definite discussion of the subject has been put off for one cause or another, and that is my reason for urging that it should be brought up at the directors' meeting tomorrow."

There was another pause, during which Bessy glanced tentatively at Mr. Tredegar, and then said, with a lovely rise of colour: "But, John, I sometimes think you forget how much has been done at Westmore—the Mothers' Club, and the play-ground, and all—in the way of carrying out your ideas."

Mr. Tredegar discreetly dropped his glance to his cigar, and Mr. Langhope sounded an irrepressible note of approval and encouragement.

Amherst smiled. "No, I have not forgotten; and I am grateful to you for giving my ideas a trial. But what has been done hitherto is purely superficial." Bessy's eyes clouded, and he added hastily: "Don't think I undervalue it for that reason—heaven knows the surface of life needs improving! But it's like picking flowers and sticking them in the ground to make a garden—unless you transplant the flower with its roots, and prepare the soil to receive it, your garden will be faded tomorrow. No radical changes have yet been made at Westmore; and it is of radical changes that I want to speak."

Bessy's look grew more pained, and Mr. Langhope exclaimed with unwonted irascibility: "Upon my soul, Amherst, the tone you take about what your wife has done doesn't strike me as the likeliest way of encouraging her to do more!"

"I don't want to encourage her to do more on such a basis—the sooner she sees the futility of it the better for Westmore!"

"The futility—?" Bessy broke out, with a flutter of tears in her voice; but before her father could intervene Mr. Tredegar had raised his hand with the gesture of one accustomed to wield the gavel.

"My dear child, I see Amherst's point, and it is best, as he says, that you should see it too. What he desires, as I understand it, is the complete reconstruction of the present state of things at Westmore; and he is right in saying that all your good works there—night-schools, and nursery, and so forth—leave that issue untouched."

A smile quivered under Mr. Langhope's moustache. He and Amherst both knew that Mr. Tredegar's feint of recognizing the justice of his adversary's claim was merely the first step to annihilating it; but Bessy could never be made to understand this, and always felt herself deserted and betrayed when any side but her own was given a hearing.

"I'm sorry if all I have tried to do at Westmore is useless—but I suppose I shall never understand business," she murmured, vainly seeking consolation in her father's eye.

"This is not business," Amherst broke in. "It's the question of your personal relation to the people there—the last thing that business considers."

Mr. Langhope uttered an impatient exclamation. "I wish to heaven the owner of the mills had made it clear just what that relation was to be!"

"I think he did, sir," Amherst answered steadily, "in leaving his wife the unrestricted control of the property."

He had reddened under Mr. Langhope's thrust, but his voice betrayed no irritation, and Bessy rewarded him with an unexpected beam of sympathy: she was always up in arms at the least sign of his being treated as an intruder.

"I am sure, papa," she said, a little tremulously, "that poor Richard, though he knew I was not clever, felt he could trust me to take the best advice——"

"Ah, that's all we ask of you, my child!" her father sighed, while Mr. Tredegar drily interposed: "We are merely losing time by this digression. Let me suggest that Amherst should give us an idea of the changes he wishes to make at Westmore."

Amherst, as he turned to answer, remembered with what ardent faith in his powers of persuasion he had responded to the same appeal three years earlier. He had thought then that all his cause needed was a hearing; now he knew that the practical man's readiness to let the idealist talk corresponds with the busy parent's permission to destructive infancy to "run out and play." They would let him state his case to the four corners of the earth—if only he did not expect them to act on it! It was their policy to let him exhaust himself in argument and exhortation, to listen to him so politely and patiently that if he failed to enforce his ideas it should not be for lack of opportunity to expound them. . . And the alternative struck him as hardly less to be feared. Supposing that the incredible happened, that his reasons prevailed with his wife, and, through her, with the others—at what cost would the victory be won? Would Bessy ever forgive him for winning it? And what would his situation be, if it left him in control of Westmore but estranged from his wife?

He recalled suddenly a phrase he had used that afternoon to the dark-eyed girl at the garden-party: "What risks we run when we scramble into the chariot of the gods!" And at the same instant he heard her retort, and saw her fine gesture of defiance. How could he ever have doubted that the thing was worth doing at whatever cost? Something in him—some secret lurking element of weakness and evasion—shrank out of sight in the light of her question: "Do *you* act on that?" and the "God forbid!" he had instantly flashed back to her. He turned to Mr. Tredegar with his answer.

Amherst knew that any large theoretical exposition of the case would be as much wasted on the two men as on his wife. To gain his point he must take only one step at a time, and it seemed to him that the first thing needed at Westmore was that the hands should work and live under healthier conditions. To attain this, two important changes were necessary: the floor-space of the mills must be enlarged, and the company must cease to rent out tenements, and give the operatives the opportunity to buy land for themselves. Both these changes involved the upheaval of the existing order. Whenever the Westmore mills had been enlarged, it had been for the sole purpose of increasing the revenues of the company; and now Amherst asked that these revenues should be materially and permanently reduced. As to the suppression of the company tenement, such a measure struck at the roots of the baneful paternalism which was choking out every germ of initiative in the workman. Once the operatives had room to work in, and the hope of homes of their own to go to when work was over, Amherst was willing to trust to time for the satisfaction of their other needs. He believed that a sounder understanding of these needs would develop on both sides the moment the employers proved their good faith by the deliberate and permanent sacrifice of excessive gain to the well-being of the employed; and once the two had learned to regard each other not as antagonists but as collaborators, a long step would have been taken toward a readjustment of the whole industrial relation. In regard to general and distant results, Amherst tried not to be too sanguine, even in his own thoughts. His aim was to remedy the abuse nearest at hand, in the hope of thus getting gradually closer to the central evil; and, had his action been unhampered, he would still have preferred the longer and more circuitous path of practical experiment to the sweeping adoption of a new industrial system.

But his demands, moderate as they were, assumed in his hearers the consciousness of a moral claim superior to the obligation of making one's business "pay"; and it was the futility of this assumption that chilled the arguments on his lips, since in the orthodox creed of the business world it was a weakness and not a strength to be content with five per cent where ten was obtainable. Business was one thing, philanthropy another; and the enthusiasts who tried combining them were usually reduced, after a brief flight, to paying fifty cents on the dollar, and handing over their stock to a promoter presumably unhampered by humanitarian ideals.

Amherst knew that this was the answer with which his plea would be met; knew, moreover, that the plea was given a hearing simply because his judges deemed it so pitiably easy to refute. But the knowledge, once he had begun to speak, fanned his argument to a white heat of pleading, since, with failure so plainly ahead, small concessions and compromises were not worth making. Reason would be wasted on all; but eloquence might at least prevail with Bessy. . .

When, late that night, he went upstairs after long pacings of the garden, he was surprised to see a light in her room. She was not given to midnight study, and fearing that she might be ill he knocked at her door. There was no answer, and after a short pause he turned the handle and entered.

In the great canopied Westmore couch, her arms flung upward and her hands clasped beneath her head, she lay staring fretfully at the globe of electric light which hung from the centre of the embossed and gilded ceiling. Seen thus, with the soft curves of throat and arms revealed, and her face childishly set in a cloud of loosened hair, she looked no older than Cicely—and, like Cicely, inaccessible to grown-up arguments and the stronger logic of experience.

It was a trick of hers, in such moods, to ignore any attempt to attract her notice; and Amherst was prepared for her remaining motionless as he paused on the threshold and then advanced toward the middle of the room. There had been a time when he would have been exasperated by her pretense of not seeing him, but a deep weariness of spirit now dulled him to these surface pricks.

"I was afraid you were not well when I saw the light burning," he began.

"Thank you—I am quite well," she answered in a colourless voice, without turning her head.

"Shall I put it out, then? You can't sleep with such a glare in your eyes."

"I should not sleep at any rate; and I hate to lie awake in the dark."

"Why shouldn't you sleep?" He moved nearer, looking down compassionately on her perturbed face and struggling lips.

She lay silent a moment; then she faltered out: "B—because I'm so unhappy!"

The pretense of indifference was swept away by a gush of childish sobs as she flung over on her side and buried her face in the embroidered pillows.

Amherst, bending down, laid a quieting hand on her shoulder. Bessy——"

She sobbed on.

He seated himself silently in the arm-chair beside the bed, and kept his soothing hold on her shoulder. The time had come when he went through all these accustomed acts of pacification as mechanically as a nurse soothing a fretful child. And once he had thought her weeping eloquent! He looked about him at the spacious room, with its heavy hangings of damask and the thick velvet carpet which stifled his steps. Everywhere were the graceful tokens of her presence—the vast lace-draped toilet-table strewn with silver and crystal, the embroidered muslin cushions heaped on the lounge, the little rose-lined slippers she had just put off, the lace wrapper, with a scent of violets in its folds, which he had pushed aside when he sat down beside her; and he remembered how full of a mysterious and intimate charm these things had once appeared to him. It was characteristic that the remembrance made him more patient with her now. Perhaps, after all, it was his failure that she was crying over. . .

"Don't be unhappy. You decided as seemed best to you," he said.

She pressed her handkerchief against her lips, still keeping her head averted. "But I hate all these arguments and disputes. Why should you unsettle everything?" she murmured.

His mother's words! Involuntairly he removed his

hand from her shoulder, though he still remained seated by the bed.

"You are right. I see the uselessness of it," he assented, with an uncontrollable note of irony.

She turned her head at the tone, and fixed her plaintive brimming eyes on him. "You *are* angry with me!"

"Was that troubling you?" He leaned forward again, with compassion in his face. *Sancta simplicitas!* was the thought within him.

"I am not angry," he went on; "be reasonable and try to sleep."

She started upright, the light masses of her hair floating about her like silken sea-weed lifted on an invisible tide. "Don't talk like that! I can't endure to be humoured like a baby. I am unhappy because I can't see why all these wretched questions should be dragged into our life. I hate to have you always disagreeing with Mr. Tredegar, who is so clever and has so much experience; and yet I hate to see you give way to him, because that makes it appear as if. . . as if. . ."

"He didn't care a straw for my ideas?" Amherst smiled. "Well, he doesn't—and I never dreamed of making him. So don't worry about that either."

"You never dreamed of making him care for your ideas? But then why do you——"

"Why do I go on setting them forth at such great length?" Amherst smiled again "To convince you —that's my only ambition."

She stared at him, shaking her head back to toss a loose lock from her puzzled eyes. A tear still shone on her lashes, but with the motion it fell and trembled down her cheek.

"To convince *me?* But you know I am so ignorant of such things."

"Most women are."

"I never pretended to understand anything about— economics, or whatever you call it."

"No."

"Then how——"

He turned and looked at her gently. "I thought you might have begun to understand something about *me*."

"About you?" The colour flowered softly under her clear skin.

"About what my ideas on such subjects were likely to be worth—judging from what you know of me in other respects." He paused and glanced away from her. "Well," he concluded deliberately, "I suppose I've had my answer tonight."

"Oh, John——!"

He rose and wandered across the room, pausing a moment to finger absently the trinkets on the dressing-table. The act recalled with a curious vividness certain dulled sensastions of their first days together, when to handle and examine these frail little accessories of her toilet had been part of the wonder and amusement of his new existence. He could still hear her laugh as she leaned over him, watching his mystified look in the glass, till their reflected eyes met there and drew down her lips to his. He laid down the fragrant powder-puff he had been turning slowly between his fingers, and moved back toward the bed. In the interval he had reached a decision.

"Well—isn't it natural that I should think so?" he began again, as he stood beside her. "When we married I never expected you to care or know much about economics. It isn't a quality a man usually chooses his wife for. But I had a fancy—perhaps it shows my conceit—that when we had lived together a year or two, and you'd found out what kind of a fellow I was in other ways—ways any woman can judge of—I had a fancy that you might take my opinions on faith when it came to my own special business—the thing I'm generally supposed to know about."

He knew that he was touching a sensitive chord, for Bessy had to the full her sex's pride of possessorship. He was human and faulty till others criticized him—then he became a god. But in this case a conflicting influence restrained her from complete response to his appeal.

"I *do* feel sure you know—about the treatment of the hands and all that; but you said yourself once—the first time we ever talked about Westmore—that the business part was different——"

Here it was again, the ancient ineradicable belief in the separable body and soul! Even an industrial organization was supposed to be subject to the old theological distinction, and Bessy was ready to co-operate with her husband in the emancipation of Westmore's spiritual part if only its body remained under the law.

Amherst controlled his impatience, as it was always easy for him to do when he had fixed on a definite line of conduct.

"It was my situation that was different; not what you call the business part. That is inextricably bound up with the treatment of the hands. If I am to have anything to do with the mills now I can deal with them only as your representative; and as such I am bound to take in the whole question."

Bessy's face clouded: was he going into it all again? But he read her look and went on reassuringly: "That was what I meant by saying that I hoped you would take me on faith. If I want the welfare of Westmore it's above all, I believe, because I want Westmore to see you as *I* do—as the dispenser of happiness, who could not endure to benefit by any wrong or injustice to others."

"Of course, of course I don't want to do them injustice!"

"Well, then——"

He had seated himself beside her again, clasping in his the hand with which she was fretting the lace-edged sheet. He felt her restless fingers surrender slowly, and her eyes turned to him in appeal.

"But I care for what people say of you too! And you know—it's horrid, but one must consider it—if they say you're spending my money imprudently. . ." The blood rose to her neck and face. "I don't mind for myself. . . even if I have to give up as many things as papa and Mr. Tredegar think. . . but there is Cicely . . . and if people said. . ."

"If people said I was spending Cicely's money on improving the condition of the people to whose work she will some day owe all her wealth—" Amherst paused: "Well, I would rather hear that said of me than any other thing I can think of, except one."

"Except what?"

"That I was doing it with her mother's help and approval."

She drew a long tremulous sigh: he knew it was always a relief to her to have him assert himself strongly. But a residue of resistance still clouded her mind.

"I should always want to help you, of course; but if

Mr. Tredegar and Halford Gaines think your plan unbusinesslike——"

"Mr. Tredegar and Halford Gaines are certain to think it so. And that is why I said, just now, that it comes, in the end, to your choosing between us; taking them on experience or taking me on faith."

She looked at him wistfully. "Of course I should expect to give up things. . . You wouldn't want me to live here?"

"I should not ask you to," he said, half-smiling.

"I suppose there would be a good many things we couldn't do——"

"You would certainly have less money for a number of years; after that, I believe you would have more rather than less; but I should not want you to think that, beyond a reasonable point, the prosperity of the mills was ever to be measured by your dividends."

"No." She leaned back wearily among the pillows. "I suppose, for instance, we should have to give up Europe this summer——?"

Here at last was the bottom of her thought! It was always on the immediate pleasure that her soul hung: she had not enough imagination to look beyond, even in the projecting of her own desires. And it was on his knowledge of this limitation that Amherst had deliberately built.

"I don't see how you could go to Europe," he said.

"The doctor thinks I need it," she faltered.

"In that case, of course—" He stood up, not abruptly, or with any show of irritation, but as if accepting this as her final answer. "What you need most, in the meantime, is a little sleep," he said. "I will tell your maid not to disturb you in the morning." He had returned to his soothing way of speech, as though definitely resigned to the inutility of farther argument. "And I will say goodbye now," he continued, "because I shall probably take an early train, before you wake——"

She sat up with a start. "An early train? Why, where are you going?"

"I must go to Chicago some time this month, and as I shall not be wanted here tomorrow I might as well run out there at once, and join you next week at Lynbrook."

Bessy had grown pale. "But I don't understand——"

Their eyes met. "Can't you understand that I am human enough to prefer, under the circumstances, not being present at tomorrow's meeting?" he said with a dry laugh.

She sank back with a moan of discouragement, turning her face away as he began to move toward his room.

"Shall I put the light out?" he asked, pausing with his hand on the electric button.

"Yes, please."

He pushed in the button and walked on, guided through the obscurity by the line of light under his door. As he reached the threshold he heard a little choking cry.

"John—oh, John!"

He paused.

"I can't *bear* it!" The sobs increased.

"Bear what?"

"That you should hate me——"

"Don't be foolish," he said, groping for his door-handle.

"But you do hate me—and I deserve it!"

"Nonsense, dear. Try to sleep."

"I can't sleep till you've forgiven me. Say you don't hate me! I'll do anything. . . only say you don't hate me!"

He stood still a moment, thinking; then he turned back, and made his way across the room to her side. As he sat down beside her, he felt her arms reach for his neck and her wet face press itself against his cheek.

"I'll do anything . . ." she sobbed; and in the darkness he held her to him and hated his victory.

XIII

MRS. ANSELL was engaged in what she called picking up threads. She had been abroad for the summer—had, in fact, transferred herself but a few hours earlier from her returning steamer to the little station at Lynbrook—and was now, in the bright September afternoon, which left her in sole possession of the terrace of Lynbrook House, using that pleasant eminence as a point of observation from which to gather up some of the loose ends of history dropped at her departure.

It might have been thought that the actual scene outspread below her—the descending gardens, the tennis-courts, the farm-lands sloping away to the blue sea-like shimmer of the Hempstead plains—offered, at the moment, little material for her purpose; but that was to view them with a superficial eye. Mrs. Ansell's trained gaze was, for example, greatly enlightened by the fact that the tennis-courts were fringed by a group of people indolently watchful of the figures agitating themselves about the nets; and that, as she turned her head toward the entrance avenue, the receding view of a station omnibus, followed by a luggage-cart, announced that more guests were to be added to those who had almost taxed to its limits the expansibility of the luncheon-table.

All this, to the initiated eye, was full of suggestion; but its significance was as nothing to that presented by the approach of two figures which, as Mrs. Ansell watched, detached themselves from the cluster about the tennis-ground and struck, obliquely and at a desultory pace, across the lawn toward the terrace. The figures—those of a slight young man with stooping shoulders, and of a lady equally youthful but slenderly erect—moved forward in absorbed communion, as if unconscious of their surroundings and indefinite as to their direction, till, on the brink of the wide grass terrace just below their observer's parapet, they paused a moment and faced each other in closer speech. This interchange of words, though brief in measure of time, lasted long enough to add a vivid strand to Mrs. Ansell's thickening skein; then, on a gesture of the lady's, and without signs of formal leave-taking, the young man struck into a path which regained the entrance avenue, while his companion, quickening her pace, crossed the grass terrace and mounted the wide stone steps sweeping up to the house.

These brought her out on the upper terrace a few yards from Mrs. Ansell's post, and exposed her, unprepared, to the full beam of welcome which that lady's rapid advance threw like a searchlight across her path.

"Dear Miss Brent! I was just wondering how it was that I hadn't seen you before." Mrs. Ansell, as she spoke, drew the girl's hand into a long soft clasp which served to keep them confronted while she delicately groped for whatever thread the encounter seemed to proffer.

Justine made no attempt to evade the scrutiny to which she found herself exposed; she merely released her hand by a movement instinctively evasive of the mechanical endearment, explaining, with a smile that softened the gesture: "I was out with Cicely when you arrived. We've just come in."

"The dear child! I haven't seen her either." Mrs. Ansell continued to bestow upon the speaker's clear dark face an intensity of attention in which, for the moment, Cicely had no perceptible share. "I hear you are teaching her botany, and all kinds of wonderful things."

Justine smiled again. "I am trying to teach her to wonder: that is the hardest faculty to cultivate in the modern child."

"Yes—I suppose so; in myself," Mrs. Ansell admitted with a responsive brightness, "I find it develops with age. The world is a remarkable place." She threw this off absently, as though leaving Miss Brent to apply it either to the inorganic phenomena with which Cicely was supposed to be occupied, or to those subtler manifestations that engaged her own attention.

"It's a great thing," she continued, "for Bessy to have had your help—for Cicely, and for herself too.

There is so much that I want you to tell me about her. As an old friend I want the benefit of your fresher eye."

"About Bessy?" Justine hesitated, letting her glance drift to the distant group still anchored about the tennis-nets. "Don't you find her looking better?"

"Than when I left? So much so that I was unduly disturbed, just now, by seeing that clever little doctor—it *was* he, wasn't it, who came up the lawn with you?"

"Dr. Wyant? Yes." Miss Brent hesitated again. "But he merely called—with a message."

"Not professionally? *Tant mieux!* The truth is, I was anxious about Bessy when I left—I thought she ought to have gone abroad for a change. But, as it turns out, her little excursion with you did as well."

"I think she only needed rest. Perhaps her six weeks in the Adirondacks were better than Europe."

"Ah, under *your* care—that made them better!" Mrs. Ansell in turn hesitated, the lines of her face melting and changing as if a rapid stage-hand had shifted them. When she spoke again they were as open as a public square, but also as destitute of personal significance, as flat and smooth as the painted drop before the real scene it hides.

"I have always thought that Bessy, for all her health and activity, needs as much care as Cicely—the kind of care a clever friend can give. She is so wasteful of her strength and her nerves, and so unwilling to listen to reason. Poor Dick Westmore watched over her as if she were a baby; but perhaps Mr. Amherst, who must have been used to such a different type of woman, doesn't realize. . . and then he's so little here. . ." The drop was lit up by a smile that seemed to make it more impenetrable. "As an old friend I can't help telling you how much I hope she is to have you with her for a long time—a long, long time."

Miss Brent bent her head in slight acknowledgment of the tribute. "Oh, soon she will not need any care——"

"My dear Miss Brent, she will always need it!" Mrs. Ansell made a movement inviting the young girl to share the bench from which, at the latter's approach, she had risen. "But perhaps there is not enough in such a life to satisfy your professional energies."

She seated herself, and after an imperceptible pause Justine sank into the seat beside her. "I am very glad, just now, to give my energies a holiday," she said, leaning back with a little sigh of retrospective weariness.

"You are tired too? Bessy wrote me you had been quite used up by a trying case after we saw you at Hanaford."

Miss Brent smiled. "When a nurse is fit for work she calls a trying case a 'beautiful' one."

"But meanwhile—?" Mrs. Ansell shone on her with elder-sisterly solicitude. "Meanwhile, why not stay on with Cicely—above all, with Bessy? Surely she's a 'beautiful' case too."

"Isn't she?" Justine laughingly agreed.

"And if you want to be tried—" Mrs. Ansell swept the scene with a slight lift of her philosophic shoulders—"you'll find there are trials enough everywhere."

Her companion started up with a glance at the small watch on her breast. "One of them is that it's already after four, and that I must see that tea is sent down to the tennis-ground, and the new arrivals looked after."

"I saw the omnibus on its way to the station. Are many more people coming?"

"Five or six, I believe. The house is usually full for Sunday."

Mrs. Ansell made a slight motion to detain her. "And when is Mr. Amherst expected?"

Miss Brent's pale cheek seemed to take on a darker tone of ivory, and her glance dropped from her companion's face to the vivid stretch of gardens at their feet. "Bessy has not told me," she said.

"Ah—" the older woman rejoined, looking also toward the gardens, as if to intercept Miss Brent's glance in its flight. The latter stood still a moment, with the appearance of not wishing to evade whatever else her companion might have to say; then she moved away, entering the house by one window just as Mr. Langhope emerged from it by another.

The sound of his stick tapping across the bricks roused Mrs. Ansell from her musings, but she showed her sense of his presence simply by returning to the bench she had just left; and accepting this mute invitation, Mr. Langhope crossed the terrace and seated himself at her side.

When he had done so they continued to look at each other without speaking, after the manner of old friends possessed of occult means of communication; and as the result of this inward colloquy Mr. Langhope at length said: "Well, what do you make of it?"

"What do *you?*" she rejoined, turning full upon him a face so released from its usual defences and disguises that it looked at once older and more simple than the countenance she presented to the world.

Mr. Langhope waved a deprecating hand. "I want your fresher impressions."

"That's what I just now said to Miss Brent."

"You've been talking to Miss Brent?"

"Only a flying word—she had to go and look after the new arrivals."

Mr. Langhope's attention deepened. "Well, what did you say to her?"

"Wouldn't you rather hear what she said to *me?*"

He smiled. "A good cross-examiner always gets the answers he wants. Let me hear your side, and I shall know hers."

"I should say that applied only to stupid cross-examiners; or to those who have stupid subjects to deal with. And Miss Brent is not stupid, you know."

"Far from it! What else do you make out?"

"I make out that she's in possession."

"Here?"

"Don't look startled. Do you dislike her?"

"Heaven forbid—with those eyes! She has a wit of her own, too—and she certainly makes things easier for Bessy."

"She guards her carefully, at any rate. I could find out nothing."

"About Bessy?"

"About the general situation."

"Including Miss Brent?"

Mrs. Ansell smiled faintly. "I made one little discovery about her."

"Well?"

"She's intimate with the new doctor."

"Wyant?" Mr. Langhope's interest dropped. "What of that? I believe she knew him before."

"I daresay. It's of no special importance, except as giving us a possible clue to her character. She strikes me as interesting and mysterious."

Mr. Langhope smiled. "The things your imagination does for you!"

"It helps me to see that we may find Miss Brent useful as a friend."

"A friend?"

"An ally." She paused, as if searching for a word. "She may restore the equilibrium."

Mr. Langhope's handsome face darkened. "Open Bessy's eyes to Amherst? Damn him!" he said quietly.

Mrs. Ansell let the imprecation pass. "When was he last here?" she asked.

"Five or six weeks ago—for one night. His only visit since she came back from the Adirondacks."

"What do you think his motive is? He must know what he risks in losing his hold on Bessy."

"His motive? With your eye for them, can you ask? A devouring ambition, that's all! Haven't you noticed that, in all except the biggest minds, ambition takes the form of wanting to command where one has had to obey? Amherst has been made to toe the line at Westmore, and now he wants Truscomb—yes, and Halford Gaines, too!—to do the same. That's the secret of his servant-of-the-people pose—gad, I believe it's the whole secret of his marriage! He's devouring my daughter's substance to pay off an old score against the mills. He'll never rest till he has Truscomb out, and some creature of his own in command—and then, *vogue la galère!* If it were women, now," Mr. Langhope summed up impatiently, "one could understand it, at his age, and with that damned romantic head—but to be put aside for a lot of low mongrelly socialist mill-hands —ah, my poor girl—my poor girl!"

Mrs. Ansell mused. "You didn't write me that things were so bad. There's been no actual quarrel?" she asked.

"How can there be, when the poor child does all he wants? He's simply too busy to come and thank her!"

"Too busy at Hanaford?"

"So he says. Introducing the golden age at Westmore—it's likely to be the age of copper at Lynbrook."

Mrs. Ansell drew a meditative breath. "I was thinking of that. I understood that Bessy would have to retrench while the changes at Westmore were going on."

"Well—didn't she give up Europe, and cable over to countermand her new motor?"

"But the life here! This mob of people! Miss Brent tells me the house is full for every week-end."

"Would you have my daughter cut off from all her friends?"

Mrs. Ansell met this promptly. "From some of the new ones, at any rate! Have you heard who has just arrived?"

Mr. Langhope's hesitation showed a tinge of embarrassment. "I'm not sure—some one has always just arrived."

"Well, the Fenton Carburys, then!" Mrs. Ansell left it to her tone to annotate the announcement.

Mr. Langhope raised his eyebrows slightly. "Are they likely to be an exceptionally costly pleasure?"

"If you're trying to prove that I haven't kept to the point—I can assure you that I'm well within it!"

"But since the good Blanche has got her divorce and married Carbury, wherein do they differ from other week-end automata?"

"Because most divorced women marry again to be respectable."

Mr. Langhope smiled faintly. "Yes—that's their punishment. But it would be too dull for Blanche."

"Precisely. *She* married again to see Ned Bowfort!"

"Ah—that may yet be hers!"

Mrs. Ansell sighed at his perversity. "Meanwhile, she's brought him here, and it is unnatural to see Bessy lending herself to such combinations."

"You're corrupted by a glimpse of the old societies. Here Bowfort and Carbury are simply hands at bridge."

"Old hands at it—yes! And the bridge is another point: Bessy never used to play for money."

"Well, she may make something, and offset her husband's prodigalities."

"There again—with this *train de vie*, how on earth are both ends to meet?"

Mr. Langhope grown suddenly grave, struck his cane resoundingly on the terrace. "Westmore and Lynbrook? I don't want them to—I want them to get farther and farther apart!"

She cast on him a look of startled divination. "You want Bessy to go on spending too much money?"

"How can I help it if it costs?"

"If what costs—?" She stopped, her eyes still wide; then their glances crossed, and she exclaimed: "If your scheme costs? It *is* your scheme, then?"

He shrugged his shoulders again. "It's a passive attitude——"

"Ah, the deepest plans are that!" Mr. Langhope uttered no protest, and she continued to piece her conjectures together. "But you expect it to lead up to something active. Do you want a rupture?"

"I want him brought back to his senses."

"Do you think that will bring him back to *her?*"

"Where the devil else will he have to go?"

Mrs. Ansell's eyes dropped toward the gardens, across which desultory knots of people were straggling back from the ended tennis-match. "Ah, here they all come," she said, rising with a half-sigh; and as she stood watching the advance of the brightly-tinted groups she added slowly: "It's ingenious—but you don't understand him."

Mr. Langhope stroked his moustache. "Perhaps

not," he assented thoughtfully. "But suppose we go in before they join us? I want to show you a set of Ming I picked up the other day for Bessy. I flatter myself I *do* understand Ming."

XIV

JUSTINE BRENT, her household duties discharged, had gone upstairs to her room, a little turret chamber projecting above the wide terrace below, from which the sounds of lively intercourse now rose increasingly to her window.

Bessy, she knew, would have preferred to have her remain with the party from whom these evidences of gaiety proceeded. Mrs. Amherst had grown to depend on her friend's nearness. She liked to feel that Justine's quick hand and eye were always in waiting on her impulses, prompt to interpret and execute them without any exertion of her own. Bessy combined great zeal in the pursuit of sport—a tireless passion for the saddle, the golf-course, the tennis-court—with an almost oriental inertia within doors, an indolence of body and brain that made her shrink from the active obligations of hospitality, though she had grown to depend more and more on the distractions of a crowded house.

But Justine, though grateful, and anxious to show her gratitude, was unwilling to add to her other duties that of joining in the amusements of the house-party. She made no pretense of effacing herself when she thought her presence might be useful—but, even if she had cared for the diversions in favour at Lynbrook, a certain unavowed pride would have kept her from participating in them on the same footing with Bessy's guests. She was not in the least ashamed of her position in the household, but she chose that every one else should be aware of it, that she should not for an instant be taken for one of the nomadic damsels who form the camp-followers of the great army of pleasure. Yet even on this point her sensitiveness was not exaggerated. Adversity has a deft hand at gathering loose strands of impulse into character, and Justine's early contact with different phases of experience had given her a fairly clear view of life in the round, what might be called a sound working topography of its relative heights and depths. She was not seriously afraid of being taken for anything but what she really was, and still less did she fear to become, by force of propinquity and suggestion, the kind of being for whom she might be temporarily taken.

When, at Bessy's summons, she had joined the latter at her camp in the Adirondacks, the transition from a fatiguing "case" at Hanaford to a life in which sylvan freedom was artfully blent with the most studied personal luxury, had come as a delicious refreshment to body and brain. She was weary, for the moment, of ugliness, pain and hard work, and life seemed to recover its meaning under the aspect of a graceful leisure. Lynbrook also, whither she had been persuaded to go with Bessy at the end of their woodland cure, had at first amused and interested her. The big house on its spreading terraces, with windows looking over bright gardens to the hazy distances of the plains, seemed a haven of harmless ease and gaiety. Justine was sensitive to the finer graces of luxurious living, to the warm lights on old pictures and bronzes, the soft mingling of tints in faded rugs and panellings of time-warmed oak. And the existence to which this background formed a setting seemed at first to have the same decorative qualities. It was pleasant, for once, to be among people whose chief business was to look well and take life lightly, and Justine's own buoyancy of nature won her immediate access among the amiable persons who peopled Bessy's week-end parties. If they had only abounded a little more in their own line she might have succumbed to their spell. But it seemed to her that they missed the poetry of their situation, transacting their pleasures with the dreary method and shortness of view of a race tethered to the ledger. Even the verbal flexibility which had made her feel that she was in a world of freer ideas, soon revealed itself as a form of flight from them, in which the race was distinctly to the swift; and Justine's phase of passive enjoyment passed with the return of her physical and mental activity. She was a creature tingling with energy, a little fleeting particle of the power that moves the sun and the other stars, and the deadening influences of the life at Lynbrook roused these tendencies to greater intensity, as a suffocated person will suddenly develop abnormal strength in the struggle for air.

She did not, indeed, regret having come. She was glad to be with Bessy, partly because of the childish friendship which had left such deep traces in her lonely heart, and partly because what she had seen of her friend's situation stirred in her all the impulses of sympathy and service; but the idea of continuing in such a life, of sinking into any of the positions of semi-dependence that an adroit and handsome girl may create for herself in a fashionable woman's train—this possibility never presented itself to Justine till Mrs. Ansell, that afternoon, had put it into words. And to hear it was to revolt from it with all the strength of her inmost nature. The thought of the future troubled her, not so much materially—for she had a light bird-like trust in the morrow's fare—but because her own tendencies seemed to have grown less clear, because she could not rest in them for guidance as she had once done. The renewal of bodily activity had not brought back her faith in her calling: her work had lost the light of consecration. She no longer felt herself predestined to nurse the sick for the rest of her life, and in her inexperience she reproached herself with this instability. Youth and womanhood were in fact crying out in her for their individual satisfaction; but instincts as deep-seated protected her from even a momentary illusion as to the nature of this demand. She wanted happiness, and a life of her own, as passionately as young flesh-and-blood had ever wanted them; but they must come bathed in the light of imagination and penetrated by the sense of larger affinities. She could not conceive of shutting herself into a little citadel of personal well-being while the great tides of existence rolled on unheeded outside. Whether they swept treasure to her feet, or strewed her life with wreckage, she felt, even now, that her place was there, on the banks, in sound and sight of the great current; and just in proportion as the scheme of life at Lynbrook succeeded in shutting out all sense of that vaster human consciousness, so did its voice speak more thrillingly within her.

Somewhere, she felt—but, alas! still out of reach—was the life she longed for, a life in which high chances of doing should be mated with the finer forms of enjoying. But what title had she to a share in such an existence? Why, none but her sense of what it was worth—and what did that count for, in a world which used all its resources to barricade itself against all its opportunities? She knew there were girls who sought, by what is called a "good" marriage, an escape into the outer world of doing and thinking—utilizing an empty brain and full pocket as the key to these envied fields. Some such chance the life at Lynbrook seemed likely enough to offer—one is not, at Justine's age and with her penetration, any more blind to the poise of one's head than to the turn of one's ideas; but here the subtler obstacles of taste and pride intervened. Not even Bessy's transparent manœuvrings, her tender solicitude for her friend's happiness, could for a moment weaken Justine's resistance. If she must marry without love—and this was growing conceivable to her—she must at least merge her craving for personal happiness in some view of life in harmony with hers.

A tap on her door interrupted these musings, to one aspect of which Bessy Amherst's entrance seemed suddenly to give visible expression.

"Why did you run off, Justine? You promised to be down-stairs when I came back from tennis."

"*Till* you came back—wasn't it, dear?" Justine corrected with a smile, pushing her arm-chair forward as Bessy continued to linger irresolutely in the doorway. "I saw that there was a fresh supply of tea in the drawing-room, and I knew you would be there before the omnibus came from the station."

"Oh, I was there—but everybody was asking for you——"

"Everybody?" Justine gave a mocking lift to her dark eyebrows.

"Well—Westy Gaines, at any rate; the moment he set foot in the house!" Bessy declared with a laugh as she dropped into the arm-chair.

Justine echoed the laugh, but offered no comment on the statement which accompanied it, and for a moment both women were silent, Bessy tilting her pretty discontented head against the back of the chair, so that her eyes were on a level with those of her friend, who leaned near her in the embrasure of the window.

"I can't understand you, Justine. You know well enough what he's come back for."

"In order to dazzle Hanaford with the fact that he has been staying at Lynbrook!"

"Nonsense—the novelty of that has worn off. He's been here three times since we came back."

"You are admirably hospitable to your family——"

Bessy let her pretty ringed hands fall with a discouraged gesture. "Why do you find him so much worse than—than other people?"

Justine's eye-brows rose again. "In the same capacity? You speak as if I had boundless opportunities of comparison."

"Well, you've Dr. Wyant!" Mrs. Amherst suddenly flung back at her.

Justine coloured under the unexpected thrust, but met her friend's eyes steadily. "As an alternative to Westy? Well, if I were on a desert island—but I'm not!" she concluded with a careless laugh.

Bessy frowned and sighed. "You can't mean that, of the two—?" She paused and then went on doubtfully: "It's because he's cleverer?"

"Dr. Wyant?" Justine smiled. "It's not making an enormous claim for him!"

"Oh, I know Westy's not brilliant; but stupid men are not always the hardest to live with." She sighed again, and turned on Justine a glance charged with conjugal experience.

Justine had sunk into the window-seat, her thin hands clasping her knee, in the attitude habitual to her meditative moments. "Perhaps not," she assented; "but I don't know that I should care for a man who made life easy; I should want some one who made it interesting."

Bessy met this with a pitying exclamation. "Don't imagine you invented that! Every girl thinks it. Afterwards she finds out that it's much pleasanter to be thought interesting herself."

She spoke with a bitterness that issued strangely from her lips. It was this bitterness which gave her soft personality the sharp edge that Justine had felt in it on the day of their meeting at Hanaford.

The girl, at first, had tried to defend herself from these scarcely-veiled confidences, distasteful enough in themselves, and placing her, if she listened, in an attitude of implied disloyalty to the man under whose roof they were spoken. But a precocious experience of life had taught her that emotions too strong for the nature containing them turn, by some law of spiritual chemistry, into a rankling poison; and she had therefore resigned herself to serving as a kind of outlet for Bessy's pent-up discontent. It was not that her friend's grievance appealed to her personal sympathies; she had learned enough of the situation to give her moral assent unreservedly to the other side. But it was characteristic of Justine that where she sympathized least she sometimes pitied most. Like all quick spirits she was often intolerant of dulness; yet when the intolerance passed it left a residue of compassion for the very incapacity at which she chafed. It seemed to her that the tragic crises in wedded life usually turned on the stupidity of one of the two concerned; and of the two victims of such a catastrophe she felt most for the one whose limitations had probably brought it about. After all, there could be no imprisonment as cruel as that of being bounded by a hard small nature. Not to be penetrable at all points to the shifting lights, the wandering music of the world—she could imagine no physical disability as cramping as that. How the little parched soul, in solitary confinement for life, must pine and dwindle in its blind cranny of self-love!

To be one's self wide open to the currents of life does not always contribute to an understanding of narrower natures; but in Justine the personal emotions were enriched and deepened by a sense of participation in all that the world about her was doing, suffering and enjoying; and this sense found expression in the instinct of ministry and solace. She was by nature a redresser, a restorer; and in her work, as she had once told Amherst, the longing to help and direct, to hasten on by personal intervention time's slow and clumsy processes, had often been in conflict with the restrictions imposed by her profession. But she had no idle desire to probe the depths of other lives; and where there seemed no hope of serving she shrank from fruitless confidences. She was beginning to feel this to be the case with Bessy Amherst. To touch the rock was not enough, if there were but a few drops within it; yet in this barrenness lay the pathos of the situation—and after all, may not the scanty spring be fed from a fuller current?

"I'm not sure about that," she said, answering her friend's last words after a deep pause of deliberation. "I mean about its being so pleasant to be found interesting. I'm sure the passive part is always the dull one: life has been a great deal more thrilling since we found out that we revolved about the sun, instead of sitting still and fancying that all the planets were dancing attendance on us. After all, they were *not;* and it's rather humiliating to think how the morning stars must have laughed together about it!"

There was no self-complacency in Justine's eagerness to help. It was far easier for her to express it in action than in counsel, to grope for the path with her friend than to point the way to it; and when she had to speak she took refuge in figures to escape the pedantry of appearing to advise. But it was not only to Mrs. Dressel that her parables were dark, and the blank look in Bessy's eyes soon snatched her down from the height of metaphor.

"I mean," she continued with a smile, "that, as human nature is constituted, it has got to find its real self—the self to be interested in—outside of what we conventionally call 'self': the particular Justine or Bessy who is clamouring for her particular morsel of life. You see, self isn't a thing one can keep in a box—bits of it keep escaping, and flying off to lodge in all sorts of unexpected crannies; we come across scraps of ourselves in the most unlikely places—as I believe you would in Westmore, if you'd only go back there and look for them!"

Bessy's lip trembled and the colour sprang to her face; but she answered with a flash of irritation: "Why doesn't *he* look for me there, then—if he still wants to find me?"

"Ah—it's for him to look here—to find himself *here*," Justine murmured.

"Well, he never comes here! That's his answer."

"He will—he will! Only, when he does, let him find you."

"Find me? I don't understand. How can he, when he never sees me? I'm no more to him than the carpet on the floor!"

Justine smiled again. "Well—be that then! The thing is to *be*."

"Under his feet? Thank you! Is that what you mean to marry for? It's not what husbands admire in one, you know!"

"No." Justine stood up with a sense of stealing discouragement. "But I don't think I want to be admired——"

"Ah, that's because you know you are!" broke from the depths of the other's bitterness.

The tone smote Justine, and she dropped into the seat at her friend's side, silently laying a hand on Bessy's feverishly-clasped fingers.

"Oh, don't let us talk about me," complained the latter, from whose lips the subject was never long absent. "And you mustn't think I *want* you to marry, Justine; not for myself, I mean—I'd so much rather keep you here. I feel much less lonely when you're with me. But you say you won't stay—and it's too dreadful to think of your going back to that dreary hospital."

"But you know the hospital's not dreary to me," Justine interposed; "it's the most interesting place I've ever known."

Mrs. Amherst smiled indulgently on this extravagance. "A great many people go through the craze for philanthropy—" she began in the tone of mature experience; but Justine interrupted her with a laugh.

"Philanthropy? I'm not philanthropic. I don't think I ever felt inclined to do good in the abstract—any more than to do ill! I can't remember that I ever planned out a course of conduct in my life. It's only," she went on, with a puzzled frown, as if honestly trying to analyze her motives, "it's only that I'm so fatally interested in people that before I know it I've slipped into their skins; and then, of course, if anything goes wrong with them, it's just as if it had gone wrong with me; and I can't help trying to rescue myself from *their* troubles! I suppose it's what you'd call meddling—and so should I, if I could only remember that the other people were not myself!"

Bessy received this with the mild tolerance of superior wisdom. Once safe on the tried ground of traditional authority, she always felt herself Justine's superior. "That's all very well now—you see the romantic side of it," she said, as if humouring her friend's vagaries. "But in time you'll want something else; you'll want a husband and children—a life of your own. And then you'll have to be more practical. It's ridiculous to pretend that comfort and money don't make a difference. And if you married a rich man, just think what a lot of good you could do! Westy will be very well off—and I'm sure he'd let you endow hospitals and things. Think how interesting it would be to build a ward in the very hospital where you'd been a nurse! I read something like that in a novel the other day—it was beautifully described. All the nurses and doctors that the heroine had worked with were there to receive her. . . and her little boy went about and gave toys to the crippled children. . ."

If the speaker's concluding instance hardly produced the effect she had intended, it was perhaps only because Justine's attention had been arrested by the earlier part of the argument. It was strange to have marriage urged on her by a woman who had twice failed to find happiness in it—strange, and yet how vivid a sign that, even to a nature absorbed in its personal demands, not happiness but completeness is the inmost craving! "A life of your own"—that was what even Bessy, in her obscure way, felt to be best worth suffering for. And how was a spirit like Justine's, thrilling with youth and sympathy, to conceive of an isolated existence as the final answer to that craving? A life circumscribed by one's own poor personal consciousness would not be life at all—far better the "adventure of the diver" than the shivering alone on the bank! Bessy, reading encouragement in her silence, returned her hand-clasp with an affectionate pressure.

"You *would* like that, Justine?" she said, secretly proud of having hit on the convincing argument.

"To endow hospitals with your cousin's money? No; I should want something much more exciting!"

Bessy's face kindled. "You mean travelling abroad —and I suppose New York in winter?"

Justine broke into a laugh. "I was thinking of your cousin himself when I spoke." And to Bessy's disappointed cry—"Then it *is* Dr. Wyant, after all?" she answered lightly, and without resenting the challenge: "I don't know. Suppose we leave it to the oracle."

"The oracle?"

"Time. His question-and-answer department is generally the most reliable in the long run." She started up, gently drawing Bessy to her feet. "And just at present he reminds me that it's nearly six, and that you promised Cicely to go and see her before you dress for dinner."

Bessy rose obediently. "Does he remind you of *your* promises too? You said you'd come down to dinner tonight."

"Did I?" Justine hesitated. "Well, I'm coming," she said, smiling and kissing her friend.

XV

WHEN the door closed on Mrs. Amherst a resolve which had taken shape in Justine's mind during their talk together made her seat herself at her writing-table, where, after a moment's musing over her suspended pen, she wrote and addressed a hurried note. This business despatched, she put on her hat and jacket, and letter in hand passed down the corridor from her room, and descended to the entrance-hall below. She might have consigned her missive to the post-box which conspicuously tendered its services from a table near the door; but to do so would delay the letter's despatch till morning, and she felt a sudden impatience to see it start.

The tumult on the terrace had transferred itself within doors, and as Justine went down the stairs she heard the click of cues from the billiard-room, the talk and laughter of belated bridge-players, the movement of servants gathering up tea-cups and mending fires. She had hoped to find the hall empty, but the sight of Westy Gaines's figure looming watchfully on the threshold of the smoking-room gave her, at the last bend of the stairs, a little start of annoyance. He would want to know where she was going, he would offer to go with her, and it would take some time and not a little emphasis to make him understand that his society was not desired.

This was the thought that flashed through Justine's mind as she reached the landing; but the next moment it gave way to a contradictory feeling. Westy Gaines was not alone in the hall. From under the stairway rose the voices of a group ensconced in that popular retreat about a chess-board; and as Justine reached the last turn of the stairs she perceived that Mason Winch, an earnest youth with advanced views on political economy, was engaged, to the diversion of a circle of spectators, in teaching the Telfer girls chess. The futility of trying to fix the spasmodic attention of this effervescent couple, and their instructor's grave unconsciousness of the fact, constituted, for the lookers-on, the peculiar diversion of the scene. It was of course inevitable that young Winch, on his arrival at Lynbrook, should have succumbed at once to the tumultuous charms of the Telfer manner, which was equally attractive to inarticulate youth and to tired and talked-out middle-age; but that he should have perceived no resistance in their minds to the deliberative processes of the game of chess, was, even to the Telfers themselves, a source of unmitigated gaiety. Nothing seemed to them funnier than that any one should credit them with any mental capacity; and they had inexhaustibly amusing ways of drawing out and showing off each other's ignorance.

It was on this scene that Westy's appreciative eyes had been fixed till Justine's appearance drew them to herself. He pronounced her name joyfully, and moved forward to greet her; but as their hands met she understood that he did not mean to press his company upon her. Under the eye of the Lynbrook circle he was chary of marked demonstrations, and even Mrs. Amherst's approval could not, at such moments, bridge over the gap between himself and the object of his attentions. A Gaines was a Gaines in the last analysis, and apart from any pleasing accident of personality; but what was Miss Brent but the transient vehicle of those graces which Providence has provided for the delectation of the privileged sex?

These influences were visible in the temperate warmth of Westy's manner, and in his way of keeping a backward eye on the mute interchange of comment about the chess-board. At another time his embarrassment would have amused Justine; but the feelings stirred by her talk with Bessy had not subsided, and she recognized with a sting of mortification the resemblance between her view of the Lynbrook set and its estimate of herself. If Bessy's friends were negligible to her she was almost non-existent to them; and, as against herself, they were overwhelmingly provided with tangible means of proving their case.

Such considerations, at a given moment, may prevail decisively even with a nature armed against them by insight and irony; and the mere fact that Westy Gaines did not mean to join her, and that he was withheld from doing so by the invisible pressure of the Lynbrook standards, had the effect of precipitating Justine's floating intentions.

If anything farther had been needed to hasten this result, it would have been accomplished by the sound of footsteps which, over-taking her a dozen yards from the house, announced her admirer's impetuous if tardy pursuit. The act of dismissing him, though it took but a word and was effected with a laugh, left her pride quivering with a hurt the more painful because she would not acknowledge it. That she should waste a moment's resentment on the conduct of a person so unimportant as poor Westy, showed her in a flash the intrinsic falseness of her position at Lynbrook. She saw that to disdain the life about her had not kept her intact from it; and the knowledge made her feel anew the need of some strong decentralizing influence, some purifying influx of emotion and activity.

She had walked on quickly through the clear October twilight, which was still saturated with the after-glow of a vivid sunset; and a few minutes brought her to the village stretching along the turnpike beyond the Lynbrook gates. The new post-office dominated the row of shabby houses and "stores" set disjointedly under reddening maples, and its arched doorway formed the centre of Lynbrook's evening intercourse.

Justine, hastening toward the knot of loungers on the threshold, had no consciousness of anything outside of her own thoughts; and as she mounted the steps she was surprised to see Dr. Wyant detach himself from the group and advance to meet her.

"May I post your letter?" he asked, lifting his hat.

His gesture uncovered the close-curling hair of a small delicately-finished head just saved from effeminacy by the vigorous jut of heavy eye-brows meeting above full grey eyes. The eyes again, at first sight, might have struck one as too expressive, or as expressing things too purely decorative for the purposes of a young country doctor with a growing practice; but this estimate was corrected by an unexpected abruptness in their owner's voice and manner. Perhaps the final impression produced on a close observer by Dr. Stephen Wyant would have been that the contradictory qualities of which he was compounded had not yet been brought into equilibrium by the hand of time.

Justine, in reply to his question, had drawn back a step, slipping her letter into the breast of her jacket.

"That is hardly worth while, since it was addressed to you," she answered with a slight smile as she turned to descend the post-office steps.

Wyant, still carrying his hat, and walking with quick uneven steps, followed her in silence till they had passed beyond earshot of the loiterers on the threshold; then, in the shade of the maple boughs, he pulled up and faced her.

"You've written to say that I may come tomorrow?"

Justine hesitated. "Yes," she said at length.

"Good God! You give royally!" he broke out, pushing his hand with a nervous gesture through the thin dark curls on his forehead.

Justine laughed, with a trace of nervousness in her own tone. "And you talk—well, imperially! Aren't you afraid to bankrupt the language?"

"What do you mean?" he said, staring.

"What do *you* mean? I have merely said that I would see you tomorrow——"

"Well," he retorted, "that's enough for my happiness!"

She sounded her light laugh again. "I'm glad to know you're so easily pleased."

"I'm not! But you couldn't have done a cruel thing without a struggle; and since you're ready to give me my answer tomorrow, I know it can't be a cruel one."

They had begun to walk onward as they talked, but at this she halted. "Please don't take that tone. I dislike sentimentality!" she exclaimed, with a tinge of imperiousness that was a surprise to her own ears.

It was not the first time in the course of her friendship with Stephen Wyant that she had been startled by this intervention of something within her that resisted and almost resented his homage. When they were apart, she was conscious only of the community of interests and sympathies that had first drawn them together. Why was it then—since his looks were of the kind generally thought to stand a suitor in good stead—that whenever they had met of late she had been subject to these rushes of obscure hostility, the half-physical, half-moral shrinking from some indefinable element in his nature against which she was constrained to defend herself by perpetual pleasantry and evasion?

To Wyant, at any rate, the answer was not far to seek. His pale face reflected the disdain in hers as he returned ironically: "A thousand pardons; I know I'm not always in the key."

"The key?"

"I haven't yet acquired the Lynbrook tone. You must make allowances for my lack of opportunity."

The retort on Justine's lips dropped to silence, as

though his words had in fact brought an answer to her inward questioning. Could it be that he was right—that her shrinking from him was the result of an increased sensitiveness to faults of taste that she would once have despised herself for noticing? When she had first known him, in her work at St. Elizabeth's some three years earlier, his excesses of manner had seemed to her merely the boyish tokens of a richness of nature not yet controlled by experience. Though Wyant was somewhat older than herself there had always been an element of protection in her feeling for him, and it was perhaps this element which formed the real ground of her liking. It was, at any rate, uppermost as she returned, with a softened gleam of mockery: "Since you are so sure of my answer I hardly know why I should see you tomorrow."

"You mean me to take it now?" he exclaimed.

"I don't mean you to take it at all till it's given—above all not to take it for granted!"

His jutting brows drew together again. "Ah, I can't split hairs with you. Won't you put me out of my misery?"

She smiled, but not unkindly. "Do you want an anæsthetic?"

"No—a clean cut with the knife!"

"You forget that we're not allowed to despatch hopeless cases—more's the pity!"

He flushed to the roots of his thin hair. "Hopeless cases? That's it, then—that's my answer?"

They had reached the point where, at the farther edge of the straggling settlement, the tiled roof of the railway-station fronted the post-office cupola; and the shriek of a whistle now reminded Justine that the spot was not propitious to private talk. She halted a moment before speaking.

"I have no answer to give you now but the one in my note—that I'll see you tomorrow."

"But if you're sure of knowing tomorrow you must know now!"

Their eyes met, his eloquently pleading, hers kind but still impenetrable. "If I knew now, you should know too. Please be content with that," she rejoined.

"How can I be, when a day may make sucn a difference? When I know that every influence about you is fighting against me?"

The words flashed a refracted light far down into the causes of her own uncertainty.

"Ah," she said, drawing a little away from him, "I'm not so sure that I don't like a fight!"

"Is that why you won't give in?" He moved toward her with a despairing gesture. "If I let you go now, you're lost to me!"

She stood her ground, facing him with a quick lift of

the head. "If you don't let me go I certainly am," she said; and he drew back, as if conscious of the uselessness of the struggle. His submission, as usual, had a disarming effect on her irritation, and she held out her hand. "Come tomorrow at three," she said, her voice and manner suddenly seeming to give back the hope she had withheld from him.

He seized on her hand with an inarticulate murmur; but at the same moment a louder whistle and the thunder of an approaching train reminded her of the impossibility of prolonging the scene. She was ordinarily careless of appearances, but while she was Mrs. Amherst's guest she did not care to be seen romantically loitering through the twilight with Stephen Wyant; and she freed herself with a quick goodbye.

He gave her a last look, hesitating and imploring; then, in obedience to her gesture, he turned away and strode off in the opposite direction.

As soon as he had left her she began to retrace her steps toward Lynbrook House; but instead of traversing the whole length of the village she passed through a turnstile in the park fencing, taking a more circuitous but quieter way home.

She walked on slowly through the dusk, wishing to give herself time to think over her conversation with Wyant. Now that she was alone again, it seemed to her that the part she had played had been both inconsistent and undignified. When she had written to Wyant that she would see him on the morrow she had done so with the clear understanding that she was to give, at that meeting, a definite answer to his offer of marriage; and during her talk with Bessy she had suddenly, and, as it seemed to her, irrevocably, decided that the answer should be favourable. From the first days of her acquaintance with Wyant she had appreciated his intelligence and had been stimulated by his zeal for his work. He had remained only six months at Saint Elizabeth's, and though his feeling for her had even then been manifest, it had been kept from expression by the restraint of their professional relation, and by her absorption in her duties. It was only when they had met again at Lynbrook that she had begun to feel a personal interest in him. His youthful promise seemed nearer fulfillment than she had once thought possible, and the contrast he presented to the young men in Bessy's train was really all in his favour. He had gained in strength and steadiness without losing his high flashes of enthusiasm; and though, even now, she was not in love with him, she began to feel that the union of their common interests might create a life full and useful enough to preclude the possibility of vague repinings. It would, at any rate, take her out of the stagnant circle of her present existence, and restore her to contact with the fruitful energies of life.

All this had seemed quite clear when she wrote her letter; why, then, had she not made use of their chance encounter to give her answer, instead of capriciously postponing it? The act might have been that of a self-conscious girl in her teens; but neither inexperience nor coquetry had prompted it. She had merely yielded to the spirit of resistance that Wyant's presence had of late aroused in her; and the possibility that this resistance might be due to some sense of his social defects, his lack of measure and facility, was so humiliating that for a moment she stood still in the path, half-meaning to turn back and overtake him——

As she paused she was surprised to hear a man's step behind her; and the thought that it might be Wyant's brought about another revulsion of feeling. What right had he to pursue her in this way, to dog her steps even into the Lynbrook grounds? She was sure that his persistent attentions had already attracted the notice of Bessy's visitors; and that he should thus force himself on her after her dismissal seemed suddenly to make their whole relation ridiculous.

She turned about to rebuke him, and found herself face to face with John Amherst.

XVI

AMHERST, on leaving the train at Lynbrook, had paused in doubt on the empty platform. His return was unexpected, and no carriage awaited him; but he caught the signal of the village cab-driver's ready whip. Amherst, however, felt a sudden desire to postpone the moment of arrival, and consigning his luggage to the cab he walked away toward the turnstile through which Justine had passed. In thus taking the longest way home he was yielding another point to his reluctance. He knew that at that hour his wife's visitors might still be assembled in the drawing-room, and he wished to avoid making his unannounced entrance among them.

It was not till now that he felt the embarrassment of such an arrival. For some time past he had known that he ought to go back to Lynbrook, but he had not known how to tell Bessy that he was coming. Lack of habit made him inexpert in the art of easy transitions, and his inability to bridge over awkward gaps had often put him at a disadvantage with his wife and her friends. He had not yet learned the importance of observing the forms which made up the daily ceremonial of their lives, and at present there was just enough soreness between himself and Bessy to make such observances more difficult than usual.

There had been no open estrangement, but peace had been preserved at the cost of a slowly accumulated tale of grievances on both sides. Since Amherst had won his point about the mills, the danger he had foreseen had been realized: his victory at Westmore had been a defeat at Lynbrook. It would be too crude to say that his wife had made him pay for her public concession by the private disregard of his wishes; and if something of this sort had actually resulted, his sense of fairness told him that it was merely the natural reaction of a soft nature against the momentary strain of self-denial At first he had been hardly aware of this consequence of his triumph. The joy of being able to work his will at Westmore obscured all lesser emotions; and his sentiment for Bessy had long since shrunk into one of those shallow pools of feeling which a sudden tide might fill, but which could never again be the deep perennial spring from which his life was fed.

The need of remaining continuously at Hanaford while the first changes were making had increased the strain of the situation. He had never expected that Bessy would stay there with him—had perhaps, at heart, hardly wished it—and her plan of going to the Adirondacks with Miss Brent seemed to him a satisfactory alternative to the European trip she had renounced. He felt as relieved as though some one had taken off his hands the task of amusing a restless child, and he let his wife go without suspecting that the moment might be a decisive one between them. But it had not occurred to Bessy that any one could regard six weeks in the Adirondacks as an adequate substitute for a summer abroad. She felt that her sacrifice deserved recognition, and personal devotion was the only form of recognition which could satisfy her. She had expected Amherst to join her at the camp, but he did not come; and when she went back to Long Island she did not stop to see him, though Hanaford lay in her way. At the moment of her return the work at the mills made it impossible for him to go to Lynbrook; and thus the weeks drifted on without their meeting.

At last, urged by his mother, he had gone down to Long Island for a night; but though, on that occasion, he had announced his coming, he found the house full, and the whole party except Mr. Langhope in the act of starting off to a dinner in the neighbourhood. He was of course expected to go too, and Bessy appeared hurt when he declared that he was too tired and preferred to remain with Mr. Langhope; but she did not suggest staying at home herself, and drove off in a mood of exuberant gaiety. Amherst had been too busy all his life to know what intricacies of perversion a sentimental grievance may develop in an unoccupied mind, and he saw in Bessy's act only a sign of indifference. The next day she complained to him of money difficulties, as though surprised that her income had been suddenly cut down; and when he reminded her that she had consented of her own will to this temporary reduction, she burst into tears and accused him of caring only for Westmore.

He went away exasperated by her inconsequence, and bills from Lynbrook continued to pour in on him. In the first days of their marriage, Bessy had put him in charge of her exchequer, and she was too indolent—and at heart perhaps too sensitive—to ask him to renounce the charge. It was clear to him, therefore, how little she was observing the spirit of their compact, and his mind was tormented by the anticipation of financial embarrassments. He wrote her a letter of gentle expostulation, but in her answer she ignored his remonstrance; and after that silence fell between them.

The only way to break this silence was to return to Lynbrook; but now that he had come back, he did not know what step to take next. Something in the atmosphere of his wife's existence seemed to paralyze his will-power. When all about her spoke a language so different from his own, how could he hope to make himself heard? He knew that her family and her immediate friends—Mr. Langhope, the Gaineses, Mrs. Ansell and Mr. Tredegar—far from being means of communication, were so many sentinels ready to raise the drawbridge and drop the portcullis at his approach. They were all in league to stifle the incipient feelings he had roused in Bessy, to push her back into the deadening routine of her former life, and the only voice that might conceivably speak for him was Miss Brent's.

The "case" which, unexpectedly presented to her by one of the Hope Hospital physicians, had detained Justine at Hanaford during the month of June, was the means of establishing a friendship between herself and Amherst. They did not meet often, or get to know each other very well; but he saw her occasionally at his mother's and at Mrs. Dressel's, and once he took her out to Westmore, to consult her about the emergency hospital which was to be included among the first improvements there. The expedition had been memorable to both; and when, some two weeks later, Bessy wrote suggesting that she should take Miss Brent to the Adirondacks, it seemed to Amherst that there was no one whom he would rather have his wife choose as her companion.

He was much too busy at the time to cultivate or analyze his feeling for Miss Brent; he rested vaguely in the thought of her, as of the "nicest" girl he had ever met, and was frankly pleased when accident brought them together; but the seeds left in both their minds by these chance encounters had not yet begun to germinate.

So unperceived had been their gradual growth in intimacy that it was a surprise to Amherst to find himself suddenly thinking of her as a means of communication with his wife; but the thought gave him such encouragement that, when he saw Justine in the path before him he went toward her with unusual eagerness.

Justine, on her part, felt an equal pleasure. She knew that Bessy did not expect her husband, and that his prolonged absence had already been the cause of malicious comment at Lynbrook; and she caught at the hope that this sudden return might betoken a more favourable turn of affairs.

"Oh, I am so glad to see you!" she exclaimed; and her tone had the effect of completing his reassurance, his happy sense that she would understand and help him.

"I wanted to see you too," he began confusedly; then, conscious of the intimacy of the phrase, he added with a slight laugh: "The fact is, I'm a culprit looking for a peace-maker."

"A culprit?"

"I've been so tied down at the mills that I didn't know, till yesterday, just when I could break away; and in the hurry of leaving—" He paused again, checked by the impossibility of uttering, to the girl before him, the little conventional falsehoods which formed the small currency of Bessy's circle. Not that any scruple of probity restrained him: in trifling matters he recognized the usefulness of such counters in the social game; but when he was with Justine he always felt the obscure need of letting his real self be seen.

"I was stupid enough not to telegraph," he said, "and I am afraid my wife will think me negligent: she often has to reproach me for my sins of omission, and this time I know they are many."

The girl received this in silence, less from embarrassment than from surprise; for she had already guessed that it was as difficult for Amherst to touch, even lightly, on his private affairs, as it was instinctive with his wife to pour her grievances into any willing ear. Justine's first thought was one of gratification that he should have spoken, and of eagerness to facilitate the saying of whatever he wished to say; but before she could answer he went on hastily: "The fact is, Bessy does not know how complicated the work at Westmore is; and when I caught sight of you just now I was thinking that you are the only one of her friends who has any technical understanding of what I am trying to do, and who might consequently help her to see how hard it is for me to take my hand from the plough."

Justine listened gravely, longing to cry out her comprehension and sympathy, but restrained by the sense that the moment was a critical one, where impulse must not be trusted too far. It was quite possible that a reaction of pride might cause Amherst to repent even so guarded an avowal; and if that happened, he might never forgive her for having encouraged him to speak. She looked up at him with a smile.

"Why not tell Bessy yourself? Your understanding of the case is a good deal clearer than mine or any one else's."

"Oh, Bessy is tired of hearing about it from me; and besides—" She detected a shade of disappointment in his tone, and was sorry she had said anything which might seem meant to discourage his confidence. It occurred to her also that she had been insincere in not telling him at once that she had already been let into the secret of his domestic differences: she felt the same craving as Amherst for absolute openness between them.

"I know," she said, almost timidly, "that Bessy has not been quite content of late to have you give so much time to Westmore, and perhaps she herself thinks it is because the work there does not interest her; but I believe it is for a different reason."

"What reason?" he asked with a look of surprise.

"Because Westmore takes you from her; because she thinks you are happier there than at Lynbrook."

The day had faded so rapidly that it was no longer possible for the speakers to see each other's faces, and it was easier for both to communicate through the veil of deepening obscurity.

"But, good heavens, she might be there with me—she's as much needed there as I am!" Amherst exclaimed.

"Yes; but you must remember that it's against all her habits—and against the point of view of every one about her—that she should lead that kind of life; and meanwhile——"

"Well?"

"Meanwhile, isn't it expedient that you should, a little more, lead hers?"

Always the same answer to his restless questioning! His mother's answer, the answer of Bessy and her friends. He had somehow hoped that the girl at his side would find a different solution to the problem, and his disappointment escaped in a bitter exclamation.

"But Westmore is my life—hers too, if she knew it! I can't desert it now without being as false to her as to myself!"

As he spoke, he was overcome once more by the hopelessness of trying to put his case clearly. How could Justine, for all her quickness and sympathy, understand a situation of which the deeper elements were necessarily unknown to her? The advice she gave him was natural enough, and on her lips it seemed not the counsel of a shallow expediency, but the plea of compassion and understanding. But she knew nothing of the long struggle for mutual adjustment which had culminated in this crisis between himself and his wife, and she could therefore not see that, if he yielded his point, and gave up his work at Westmore, the concession would mean not renewal but destruction. He felt that he should hate Bessy if he won her back at that price; and the violence of his feeling frightened him. It was, in truth, as he had said, his own life that he was fighting for. If he gave up Wetsmore he could not fall back on the futile activities of Lynbrook, and fate might yet have some lower alternative to offer. He could trust to his own strength and self-command while his energies had a normal outlet; but idleness and self-indulgence might work in him like a dangerous drug.

Justine kept steadily to her point. "Westmore must be foremost to both of you in time; I don't see how either of you can escape that. But the realization of it must come to Bessy through *you*, and for that reason I think that you ought to be more patient—that you ought even to put the question aside for a time and enter a little more into her life while she is learning to understand yours." As she ended, it seemed to her that what she had said was trite and ineffectual, and yet that it might have passed the measure of discretion; and, torn between two doubts, she added hastily:

"But you have done just that in coming back now—that is the real solution of the problem."

While she spoke they passed out of the wood-path they had been following, and rounding a mass of shrubbery emerged on the lawn below the terraces. The long bulk of the house lay above them, dark against the lingering gleam of the west, with brightly-lit windows marking its irregular outline; and the sight produced in Amherst and Justine a vague sense of helplessness and constraint. It was impossible to speak with the same freedom, confronted by that substantial symbol of the accepted order, which seemed to glare down on them in massive disdain of their puny efforts to deflect the course of events; and Amherst, without reverting to her last words, asked after a moment if his wife had many guests.

He listened in silence while Justine ran over the list of names—the Telfer girls and their brother, Mason Winch and Westy Gaines, a cluster of young bridge-playing couples, and, among the last arrivals, the Fenton Carburys and Ned Bowfort. The names were all familiar to Amherst—he knew they represented the flower of week-end fashion; but he did not remember having seen the Carburys among his wife's guests, and his mind paused on the name, seeking to regain some lost impression connected with it. But it evoked, like the others, merely the confused sense of stridency and unrest which he had brought away from his last Lynbrook visit; and this reminiscence made him ask Miss Brent, when her list was ended, if she did not think that so continuous a succession of visitors was too tiring for Bessy.

"I sometimes think it tires her more than she knows; but I hope she can be persuaded to take better care of herself now that Mrs. Ansell has come back."

Amherst halted abruptly. "Is Mrs. Ansell here?"

"She arrived from Europe today."

"And Mr. Langhope too, I suppose?"

"Yes. He came from Newport about ten days ago."

Amherst checked himself, conscious that his questions betrayed the fact that he and his wife no longer wrote to each other. The same thought appeared to strike Justine, and they walked across the lawn in silence, hastening their steps involuntarily, as though to escape the oppressive weight of the words which had passed between them. But Justine was unwilling that this fruitless sense of oppression should be the final outcome of their talk; and when they reached the upper terrace she paused and turned impulsively to Amherst. As she did so, the light from an uncurtained window fell on her face, which glowed with the inner brightness kindled in it by moments of strong feeling.

"I am sure of one thing—Bessy will be very, very glad that you have come," she exclaimed.

"Thank you," he answered.

Their hands met mechanically, and she turned away and entered the house.

XVII

BESSY had not seen her little girl that day, and filled with compunction by Justine's reminder, she hastened directly to the school-room.

Of late, in certain moods, her maternal tenderness had been clouded by a sense of uneasiness in the child's presence, for Cicely was the argument most effectually used by Mr. Langhope and Mr. Tredegar in their efforts to check the triumph of Amherst's ideas. Bessy, still unable to form an independent opinion on the harassing question of the mills, continued to oscillate between the views of the contending parties, now regarding Cicely as an innocent victim and herself as an unnatural mother, sacrificing her child's prospects to further Amherst's enterprise, and now conscious of a vague animosity against the little girl, as the chief cause of the dissensions which had so soon clouded the skies of her second marriage. Then again, there were moments when Cicely's rosy bloom reminded her bitterly of the child she had lost—the son on whom her ambitions had been fixed. It seemed to her now that if their boy had lived she might have kept Amherst's love and have played a more important part in his life; and brooding on the tragedy of the child's sickly existence she resented the contrast of Cicely's brightness and vigour. The result was that in her treatment of her daughter she alternated between moments of exaggerated devotion and days of neglect, never long happy away from the little girl, yet restless and self-tormenting in her presence.

After her talk with Justine she felt more than usually disturbed, as she always did when her unprofitable impulses of self-exposure had subsided. Bessy's mind was not made for introspection, and chance had burdened it with unintelligible problems. She felt herself the victim of circumstances to which her imagination attributed the deliberate malice that children ascribe to the furniture they run against in playing. This helped her to cultivate a sense of helpless injury and to disdain in advance the advice she was perpetually seeking. How absurd it was, for instance, to suppose that a girl could understand the feelings of a married woman! Justine's suggestion that she should humble herself still farther to Amherst merely left in Bessy's mind a rankling sense of being misunderstood and undervalued by those to whom she turned in her extremity, and she said to herself, in a phrase that sounded well in her own ears, that sooner or later every woman must learn to fight her battles alone.

In this mood she entered the room where Cicely was at supper with her governess, and enveloped the child in a whirl of passionate caresses. But Cicely had inherited the soberer Westmore temper, and her mother's spasmodic endearments always had a repressive effect on her. She dutifully returned a small fraction of Bessy's kisses, and then, with an air of relief, addressed herself once more to her bread and marmalade.

"You don't seem a bit glad to see me!" Bessy exclaimed, while the little governess made a nervous pretence of being greatly amused at this prodigious paradox, and Cicely, setting down her silver mug, asked judicially: "Why should I be gladder than other days? It isn't a birthday."

This Cordelia-like answer cut Bessy to the quick. "You horrid child to say such a cruel thing when you know I love you better and better every minute! But you don't care for me any longer because Justine has taken you away from me!"

This last charge had sprung into her mind in the act of uttering it, but now that it was spoken it instantly assumed the proportions of a fact, and seemed to furnish another justification for her wretchedness. Bessy was not naturally jealous, but her imagination was thrall to the spoken word, and it gave her a sudden incomprehensible relief to associate Justine with the obscure causes of her suffering.

"I know she's cleverer than I am, and more amusing, and can tell you about plants and animals and things. . . and I daresay she tells you how tiresome and stupid I am. . ."

She sprang up suddenly, abashed by Cicely's astonished gaze, and by the governess's tremulous attempt to continue to treat the scene as one of "Mamma's" most successful pleasantries.

"Don't mind me—my head aches horribly. I think I'll rush off for a gallop on Impulse before dinner. Miss Dill, Cicely's nails are a sight—I suppose that comes of grubbing up wild-flowers."

And with this parting shot at Justine's pursuits she swept out of the school-room, leaving pupil and teacher plunged in a stricken silence from which Cicely at length emerged to say, with the candour that Miss Dill dreaded more than any punishable offense: "Mother's prettiest—but I do like Justine the best."

It was nearly dark when Bessy mounted the horse which had been hastily saddled in response to her order; but it was her habit to ride out alone at all hours, and of late nothing but a hard gallop had availed to quiet her nerves. Her craving for occupation had increased as her life became more dispersed and agitated, and the need to fill every hour drove her to excesses of bodily exertion, since other forms of activity were unknown to her.

As she cantered along under the twilight sky, with a strong sea-breeze in her face, the rush of air and the effort of steadying her nervous thoroughbred filled her with a glow of bodily energy from which her thoughts emerged somewhat cleansed of their bitterness.

She had been odious to poor little Cicely, for whom she now felt a sudden remorseful yearning which almost made her turn her horse's head homeward, that she might dash upstairs and do penance beside the child's bed. And that she should have accused Justine of taking Cicely from her! It frightened her to find herself thinking evil of Justine. Bessy, whose perceptions were keen enough in certain directions, knew that her second marriage had changed her relation to all her former circle of friends. Though they still rallied about her, keeping up the convenient habit of familiar intercourse, she had begun to be aware that their view of her had in it an element of criticism and compassion. She had once fancied that Amherst's good looks, and the other qualities she had seen in him, would immediately make him free of the charmed circle in which she moved; but she was discouraged by his disregard of his opportunities, and above all by the fundamental differences in his view of life. He was never common or ridiculous, but she saw that he would never acquire the small social facilities. He was fond of exercise, but it bored him to talk of it. The men's smoking-room anecdotes did not amuse him, he was unmoved by the fluctuations of the stock-market, he could not tell one card from another, and his perfunctory attempts at billiards had once caused Mr. Langhope to murmur, in his daughter's hearing: "Ah, that's the test—I always said so!"

Thus debarred from what seemed to Bessy the chief points of contact with life, how could Amherst hope to impose himself on minds versed in these larger relations? As the sense of his social insufficiency grew on her, Bessy became more sensitive to that latent criticism of her marriage which—intolerable thought!—involved a judgment on herself. She was increasingly eager for the approval and applause of her little audience, yet increasingly distrustful of their sincerity, and more miserably persuaded that she and her husband were the butt of some of their most effective stories. She knew also that rumours of the disagreement about Westmore were abroad, and the suspicion that Amherst's conduct was the subject of unfriendly comment provoked in her a reaction of loyalty to his ideas. . .

From this turmoil of conflicting influences only her friendship with Justine Brent remained secure. Though Justine's adaptability made it easy for her to fit into the Lynbrook life, Bessy knew that she stood as much outside of it as Amherst. She could never, for instance, be influenced by what Maria Ansell and the Gaineses and the Telfers thought. She had her own criteria of conduct, unintelligible to Bessy, but giving her an independence of mind on which her friend leaned in a kind of blind security. And that even her faith in Justine should suddenly be poisoned by a jealous thought seemed to prove that the consequences of her marriage were gradually infecting her whole life. Bessy could conceive of masculine devotion only as subservient to its divinity's least wish, and she argued that if Amherst had really loved her he could not so lightly have disturbed the foundations of her world. And so her tormented thoughts, perpetually circling on themselves, reverted once more to their central grievance—the failure of her marriage. If her own love had died out it would have been much simpler—she was surrounded by examples of the mutual evasion of a troublesome tie. There was Blanche Carbury, for instance, with whom she had lately struck up an absorbing friendship. . . it was perfectly clear that Blanche Carbury wondered how much more she was going to stand! But it was the torment of Bessy's situation that it involved a radical contradiction, that she still loved Amherst though she could not forgive him for having married her.

Perhaps what she most suffered from was his too-prompt acceptance of the semi-estrangement between them. After nearly three years of marriage she had still to learn that it was Amherst's way to wrestle with the angel till dawn, and then to go about his other business. Her own mind could revolve in the same grievance as interminably as a squirrel in its wheel, and her husband's habit of casting off the accepted fact seemed to betoken poverty of feeling. If only he had striven a little harder to keep her—if, even now, he would come back to her, and make her feel that she was more to him than those wretched mills!

When she turned her mare toward Lynbrook, the longing to see Amherst was again uppermost. He had not written for weeks—she had been obliged to tell Maria Ansell that she knew nothing of his plans, and it mortified her to think that every one was aware of his neglect. Yet, even now, if on reaching the house she should find a telegram to say that he was coming, the weight of loneliness would be lifted, and everything in life would seem different. . .

Her high-strung mare, scenting the homeward road, and excited by the fantastic play of wayside lights and shadows, swept her along at a wild gallop with which the fevered rush of her thoughts kept pace, and when she reached the house she dropped from the saddle with aching wrists and brain benumbed.

She entered by a side door, to avoid meeting any one, and ran upstairs at once, knowing that she had barely time to dress for dinner. As she opened the door of her sitting-room some one rose from the chair by the fire, and she stood still, facing her husband. . .

It was the moment both had desired, yet when it came it found them tongue-tied and helpless.

Bessy was the first to speak. "When did you get here? You never wrote me you were coming!"

Amherst advanced toward her, holding out his hand. "No; you must forgive me. I have been very busy," he said.

Always the same excuse! The same thrusting at her of the hateful fact that Westmore came first, and that she must put up with whatever was left of his time and thoughts!

"You are always too busy to let me hear from you," she said coldly, and the hand which had sprung toward his fell back to her side.

Even then, if he had only said frankly: "It was too difficult—I didn't know how," the note of truth would have reached and moved her; but he had striven for the tone of ease and self-restraint that was habitual among her friends, and as usual his attempt had been a failure.

"I am sorry—I'm a bad hand at writing," he rejoined; and his evil genius prompted him to add: "I hope my coming is not inconvenient?"

The colour rose to Bessy's face. "Of course not. But it must seem rather odd to our visitors that I should know so little of your plans."

At this he humbled himself still farther. "I know I don't think enough about appearances—I'll try to do better the next time."

Appearances! He spoke as if she had been reproaching him for a breach of etiquette. . . it never occurred to him that the cry came from her humiliated heart! The tide of warmth that always enveloped her in his presence was receding, and in its place a chill fluid seemed to creep up slowly to her throat and lips.

In Amherst, meanwhile, the opposite process was taking place. His wife was still to him the most beautiful woman in the world, or rather, perhaps, the only woman to whose beauty his eyes had been opened. That beauty could never again penetrate to his heart, but it still touched his senses, not with passion but with a caressing kindliness, such as one might feel for the bright movements of a bird or a kitten. It seemed to plead with him not to ask of her more than she could give—to be content with the outward grace and not seek in it an inner meaning. He moved toward her again, and took her passive hands in his.

"You look tired. Why do you ride so late?"

"Oh, I just wanted to give Impulse a gallop. I hadn't time to take her out earlier, and if I let the grooms exercise her they'll spoil her mouth."

Amherst frowned. "You ought not to ride that mare alone at night. She shies at everything after dark."

"She's the only horse I care for—the others are all cows," she murmured, releasing her hands impatiently.

"Well, you must take me with you the next time you ride her."

She softened a little, in spite of herself. Riding was the only amusement he cared to share with her, and the thought of a long gallop across the plains at his side brought back the warmth to her veins.

"Yes, we'll go tomorrow. How long do you mean to stay?" she asked, looking up at him eagerly.

He was pleased that she should wish to know, yet the question embarrassed him, for it was necessary that he should be back at Westmore within three days, and he could not put her off with an evasion.

Bessy saw his hesitation, and her colour rose again. "I only asked," she explained, "because there is to be a fancy ball at the Hunt Club on the twentieth, and I thought of giving a big dinner here first."

Amherst did not understand that she too had her inarticulate moments, and that the allusion to the fancy ball was improvised to hide an eagerness to which he had been too slow in responding. He thought she had enquired about his plans only that he might not again interfere with the arrangements of her dinner-table. If that was all she cared about, it became suddenly easy to tell her that he could not stay, and he answered lightly: "Fancy balls are a little out of my line; but at any rate I shall have to be back at the mills the day after tomorrow."

The disappointment brought a rush of bitterness to her lips. "The day after tomorrow? It seems hardly worth while to have come so far for two days!"

"Oh, I don't mind the journey—and there are one or two matters I must consult you about."

There could hardly have been a more ill-advised answer, but Amherst was reckless now. If she cared for his coming only that he might fill a place at a fancy-dress dinner, he would let her see that he had come only because he had to go through the form of submitting to her certain measures to be taken at Westmore.

Bessy was beginning to feel the physical reaction of her struggle with the mare. The fatigue which at first had deadened her nerves now woke them to acuter sensibility, and an appealing word from her husband would have drawn her to his arms. But his answer seemed to drive all the blood back to her heart.

"I don't see why you still go through the form of consulting me about Westmore, when you have always done just as you pleased there, without regard to me or Cicely."

Amherst made no answer, silenced by the discouragement of hearing the same old grievance on her lips; and she too seemed struck, after she had spoken, by the unprofitableness of such retorts.

"It doesn't matter—of course I'll do whatever you wish," she went on listlessly. "But I could have sent my signature, if that is all you came for——"

"Thanks," said Amherst coldly. "I shall remember that the next time."

They stood silent for a moment, he with his eyes fixed on her, she with averted head, twisting her riding-whip between her fingers; then she said suddenly: "We shall be late for dinner," and passing into her dressing-room she closed the door.

Amherst roused himself as she disappeared.

"Bessy!" he exclaimed, moving toward her; but as he approached the door he heard her maid's voice within, and turning away he went to his own room

Bessy came down late to dinner, with vivid cheeks and an air of improvised ease; and the manner of her entrance, combined with her husband's unannounced arrival, produced in their observant guests the sense of latent complications. Mr. Langhope, though evidently unaware of his son-in-law's return till they greeted each other in the drawing-room, was too good a card-player to betray surprise, and Mrs. Ansell outdid herself in the delicate art of taking everything for granted; but these very dissimulations sharpened the perception of the other guests, whom long practice had rendered expert in interpreting such signs.

Of all this Justine Brent was aware; and conscious also that, by every one but herself, the suspected estrangement between the Amhersts was regarded as turning merely on the question of money. To the greater number of persons present there was, in fact, no other conceivable source of conjugal discord, since every known complication could be adjusted by means of the universal lubricant. It was this unanimity of view which bound together in the compactness of a new feudalism the members of Bessy Amherst's world; which supplied them with their pass-words and social tests, and defended them securely against the insidious attack of ideas

The Genius of History, capriciously directing the antics of its marionettes, sometimes lets the drama languish through a series of unrelated episodes, and then, suddenly quickening the pace, packs into one scene the stuff of a dozen. The chance meeting of Amherst and Justine, seemingly of no significance to either, contained the germ of developments of which both had begun to be aware before the evening was over. Their short talk—the first really intimate exchange of words between them—had the effect of creating a sense of solidarity that grew apace in the atmosphere of the Lynbrook dinner-table.

Justine was always reluctant to take part in Bessy's

week-end dinners, but as she descended the stairs that evening she did not regret having promised to be present. She frankly wanted to see Amherst again—his tone, his view of life, reinforced her own convictions, restored her faith in the reality and importance of all that Lynbrook ignored and excluded. Her extreme sensitiveness to surrounding vibrations of thought and feeling told her, as she glanced at him between the flowers and candles of the long dinner-table, that he too was obscurely aware of the same effect; and it flashed across her that they were unconsciously drawn together by the fact that they were the only two strangers in the room. Every one else had the same standpoint, spoke the same language, drew on the same stock of allusions, used the same weights and measures in estimating persons and actions. Between Mr. Langhope's indolent acuteness of mind and the rudimentary processes of the rosy Telfers there was a difference of degree but not of kind. If Mr. Langhope viewed the spectacle more objectively, it was not because he had outlived the sense of its importance, but because years of experience had familiarized him with its minutest details; and this familiarity with the world he lived in had bred a profound contempt for any other.

In no way could the points of contact between Amherst and Justine Brent have been more vividly brought out than by their tacit exclusion from the currents of opinion about them. Amherst, seated in unsmiling endurance at the foot of the table, between Mrs. Ansell, with her carefully-distributed affabilities, and Blanche Carbury, with her reckless hurling of conversational pebbles, seemed to Justine as much of a stranger as herself among the people to whom his marriage had introduced him. So strongly did she feel the sense of their common isolation that it was no surprise to her, when the men reappeared in the drawing-room after dinner, to have her host thread his way, between the unfolding bridge-tables, straight to the corner where she sat. Amherst's methods in the drawing-room were still as direct as in the cotton-mill. He always went up at once to the person he sought, without preliminary waste of tactics; and on this occasion Justine, without knowing what had passed between himself and Bessy, suspected from the appearance of both that their talk had resulted in increasing Amherst's desire to be with some one to whom he could speak freely and naturally on the subject nearest his heart.

She began at once to question him about Westmore, and the change in his face showed that his work was still a refuge from all that made life disheartening and unintelligible. Whatever convictions had been thwarted or impaired in him, his faith in the importance of his task remained unshaken; and the firmness with which he held to it filled Justine with a sense of his strength.

The feeling kindled her own desire to escape again into the world of deeds, yet by a sudden reaction it checked the growing inclination for Stephen Wyant that had resulted from her revolt against Lynbrook. Here was a man as careless as Wyant of the minor forms, yet her appreciation of him was not affected by the lack of adaptability that she accused herself of criticizing in her suitor. She began to see that it was not the sense of Wyant's social deficiencies that had held her back; and the discovery at once set free her judgment of him, enabling her to penetrate to the real causes of her reluctance. She understood now that the flaw she felt was far deeper than any defect of manner. It was the sense in him of something unstable and incalculable, something at once weak and violent, that was brought to light by the contrast of Amherst's quiet resolution. Here was a man whom no gusts of chance could deflect from his purpose; while she felt that the career to which Wyant had so ardently given himself would always be at the mercy of his passing emotions.

As the distinction grew clearer, Justine trembled to think that she had so nearly pledged herself, without the excuse of love, to a man whose failings she could judge so lucidly. . . But had she ever really thought of marrying Wyant? While she continued to talk with Amherst such a possibility became more and more remote, till she began to feel it was no more than a haunting dream. But her promise to see Wyant the next day reminded her of the nearness of her peril. How could she have played with her fate so lightly—she, who held her life so dear because she felt in it such untried powers of action and emotion? She continued to listen to Amherst's account of his work, with enough outward self-possession to place the right comment and put the right question, yet conscious only of the quiet strength she was absorbing from his presence, of the way in which his words, his voice, his mere nearness were slowly steadying and clarifying her will.

In the smoking-room, after the ladies had gone upstairs, Amherst continued to acquit himself mechanically of his duties, against the incongruous back-ground of his predecessor's remarkable sporting-prints—for it was characteristic of his relation to Lynbrook that his life there was carried on in the setting of foils and boxing-gloves, firearms and racing-trophies, which had expressed Dick Westmore's ideals. Never very keenly alive to his material surroundings, and quite unconscious of the irony of this proximity, Amherst had come to accept his wife's guests as unquestioningly as their background, and with the same sense of their being an inevitable part of his new life. Their talk was no more intelligible to him than the red and yellow hieroglyphics of the racing-prints, and he smoked in silence while Mr. Langhope discoursed to Westy Gaines on the recent sale of Chinese porcelains at which he had been lucky enough to pick up the set of Ming for his daughter, and Mason Winch expounded to a group of languid listeners the essential dependence of the labouring-man on the prosperity of Wall Street. In a retired corner, Ned Bowfort was imparting facts of a more personal nature to a chosen following who hailed with suppressed enjoyment the murmured mention of proper names; and now and then Amherst found himself obliged to say to Fenton Carbury, who with one accord had been left on his hands, "Yes, I understand the flat-tread tire is best," or, "There's a good deal to be said for the low tension magneto——"

But all the while his conscious thoughts were absorbed in the remembrance of his talk with Justine Brent. He had left his wife's presence in that state of moral lassitude when the strongest hopes droop under the infection of indifference and hostility, and the effort of attainment seems out of all proportion to the end in view; but as he listened to Justine all his energies sprang to life again. Here at last was some one who felt the urgency of his task: her every word and look confirmed her comment of the afternoon: "Westmore must be foremost to you both in time—I don't see how either of you can escape it."

She saw it, as he did, to be the special outlet offered for the expression of what he was worth to the world;

and with the knowledge that one other person recognized his call, it sounded again loudly in his heart. Yes, he would go on, patiently and persistently, conquering obstacles, suffering delay, enduring criticism—hardest of all, bearing with his wife's deepening indifference and distrust. Justine had said "Westmore must be foremost to you both," and he would prove that she was right—spite of the powers leagued against him he would win over Bessy in the end!

Those observers who had been struck by the length and animation of Miss Brent's talk with her host—and among whom Mrs. Ansell and Westy Gaines were foremost—would hardly have believed how small a part her personal charms had played in attracting him. Amherst was still under the power of the other kind of beauty—the soft graces personifying the first triumph of sex in his heart—and Justine's dark slenderness could not at once dispel the milder image. He watched her with pleasure while she talked, but her face interested him only as the vehicle of her ideas—she looked as a girl must look who felt and thought as she did. He was aware that everything about her was quick and fine and supple, and that the muscles of character lay close to the surface of feeling; but the interpenetration of spirit and flesh that made her body seem like the bright projection of her mind left him unconscious of anything but the oneness of their thoughts.

So these two, in their hour of doubt, poured strength into each other's hearts, each unconscious of what they gave, and of its hidden power of renewing their own purposes.

XVIII

IF Mr. Langhope had ever stooped to such facile triumphs as that summed up in the convenient "I told you so," he would have loosed the phrase on Mrs. Ansell in the course of a colloquy which these two, the next afternoon, were at some pains to defend from the incursions of the Lynbrook house-party.

Mrs. Ansell was the kind of woman who could encircle herself with privacy on an excursion-boat and create a nook in an hotel drawing-room, but it taxed even her ingenuity to segregate herself from the Telfers. When the feat was accomplished, and it became evident that Mr. Langhope could yield himself securely to the joys of confidential discourse, he paused on the brink of disclosure to say: "It's as well I saved that Ming from the ruins."

"What ruins?" she exclaimed, her startled look giving him the full benefit of the effect he was seeking to produce.

He addressed himself deliberately to the selecting and lighting of a cigarette. "Truscomb is down and out—resigned, 'the wise it call.' And the alterations at Westmore are going to cost a great deal more than my experienced son-in-law expected. This is Westy's morning budget—he and Amherst had it out last night. I tell my poor girl that at least she'll lose nothing when the *bibelots* I've bought for her go up the spout."

Mrs. Ansell received this with a troubled countenance. "What has become of Bessy? I've not seen her since luncheon."

"No. She and Blanche Carbury have motored over to dine with the Nick Ledgers at Islip."

"Did you see her before she left?"

"For a moment, but she said very little. Westy tells me that Amherst hints at leasing the New York house. One can understand that she's left speechless."

Mrs. Ansell, at this, sat bolt upright. "The New York house?" But she broke off to add, with seeming irrelevance: "If you knew how I detest Blanche Carbury!"

Mr. Langhope made a gesture of semi-acquiescence. "She is not the friend I should have chosen for Bessy—but we know that Providence makes use of strange instruments."

"Providence and Blanche Carbury?" She stared at him. "Ah, you are profoundly corrupt!"

"I have the coarse masculine habit of looking facts in the face. Woman-like, you prefer to make use of them privately, and cut them when you meet in public."

"Blanche is not the kind of fact I should care to make use of under any circumstances whatever!"

"No one asks you to. Simply regard her as a force of nature—let her alone, and don't put up too many lightning-rods."

She raised her eyes to his face. "Do you really mean that you want Bessy to get a divorce?"

"Your style is elliptical, dear Maria; but divorce does not frighten me very much. It has grown almost as painless as modern dentistry."

"It's our odious insensibility that makes it so!"

Mr. Langhope received this with the mildness of suspended judgment. "How else, then, do you propose that Bessy shall save what is left of her money?"

"I would rather see her save what is left of her happiness. Bessy will never be happy in the new way."

"What do you call the new way?"

"Launching one's boat over a human body—or several, as the case may be!"

"But don't you see that, as an expedient to bring this madman to reason——"

"I've told you that you don't understand him!"

Mr. Langhope turned on her with what would have been a show of temper in any one less provided with shades of manner. "Well, then, explain him, for God's sake!"

"I might explain him by saying that she's still in love with him."

"Ah, if you're still imprisoned in the old formulas!"

Mrs. Ansell confronted him with a grave face. "Isn't that precisely what Bessy is? Isn't she one of the most harrowing victims of the plan of bringing up our girls in the double bondage of expediency and unreality, corrupting their bodies with luxury and their brains with sentiment, and leaving them to reconcile the two as best they can, or lose their souls in the attempt?"

Mr. Langhope smiled. "I may observe that, with my poor child so early left alone to me, I supposed I was doing my best in committing her guidance to some of the most admirable women I know."

"Of whom I was one—and not the least lamentable example of the system! Of course the only thing that saves us from their vengeance," Mrs. Ansell added, "is that so few of them ever stop to think. . ."

"And yet, as I make out, it's precisely what you would have Bessy do!"

"It's what neither you nor I can help her doing. You've given her just acuteness enough to question, without consecutiveness enough to explain. But if she must perish in the struggle—and I see no hope for her—" cried Mrs. Ansell, starting suddenly and dramatically to her feet, "at least let her perish defending her ideals and not denying them—even if she has to sell the New York house and all your china pots into the bargain!"

Mr. Langhope, rising also, deprecatingly lifted his hands, "If that's what you call saving me from her vengeance—sending the crockery crashing round my ears!" And, as she turned away without any pretense of capping his pleasantry, he added, with a gleam of friendly malice: "I suppose you're going to the Hunt ball as Cassandra?"

Amherst, that morning, had sought out his wife with the definite resolve to efface the unhappy impression of their previous talk. He blamed himself for having been too easily repelled by her impatience. As the stronger of the two, with the power of a fixed purpose to sustain him, he should have allowed for the instability of her impulses, and above all for the automatic influences of habit.

Knowing that she did not keep early hours he delayed till ten o'clock to present himself at her sitting-room door, but the maid who answered his knock informed him that Mrs. Amherst was not yet up.

His reply that he would wait did not appear to hasten the leisurely process of her toilet, and he had the room to himself for a full half-hour. Many months had passed since he had spent so long a time in it, and though habitually unobservant of external details, he now found an outlet for his restlessness in mechanically noting the intimate appurtenances of Bessy's life. He was at first merely conscious of a soothing harmony of line and colour, extending from the blurred tints of the rug to the subdued gleam of light on old picture-frames and on the slender flanks of porcelain vases; but gradually he began to notice how every chair and screen and cushion, and even every trifling utensil on the inlaid writing-desk, had been chosen with reference to the whole composition, and to the minutest requirements of a fastidious leisure. A few months ago this studied setting, if he had thought of it at all, would have justified itself as expressing the pretty woman's natural affinity with pretty toys; but now it was the cost of it that struck him. He was beginning to learn from Bessy's bills that no commodity is taxed as high as beauty, and the beauty about him filled him with sudden repugnance, as the disguise of the evil influences that were separating his wife's life from his.

But with her entrance he dismissed the thought, and tried to meet her as if nothing stood in the way of their full communion. Her hair, still wet from the bath, broke from its dryad-like knot in dusky rings and spirals threaded with gold, and from her loose flexible draperies, and her whole person as she moved, there came a scent of youth and morning freshness. Her beauty touched him, and made it easier for him to humble himself.

"I was stupid and disagreeable last night. I can never say what I want when I have to count the minutes, and I've come back now for a quiet talk," he began.

A shade of distrust passed over Bessy's face. "About business?" she asked, pausing a few feet away from him.

"Don't let us give it that name!" He went up to her and drew her two hands into his. "You used to call it our work—won't you go back to that way of looking at it?"

Her hands resisted his pressure. "I didn't know, then, that it was going to be the only thing you cared for——"

But for her own sake he would not let her go on. "Some day I shall make you see how much my caring for it means my caring for you. But meanwhile," he urged, "won't you overcome your aversion to the subject, and bear with it as my work, if you no longer care to think of it as yours?"

Bessy, freeing herself, sat down on the edge of the straight-backed chair near the desk, as though to mark the parenthetical nature of the interview.

"I know you think me stupid—but wives are not usually expected to go into all the details of their husband's business. I have told you to do whatever you wish at Westmore, and I can't see why that is not enough."

Amherst looked at her in surprise. Something in her quick mechanical utterance suggested that not only the thought but the actual words she spoke had been inspired, and he fancied he heard in them an echo of Blanche Carbury's tones. Though Bessy's intimacy with Mrs. Carbury was of such recent date, fragments of unheeded smoking-room gossip now recurred to confirm the vague antipathy which Amherst had felt for her the previous evening.

"I know that, among your friends, wives are not expected to interest themselves in their husbands' work, and if the mills were mine I should try to conform to the custom, though I should always think it a pity that the questions that fill a man's thoughts should be ruled out of his talk with his wife; but as it is, I am only your representative at Westmore, and I don't see how we can help having the subject come up between us."

Bessy remained silent, not as if acquiescing in his plea, but as though her own small stock of arguments had temporarily failed her; and he went on, enlarging on his theme with a careful avoidance of technical terms, and with the constant effort to keep the human and personal side of the question before her.

She listened without comment, her eyes fixed on a little jewelled letter-opener which she had picked up from the writing-table, and which she continued to turn in her fingers while he spoke.

The full development of Amherst's plans at Westmore, besides resulting, as he had foreseen, in Truscomb's resignation, and in Halford Gaines's outspoken resistance to the new policy, had necessitated a larger immediate outlay of capital than the first estimates demanded, and Amherst, in putting his case to Bessy, was prepared to have her meet it on the old ground of the disapproval of all her advisers. But when he had ended she merely said, without looking up from the toy in her hand: "I always expected that you would need a great deal more money than you thought."

The comment touched him at his most vulnerable point. "But you see why? You understand how the work has gone on growing—?"

His wife lifted her head to glance at him for a moment. "I am not sure that I understand," she said indifferently; "but if another loan is necessary, of course I will sign the note for it."

The words checked his reply by bringing up, before he was prepared to deal with it, the other and more embarrassing aspect of the question. He had hoped to reawaken in Bessy some feeling for the urgency of his task before having to take up the subject of its cost; but her cold anticipation of his demands as part of a disagreeable business to be despatched and put out of mind, doubled the difficulty of what he had left to say; and it occurred to him that she had perhaps foreseen and reckoned on this result.

He met her eyes gravely. "Another loan *is* necessary; but if any proper provision is to be made for paying it back, your expenses will have to be cut down a good deal for the next few months."

The blood leapt to Bessy's face. "My expenses? You seem to forget how much I've had to cut them down already."

"The household bills certainly don't show it. They are increasing steadily, and there have been some very heavy incidental payments lately."

"What do you mean by incidental payments?"

"Well, there was the pair of cobs you bought last month——"

She returned to a resigned contemplation of the letter-opener. "With only one motor, one must have more horses, of course."

"The stables seemed to me fairly full before. But if you required more horses, I don't see why, at this particular moment, it was also necessary to buy a set of Chinese vases for twenty-five hundred dollars."

Bessy, at this, lifted her head with an air of decision that surprised him. Her blush had faded as quickly as it came, and he noticed that she was pale to the lips.

"I know you don't care about such things; but I had an exceptional chance of securing the vases at a low price—they are really worth twice as much—and Dick always wanted a set of Ming for the drawing-room mantelpiece."

Richard Westmore's name was always tacitly avoided between them, for in Amherst's case the disagreeable sense of dependence on a dead man's bounty increased that feeling of obscure constraint and repugnance which any reminder of the first husband's existence is wont to produce in his successor.

He reddened at the reply, and Bessy, profiting by an embarrassment which she had perhaps consciously provoked, went on hastily, and as if by rote: "I have left you perfectly free to do as you think best at the mills, but this perpetual discussion of my personal expenses is very unpleasant to me, as I am sure it must be to you, and in future I think it would be much better for us to have separate accounts."

"Separate accounts?" Amherst echoed in genuine astonishment.

"I should like my personal expenses to be under my own control again—I have never been used to accounting for every penny I spend."

The vertical lines deepened between Amherst's brows. "You are of course free to spend your money as you like—and I thought you were doing so when you authorized me, last spring, to begin the changes at Westmore."

Her lip trembled. "Do you reproach me for that? I didn't understand. . . you took advantage. . ."

"Oh!" he exclaimed.

At his tone the blood rushed back to her face. "It was my fault, of course— I only wanted to please you——"

Amherst was silent, confronted by the sudden sense of his own responsibility. What she said was true— he had known, when he exacted the sacrifice, that she made it only to please him, on an impulse of reawakened feeling, and not from any real recognition of a larger duty. The perception of this made him answer gently: "I am willing to take any blame you think I deserve; but it won't help us now to go back to the past. It is more important that we should come to an understanding about the future. If by keeping your personal account separate, you mean that you wish to resume control of your whole income, then you ought to understand that the improvements at the mills will have to be dropped at once, and things there go back to their old state."

She started up with an impatient gesture. "Oh, I should like never to hear of the mills again!"

He looked at her a moment in silence. "Am I to take that as your answer?"

She walked toward her door without returning his look. "Of course," she murmured, "you will end by doing as you please."

The retort moved him, for he heard in it the cry of her wounded pride. He longed to be able to cry out in return that Westmore was nothing to him, that all he asked was to see her happy. . . But it was not true, and his manhood revolted from the deception. Besides, its effect would be only temporary—would wear no better than her vain efforts to simulate an interest in his work. Between them, forever, were the insurmountable barriers of character, of education, of habit—and yet it was not in him to believe that any barrier was insurmountable.

"Bessy," he exclaimed, following her, "don't let us part in this way——"

She paused with her hand on her dressing-room door. "It is time to dress for church," she objected, turning to glance at the little gilt clock on the chimney-piece.

"For church?" Amherst stared, wondering that at such a crisis she should have remained detached enough to take note of the hour.

"You forget," she replied, with an air of gentle reproof, "that before we married I was in the habit of going to church every Sunday."

"Yes—to be sure. Would you not like me to go with you?" he rejoined gently, as if roused to the consciousness of another omission in the long list of his social shortcomings; for church-going, at Lynbrook, had always struck him as a purely social observance.

But Bessy had opened the door of her dressing-room. "I much prefer that you should do what you like," she said as she passed from the room.

Amherst made no farther attempt to detain her, and the door closed on her as though it were closing on a chapter in their lives.

"That's the end of it!" he murmured, picking up the letter-opener she had been playing with, and twirling it absently in his fingers. But nothing in life ever ends, and the next moment a new question confronted him—how was the next chapter to open?

BOOK III

XIX

IT was late in October when Amherst returned to Lynbrook.

He had begun to learn, in the interval, the lesson most difficult to his direct and trenchant nature: that compromise is the law of married life. On the afternoon of his talk with his wife he had sought her out, determined to make a final effort to clear up the situation between them; but he learned that, immediately after luncheon, she had gone off in the motor with Mrs. Carbury and two men of the party, leaving word that they would probably not be back till evening. It cost Amherst a struggle, when he had humbled himself to receive this information from the butler, not to pack his portmanteau and take the first train for Hanaford; but he was still under the influence of Justine Brent's words, and also of his own feeling that, at this juncture, a break between himself and Bessy would be final.

He stayed on accordingly, enduring as best he might the mute observation of the household, and the gentle irony of Mr. Langhope's attentions; and before he left Lynbrook, two days later, a provisional understanding had been reached.

His wife proved more firm than he had foreseen in her resolve to regain control of her income, and the talk between them ended in reciprocal concessions, Bessy consenting to let the town house for the winter and remain at Lynbrook, while Amherst agreed to restrict his improvements at Westmore to such alterations as had already been begun, and to reduce the expenditure on these as much as possible. It was virtually the defeat of his policy, and he had to suffer the decent triumph of the Gaineses, as well as the bitterer pang of his foiled aspirations. In spite of the opposition of the directors, he had taken advantage of Truscomb's resignation to put Duplain at the head of the mills; but the new manager's outspoken disgust at the company's change of plan made it clear that he would not remain long at Westmore, and it was one of the miseries of Amherst's situation that he could not give the reasons for his defection, but must bear to figure in Duplain's terse vocabulary as a "quitter." The difficulty of finding a new manager expert enough to satisfy the directors, yet in sympathy with his own social theories, made Amherst fear that Duplain's withdrawal would open the way for Truscomb's reinstatement, an outcome on which he suspected Halford Gaines had always counted; and this possibility loomed before him as the final defeat of his hopes.

Meanwhile the issues ahead had at least the merit of

keeping him busy. The task of modifying and retrenching his plans contrasted drearily with the hopeful activity of the past months, but he had an iron capacity for hard work under adverse conditions, and the fact of being too busy for thought helped him to wear through the days. This pressure of work relieved him, at first, from too close consideration of his relation to Bessy. He had yielded up his dearest hopes at her wish, and for the moment his renunciation had set a chasm between them; but gradually he saw that, as he was patching together the ruins of his Westmore plans, so he must presently apply himself to the reconstruction of his married life.

Before leaving Lynbrook he had had a last word with Miss Brent; not a word of confidence—for the same sense of reserve kept both from any explicit renewal of their moment's intimacy—but one of those exchanges of commonplace phrase that circumstances may be left to charge with special meaning. Justine had merely asked if he were really leaving and, on his assenting, had exclaimed quickly: "But you will come back soon?"

"I shall certainly come back," he answered; and after a pause he added: "I shall find you here? You will remain at Lynbrook?"

On her part also there was a shade of hesitation; then she said with a smile: "Yes, I shall stay."

His look brightened. "And you'll write me if anything—if Bessy should not be well?"

"I will write you," she promised; and a few weeks after his return to Hanaford he had, in fact, received a short note from her. Its ostensible purpose was to reassure him as to Bessy's health, which had certainly grown stronger since Dr. Wyant had persuaded her, at the close of the last house-party, to accord herself a period of quiet; but (the writer added) now that Mr. Langhope and Mrs. Ansell had also left, the quiet was perhaps too complete, and Bessy's nerves were beginning to suffer from the reaction.

Amherst had no difficulty in interpreting this brief communication. "I have succeeded in dispersing the people who are always keeping you and your wife apart; now is your chance: come and take it." That was what Miss Brent's letter meant; and his answer was a telegram to Bessy, announcing his return to Long Island.

The step was not an easy one; but decisive action, however hard, was always easier to Amherst than the ensuing interval of readjustment. To come to Lynbrook had required a strong effort of will; but the effort of remaining there called into play less disciplined faculties.

Amherst had always been used to doing things; now he had to resign himself to enduring a state of things.

The material facilities of the life about him, the way in which the machinery of the great empty house ran on like some complex apparatus working in the void, increased the exasperation of his nerves. Dr. Wyant's suggestion—which Amherst suspected Justine of having prompted—that Mrs. Amherst should cancel her autumn engagements, and give herself up to a quiet outdoor life with her husband, seemed to present the very opportunity these two distracted spirits needed to find and repossess each other. But, though Amherst was grateful to Bessy for having dismissed her visitors—partly to please him, as he guessed—yet he found the routine of the establishment more oppressive than when the house was full. If he could have been alone with her in a quiet corner—the despised cottage at Westmore, even!—he fancied they might still have been brought together by restricted space and the familiar exigencies of life. All the primitive necessities which bind together, through their recurring daily wants, natures fated to find no higher point of union, had been carefully eliminated from the life at Lynbrook, where material needs were not only provided for but anticipated by a hidden mechanism that filled the house with the perpetual sense of invisible attendance. Though Amherst knew that he and Bessy could never meet in the region of great issues, he thought he might have regained the way to her heart, and found relief from his own inaction, in the small ministrations of daily life; but the next moment he smiled to picture Bessy in surroundings where the clocks were not wound of themselves and the doors did not fly open at her approach. Those thick-crowding cares and drudgeries which serve as merciful screens between so many discordant natures would have been as intolerable to her as was to Amherst the great glare of leisure in which he and she were now confronted.

He saw that Bessy was in the state of propitiatory eagerness which always followed on her gaining a point in their long duel; and he could guess that she was tremulously anxious not only to make up to him, by all the arts she knew, for the sacrifice she had exacted, but also to conceal from every one the fact that, as Mr. Langhope bluntly put it, he had been "brought to terms." Amherst was touched by her efforts, and half-ashamed of his own inability to respond to them. But his mind, released from its normal preoccupations, had become a dangerous instrument of analysis and disintegration, and conditions which, a few months before, he might have accepted with the wholesome tolerance of the busy man, now pressed on him unendurably. He saw that he and his wife were really face to face for the first time since their marriage. Hitherto something had always intervened between them—first the spell of her grace and beauty, and the brief joy of her participation in his work; then the sorrow of their child's death, and after that the temporary exhilaration of carrying out his ideas at Westmore—but now that the last of these veils had been torn away they faced each other as strangers.

The habit of keeping factory hours always drove Amherst forth long before his wife's day began, and in the course of one of his early tramps he met Miss Brent and Cicely setting out for a distant swamp where rumour had it that a rare native orchid might be found. Justine's sylvan tastes had developed in the little girl a passion for such pillaging expeditions, and Cicely, who had discovered that her step-father knew almost as much about birds and squirrels as Miss Brent did about flowers, was not to be appeased till Amherst had scrambled into the pony-cart, wedging his long legs between a fern-box and a lunch-basket, and balancing a Scotch terrier's telescopic body across his knees.

The season was so mild that only one or two light windless frosts had singed the foliage of oaks and beeches, and gilded the roadsides with a smooth carpeting of maple leaves. The morning haze rose like smoke from burnt-out pyres of sumach and sugar-maple; a silver bloom lay on the furrows of the ploughed fields; and now and then, as they drove on, the wooded road showed at its end a tarnished disk of light, where sea and sky were merged.

At length they left the road for a winding track through scrub-oaks and glossy thickets of mountain-laurel; the track died out at the foot of a wooded knoll, and clambering along its base they came upon the swamp. There it lay in charmed solitude, shut in by a tawny growth of larch and swamp-maple, its edges burnt out to smouldering shades of russet, ember-red and ashen-grey, while the quaking centre still preserved a jewel-like green, where hidden lanes of moisture wound between islets tufted with swamp-cranberry and with the charred browns of fern and wild rose and bay. Sodden earth and decaying branches gave forth a strange sweet odour, as of the aromatic essences embalming a dead summer; and the air charged with this scent was so still that the snapping of witch-hazel pods, the drop of a nut, the leap of a startled frog, pricked the silence with separate points of sound.

The pony made fast, the terrier released, and fern-box and lunch-basket slung over Amherst's shoulder, the three explorers set forth on their journey. Amherst, as became his sex, went first; but after a few absent-minded plunges into the sedgy depths between the islets, he was ordered to relinquish his command and fall to the rear, where he might perform the humbler service of occasionally lifting Cicely over unspannable gulfs of moisture.

Justine, leading the way, guided them across the treacherous surface as fearlessly as a king-fisher, lighting instinctively on every grass-tussock and submerged tree-stump of the uncertain path. Now and then she paused, her feet drawn close on their narrow perch, and her slender body swaying over as she reached down for some rare growth detected among the withered reeds and grasses; then she would right herself again by a backward movement as natural as the upward spring of a branch—so free and flexible in all her motions that she seemed akin to the swaying reeds and curving brambles which caught at her as she passed.

At length the explorers reached the mossy corner where the orchids grew, and Cicely, securely balanced on a fallen tree-trunk, was allowed to dig the coveted roots. When they had been packed away, it was felt that this culminating moment must be celebrated with immediate libations of jam and milk; and having climbed to a dry slope among the pepper-bushes, the party fell on the contents of the lunch-basket. It was just the hour when Bessy's maid was carrying her breakfast-tray, with its delicate service of old silver and porcelain, into the darkened bed-room at Lynbrook; but early rising and hard scrambling had whetted the appetites of the naturalists, and the nursery fare which Cicely spread before them seemed a sumptuous reward for their toil.

"I do like this kind of picnic much better than the ones where mother takes all the footmen, and the mayonnaise has to be scraped off things before I can eat them," Cicely declared, lifting her foaming mouth from a beaker of milk.

Amherst, lighting his pipe, stretched himself contentedly among the pepper-bushes, steeped in that unreflecting peace which is shed into some hearts by communion with trees and sky. He too was glad to get away from the footmen and the mayonnaise, and he imagined that his stepdaughter's exclamation summed up all the reasons for his happiness. The boyish wood-craft which he had cultivated in order to encourage the same taste in his factory lads came to life in this sudden return to nature, and he redeemed his clumsiness in crossing the swamp by spying a marsh-wren's nest that had escaped Justine, and detecting in a swiftly-flitting olive-brown bird a belated tanager in autumn incognito.

Cicely sat rapt while he pictured the bird's winter pilgrimage, with glimpses of the seas and islands that fled beneath him till his long southern flight ended in the dim glades of the equatorial forests.

"Oh, what a good life—how I should like to be a wander-bird, and look down people's chimneys twice a year!" Justine laughed, tilting her head back to catch a last glimpse of the tanager.

The sun beamed full on their ledge from a sky of misty blue, and she had thrown aside her hat, uncovering her thick waves of hair, blue-black in the hollows, with warm rusty edges where they took the light. Cicely dragged down a plumy spray of traveller's joy and wound it above her friend's forehead; and thus wreathed, with her bright pallour relieved against the dusky autumn tints, Justine looked like a wood-spirit who had absorbed into herself the last golden juices of the year.

She leaned back laughing against a tree-trunk, pelting Cicely with witch-hazel pods, making the terrier waltz for scraps of ginger-bread, and breaking off now and then to imitate, with her clear full notes, the call of some hidden marsh-bird, or the scolding chatter of a squirrel in the scrub-oaks.

"Is that what you'd like most about the journey—looking down the chimneys?" Amherst asked with a smile.

"Oh, I don't know—I should love it all! Think of the joy of skimming over half the earth—seeing it born again out of darkness every morning! Sometimes, when I've been up all night with a patient, and have seen the world *come back to me* like that, I've been almost mad with its beauty; and then the thought that

I've never seen more than a little corner of it makes me feel as if I were chained. But I think if I had wings I should choose to be a house-swallow; and then, after I'd had my fill of wonders, I should come back to my familiar corner, and my house full of busy humdrum people, and fly low to warn them of rain, and wheel up high to show them it was good haying weather, and know what was going on in every room in the house, and every house in the village; and all the while I should be hugging my wonderful big secret—the secret of snow-plains and burning deserts, and coral islands and buried cities—and should put it all into my chatter under the eaves, that the people in the house were always too busy to stop and listen to—and when winter came I'm sure I should hate to leave them, even to go back to my great Brazilian forests full of orchids and monkeys!"

"But, Justine, in winter you could take care of the monkeys," the practical Cicely suggested.

"Yes—and that would remind me of home!" Justine cried, swinging about to pinch the little girl's chin.

She was in one of the buoyant moods when the spirit of life caught her in its grip, and shook and tossed her on its mighty waves as a sea-bird is tossed through the spray of flying rollers. At such moments all the light and music of the world seemed distilled into her veins, and forced up in bubbles of laughter to her lips and eyes. Amherst had never seen her thus, and he watched her with the sense of relaxation which the contact of limpid gaiety brings to a mind obscured by failure and self-distrust. The world was not so dark a place after all, if such springs of merriment could well up in a heart as sensitive as hers to the burden and toil of existence.

"Isn't it strange," she went on with a sudden drop to gravity, "that the bird whose wings carry him farthest and show him the most wonderful things, is the one who always comes back to the eaves, and is happiest in the thick of everyday life?"

Her eyes met Amherst's. "It seems to me," he said, "that you're like that yourself—loving long flights, yet happiest in the thick of life."

She raised her dark brows laughingly. "So I imagine—but then you see I've never had the long flight!"

Amherst smiled. "Ah, there it is—one never knows—one never says, *This is the moment!* because, however good it is, it always seems the door to a better one beyond. Faust never said it till the end, when he'd nothing left of all he began by thinking worth while; and then, with what a difference it was said!"

She pondered. "Yes—but it *was* the best, after all—the moment in which he had nothing left. . ."

"Oh," Cicely broke in suddenly, "do look at the

squirrel up there! See, father—he's off! Let's follow him!"

As she crouched there, with head thrown back, and sparkling lips and eyes, her fair hair—of her mother's very hue—making a shining haze about her face, Amherst recalled the winter evening at Hopewood, when he and Bessy had tracked the grey squirrel under the snowy beeches. Scarcely three years ago—and how bitter memory had turned! A chilly cloud spread over his spirit, reducing everything once more to the leaden hue of reality. . .

"It's too late for any more adventures—we must be going," he said.

XX

AMHERST'S morning excursions with his step-daughter and Miss Brent renewed themselves more than once. He welcomed any pretext for escaping from the unprofitable round of his thoughts, and these woodland explorations, with their gay rivalry of search for some rare plant or elusive bird, and the contact with the child's happy wonder, and with the morning brightness of Justine's mood, gave him his only moments of self-forgetfulness.

But the first time that Cicely's chatter carried home an echo of their adventures, Amherst saw a cloud on his wife's face. Her resentment of Justine's influence over the child had long since subsided, and in the temporary absence of the governess she was glad to have Cicely amused; but she was never quite satisfied that those about her should have pursuits and diversions in which she did not share. Her jealousy did not concentrate itself on her husband and Miss Brent: Amherst had never shown any inclination for the society of other women, and if the possibility had been suggested to her, she would probably have said that Justine was not "in his style"—so unconscious is a pretty woman apt to be of the versatility of masculine tastes. But Amherst saw that she felt herself excluded from amusements in which she had no desire to join, and of which she consequently failed to see the purpose; and he gave up accompanying his step-daughter.

Bessy, as if in acknowledgment of his renunciation, rose earlier in order to prolong their rides together. Dr. Wyant had counselled her against the fatigue of following the hounds, and she instinctively turned their horses away from the course the hunt was likely to take; but now and then the cry of the pack, or the flash of red on a distant slope, sent the blood to her face and made her press her mare to a gallop. When they escaped such encounters she showed no great zest in the exercise, and their rides resolved themselves into a spiritless middle-aged jog along the autumn lanes.

In the early days of their marriage the joy of a canter side by side had merged them in a community of sensation beyond need of speech; but now that the physical spell had passed they felt the burden of a silence that neither knew how to break.

Once only, a moment's friction galvanized these lifeless rides. It was one morning when Bessy's wild mare Impulse, under-exercised and over-fed, suddenly broke from her control, and would have unseated her but for Amherst's grasp on the bridle.

"The horse is not fit for you to ride," he exclaimed, as the hot creature, with shudders of defiance rippling her flanks, lapsed into sullen subjection.

"It's only because I don't ride her enough," Bessy panted. "That new groom is ruining her mouth."

"You must not ride her alone, then."

"I shall not let that man ride her."

"I say you must not ride her alone."

"It's ridiculous to have a groom at one's heels!"

"Nevertheless you must, if you ride Impulse."

Their eyes met, and she quivered and yielded like the horse. "Oh, if you say so—" She always hugged his brief flashes of authority.

"I do say so. You promise me?"

"If you like——"

Amherst had made an attempt to occupy himself with

the condition of Lynbrook, one of those slovenly villages, without individual character or the tradition of self-respect, which spring up in America on the skirts of the rich summer colonies. But Bessy had never given Lynbrook a thought, and he realized the futility of hoping to interest her in its mongrel population of day-labourers and publicans so soon after his glaring failure at Westmore. The sight of the village irritated him whenever he passed through the Lynbrook gates, but having perforce accepted the situation of prince consort, without voice in the government, he tried to put himself out of relation with all the questions which had hitherto engrossed him, and to see life simply as a spectator. He could even conceive that, under certain conditions, there might be compensations in the passive attitude; but unfortunately these conditions were not such as the life at Lynbrook presented.

The temporary cessation of Bessy's week-end parties had naturally not closed her doors to occasional visitors, and glimpses of the autumnal animation of Long Island passed now and then across the Amhersts' horizon. Blanche Carbury had installed herself at Mapleside, a fashionable colony half-way between Lynbrook and Clifton, and even Amherst, unused as he was to noting the seemingly inconsecutive movements of idle people, could not but remark that her visits to his wife almost invariably coincided with Ned Bowfort's cantering over unannounced from the Hunt Club, where he had taken up his autumn quarters.

There was something very likeable about Bowfort, to whom Amherst was attracted by the fact that he was one of the few men of Bessy's circle who knew what was going on in the outer world. Throughout an existence which one divined to have been both dependent and desultory, he had preserved a sense of wider relations and acquired a smattering of information to which he applied his only independent faculty, that of clear thought. He could talk intelligently and not too inaccurately of the larger questions which Lynbrook ignored, and a gay indifference to the importance of money seemed the crowning grace of his nature, till Amherst suddenly learned that this attitude of detachment was generally ascribed to the liberality of Mrs. Fenton Carbury. "Everybody knows she married Fenton to provide for Ned," some one let fall in the course of one of the smoking-room dissertations on which the host of Lynbrook had such difficulty in fixing his attention; and the speaker's matter-of-course tone, and the careless acquiescence of his hearers, were more offensive to Amherst than the fact itself. In the first flush of his disgust he classed the story as one of the lies bred in the malarious air of after-dinner gossip; but gradually he saw that, whether true or not, it had sufficient circulation to cast a shade of ambiguity on the persons concerned. Bessy alone seemed deaf to the rumours about her friend. There was something captivating to her in Mrs. Carbury's slang and noise, in her defiance of decorum and contempt of criticism. "I like Blanche because she doesn't pretend," was Bessy's vague justification of the lady; but in reality she was under the mysterious spell which such natures cast over the less venturesome imaginations of their own sex.

Amherst at first tried to deaden himself to the situation, as part of the larger coil of miseries in which he found himself; but all his traditions were against such tolerance, and they were roused to revolt by the receipt of a newspaper clipping, sent by an anonymous hand, enlarging on the fact that the clandestine meetings of a fashionable couple were being facilitated by the connivance of a Long Island *châtelaine*. Amherst, hot from the perusal of this paragraph, sprang into the first train, and laid the clipping before his father-in-law, who chanced to be passing through town on his way from the Hudson to the Hot Springs.

Mr. Langhope, ensconced in the cushioned privacy of the reading-room at the Amsterdam Club, where he had invited his son-in-law to meet him, perused the article with the cool eye of the collector to whom a new curiosity is offered.

"I suppose," he mused, "that in the time of the

Pharaohs the Morning Papyrus used to serve up this kind of thing"— and then, as the nervous tension of his hearer expressed itself in an abrupt movement, he added, handing back the clipping with a smile: "What do you propose to do? Kill the editor, and forbid Blanche and Bowfort the house?"

"I mean to do something," Amherst began, suddenly chilled by the realization that his wrath had not yet shaped itself into a definite plan of action.

"Well, it must be that or nothing," said Mr. Langhope, drawing his stick meditatively across his knee. "And, of course, if it's *that*, you'll land Bessy in a devil of a mess."

Without giving his son-in-law time to protest, he touched rapidly but vividly on the inutility and embarrassment of libel suits, and on the devices whereby the legal means of vindication from such attacks may be turned against those who have recourse to them; and Amherst listened with a sickened sense of the incompatibility between abstract standards of honour and their practical application.

"What should you do, then?" he murmured, as Mr. Langhope ended with his light shrug and a "See Tredegar, if you don't believe me"—; and his father-in-law replied with an evasive gesture: "Why, leave the responsibility where it belongs!"

"Where it belongs?"

"To Fenton Carbury, of course. Luckily it's nobody's business but his, and if he doesn't mind what is said about his wife I don't see how you can take up the cudgels for her without casting another shade on her somewhat chequered reputation."

Amherst stared. "His wife? What do I care what's said of her? I'm thinking of mine!"

"Well, if Carbury has no objection to his wife's meeting Bowfort, I don't see how you can object to her meeting him at your house. In such matters, as you know, it has mercifully been decided that the husband's attitude shall determine other people's; otherwise we should be deprived of the legitimate pleasure of slandering our neighbours." Mr. Langhope was always careful to temper his explanations with an "as you know": he would have thought it ill-bred to omit this parenthesis in elucidating the social code to his son-in-law.

"Then you mean that I can do nothing?" Amherst exclaimed.

Mr. Langhope smiled. "What applies to Carbury applies to you—by doing nothing you establish the fact that there's nothing to do; just as you create the difficulty by recognizing it." And he added, as Amherst sat silent: "Take Bessy away, and they'll have to see each other elsewhere."

Amherst returned to Lynbrook with the echoes of this

casuistry in his brain. It seemed to him but a part of the ingenious system of evasion whereby a society bent on the undisturbed pursuit of amusement had contrived to protect itself from the intrusion of the disagreeable: a policy summed up in Mr. Langhope's concluding advice that Amherst should take his wife away. Yes—that was wealth's contemptuous answer to every challenge of responsibility: duty, sorrow and disgrace were equally to be evaded by a change of residence, and nothing in life need be faced and fought out while one could pay for a passage to Europe!

In a calmer mood Amherst's sense of humour would have preserved him from such a view of his father-in-law's advice; but just then it fell like a spark on his smouldering prejudices. He was clear-sighted enough to recognize the obstacles to legal retaliation; but this only made him the more resolved to assert his will in his own house. He no longer paused to consider the possible effect of such a course on his already strained relations with his wife: the man's will rose in him and spoke.

The scene between Bessy and himself was short and sharp; and it ended in a way that left him more than ever perplexed at the ways of her sex. Impatient of preamble, he had opened the attack with his ultimatum: the suspected couple were to be denied the house. Bessy flamed into immediate defence of her friend;

but to Amherst's surprise she no longer sounded the note of her own rights. Husband and wife were animated by emotions deeper-seated and more instinctive than had ever before confronted them; yet while Amherst's resistance was gathering strength from the conflict, Bessy unexpectedly collapsed in tears and submission. She would do as he wished, of course—give up seeing Blanche, dismiss Bowfort, wash her hands, in short, of the imprudent pair—in such matters a woman needed a man's guidance, a wife must of necessity see with her husband's eyes; and she looked up into his through a mist of penitence and admiration. . .

XXI

IN the first reaction from her brief delusion about Stephen Wyant, Justine accepted with a good grace the necessity of staying on at Lynbrook. Though she was now well enough to return to her regular work, her talk with Amherst had made her feel that, for the present, she could be of more use by remaining with Bessy; and she was not sorry to have a farther period of delay and reflection before taking the next step in her life. These at least were the reasons she gave herself for deciding not to leave; and if any less ostensible lurked beneath, they were not as yet visible even to her searching self-scrutiny.

At first she was embarrassed by the obligation of meeting Dr. Wyant, on whom her definite refusal had produced an effect for which she could not hold herself blameless. She had not kept her promise of seeing him on the day after their encounter at the post-office, but had written, instead, in terms which obviously made such a meeting unnecessary. But all her efforts to soften the abruptness of her answer could not conceal, from either herself or her suitor, that it was not the one she had led him to expect; and she foresaw that if she remained at Lynbrook she could not escape a scene of recrimination.

When the scene took place, Wyant's part in it went far toward justifying her decision; yet his vehement reproaches contained a sufficient core of truth to humble her pride. It was lucky for her somewhat exaggerated sense of fairness that he overshot the mark by charging her with a coquetry of which she knew herself innocent, and laying on her the responsibility for any follies to which her rejection might drive him. Such threats, as a rule, no longer move the feminine imagination; yet Justine's pity for all forms of weakness made her recognize, in the very heat of her contempt for Wyant, that his reproaches were not the mere cry of wounded vanity but the appeal of a nature conscious of its lack of recuperative power. It seemed to her as though she had done him irreparable harm, and the feeling might have betrayed her into too great a show of compassion had she not been restrained by a salutary fear of the result.

The state of Bessy's nerves necessitated frequent visits from her physician, but Justine, on these occasions, could usually shelter herself behind the professional reserve which kept even Wyant from any open expression of feeling. One day, however, they chanced to find themselves alone before Bessy's return from her ride. The servant had ushered Wyant into the library where Justine was writing, and when she had replied to his enquiries about his patient they found themselves face to face with an awkward period of waiting. Justine was too proud to cut it short by leaving the room; but Wyant answered her commonplaces at random, stirring uneasily to and fro between window and fireside, and at length halting behind the table at which she sat.

"May I ask how much longer you mean to stay here?" he said in a low voice, his eyes darkening under the sullen jut of the brows.

As she glanced up in surprise she noticed for the first time an odd contraction of his pupils, and the discovery, familiar enough in her professional experience, made her disregard the abruptness of his question and softened the tone in which she answered. "I hardly know—I suppose as long as I am needed."

Wyant laughed. "Needed by whom? By John Amherst?"

A moment passed before Justine took in the full significance of the retort; then the blood rushed to her face. "Yes—I believe both Mr. and Mrs. Amherst need me," she answered, keeping her eyes on his; and Wyant laughed again.

"You didn't think so till Amherst came back from Hanaford. His return seems to have changed your plans in several respects."

She looked away from him, for even now his eyes moved her to pity and self-reproach. "Dr. Wyant, you are not well; why do you wait to see Mrs. Amherst?" she said.

He stared at her and then his glance fell. "I'm much obliged—I'm as well as usual," he muttered, pushing the hair from his forehead with a shaking hand; and at that moment the sound of Bessy's voice gave Justine a pretext for escape.

In her own room she sank for a moment under a rush of self-disgust; but it soon receded before the saner forces of her nature, leaving only a residue of pity for the poor creature whose secret she had surprised. She had never before suspected Wyant of taking a drug, nor did she now suppose that he did so habitually; but to see him even momentarily under such an influence explained her instinctive sense of his weakness. She felt now that what would have been an insult on other lips was only a cry of distress from his; and once more she blamed herself and forgave him.

But if she had been inclined to any morbidness of self-reproach she would have been saved from it by other cares. For the moment she was more concerned with Bessy's fate than with her own—her poor friend seemed to have so much more at stake, and so much less strength to bring to the defence of her happiness. Justine was always saved from any excess of self-compassion by the sense, within herself, of abounding forces of growth and self-renewal, as though from every lopped aspiration a fresh shoot of energy must spring; but she felt that Bessy had no such sources of renovation, and that every disappointment left an arid spot in her soul.

Even without her friend's confidences, Justine would have had no difficulty in following the successive stages of the Amhersts' inner history. She knew that Amherst had virtually resigned his rule at Westmore, and that his wife, in return for the sacrifice, was trying to conform to the way of life she thought he preferred; and the futility of both attempts was more visible to Justine than to either of the two concerned. She saw that the failure of the Amhersts' marriage lay not in any accident of outward circumstances but in the lack of all natural points of contact. As she put it to herself, they met neither underfoot nor overhead: practical necessities united them no more than imaginative joys.

There were moments when Justine thought Amherst hard to Bessy, as she suspected that he had once been hard to his mother—as the leader of men must perhaps always be hard to the hampering sex. Yet she did justice to his efforts to accept the irretrievable, and to waken in his wife some capacity for sharing in his minor interests, since she had none of her own with which to fill their days.

Amherst had always been a reader; not, like Justine herself, a flame-like devourer of the page, but a slow absorber of its essence; and in the early days of his marriage he had fancied it would be easy to make Bessy share this taste. Though his mother was not a bookish woman, he had breathed at her side an air rich in allusion and filled with the bright presences of romance; and he had always regarded this commerce of the imagination as one of the normal conditions of life. The discovery that there were no books at Lynbrook save a few morocco "sets" imprisoned behind the brass trellisings of the library had been one of the many surprises of his new state. But in his first months with Bessy there was no room for books, and if he thought of the matter it was only in a glancing vision of future evenings, when he and she, in the calm afterglow of happiness, should lean together over some cherished page. Her lack of response to any reference outside the small circle of daily facts had long since dispelled that vision; but now that his own mind felt the need of inner sustenance he began to ask himself whether he might not have done more to rouse her imagination. During the long evenings over the library fire he tried to lead the talk to books, with a parenthesis, now and again, from the page beneath his eye; and Bessy met the experiment with conciliatory eagerness. She showed, in especial, a hopeful but misleading preference for poetry, leaning back with dreaming lids and lovely parted lips while he rolled out the immortal measures; but her outward signs of attention never ripened into any expression of opinion, or any after-allusion to what she heard, and before long he discovered that Justine Brent was his only listener. It was to her that the words he read began to be unconsciously addressed; her comments directed him in his choice of subjects, and the ensuing discussions restored him to some semblance of mental activity.

Bessy, true to her new rôle of acquiescence, shone silently on this interchange of ideas; Amherst even detected in her a vague admiration for his power of conversing on subjects which she regarded as abstruse; and this childlike approval, combined with her submission to his will, deluded him with a sense of recovered power over her. He could not but note that the new phase in their relations had coincided with his first assertion of mastery; and he rashly concluded that, with the removal of the influences tending to separate them, his wife might gradually be won back to her earlier sympathy with his views.

To accept this theory was to apply it; for nothing could long divert Amherst from his main purpose, and all the thwarted strength of his will was only gathering to itself fresh stores of energy. He had never been a skilful lover, for no woman had as yet stirred in him those feelings which call the finer perceptions into play; and there was no instinct to tell him that Bessy's sudden conformity to his wishes was as unreasoning as her surrender to his first kiss. He fancied that he and she were at length reaching some semblance of that moral harmony which should grow out of the physical accord, and that, poor and incomplete as the understanding was, it must lift and strengthen their relation.

He waited till early winter had brought solitude to Lynbrook, dispersing the hunting colony to various points of the compass, and sending Mr. Langhope to Egypt and the Riviera, while Mrs. Ansell, as usual, took up her annual tour of a social circuit whose extreme points were marked by Boston and Baltimore—and then he made his final appeal to his wife.

His pretext for speaking was a letter from Duplain,

definitely announcing his resolve not to remain at Westmore. A year earlier Amherst, deeply moved by the letter, would have given it to his wife in the hope of its producing the same effect on her. He knew better now—he had learned her instinct for detecting "business" under every serious call on her attention. His only hope, as always, was to reach her through the personal appeal; and he put before her the fact of Duplain's withdrawal as the open victory of his antagonists. But he saw at once that even this could not infuse new life into the question.

"If I go back he'll stay—I can hold him, can gain time till things take a turn," he urged.

"Another? I thought they were definitely settled," she objected languidly.

"No—they're not; they can't be, on such a basis," Amherst broke out with sudden emphasis. He walked across the room, and came back to her side with a determined face. "It's a delusion, a deception," he exclaimed, "to think I can stand by any longer and see things going to ruin at Westmore! If I've made you think so, I've unconsciously deceived us both. As long as you're my wife we've only one honour between us, and that honour is mine to take care of."

"Honour? What an odd expression!" she said with a forced laugh, and a little tinge of pink in her cheek. "You speak as if I had—had made myself talked about

—when you know I've never even looked at another man!"

"Another man?" Amherst looked at her in wonder. "Good God! Can't you conceive of any vow to be kept between husband and wife but the primitive one of bodily fidelity? Heaven knows I've never looked at another woman—but, by my reading of our compact, I shouldn't be keeping faith with you if I didn't help you to keep faith with better things. And you owe me the same help—the same chance to rise through you, and not sink by you—else we've betrayed each other more deeply than any adultery could make us!"

She had drawn back, turning pale again, and shrinking a little at the sound of words which, except when heard in church, she vaguely associated with oaths, slammed doors, and other evidences of ill-breeding; but Amherst had been swept too far on the flood of his indignation to be checked by such small signs of disapproval.

"You'll say that what I'm asking you is to give me back the free use of your money. Well! Why not? Is it so much for a wife to give? I know you all think that a man who marries a rich woman forfeits his self-respect if he spends a penny without her approval. But that's because money is so sacred to you all! It seems to me the least important thing that a woman entrusts to her husband. What of her dreams and her hopes, her belief in justice and goodness and decency? If he takes those and destroys them, he'd better have had a mill-stone about his neck. But nobody has a word to say till he touches her dividends—then he's a calculating brute who has married her for her fortune!"

He had come close again, facing her with outstretched hands, half-commanding, half in appeal. "Don't you see that I can't go on in this way—that I've *no right* to let you keep me from Westmore?"

Bessy was looking at him coldly, under the half-dropped lids of indifference. "I hardly know what you mean—you use such peculiar words; but I don't see why you should expect me to give up all the ideas I was brought up in. Our standards *are* different—but why should yours always be right?"

"You believed they were right when you married me—have they changed since then?"

"No; but——" Her face seemed to harden and contract into a small expressionless mask, in which he could no longer read anything but blank opposition to his will.

"You trusted my judgment not long ago," he went on, "when I asked you to give up seeing Mrs. Carbury——"

She flushed, but with anger, not compunction. "It seems to me that should be a reason for your not asking me to make other sacrifices! When I gave up Blanche

I thought you would see that I wanted to please you—and that you would do something for me in return. . ."

Amherst interrupted her with a laugh. "Thank you for telling me your real reasons. I was fool enough to think you acted from conviction—not that you were simply striking a bargain——"

He broke off, and they looked at each other with a kind of fear, each hearing between them the echo of irreparable words. Amherst's only clear feeling was that he must not speak again till he had beaten down the horrible sensation in his breast—the rage of hate which had him in its grip, and which made him almost afraid, while it lasted, to let his eyes rest on the fair weak creature before him. Bessy, too, was in the clutch of a mute anger which slowly poured its benumbing current around her heart. Strong waves of passion did not quicken her vitality: she grew inert and cold under their shock. Only one little pulse of self-pity continued to beat in her, trembling out at last on the cry: "Ah, I know it's not because you care so much for Westmore—it's only because you want to get away from me!"

Amherst stared as if her words had flashed a light into the darkest windings of his misery. "Yes—I want to get away. . ." he said; and he turned and walked out of the room.

He went down to the smoking-room, and ringing

for a servant, ordered his horse to be saddled. The foot-man who answered his summons brought the afternoon's mail, and Amherst, throwing himself down on the sofa, began to tear open his letters while he waited.

He ran through the first few without knowing what he read; but presently his attention was arrested by the hand-writing of a man he had known well in college, and who had lately come into possession of a large cotton-mill in the South. He wrote now to ask if Amherst could recommend a good manager—"not one of your old routine men, but a young fellow with the new ideas. Things have been in pretty bad shape down here," the writer added, "and now that I'm in possession I want to see what can be done to civilize the place"; and he went on to urge that Amherst should come down himself to inspect the mills, and propose such improvements as his experience suggested. "We've all heard of the great things you're doing at Westmore," the letter ended; and Amherst cast it from him with a groan. . .

It was Duplain's chance, of course. . . that was his first thought. He took up the letter and read it over. He knew the man who wrote—no sentimentalist seeking emotional variety from vague philanthropic experiments, but a serious student of social conditions, now unexpectedly provided with the opportunity to apply his ideas. Yes, it was Duplain's chance—if indeed it might not be his own! . . . Amherst sat upright, dazzled by the thought. Why Duplain—why not himself? Bessy had spoken the illuminating word—what he wanted was to get away—to get away at any cost! Escape had become his one thought: escape from the bondage of Lynbrook, from the bitter memory of his failure at Westmore; and here was the chance to escape back into life—into independence, activity and usefulness! Every atrophied faculty in him suddenly started from its torpor, and his brain throbbed with the pain of the awakening. . . The servant came to tell him that his horse waited, and he sprang up, took his riding-whip from the rack, stared a moment, absently, after the man's retreating back, and then dropped down again on the sofa. . .

What was there to keep him from accepting? His wife's affection was dead—if her sentimental fancy for him had ever deserved the name! And his passing mastery over her was gone too—he smiled to remember that, hardly two hours earlier, he had been fatuous enough to think he could still regain it! Now he said to himself that she would sooner desert a friend to please him than sacrifice a fraction of her income; and the discovery cast a stain of sordidness on their whole relation. He could still imagine struggling to win her back from another man, or even to save her from some folly into which mistaken judgment or perverted enthusiasm might have hurried her; but to go on battling against the dull unimaginative subservience to personal luxury—the slavery to houses and servants and clothes—ah, no, while he had any fight left in him it was worth spending in a better cause than that!

Through the open window he could hear, in the mild December stillness, his horse's feet coming and going on the gravel. *Her* horse, led up and down by *her* servant, at the door of *her* house! . . . The sound symbolized his whole future. . . the situation his marriage had made for him, and to which he must henceforth bend, unless he broke with it then and there. . . He tried to look ahead, to follow up, one by one, the consequences of such a break. That it would be final he had no doubt. There are natures which seem to be drawn closer by dissension, to depend, for the renewal of understanding, on the spark of generosity and compunction that anger strikes out of both; but Amherst knew that between himself and his wife no such clearing of the moral atmosphere was possible. The indignation which left him with tingling nerves and a burning need of some immediate escape into action, crystallized in Bessy into a hard kernel of obstinacy, into which, after each fresh collision, he felt that a little more of herself had been absorbed. . . No, the break between them would be final—if he went now he would not come back. And it flashed across him that this solution might have been foreseen by his wife —might even have been deliberately planned and led up to by those about her. His father-in-law had never liked him—the disturbing waves of his activity had rippled even the sheltered surface of Mr. Langhope's existence. He must have been horribly in their way! Well—it was not too late to take himself out of it. In Bessy's circle the severing of such ties was regarded as an expensive but unhazardous piece of surgery—nobody bled to death of the wound. . . The footman came back to remind him that his horse was waiting, and Amherst rose to his feet.

"Send him back to the stable," he said with a glance at his watch, "and order a trap to take me to the next train."

XXII

WHEN Amherst woke, the next morning, in the hotel to which he had gone up from Lynbrook, he was oppressed by the sense that the hardest step he had to take still lay before him. It had been almost easy to decide that the moment of separation had come, for circumstances seemed to have closed every other issue from his unhappy situation; but how tell his wife of his decision? Amherst, to whom action was the first necessity of being, became a weak procrastinator when he was confronted by the need of writing instead of speaking.

To account for his abrupt departure from Lynbrook he had left word that he was called to town on business; but, since he did not mean to return, some farther explanation was now necessary, and he was paralyzed by the difficulty of writing. He had already telegraphed to his friend that he would be at the mills the next day; but the southern express did not leave till the afternoon, and he still had several hours in which to consider what he should say to his wife. To postpone the dreaded task, he invented the pretext of some business to be despatched, and taking the Subway to Wall Street consumed the morning in futile activities. But since the renunciation of his work at Westmore he had no active concern with the financial world, and by twelve o'clock he had exhausted his imaginary affairs and was journeying up town again. He left the train at Union Square, and walked along Fourth Avenue, now definitely resolved to go back to the hotel and write his letter before lunching.

At Twenty-sixth Street he had struck into Madison Avenue, and was striding onward with the fixed eye and aimless haste of the man who has empty hours to fill, when a hansom drew up ahead of him and Justine Brent sprang out. She was trimly dressed, as if for travel, with a small bag in her hand; but at sight of him she paused with a cry of pleasure.

"Oh, Mr. Amherst, I'm so glad! I was afraid I might not see you for goodbye."

"For goodbye?" Amherst paused, embarrassed. How had she guessed that he did not mean to return to Lynbrook?

"You know," she reminded him, "I'm going to some friends near Philadelphia for ten days"—and he remembered confusedly that a long time ago—probably yesterday morning—he had heard her speak of her projected visit.

"I had no idea," she continued, "that you were coming up to town yesterday, or I should have tried to see you before you left. I wanted to ask you to send me a line if Bessy needs me—I'll come back at once if she does." Amherst continued to listen blankly, as if making a painful effort to regain some consciousness of what was being said to him, and she went on: "She seemed so nervous and poorly yesterday evening that I was sorry I had decided to go——"

Her intent gaze reminded him that the emotions of the last twenty-four hours must still be visible in his face; and the thought of what she might detect helped to restore his self-possession. "You must not think of giving up your visit," he began hurriedly—he had meant to add "on account of Bessy," but he found himself unable to utter his wife's name.

Justine was still looking at him. "Oh, I'm sure

everything will be all right," she rejoined. "You go back this afternoon, I suppose? I've left you a little note, with my address, and I want you to promise——"

She paused, for Amherst had made a motion as though to interrupt her. The old confused sense that there must always be truth between them was struggling in him with the strong restraints of habit and character; and suddenly, before he was conscious of having decided to speak, he heard himself say: "I ought to tell you that I am not going back."

"Not going back?" A flash of apprehension crossed Justine's face. "Not till tomorrow, you mean?" she added, recovering herself.

Amherst hesitated, glancing vaguely up and down the street. At that noonday hour it was nearly deserted, and Justine's driver dozed on his perch above the hansom. They could speak almost as openly as if they had been in one of the wood-paths at Lynbrook.

"Nor tomorrow," Amherst said in a low voice. There was another pause before he added: "It may be some time before—" He broke off, and then continued with an effort: "The fact is, I am thinking of going back to my old work."

She caught him up with an exclamation of surprise and sympathy. "Your old work? You mean at——"

She was checked by the quick contraction of pain in his face. "Not that! I mean that I'm thinking of taking a new job—as manager of a Georgia mill. . . It's the only thing I know how to do, and I've got to do something—" He forced a laugh. "The habit of work is incurable!"

Justine's face had grown as grave as his. She hesitated a moment, looking down the street toward the angle of Madison Square, which was visible from the corner where they stood.

"Will you walk back to the square with me? Then we can sit down a moment."

She began to move as she spoke, and he walked beside her in silence till they had gained the seat she pointed out. Her hansom trailed after them, drawing up at the corner.

As Amherst sat down beside her, Justine turned to him with an air of quiet resolution. "Mr. Amherst—will you let me ask you something? Is this a sudden decision?"

"Yes. I decided yesterday."

"And Bessy——?"

His glance dropped for the first time, but Justine pressed her point. "Bessy approves?"

"She—she will, I think—when she knows——"

"When she knows?" Her emotion sprang into her face. "When she knows? Then she does not—yet?"

"No. The offer came suddenly. I must go at once."

"Without seeing her?" She cut him short with a quick commanding gesture. "Mr. Amherst, you can't do this—you won't do it! You will not go away without seeing Bessy!" she said.

Her eyes sought his and drew them upward, constraining them to meet the full beam of her rebuking gaze.

"I must do what seems best under the circumstances," he answered hesitatingly. "She will hear from me, of course; I shall write today—and later——"

"Not later! *Now*—you will go back now to Lynbrook! Such things can't be told in writing—if they must be said at all, they must be spoken. Don't tell me that I don't understand—or that I'm meddling in what doesn't concern me. I don't care a fig for that! I've always meddled in what didn't concern me—I always shall, I suppose, till I die! And I understand enough to know that Bessy is very unhappy—and that you're the wiser and stronger of the two. I know what it's been to you to give up your work—to feel yourself useless," she interrupted herself, with softening eyes, "and I know how you've tried. . . I've watched you. . . but Bessy has tried too; and even if you've both failed—if you've come to the end of your resources—it's for you to face the fact, and help her face it—not to run away from it like this!"

Amherst sat silent under the assault of her eloquence.

He was conscious of no instinctive resentment, no sense that she was, as she confessed, meddling in matters which did not concern her. His ebbing spirit was revived by the shock of an ardour like his own. She had not shrunk from calling him a coward—and it did him good to hear her call him so! Her words put life back into its true perspective, restored their meaning to obsolete terms: to truth and manliness and courage. He had lived so long among equivocations that he had forgotten how to look a fact in the face; but here was a woman who judged life by his own standards—and by those standards she had found him wanting!

Still, he could not forget the last bitter hours, or change his opinion as to the futility of attempting to remain at Lynbrook. He felt as strongly as ever the need of moral and mental liberation—the right to begin life again on his own terms. But Justine Brent had made him see that his first step toward self-assertion had been the inconsistent one of trying to evade its results.

"You are right—I will go back," he said.

She thanked him with her eyes, as she had thanked him on the terrace at Lynbrook, on the autumn evening which had witnessed their first broken exchange of confidences; and he was struck once more with the change that feeling produced in her. Emotions flashed across her face like the sweep of sun-rent clouds over a quiet landscape, bringing out the gleam of hidden waters, the fervour of smouldering colours, all the subtle delicacies of modelling that are lost under the light of an open sky. And it was extraordinary how she could infuse into a principle the warmth and colour of a passion! If conduct, to most people, seemed a cold matter of social prudence or inherited habit, to her it was always the newly-discovered question of her own relation to life—as most women see the great issues only through their own wants and prejudices, so she seemed always to see her personal desires in the light of the larger claims.

"But I don't think," Amherst went on, "that anything can be said to convince me that I ought to alter my decision. These months of idleness have shown me that I'm one of the members of society who are a danger to the community if their noses are not kept to the grindstone——"

Justine lowered her eyes musingly, and he saw she was undergoing the reaction of constraint which always followed on her bursts of unpremeditated frankness.

"That is not for me to judge," she answered after a moment. "But if you decide to go away for a time—surely it ought to be in such a way that your going does not seem to cast any reflection on Bessy, or subject her to any unkind criticism."

Amherst, reddening slightly, glanced at her in surprise. "I don't think you need fear that—I shall be the only one criticized," he said drily.

"Are you sure—if you take such a position as you spoke of? So few people understand the love of hard work for its own sake. They will say that your quarrel with your wife has driven you to support yourself—and that will be cruel to Bessy."

Amherst shrugged his shoulders. "They'll be more likely to say I tried to play the gentleman and failed, and wasn't happy till I got back to my own place in life—which is true enough," he added with a touch of irony.

"They may say that too; but they will make Bessy suffer first—and it will be your fault if she is humiliated in that way. If you decide to take up your factory work for a time, can't you do so without—without accepting a salary? Oh, you see I stick at nothing," she broke in upon herself with a laugh, "and Bessy has said things which make me see that she would suffer horribly if—if you put such a slight on her." He remained silent, and she went on urgently: "From Bessy's standpoint it would mean a decisive break—the repudiating of your whole past. And it is a question on which you can afford to be generous, because I know. . . I think. . . it's less important in your eyes than hers. . ."

Amherst glanced at her quickly. "That particular form of indebtedness, you mean?"

She smiled. "The easiest to cancel, and therefore the least galling; isn't that the way you regard it?"

"I used to—yes; but—" He was about to add: "No one at Lynbrook does," but the flash of intelligence in her eyes restrained him, while at the same time it seemed to answer: "There's my point! To see their limitation is to allow for it, since every enlightenment brings a corresponding obligation."

She made no attempt to put into words the argument her look conveyed, but rose from her seat with a rapid glance at her watch.

"And now I must go, or I shall miss my train." She held out her hand, and as Amherst's met it, he said in a low tone, as if in reply to her unspoken appeal: "I shall remember all you have said."

It was a new experience for Amherst to be acting under the pressure of another will; but during his return journey to Lynbrook that afternoon it was pure relief to surrender himself to this pressure, and the surrender brought not a sense of weakness but of recovered energy. It was not in his nature to analyze his motives, or spend his strength in weighing closely balanced alternatives of conduct; and though, during the last purposeless months, he had grown to brood over every spring of action in himself and others, this tendency disappeared at once in contact with the deed to be done. It was as though a tributary stream, gathering its crystal speed among the hills, had been suddenly poured into the stagnant waters of his will; and he saw now how thick and turbid those waters had become—how full of the slime-bred life that chokes the springs of courage.

His whole desire now was to be generous to his wife: to bear the full brunt of whatever pain their parting brought. Justine had said that Bessy seemed nervous and unhappy: it was clear, therefore, that she also had suffered from the wounds they had dealt each other, though she kept her unmoved front to the last. Poor child! Perhaps that insensible exterior was the only way she knew of expressing courage! It seemed to Amherst that all means of manifesting the finer impulses must slowly wither in the Lynbrook air. As he approached his destination, his thoughts of her were all pitiful: nothing remained of the personal resentment which had debased their parting. He had telephoned from town to announce the hour of his return, and when he emerged from the station he half-expected to find her seated in the brougham whose lamps signalled him through the early dusk. It would be like her to undergo such a reaction of feeling, and to express it, not in words, but by taking up their relation as if there had been no break in it. He had once condemned this facility of renewal as a sign of lightness, a result of that continual evasion of serious issues which made the life of Bessy's world a thin crust of custom above a void of thought. But he now saw that, if she was the product of her environment, that constituted but another claim on his charity, and made the more precious any impulses of natural feeling that had survived the unifying pressure of her life. As he approached the brougham, he murmured mentally: "What if I were to try once more?"

Bessy had not come to meet him; but he said to himself that he should find her alone at the house, and that he would make his confession at once. As the carriage passed between the lights on the tall stone gate-posts, and rolled through the bare shrubberies of the avenue, he felt a momentary tightening of the heart—a sense of stepping back into the trap from which he had just wrenched himself free—a premonition of the way in which the smooth systematized routine of his wife's existence might draw him back into its revolutions as he had once seen a careless factory hand seized and dragged into a flying belt. . .

But it was only for a moment; then his thoughts reverted to Bessy. It was she who was to be considered—this time he must be strong enough for both.

The butler met him on the threshold, flanked by the usual array of footmen; and as he saw his portmanteau ceremoniously passed from hand to hand, Amherst once more felt the steel of the springe on his neck.

"Is Mrs. Amherst in the drawing-room, Knowles?" he asked.

"No, sir," said Knowles, who had too high a sense of fitness to volunteer any information beyond the immediate fact required of him.

"She has gone up to her sitting-room, then?" Amherst continued, turning toward the broad sweep of the stairway.

"No, sir," said the butler slowly; "Mrs. Amherst has gone away."

"Gone away?" Amherst stopped short, staring blankly at the man's smooth official mask.

"This afternoon, sir; to Mapleside."

"To Mapleside?"

"Yes, sir, by motor—to stay with Mrs. Carbury."

There was a moment's silence. It had all happened so quickly that Amherst, with the dual vision which comes at such moments, noticed that the third footman—or was it the fourth?—was just passing his portmanteau on to a shirt-sleeved arm behind the door which led to the servant's wing. . .

He roused himself to look at the tall clock. It was just six. He had telephoned from town at two.

"At what time did Mrs. Amherst leave?"

The butler meditated. "Sharp at four, sir. The maid took the three-forty with the luggage."

With the luggage! So it was not a mere one-night visit. The blood rose slowly to Amherst's face. The footmen had disappeared, but presently the door at the back of the hall reopened, and one of them came out, carrying an elaborately-appointed tea-tray toward the smoking-room. The routine of the house was going on as if nothing had happened. . . The butler looked at Amherst with respectful—too respectful—interrogation, and he was suddenly conscious that he was standing motionless in the middle of the hall, with one last intolerable question on his lips.

Well—it had to be spoken! "Did Mrs. Amherst receive my telephone message?"

"Yes, sir. I gave it to her myself."

It occurred confusedly to Amherst that a well-bred man—as Lynbrook understood the phrase—would, at this point, have made some tardy feint of being in his wife's confidence, of having, on second thoughts, no reason to be surprised at her departure. It was humiliating, he supposed, to be thus laying bare his discomfiture to his dependents—he could see that even Knowles was affected by the manifest impropriety of the situation—but no pretext presented itself to his mind, and after another interval of silence he turned slowly toward the door of the smoking-room

"My letters are here, I suppose?" he paused on the threshold to enquire; and on the butler's answering in the affirmative, he said to himself, with a last effort to suspend his judgment: "She has left a line—there will be some explanation——"

But there was nothing—neither word nor message; nothing but the reverberating retort of her departure in the face of his return—her flight to Blanche Carbury as the final answer to his final appeal.

XXIII

JUSTINE was coming back to Lynbrook.

She had been, after all, unable to stay out the ten days of her visit: the undefinable sense of being needed, so often the determining motive of her actions, drew her back to Long Island at the end of the week. She had received no word from Amherst or Bessy; only Cicely had told her, in a big round hand, that mother had been away three days, and that it had been very lonely, and that the housekeeper's cat had kittens, and she was to have one; and were kittens christened, or how did they get their names?—because she wanted to call hers Justine; and she had found in her book a bird like the one father had shown them in the swamp; and they were not alone now, because the Telfers were there, and they had all been out sleighing; but it would be much nicer when Justine came back. . .

It was as difficult to extract any sequence of facts from Cicely's letter as from an early chronicle. She made no reference to Amherst's return, which was odd, since she was fond of her step-father, yet not significant, since the fact of his arrival might have been crowded out by the birth of the kittens, or some incident equally prominent in her perspectiveless grouping of events; nor did she name the date of her mother's departure, so that Justine could not guess whether it had been contingent on Amherst's return, or wholly unconnected with it. What puzzled her most was Bessy's own silence—yet that too, in a sense, was reassuring, for Bessy thought of others chiefly when it was painful to think of herself, and her not writing implied that she had felt no present need of her friend's sympathy.

Justine did not expect to find Amherst at Lynbrook. She had felt convinced, when they parted, that he would persist in his plan of going south; and the fact that the Telfer girls were again in possession made it seem probable that he had already left. Under the circumstances, Justine thought the separation advisable; but she was eager to be assured that it had been effected amicably, and without open affront to Bessy's pride.

She arrived on a Saturday afternoon, and when she

entered the house the sound of voices from the drawing-room, and the prevailing sense of bustle and movement amid which her own coming was evidently an unconsidered detail, showed that the normal life of Lynbrook had resumed its course. The Telfers, as usual, had brought a lively throng in their train; and amid the bursts of merriment about the drawing-room tea-table she caught Westy Gaines's impressive accents, and the screaming laughter of Blanche Carbury. . .

So Blanche Carbury was back at Lynbrook! The discovery gave Justine fresh cause for conjecture. Whatever reciprocal concessions might have resulted from Amherst's return to his wife, it seemed hardly probable that they included a renewal of relations with Mrs. Carbury. Had his mission failed then—had he and Bessy parted in anger, and was Mrs. Carbury's presence at Lynbrook Bessy's retort to his assertion of independence?

In the school-room, where Justine was received with the eager outpouring of Cicely's minutest experiences, she dared not put the question that would have solved these doubts; and she left to dress for dinner without knowing whether Amherst had returned to Lynbrook. Yet in her heart she never questioned that he had done so; all her fears revolved about what had since taken place.

She saw Bessy first in the drawing-room, surrounded by her guests; and their brief embrace told her nothing, except that she had never beheld her friend more brilliant, more triumphantly in possession of recovered spirits and health.

That Amherst was absent was now made evident by Bessy's requesting Westy Gaines to lead the way to the dining-room with Mrs. Ansell, who was one of the reassembled visitors; and the only one, as Justine presently observed, not in key with the prevailing gaiety. Mrs. Ansell, usually so tinged with the colours of her environment, preserved on this occasion a grey neutrality of tone which was the only break in the general brightness. It was not in her graceful person to express anything as gross as disapproval, yet that sentiment was manifest, to the nice observer, in a delicate aloofness which made the waves of laughter fall back from her, and spread a circle of cloudy calm about her end of the table. Justine had never been greatly drawn to Mrs. Ansell. Her own adaptability was not in the least akin to the older woman's studied self-effacement; and the independence of judgment which Justine preserved in spite of her perception of divergent standpoints made her a little contemptuous of an excess of charity that seemed to have been acquired at the cost of all individual convictions. To-night for the first time she felt in Mrs. Ansell a secret sympathy with her own fears; and a sense of this tacit understanding made her examine with sudden interest the face of her unexpected ally. . . After all, what did she know of Mrs. Ansell's history—of the hidden processes which had gradually subdued her own passions and desires, making of her, as it were, a mere decorative background, a connecting link between other personalities? Perhaps, for a woman alone in the world, without the power and opportunity that money gives, there was no alternative between letting one's individuality harden into a small dry nucleus of egoism, or diffuse itself thus in the interstices of other lives—and there fell upon Justine the chill thought that just such a future might await her if she missed the liberating gift of personal happiness. . .

Neither that night nor the next day had she a private word with Bessy—and it became evident, as the hours passed, that Mrs. Amherst was deliberately postponing the moment when they should find themselves alone. But the Lynbrook party was to disperse on the Monday; and Bessy, who hated early rising, and all the details of housekeeping, tapped at Justine's door late on Sunday night to ask her to speed the departing visitors.

She pleaded this necessity as an excuse for her intrusion, and the playful haste of her manner showed a nervous shrinking from any renewal of confidence; but as she leaned in the doorway, fingering the diamond chain about her neck, while one satin-tipped foot emerged restlessly from the edge of her lace gown, her face lost the bloom of animation which talk and laughter always produced in it, and she looked so pale and weary that Justine needed no better pretext for drawing her into the room.

It was not in Bessy to resist a soothing touch in her moments of nervous reaction. She sank into the chair by the fire and let her head rest wearily against the cushion which Justine slipped behind it.

Justine dropped into the low seat beside her, and laid a hand on hers. "You don't look as well as when I went away, Bessy. Are you sure you've done wisely in beginning your house-parties so soon?"

It always alarmed Bessy to be told that she was not looking her best, and she sat upright, a wave of pink rising under her sensitive skin.

"I am quite well, on the contrary; but I was dying of inanition in this big empty house, and I suppose I haven't got the boredom out of my system yet!"

Justine recognized the echo of Mrs. Carbury's manner.

"Even if you *were* bored," she rejoined, "the inanition was probably good for you. What does Dr. Wyant say to your breaking away from his régime?" She named Wyant purposely, knowing that Bessy had that respect for the medical verdict which is the last trace of reverence for authority in the mind of the modern woman. But Mrs. Amherst laughed with gentle malice.

"Oh, I haven't seen Dr. Wyant lately. His interest in me died out the day you left."

Justine forced a laugh to hide her annoyance. She had not yet recovered from the shrinking disgust of her last scene with Wyant.

"Don't be a goose, Bessy. If he hasn't come, it must be because you've told him not to—because you're afraid of letting him see that you're disobeying him."

Bessy laughed again. "My dear, I'm afraid of nothing—nothing! Not even of your big eyes when they glare at me like coals. I suppose you must have looked at poor Wyant like that to frighten him away! And yet the last time we talked of him you seemed to like him—you even hinted that it was because of him that Westy had no chance."

Justine uttered an impatient exclamation. "If neither of them existed it wouldn't affect the other's chances in the least. Their only merit is that they both enhance the charms of celibacy!"

Bessy's smile dropped, and she turned a grave glance on her friend. "Ah, most men do that—you're so clever to have found it out!"

It was Justine's turn to smile. "Oh, but I haven't—

as a generalization. I mean to marry as soon as I get the chance!"

"The chance——?"

"To meet the right man. I'm gambler enough to believe in my luck yet!"

Mrs. Amherst sighed compassionately. "There *is* no right man! As Blanche says, matrimony's as uncomfortable as a ready-made shoe. How can one and the same institution fit every individual case? And why should we all have to go lame because marriage was once invented to suit an imaginary case?"

Justine gave a slight shrug. "You talk of walking lame—how else do we all walk? It seems to me that life's the tight boot, and marriage the crutch that may help one to hobble along!" She drew Bessy's hand into hers with a caressing pressure. "When you philosophize I always know you're tired. No one who feels well stops to generalize about symptoms. If you won't let your doctor prescribe for you, your nurse is going to carry out his orders. What you want is quiet. Be reasonable and send away everybody before Mr. Amherst comes back!"

She dropped the last phrase carelessly, glancing away as she spoke; but the stiffening of the fingers in her clasp sent a little tremor through her hand.

"Thanks for your advice. It would be excellent but for one thing—my husband is not coming back!"

The mockery in Bessy's voice seemed to pass into her features, hardening and contracting them as frost shrivels a flower. Justine's face, on the contrary, was suddenly illuminated by compassion, as though a light had struck up into it from the cold glitter of her friend's unhappiness.

"Bessy! What do you mean by not coming back?"

"I mean he's had the tact to see that we shall be more comfortable apart—without putting me to the unpleasant necessity of telling him so."

Again the piteous echo of Blanche Carbury's phrases! The laboured mimicry of her ideas!

Justine looked anxiously at her friend. It seemed horribly false not to mention her own talk with Amherst, yet she felt it wiser to feign ignorance, since Bessy could never be trusted to interpret rightly any departure from the conventional.

"Please tell me what has happened," she said at length.

Bessy, with a smile, released her hand. "John has gone back to the life he prefers—which I take to be a hint to me to do the same."

Justine hesitated again; then the pressure of truth overcame every barrier of expediency. "Bessy—I ought to tell you that I saw Mr. Amherst in town the day I went to Philadelphia. He spoke of going away for a time. . . he seemed unhappy. . . but he told me he was coming back to see you first—" She broke off, her clear eyes on her friend's; and she saw at once that Bessy was too self-engrossed to feel any surprise at her avowal. "Surely he came back?" she went on.

"Oh, yes—he came back!" Bessy sank into the cushions, watching the firelight play on her diamond chain as she repeated the restless gesture of lifting it up and letting it slip through her fingers.

"Well—and then?"

"Then—nothing! I was not here when he came."

"You were not here? What had happened?"

"I had gone over to Blanche Carbury's for a day or two. I was just leaving when I heard he was coming back, and I couldn't throw her over at the last moment."

Justine tried to catch the glance that fluttered evasively under Bessy's lashes. "You knew he was coming—and you chose that time to go to Mrs. Carbury's?"

"I didn't choose, my dear—it just happened! And it really happened for the best. I suppose he was annoyed at my going—you know he has a ridiculous prejudice against Blanche—and so the next morning he rushed off to his cotton mill."

There was a pause, while the diamonds continued to flow in threads of fire through Mrs. Amherst's fingers.

At length Justine said: "Did Mr. Amherst know that you knew he was coming back before you left for Mrs. Carbury's?"

Bessy feigned to meditate the question. "Did he know that I knew that he knew?" she mocked. "Yes —I suppose so—he must have known." She stifled a slight yawn as she drew herself languidly to her feet.

"Then he took that as your answer?"

"My answer——?"

"To his coming back——"

"So it appears. I told you he had shown unusual tact." Bessy stretched her softly tapering arms above her head and then dropped them along her sides with another yawn. "But it's almost morning—it's wicked of me to have kept you so late, when you must be up to look after all those people!"

She flung her arms with a light gesture about Justine's shoulders, and laid a dry kiss on her cheek.

"Don't look at me with those big eyes—they've eaten up the whole of your face! And you needn't think I'm sorry for what I've done," she declared. "I'm *not*—the—least—little—atom—of a bit!"

XXIV

JUSTINE was pacing the long library at Lynbrook, between the caged sets of standard authors.

She felt as much caged as they: as much a part of a conventional stage-setting totally unrelated to the action going on before it. Two weeks had passed since her return from Philadelphia; and during that time she had learned that her usefulness at Lynbrook was over. Though not unwelcome, she might almost call herself unwanted; life swept by, leaving her tethered to the stake of inaction; a bitter lot for one who chose to measure existence by deeds instead of days. She had found Bessy ostensibly busy with a succession of guests; no one in the house needed her but Cicely, and even Cicely, at times, was caught up into the whirl of her mother's life, swept off on sleighing parties and motor-trips, or carried to town for a dancing-class or an opera matinée.

Mrs. Fenton Carbury was not among the visitors who left Lynbrook on the Monday after Justine's return.

Mr. Carbury, with the other bread-winners of the party, had hastened back to his treadmill in Wall Street after a Sunday spent in silently studying the files of the Financial Record; but his wife stayed on, somewhat aggressively in possession, criticizing and rearranging the furniture, ringing for the servants, making sudden demands on the stable, telegraphing, telephoning, ordering fires lighted or windows opened, and leaving everywhere in her wake a trail of cigarette ashes and cocktail glasses.

Ned Bowfort had not been included in the house-party; but on the day of its dispersal he rode over unannounced for luncheon, put up his horse in the stable, threaded his way familiarly among the dozing dogs in the hall, greeted Mrs. Ansell and Justine with just the right shade of quiet deference, produced from his pocket a new puzzle-game for Cicely, and sat down beside her mother with the quiet urbanity of the family friend who knows his privileges but is too discreet to abuse them.

After that he came every day, sometimes riding home late to the Hunt Club, sometimes accompanying Bessy and Mrs. Carbury to town for dinner and the theatre; but always with his deprecating air of having dropped in by accident, and modestly hoping that his intrusion was not unwelcome.

The following Sunday brought another influx of visitors, and Bessy seemed to fling herself with renewed enthusiasm into the cares of hospitality. She had avoided Justine since their midnight talk, contriving to see her in Cicely's presence, or pleading haste when they found themselves alone. The winter was unusually open, and she spent long hours in the saddle when her time was not taken up with her visitors. For a while she took Cicely on her daily rides; but she soon wearied of adapting her hunter's stride to the pace of the little girl's pony, and Cicely was once more given over to the coachman's care.

Then came snow and a long frost, and Bessy grew restless at her imprisonment, and grumbled that there was no way of keeping well in a winter climate which made regular exercise impossible.

"Why not build a squash-court?" Blanche Carbury proposed; and the two fell instantly to making plans under the guidance of Ned Bowfort and Westy Gaines. As the scheme developed, various advisers suggested that it was a pity not to add a bowling-alley, a swimming-tank and a gymnasium; a fashionable architect was summoned from town, measurements were taken, sites discussed, sketches compared, and engineers consulted as to the cost of artesian wells and the best system for heating the tank.

Bessy seemed filled with a feverish desire to carry out the plan as quickly as possible, and on as large a scale as even the architect's invention soared to; but it was finally decided that, before signing the contracts, she should run over to New Jersey to see a building of the same kind on which a sporting friend of Mrs. Carbury's had recently lavished a fortune.

It was on this errand that the two ladies, in company with Westy Gaines and Bowfort, had departed on the day which found Justine restlessly measuring the length of the library. She and Mrs. Ansell had the house to themselves; and it was hardly a surprise to her when, in the course of the afternoon, Mrs. Ansell, after a discreet pause on the threshold, advanced toward her down the long room.

Since the night of her return Justine had felt sure that Mrs. Ansell would speak; but the elder lady was given to hawk-like circlings about her subject, to hanging over it and contemplating it before her wings dropped for the descent.

Now, however, it was plain that she had resolved to strike; and Justine had a sense of relief at the thought. She had been too long isolated in her anxiety, her powerlessness to help; and she had a vague hope that Mrs. Ansell's worldly wisdom might accomplish what her inexperience had failed to achieve.

"Shall we sit by the fire? I am glad to find you alone," Mrs. Ansell began, with the pleasant abruptness that was one of the subtlest instruments of her indirection; and as Justine acquiesced, she added, yielding her slight lines to the luxurious depths of an arm-chair: "I have been rather suddenly asked by an invalid cousin to go to Europe with her next week, and I can't go contentedly without being at peace about our friends."

She paused, but Justine made no answer. In spite of her growing sympathy for Mrs. Ansell she could not overcome an inherent distrust, not of her methods, but of her ultimate object. What, for instance, was her conception of being at peace about the Amhersts? Justine's own conviction was that, as far as their final welfare was concerned, any terms were better between them than the external harmony which had prevailed during Amherst's stay at Lynbrook.

The subtle emanation of her distrust may have been felt by Mrs. Ansell; for the latter presently continued, with a certain nobleness: "I am the more concerned because I believe I must hold myself, in a small degree, responsible for Bessy's marriage—" and, as Justine looked at her in surprise, she added: "I thought she could never be happy unless her affections were satisfied—and even now I believe so."

"I believe so too," Justine said, surprised into assent by the simplicity of Mrs. Ansell's declaration.

"Well, then—since we are agreed in our diagnosis," the older woman went on, smiling, "what remedy do you suggest? Or rather, how can we administer it?"

"What remedy?" Justine hesitated.

"Oh, I believe we are agreed on that too. Mr. Amherst must be brought back—but how to bring him?" She paused, and then added, with a singular effect of appealing frankness: "I ask you, because I believe you to be the only one of Bessy's friends who is in the least in her husband's confidence."

Justine's embarrassment increased. Would it not be disloyal both to Bessy and Amherst to acknowledge to a third person a fact of which Bessy herself was unaware? Yet to betray embarrassment under Mrs. Ansell's eyes was to risk giving it a dangerous significance.

"Bessy has spoken to me once or twice—but I know very little of Mr. Amherst's point of view; except," Justine added, after another moment's weighing of alternatives, "that I believe he suffers most from being cut off from his work at Westmore."

"Yes—so I think; but that is a difficulty that time and expediency must adjust. All *we* can do—their friends, I mean—is to get them together again before the breach is too wide."

Justine pondered. She was perhaps more ignorant of the situation than Mrs. Ansell imagined, for since her talk with Bessy the latter had not again alluded to Amherst's absence, and Justine could merely conjecture that he had carried out his plan of taking the management of the mill he had spoken of. What she most wished to know was whether he had listened to her entreaty, and taken the position temporarily, without binding himself by the acceptance of a salary; or whether, wounded by the outrage of Bessy's flight, he had freed himself from financial dependence by engaging himself definitely as manager.

"I really know very little of the present situation," Justine said, looking at Mrs. Ansell. "Bessy merely told me that Mr. Amherst had taken up his old work in a cotton mill in the south."

As her eyes met Mrs. Ansell's it flashed across her that the latter did not believe what she said, and the perception made her instantly shrink back into herself. But there was nothing in Mrs. Ansell's tone to confirm the doubt which her look betrayed.

"Ah—I hoped you knew more," she said simply; "for, like you, I have only heard from Bessy that her husband went away suddenly to help a friend who is reorganizing some mills in Georgia. Of course, under the circumstances, such a temporary break is natural enough—perhaps inevitable—only he must not stay away too long."

Justine was silent. Mrs. Ansell's momentary self-betrayal had checked all farther possibility of frank communion, and the discerning lady had seen her error too late to remedy it.

But her hearer's heart gave a leap of joy. It was clear from what Mrs. Ansell said that Amherst had not bound himself definitely, since he would not have done so without informing his wife. And with a secret thrill of happiness Justine recalled his last word to her: "I will remember all you have said."

He had kept that word and acted on it; in spite of Bessy's last assault on his pride he had borne with her, and deferred the day of final rupture; and the sense that she had had a part in his decision filled Justine with a glow of hope. The consciousness of Mrs. Ansell's suspicions faded to insignificance—Mrs. Ansell and her kind might think what they chose, since all that mattered now was that she herself should act bravely and circumspectly in her last attempt to save her friends.

"I am not sure," Mrs. Ansell continued, gently scrutinizing her companion, "that I think it unwise of him to have gone; but if he stays too long Bessy may listen to bad advice—advice disastrous to her happiness." She paused, and turned her eyes meditatively toward the fire. "As far as I know," she said, with the same air of serious candour, "you are the only person who can tell him this."

"I?" exclaimed Justine, with a leap of colour to her pale cheeks.

Mrs. Ansell's eyes continued to avoid her. "My dear Miss Brent, Bessy has told me something of the wise counsels you have given her. Mr. Amherst is also your friend. As I said just now, you are the only person who might act as a link between them—surely you will not renounce the rôle."

Justine controlled herself. "My only rôle, as you call it, has been to urge Bessy to—to try to allow for her husband's views——"

"And have you not given the same advice to Mr. Amherst?"

The eyes of the two women met. "Yes," said Justine, after a moment.

"Then why refuse your help now? The moment is crucial."

Justine's thoughts had flown beyond the stage of resenting Mrs. Ansell's gentle pertinacity. All her faculties we e absorbed in the question as to how she could most effectually use whatever influence she possessed.

"I put it to you as one old friend to another—will you write to Mr. Amherst to come back?" Mrs. Ansell urged her.

Justine was past considering even the strangeness of this request, and its oblique reflection on the kind of power ascribed to her. Through the confused beatings of her heart she merely struggled for a clearer sense of guidance.

"No," she said slowly. "I cannot."

"You cannot? With a friend's happiness in extremity?" Mrs. Ansell paused a moment before she added. "Unless you believe that Bessy would be happier divorced?"

"Divorced—? Oh, no," Justine shuddered.

"That is what it will come to."

"No, no! In time——"

"Time is what I am most afraid of, when Blanche Carbury disposes of it."

Justine breathed a deep sigh.

"You'll write?" Mrs. Ansell murmured, laying a soft touch on her hand.

"I have not the influence you think——"

"Can you do any harm by trying?"

"I might—" Justine faltered, losing her exact sense of the words she used.

"Ah," the other flashed back, "then you *have* influence! Why will you not use it?"

Justine waited a moment; then her resolve gathered itself into words. "If I have any influence, I am not sure it would be well to use it as you suggest."

"Not to urge Mr. Amherst's return?"

"No—not now."

She caught the same veiled gleam of incredulity under Mrs. Ansell's lids—caught and disregarded it.

"It must be now or never," Mrs. Ansell insisted.

"I can't think so," Justine held out.

"Nevertheless—will you try?"

"No—no! It might be fatal."

"To whom?"

"To both." She considered. "If he came back now I know he would not stay."

Mrs. Ansell was upon her abruptly. "You *know?* Then you speak with authority?"

"No—what authority? I speak as I feel," Justine faltered.

The older woman drew herself to her feet. "Ah—then you shoulder a great responsibility!" She moved nearer to Justine, and once more laid a fugitive touch upon her. "You won't write to him?"

"No—no," the girl flung back; and the voices of the

returning party in the hall made Mrs. Ansell, with an almost imperceptible gesture of warning, turn musingly away toward the fire.

Bessy came back brimming with the wonders she had seen. A glazed "sun-room," mosaic pavements, a marble fountain to feed the marble tank—and outside a water-garden, descending in successive terraces, to take up and utilize—one could see how practically!—the overflow from the tank. If one did the thing at all, why not do it decently? She had given up her new motor, had let her town house, had pinched and stinted herself in a hundred ways—if ever woman was entitled to a little compensating pleasure, surely she was that woman!

The days were crowded with consultations. Architect, contractors, engineers, a landscape gardener, and a dozen minor craftsmen, came and went, unrolled plans, moistened pencils, sketched, figured, argued, persuaded, and filled Bessy with the dread of appearing, under Blanche Carbury's eyes, subject to any restraining influences of economy. What! She was a young woman, with an independent fortune, and she was always wavering, considering, secretly referring back to the mute criticism of an invisible judge—of the husband who had been first to shake himself free of any mutual subjection? The accomplished Blanche did not have to say this—she conveyed it by the raising of painted brows, by a smile of mocking interrogation, a judiciously placed silence or a resigned glance at the architect. So the estimates poured in, were studied, resisted—then yielded to and signed; then the hour of advance payments struck, and an imperious appeal was despatched to Mr. Tredegar, to whom the management of Bessy's affairs had been transferred.

Mr. Tredegar, to his client's surprise, answered the appeal in person. He had not been lately to Lynbrook, dreading the cold and damp of the country in winter; and his sudden arrival had therefore an ominous significance.

He came for an evening in mid-week, when even Blanche Carbury was absent, and Bessy and Justine had the house to themselves. Mrs. Ansell had sailed the week before with her invalid cousin. No farther words had passed between herself and Justine—but the latter was conscious that their talk had increased instead of lessened the distance between them. Justine herself meant to leave soon. Her hope of regaining Bessy's confidence had been deceived, and seeing herself definitely superseded, she chafed anew at her purposeless inactivity. She had already written to one or two doctors in New York, and to the matron of Saint Elizabeth's. She had made herself a name in surgical cases, and it could not be long before a summons came. . .

Meanwhile Mr. Tredegar arrived, and the three dined together, the two women bending meekly to his discourse, which was never more oracular and authoritative than when delivered to the gentler sex alone. Amherst's absence, in particular, seemed to loose the thin current of Mr. Tredegar's eloquence. He was never quite at ease in the presence of an independent mind, and Justine often reflected that, even had the two men known nothing of each other's views, there would have been between them an instinctive and irreducible hostility—they would have disliked each other if they had merely jostled elbows in the street.

Yet even freed from Amherst's presence Mr. Tredegar showed a darkling brow, and as Justine slipped away after dinner she felt that she left Bessy to something more serious than the usual business conference.

How serious, she was to learn that very night, when, in the small hours, her friend burst in on her tearfully. Bessy was ruined—ruined—that was what Mr. Tredegar had come to tell her! She might have known he would not have travelled to Lynbrook for a trifle. . . She had expected to find herself cramped, restricted—to be warned that she must "manage," hateful word! . . . But this! This was incredible! Unendurable! There was no money to build the gymnasium—none at all! And all because it had been swallowed up at Westmore—because the ridiculous changes there, the changes that nobody wanted, nobody approved of—that Truscomb and all the other experts had opposed and derided from the first—these changes, even modified and arrested, had already involved so much of her income, that it might be years—yes, he said *years!*—before she would feel herself free again—free of her own fortune, of Cicely's fortune. . . of the money poor Dick Westmore had meant his wife and child to enjoy!

Justine listened anxiously to this confused outpouring of resentments. Bessy's born incapacity for figures made it indeed possible that the facts came on her as a surprise—that she had quite forgotten the temporary reduction of her income, and had begun to imagine that what she had saved in one direction was hers to spend in another. All this was conceivable. But why had Mr. Tredegar drawn so dark a picture of the future? Or was it only that, thwarted of her immediate desire, Bessy's disappointment blackened the farthest verge of her horizon? Justine, though aware of her friend's lack of perspective, suspected that a conniving hand had helped to throw the prospect out of drawing. . .

Could it be possible, then, that Mr. Tredegar was among those who desired a divorce? That the influences at which Mrs. Ansell had hinted proceeded not only from Blanche Carbury and her group? Helpless amid this rush of forebodings, Justine could do no more than soothe and restrain—to reason would have been idle. She had never till now realized how completely she had lost ground with Bessy.

"The humiliation—before my friends! Oh, I was warned. . . my father, every one. . . for Cicely's sake I was warned. . . but I wouldn't listen—and *now!* From the first it was all he cared for—in Europe, even, he was always dragging me to factories. *Me?* —I was only the owner of Westmore! He wanted power—power, that's all—when he lost it he left me . . . oh, I'm glad now my baby is dead! Glad there's nothing between us—nothing, nothing in the world to tie us together any longer!"

The disproportion between this violent grief and its trivial cause would have struck Justine as simply grotesque, had she not understood that the incident of the gymnasium, which followed with cumulative pressure on a series of similar episodes, seemed to Bessy like the reaching out of a retaliatory hand—a mocking reminder that she was still imprisoned in the consequences of her unhappy marriage.

Such folly seemed past weeping for—it froze Justine's compassion into disdain, till she remembered that the sources of our sorrow are sometimes nobler than their means of expression, and that a baffled unappeased love was perhaps the real cause of Bessy's anger against her husband.

At any rate, the moment was a critical one, and Justine remembered with a pang that Mrs. Ansell had foreseen such a contingency, and implored her to take measures against it. She had refused, from a sincere dread of precipitating a definite estrangement—but had she been right in judging the situation so logically? With a creature of Bessy's emotional uncertainties the result of contending influences was really incalculable—it might still be that, at this juncture, Amherst's return would bring about a reaction of better feelings. . .

Justine sat and mused on these things after leaving her friend exhausted upon a tearful pillow. She felt that she had perhaps taken too large a survey of the situation—that the question whether there could ever be happiness between this tormented pair was not one to concern those who struggled for their welfare. Most marriages are a patch-work of jarring tastes and ill-assorted ambitions—if here and there, for a moment, two colours blend, two textures are the same, so much the better for the pattern! Justine, certainly, could foresee in reunion no positive happiness for either of her friends; but she saw positive disaster for Bessy in separation from her husband. . .

Suddenly she rose from her chair by the falling fire, and crossed over to the writing-table. She would write to Amherst herself—she would tell him to come. The decision once reached, hope flowed back to her heart—the joy of action so often deceived her into immediate faith in its results!

"Dear Mr. Amherst," she wrote, "the last time I saw you, you told me you would remember what I said. I ask you to do so now—to remember that I urged you not to be away too long. I believe you ought to come back now, though I know Bessy will not ask you to. I am writing without her knowledge, but with the conviction that she needs you, though perhaps without knowing it herself. . ."

She paused, and laid down her pen. Why did it make her so happy to write to him? Was it merely the sense of recovered helpfulness, or something warmer, more personal, that made it a joy to trace his name, and to remind him of their last intimate exchange of words? Well—perhaps it was that too. There were moments when she was so mortally lonely that any sympathetic contact with another life sent a glow into her veins—that she was thankful to warm herself at any fire

XXV

BESSY, languidly glancing through her midday mail some five days later, uttered a slight exclamation as she withdrew her finger-tip from the flap of the envelope she had begun to open.

It was a black sleety day, with an east wind bowing the trees beyond the drenched window-panes, and the two friends, after luncheon, had withdrawn to the library, where Justine sat writing notes for Bessy, while the latter lay back in her arm-chair, in the state of dreamy listlessness into which she always sank when not under the stimulus of amusement or exercise.

She sat suddenly upright as her eyes fell on the letter.

"I beg your pardon! I thought it was for me," she said, holding it out to Justine.

The latter reddened as she glanced at the superscription. It had not occurred to her that Amherst would reply to her appeal: she had pictured him springing on the first north-bound train, perhaps not even pausing to announce his return to his wife. . . And to receive his letter under Bessy's eye was undeniably embarrassing, since Justine felt the necessity of keeping her intervention secret.

But under Bessy's eye she certainly was—it continued to rest on her curiously, speculatively, with an undergleam of malicious significance.

"So stupid of me—I can't imagine why I should have expected my husband to write to me!" Bessy went on, leaning back in lazy contemplation of her other letters, but still obliquely including Justine in her angle of vision.

The latter, after a moment's pause, broke the seal and read.

"Millfield, Georgia.

"My dear Miss Brent,

"Your letter reached me yesterday and I have thought it over carefully. I appreciate the feeling that prompted it—but I don't know that any friend, however kind and discerning, can give the final advice in such matters. You tell me you are sure my wife will not ask me to return—well, under present conditions that seems to me a sufficient reason for staying away.

"Meanwhile, I assure you that I have remembered all you said to me that day. I have made no binding arrangement here—nothing to involve my future action—and I have done this solely because you asked it. This will tell you better than words how much I value your advice, and what strong reasons I must have for not following it now.

"I suppose there are no more exploring parties in this weather. I wish I could show Cicely some of the birds down here.

"Yours faithfully,

"John Amherst.

"Please don't let my wife ride Impulse."

Latent under Justine's acute consciousness of what this

letter meant, was the sense of Bessy's inferences and conjectures. She could feel them actually piercing the page in her hand like some hypersensitive visual organ to which matter offers no obstruction. Or rather, baffled in their endeavour, they were evoking out of the unseen, heaven knew what fantastic structure of intrigue—scrawling over the innocent page with burning evidences of perfidy and collusion. . .

One thing became instantly clear to her: she must show the letter to Bessy. She ran her eyes over it again, trying to disentangle the consequences. There was the allusion to their talk in town—well, she had told Bessy of that! But the careless reference to their woodland excursions—what might not Bessy, in her present mood, make of it? Justine's uppermost thought was of distress at the failure of her plan. Perhaps she might still have induced Amherst to come back, had it not been for this accident; but now that hope was destroyed

She raised her eyes and met Bessy's. "Will you read it?" she said, holding out the letter.

Bessy received it with lifted brows, and a protesting murmur—but as she read, Justine saw the blood mount under her clear skin, invade the temples, the nape, even the little flower-like ears; then it receded as suddenly, ebbing at last from the very lips, so that the smile with which she looked up from her reading was as white as if she had been under the stress of physical pain.

"So you have written my husband to come back?"

"As you see."

Bessy looked her straight in the eyes. "I am very much obliged to you—extremely obliged!"

Justine met the look quietly. "Which means that you resent my interference——"

"Oh, I leave you to call it that!" Bessy mocked, tossing the letter down on the table at her side.

"Bessy! Don't take it in that way. If I made a mistake I did so with the hope of helping you. How can I stand by, after all these months together, and see you deliberately destroying your life without trying to stop you?"

The smile withered on Bessy's lips. "It is very dear and good of you—I know you're never happy unless you're helping people—but in this case I can only repeat what my husband says. He and I don't often look at things in the same light—but I quite agree with him that the management of such matters is best left to—to the persons concerned."

Justine hesitated. "I might answer that, if you take that view, it was inconsistent of you to talk with me so openly. You've certainly made me feel that you wanted help—you've turned to me for it. But perhaps that does not justify my writing to Mr. Amherst without your knowing it."

Bessy laughed. "Ah, my dear, you knew that if you asked me the letter would never be sent!"

"Perhaps I did," said Justine simply. "I was trying to help you against your will."

"Well, you see the result." Bessy laid a derisive touch on the letter. "Do you understand now whose fault it is if I am alone?"

Justine faced her steadily. "There is nothing in Mr. Amherst's letter to make me change my opinion. I still think it lies with you to bring him back."

Bessy raised a glittering face to her—all hardness and laughter. "Such modesty, my dear! As if I had a chance of succeeding where you failed!"

She sprang up, brushing the curls from her temples with a petulant gesture. "Don't mind me if I'm cross—but I've had a dose of preaching from Maria Ansell, and I don't know why my friends should treat me like a puppet without any preferences of my own, and press me upon a man who has done his best to show that he doesn't want me. As a matter of fact, he and I are luckily agreed on that point too—and I'm afraid all the good advice in the world won't persuade us to change our opinion!"

Justine held her ground. "If I believed that of either of you, I shouldn't have written—I should not be pleading with you now— And Mr. Amherst doesn't believe it either," she added, after a pause, conscious of the risk she was taking, but thinking the words might act like a blow in the face of a person sinking under a deadly narcotic.

Bessy's smile deepened to a sneer. "I see you've talked me over thoroughly—and on *his* views I ought perhaps not to have risked an opinion——"

"We have not talked you over," Justine exclaimed. "Mr. Amherst could never talk of you... in the way you think..." And under the light staccato of Bessy's laugh she found resolution to add: "It is not in that way that I know what he feels."

"Ah? I should be curious to hear, then——"

Justine turned to the letter, which still lay between them. "Will you read the last sentence again? The postscript, I mean."

Bessy, after a surprised glance at her, took the letter up with the deprecating murmur of one who acts under compulsion rather than dispute about a trifle.

"The postscript? Let me see... 'Don't let my wife ride Impulse.'— *Et puis?*" she murmured, dropping the page again.

"Well, does it tell you nothing? It's a cold letter—at first I thought so—the letter of a man who believes himself deeply hurt—so deeply that he will make no advance, no sign of relenting. That's what I thought when I first read it... but the postscript undoes it all."

Justine, as she spoke, had drawn near Bessy, laying a hand on her arm, and shedding on her the radiance of a face all charity and sweet compassion. It was her rare gift, at such moments, to forget her own relation to the person for whose fate she was concerned, to cast aside all consciousness of criticism and distrust in the heart she strove to reach, as pitiful people forget their physical timidity in the attempt to help a wounded animal.

For a moment Bessy seemed to waver. The colour flickered faintly up her cheek, her long lashes drooped —she had the tenderest lids!—and all her face seemed melting under the beams of Justine's ardour. But the letter was still in her hand—her eyes, in sinking, fell upon it, and she sounded beneath her breath the fatal phrase: "'I have done this solely because you asked it.'

"After such a tribute to your influence I don't wonder you feel competent to set everybody's affairs in order! But take my advice, my dear—*don't* ask me not to ride Impulse!"

The pity froze on Justine's lip: she shrank back cut to the quick. For a moment the silence between the two women rang with the flight of arrowy, wounding thoughts; then Bessy's anger flagged, she gave one of her embarrassed half-laughs, and turning back, laid a deprecating touch on her friend's arm.

"I didn't mean that, Justine. . . but let us not talk now—I can't!"

Justine did not move: the reaction could not come as quickly in her case. But she turned on Bessy two eyes full of pardon, full of speechless pity. . . and Bessy received the look silently before she moved to the door and went out.

"Oh, poor thing—poor thing!" Justine gasped as the door closed.

She had already forgotten her own hurt—she was alone again with Bessy's sterile pain. She stood staring before her for a moment—then her eyes fell on Amherst's letter, which had fluttered to the floor between them. The fatal letter! If it had not come at that unlucky moment perhaps she might still have gained her end. . . She picked it up and re-read it. Yes—there were phrases in it that a wounded suspicious heart might misconstrue. . . Yet Bessy's last words had absolved her. . . Why had she not answered them? Why had she stood there dumb? The blow to her pride had been too deep, had been dealt too unexpectedly—for one miserable moment she had thought first of herself! Ah, that importunate, irrepressible self—the *moi haïssable* of the Christian—if only one could tear it from one's breast! She had missed an opportunity—her last opportunity perhaps! By this time, even, a hundred hostile influences, cold whispers of vanity, of selfishness, of worldly pride, might have drawn their freezing ring about Bessy's heart...

Justine started up to follow her... then paused, recalling her last words. "Let us not talk now—I can't!" She had no right to intrude on that bleeding privacy—if the chance had been hers she had lost it. She dropped back into her seat at the desk, hiding her face in her hands.

Presently she heard the clock strike, and true to her tireless instinct of activity, she lifted her head, took up her pen, and went on with the correspondence she had dropped... It was hard at first to collect her thoughts, or even to summon to her pen the conventional phrases that sufficed for most of the notes. Groping for a word, she pushed aside her writing and stared out at the sallow frozen landscape framed by the window at which she sat. The sleet had ceased, and hollows of sunless blue showed through the driving wind-clouds. A hard sky and a hard ground—frost-bound ringing earth under rigid ice-mailed trees.

As Justine looked out, shivering a little, she saw a woman's figure riding down the avenue toward the gate. The figure disappeared behind a clump of evergreens—showed again farther down, through the boughs of a skeleton beech—and revealed itself in the next open space as Bessy—Bessy in the saddle on a day of glaring frost, when no horse could keep his footing out of a walk!

Justine went to the window and strained her eyes for a confirming glimpse. Yes—it was Bessy! There was no mistaking that light flexible figure, every line swaying true to the beat of the horse's stride. But Justine remembered that Bessy had not meant to ride—had countermanded her horse because of the bad going. . . Well, she was a perfect horsewoman and had no doubt chosen her surest-footed mount. . . probably the brown cob, Tony Lumpkin.

But when did Tony's sides shine so bright through the leafless branches? And when did he sweep his rider on with such long free play of the hind-quarters? Horse and rider shot into sight again, rounding the curve of the avenue near the gates, and in a break of sunlight Justine saw the glitter of chestnut flanks—and remembered that Impulse was the only chestnut in the stables. . .

She went back to her seat and continued writing. Bessy had left a formidable heap of bills and letters; and when this was demolished, Justine had her own correspondence to despatch. She had heard that morning from the matron of Saint Elizabeth's: an interesting "case" was offered her, but she must come within two days. For the first few hours she had wavered, loath to leave Lynbrook without some definite light on her friend's future; but now Amherst's letter had shed that light—or rather, had deepened the obscurity—and she had no pretext for lingering on where her uselessness had been so amply demonstrated.

She wrote to the matron accepting the engagement; and the acceptance involved the writing of other letters, the general reorganizing of that minute polity, the life of Justine Brent. She smiled a little to think how easily she could be displaced and transplanted—how slender were her material impedimenta, how few her invisible bonds! She was as light and detachable as a dead leaf on the autumn breeze—yet she was in the season of sap and flower, when there is life and song in the trees!

But she did not think long of herself, for an undefinable anxiety ran through her thoughts like a black thread. It found expression, now and then, in the long glances she threw through the window—in her rising to consult the clock and compare her watch with it—in a nervous snatch of humming as she paced the room once or twice before going back to her desk. . .

Why was Bessy so late? Dusk was falling already—the early end of the cold slate-hued day. But Bessy always rode late—there was always a rational answer to Justine's irrational conjectures. . . It was the sight of those chestnut flanks that tormented her—she knew of Bessy's previous struggles with the mare. But the indulging of idle apprehensions was not in her nature, and when the tea-tray came, and with it Cicely, sparkling from a gusty walk, and coral-pink in her cloud of crinkled hair, Justine sprang up and cast off her cares.

It cost her a pang, again, to see the lamps lit and the curtains drawn—shutting in the warmth and brightness of the house from that wind-swept frozen twilight through which Bessy rode alone. But the icy touch of the thought slipped from Justine's mind as she bent above the tea-tray, gravely measuring Cicely's milk into a "grown-up" teacup, hearing the confidential details of the child's day, and capping them with banter and fantastic narrative.

She was not sorry to go—ah, no! The house had become a prison to her, with ghosts walking its dreary floors. But to lose Cicely would be bitter—she had not felt how bitter till the child pressed against her in the firelight, insisting raptly, with little sharp elbows stabbing her knee: "And *then* what happened, Justine?"

The door opened, and some one came in to look at the fire. Justine, through the mazes of her fairy-tale, was dimly conscious that it was Knowles, and not one of the footmen... the proud Knowles, who never mended the fires himself... As he passed out again, hovering slowly down the long room, she rose, leaving Cicely on the hearth-rug, and followed him to the door.

"Has Mrs. Amherst not come in?" she asked, not knowing why she wished to ask it out of the child's hearing.

"No, miss. I looked in myself to see—thinking she might have come by the side-door."

"She may have gone to her sitting-room."

"She's not upstairs."

They both paused. Then Justine said: "What horse was she riding?"

"Impulse, Miss." The butler looked at his large responsible watch. "It's not late—" he said, more to himself than to her.

"No. Has she been riding Impulse lately?"

"No, Miss. Not since that day the mare nearly had her off. I understood Mr. Amherst did not wish it."

Justine went back to Cicely and the fairy-tale.—As she took up the thread of the Princess's adventures, she asked herself why she had ever had any hope of helping Bessy. The seeds of disaster were in the poor creature's soul... Even when she appeared to be moved, lifted out of herself, her escaping impulses were always dragged back to the magnetic centre of hard distrust and resistance that sometimes forms the core of soft-fibred natures. As she had answered her husband's previous appeal by her flight to the woman he disliked, so she answered this one by riding the horse he feared... Justine's last illusions crumbled. The distance between two such natures was unspannable. Amherst had done well to remain away... and with a tidal rush her sympathies swept back to his side...

The governess came to claim Cicely. One of the foōtmen came to put another log on the fire. Then the rite of removing the tea-table was majestically performed—the ceremonial that had so often jarred on Amherst's nerves. As she watched it, Justine had a vague sense of the immutability of the household routine—a queer awed feeling that, whatever happened, a machine so perfectly adjusted would work on inexorably, like a natural law...

She rose to look out of the window, staring vainly into blackness between the parted curtains. As she turned back, passing the writing-table, she noticed that Cicely's irruption had made her forget to post her letters—an unusual oversight. A glance at the clock told her that she was not too late for the mail—reminding her, at the same time, that it was scarcely three hours since Bessy had started on her ride... She saw the foolishness of her fears. Even in winter, Bessy often rode for more than three hours; and now that the days were growing longer——

Suddenly reassured, Justine went out into the hall, intending to carry her batch of letters to the red pillar-box by the door. As she did so, a cold blast struck her. Could it be that for once the faultless routine of the house had been relaxed, that one of the servants had left the outer door ajar? She walked over to the vestibule—yes, both doors were wide. The night rushed in on a vicious wind. As she pushed the vestibule door shut, she heard the dogs sniffing and whining on the threshold. She crossed the vestibule, and heard voices and the tramping of feet in the darkness—then saw a lantern gleam. Suddenly Knowles shot out of the night—the lantern struck on his bleached face.

Justine, stepping back, pressed the electric button in the wall, and the wide door-step was abruptly illuminated, with its huddled, pushing, heavily-breathing group. . . black figures writhing out of darkness, strange faces distorted in the glare.

"Bessy!" she cried, and sprang forward; but suddenly Wyant was before her, his hand on her arm; and as the dreadful group struggled by into the hall, he froze her to him with a whisper: "The spine——"

XXVI

WITHIN Justine there was a moment's darkness; then, like terror-struck workers rallying to their tasks, every faculty was again at its post, receiving and transmitting signals, taking observations, anticipating orders, making her brain ring with the hum of a controlled activity.

She had known the sensation before—the transmuting of terror and pity into this miraculous lucidity of thought and action; but never had it snatched her from such depths. Oh, thank heaven for her knowledge now—for the trained mind that could take command of her senses and bend them firmly to its service!

Wyant seconded her well, after a moment's ague-fit of fear. She pitied and pardoned the moment, aware of its cause, and respecting him for the way in which he rose above it into the clear air of professional self-command. Through the first hours they worked shoulder to shoulder, conscious of each other only as of kindred will-powers, stretched to the utmost tension of discernment and activity, and hardly needing speech or look to further their swift co-operation. It was thus that she had known him in the hospital, in the heat of his youthful zeal: the doctor she liked best to work with, because no other so tempered ardour with judgment.

The great surgeon, arriving from town at midnight, confirmed his diagnosis: there was undoubted injury to the spine. Other consultants were summoned in haste, and in the winter dawn the verdict was pronounced—a fractured vertebra, and possibly lesion of the cord. . .

Justine got a moment alone when the surgeons returned to the sick-room. Other nurses were there now, capped, aproned, quickly and silently unpacking their appliances. . . She must call a halt, clear her brain again, decide rapidly what was to be done next. . . Oh, if only the crawling hours could bring Amherst! It was strange that there was no telegram yet—no, not strange, after all, since it was barely six in the morning, and her message had not been despatched till seven the night before. It was not unlikely that, in that little southern settlement, the telegraph office closed at six.

She stood in Bessy's sitting-room, her forehead pressed to the window-pane, her eyes straining out into the thin February darkness, through which the morning star swam white. As soon as she had yielded her place to the other nurses her nervous tension relaxed, and she hung again above the deeps of anguish, terrified and weak. In a moment the necessity for action would snatch her back to a firm footing—her thoughts would clear, her will affirm itself, all the wheels of the complex machine resume their functions. But now she felt only the horror. . .

She knew so well what was going on in the next room. Dr. Garford, the great surgeon, who had known her at Saint Elizabeth's, had evidently expected her to take command of the nurses he had brought from town;

but there were enough without her, and there were other cares which, for the moment, she only could assume—the despatching of messages to the scattered family, the incessant telephoning and telegraphing to town, the general guidance of the household swinging rudderless in the tide of disaster. Cicely, above all, must be watched over and guarded from alarm. The little governess, reduced to a twittering heap of fears, had been quarantined in a distant room till reason returned to her; and the child, meanwhile, slept quietly in the old nurse's care.

Cicely would wake presently, and Justine must go up to her with a bright face; other duties would press thick on the heels of this; their feet were already on the threshold. But meanwhile she could only follow in imagination what was going on in the other room. . .

She had often thought with dread of such a contingency. She always sympathized too much with her patients—she knew it was the joint in her armour. Her quick-gushing pity lay too near that professional exterior which she had managed to endue with such a bright glaze of insensibility that some sentimental patients—without much the matter—had been known to call her "a little hard." How, then, should she steel herself if it fell to her lot to witness a cruel accident to some one she loved, and to have to perform a nurse's duties, steadily, expertly, unflinchingly, while every fibre was torn with inward anguish?

She knew the horror of it now—and she knew also that her self-enforced exile from the sick-room was a hundred times worse. To stand there, knowing, with each tick of the clock, what was being said and done within—how the great luxurious room, with its pale draperies and scented cushions, and the hundred pretty trifles strewing the lace toilet-table and the delicate old furniture, was being swept bare, cleared for action like a ship's deck, drearily garnished with rows of instruments, rolls of medicated cotton, oiled silk, bottles, bandages, water-pillows—all the grim paraphernalia of the awful rites of pain: to know this, and to be able to call up with torturing vividness that poor pale face on the pillows, vague-eyed, expressionless, perhaps, as she had last seen it, or—worse yet—stirred already with the first creeping pangs of consciousness: to have these images slowly, deliberately burn themselves into her brain, and to be aware, at the same time, of that underlying moral disaster, of which the accident seemed the monstrous outward symbol—ah, this was worse than anything she had ever dreamed!

She knew that the final verdict could not be pronounced till the operation which was about to take place should reveal the extent of injury to the spine. Bessy, in falling, must have struck on the back of her head and shoulders, and it was but too probable that the fractured vertebra had caused a bruise if not a lesion of the spinal cord. In that case paralysis was certain —and a slow crawling death the almost inevitable outcome. There had been cases, of course—Justine's professional memory evoked them—cases of so-called "recovery," where actual death was kept at bay, a semblance of life preserved for years in the poor petrified body. . . But the mind shrank from such a fate for Bessy. And it might still be that the injury to the spine was not grave—though, here again, the fracturing of the fourth vertebra was ominous.

The door opened and some one came from the inner room—Wyant, in search of an instrument-case. Justine turned and they looked at each other.

"It will be now?"

"Yes. Dr. Garford asked if there was no one you could send for."

"No one but Mr. Tredegar and the Halford Gaineses. They'll be here this evening, I suppose."

They exchanged a discouraged glance, knowing how little difference the presence of the Halford Gaineses would make.

"He wanted to know if there was no telegram from Amherst."

"No."

"Then they mean to begin."

A nursemaid appeared in the doorway. "Miss Cicely—" she said; and Justine bounded upstairs.

The day's work had begun. From Cicely to the governess—from the governess to the housekeeper—from the telephone to the writing-table—Justine vibrated back and forth, quick, noiseless, self-possessed—sobering, guiding, controlling her confused and panic-stricken world. It seemed to her that half the day had elapsed before the telegraph office at Lynbrook opened—she was at the telephone at the stroke of the hour. No telegram? Only one—a message from Halford Gaines—"Arrive at eight tonight." Amherst was still silent! Was there a difference of time to be allowed for? She tried to remember, to calculate, but her brain was too crowded with other thoughts. . . She turned away from the instrument discouraged.

Whenever she had time to think, she was overwhelmed by the weight of her solitude. Mr. Langhope was in Egypt, accessible only through a London banker—Mrs. Ansell presumably wandering on the continent. Her cables might not reach them for days. And among the throng of Lynbrook habitués, she knew not to whom to turn. To loose the Telfer tribe and Mrs. Carbury upon that stricken house—her thought revolted from it, and she was thankful to know that February had dispersed their migratory flock to southern shores. But if only Amherst would come!

Cicely and the tranquillized governess had been despatched on a walk with the dogs, and Justine was returning upstairs when she met one of the servants with a telegram. She tore it open with a great throb of relief. It was her own message to Amherst—*address unknown*...

Had she misdirected it, then? In that first blinding moment her mind might so easily have failed her. But no—there was the name of the town before her... Millfield, Georgia... the same name as in his letter... She had made no mistake, but he was gone! Gone—and without leaving an address... For a moment her tired mind refused to work; then she roused herself, ran down the stairs again, and rang up the telegraph-office. The thing to do, of course, was to telegraph to the owner of the mills—of whose very name she was ignorant!—enquiring where Amherst was, and asking him to forward the message. Precious hours must be lost meanwhile—but, after all, they were waiting for no one upstairs.

The verdict had been pronounced: dislocation and fracture of the fourth vertebra, with consequent injury to the spinal cord. Dr. Garford and Wyant came out alone to tell her. The surgeon ran over the technical details, her brain instantly at attention as he developed his diagnosis and issued his orders. She asked no questions as to the future—she knew it was impossible to tell. But there were no immediate signs of a fatal ending: the patient had rallied well, and the general conditions were not unfavourable.

"You have heard from Mr. Amherst?" Dr. Garford concluded.

"Not yet. . . he may be travelling," Justine faltered, unwilling to say that her telegram had been returned. As she spoke there was a tap on the door, and a folded paper was handed in—a telegram telephoned from the village.

"Amherst gone South America to study possibilities cotton growing have cabled our correspondent Buenos Ayres."

Concealment was no longer possible. Justine handed the message to the surgeon.

"Ah—and there would be no chance of finding his address among Mrs. Amherst's papers?"

"I think not—no."

"Well—we must keep her alive, Wyant."

"Yes, sir."

At dusk, Justine sat in the library, waiting for Cicely to be brought to her. A lull had descended on the house—a new order developed out of the morning's chaos. With soundless steps, with lowered voices, the machinery of life was carried on. And Justine, caught in one of the pauses of inaction which she had fought off since morning, was reliving, for the hundredth time, her few moments at Bessy's bedside...

She had been summoned in the course of the afternoon, and stealing into the darkened room, had bent over the bed while the nurses noiselessly withdrew. There lay the white face which had been burnt into her inward vision—the motionless body, and the head stirring ceaselessly, as though to release the agitation of the imprisoned limbs. Bessy's eyes turned to her, drawing her down.

"Am I going to die, Justine?"

"No."

"The pain is... so awful..."

"It will pass... you will sleep..."

"Cicely——"

"She has gone for a walk. You'll see her presently."

The eyes faded, releasing Justine. She stole away, and the nurses came back.

Bessy had spoken of Cicely—but not a word of her husband! Perhaps her poor dazed mind groped for him, or perhaps it shrank from his name... Justine was thankful for her silence. For the moment her heart was bitter against Amherst. Why, so soon after her appeal and his answer, had he been false to the spirit of their agreement? This unannounced, unexplained departure was nothing less than a breach of his tacit pledge—the pledge not to break definitely with Lynbrook. And why had he gone to South America? She drew her aching brows together, trying to retrace a vague memory of some allusion to the cotton-growing capabilities of the region... Yes, he had spoken of it once in talking of the world's area of cotton production. But what impulse had sent him off on such an exploration? Mere unrest, perhaps—the intolerable burden of his useless life? The questions spun round and round in her head, weary, profitless, yet persistent...

It was a relief when Cicely came—a relief to measure out the cambric tea, to make the terrier beg for gingerbread, even to take up the thread of the interrupted fairy-tale—though through it all she was wrung by the thought that, just twenty-four hours earlier, she and the child had sat in the same place, listening for the trot of Bessy's horse...

The day passed: the hands of the clocks moved, food was cooked and served, blinds were drawn up or down, lamps lit and fires renewed... all these tokens of the passage of time took place before her, while her real consciousness seemed to hang in some dim central void, where nothing happened, nothing would ever happen...

And now Cicely was in bed, the last "long-distance" call was answered, the last orders to kitchen and stable had been despatched, Wyant had stolen down to her with his hourly report—"no change"—and she was waiting in the library for the Gaineses.

Carriage-wheels on the gravel: they were there at last. Justine started up and went into the hall. As she passed out of the library the outer door opened, and the gusty night swooped in—as, at the same hour the day before, it had swooped in ahead of the dreadful procession—preceding now the carriageful of Hanaford relations: Mr. Gaines, red-glazed, brief and interrogatory; Westy, small, nervous, ill at ease with his grief; and Mrs. Gaines, supreme in the possession of a consolatory yet funereal manner, and sinking on Justine's breast with the solemn whisper: "Have you sent for the clergyman?"

XXVII

THE house was empty again.

A week had passed since Bessy's accident, and friends and relations had dispersed. The household had fallen into its routine, the routine of sickness and silence, and once more the perfectly-adjusted machine was working on steadily, inexorably, like a natural law. . .

So at least it seemed to Justine's nerves, intolerably stretched, at times, on the rack of solitude, of suspense, of forebodings. She had been thankful when the Gaineses left—doubly thankful when a telegram from Bermuda declared Mrs. Carbury to be "in despair" at her inability to fly to Bessy's side—thankful even that Mr. Tredegar's professional engagements made it impossible for him to do more than come down, every second or third day, for a few hours; yet, though in some ways it was a relief to be again in sole command, there were moments when the weight of responsibility, and the inability to cry out her fears and her uncertainties, seemed almost unendurable.

Wyant was her chief reliance. He had risen so gallantly above his weakness, become again so completely the indefatigable worker of former days, that she accused herself of injustice in ascribing to physical causes the vague eye and tremulous hand which might merely have betokened a passing access of nervous sensibility. Now, at any rate, he had his nerves so well under control, and had shown such a grasp of the case, and such marked executive capacity, that on the third day after the accident Dr. Garford, withdrawing his own assistant, had left him in control at Lynbrook.

At the same time Justine had taken up her attendance in the sick-room, replacing one of the subordinate nurses who had been suddenly called away. She had done this the more willingly because Bessy, who was now conscious for the greater part of the time, had asked for her once or twice, and had seemed easier when she was in the room. But she still gave only occasional aid, relieving the other nurses when they dined or rested, but keeping herself partly free in order to have an eye on the household, and give a few hours daily to Cicely.

All this had become part of a system that already seemed as old as memory. She could hardly recall what life had been before the accident—the seven dreadful days seemed as long as the days of creation. Every morning she rose to the same report—"no change"—and every day passed without a word from Amherst. Minor news, of course, had come: poor Mr. Langhope, at length overtaken at Wady Halfa, was hastening back as fast as ship and rail could carry him; Mrs. Ansell, anchored at Algiers with her invalid, cabled anxious enquiries; but still no word from Amherst. The correspondent at Buenos Ayres had simply cabled "Not here. Will enquire"—and since then, silence.

Justine had taken to sitting in a small room beyond Amherst's bedroom, near enough to Bessy to be within call, yet accessible to the rest of the household. The walls were hung with old prints, and with two or three photographs of early Italian pictures; and in a low bookcase Amherst had put the books he had brought from Hanaford—the English poets, the Greek dramatists, some text-books of biology and kindred subjects, and a few stray well-worn volumes: Lecky's European Morals, Carlyle's translation of Wilhelm Meister, Seneca, Epictetus, a German grammar, a pocket Bacon.

It was unlike any other room at Lynbrook—even through her benumbing misery, Justine felt the relief of escaping there from the rest of the great soulless house. Sometimes she took up one of the books and read a page or two, letting the beat of the verse lull her throbbing brain, or the strong words of stoic wisdom sink into her heart. And even when there was no time for these brief flights from reality, it soothed her to feel herself in the presence of great thoughts—to know that in this room, among these books, another restless baffled mind had sought escape from the "dusty answer" of life. Her hours there made her think less bitterly of Amherst—but also, alas, made her see more clearly the irreconcilable difference between the two natures she had striven to reunite. That which was the essence of life to one was a meaningless shadow to the other; and the gulf between them was too wide for the imagination of either to bridge.

As she sat there on the seventh afternoon there was a knock on the door and Wyant entered. She had only time to notice that he was very pale—she had been struck once or twice with his look of sudden exhaustion, which passed as quickly as it came—then she saw that he carried a telegram, and her mind flew back to its central anxiety. She grew pale herself as she read the message.

"He has been found—at Corrientes. It will take him at least a month to get here."

"A month—good God!"

"And it may take Mr. Langhope longer." Their eyes met. "It's too long——?" she asked.

"I don't know—I don't know." He shivered slightly, turning away into the window.

Justine sat down to dash off messages to Mr. Tredegar and the Gaineses: Amherst's return must be made known at once. When she glanced up, Wyant was standing near her. His air of intense weariness had passed, and he looked calm and ready for action.

"Shall I take these down?"

"No. Ring, please. I want to ask you a few questions."

The servant who answered the bell brought in a tea-tray, and Justine, having despatched the telegrams, seated herself and began to pour out her tea. Food had been repugnant to her during the first anguished unsettled days, but with the resumption of the nurse's systematic habits the nurse's punctual appetite returned. Every drop of energy must be husbanded now, and only sleep and nourishment could fill the empty cisterns.

She held out a cup to Wyant, but he drew back with a gesture of aversion.

"Thanks; I'm not hungry."

"You ought to eat more."

"No, no. I'm very well."

She lifted her head, revived by the warm draught. The mechanical act of nourishment performed, her mind leapt back to the prospect of Amherst's return. A whole month before he reached Lynbrook! He had instructed her where news might find him on the way. . . but a whole month to wait!

She looked at Wyant, and they read each other's thoughts.

"It's a long time," he said.

"Yes."

"But Garford can do wonders—and she's very strong."

Justine shuddered. Just so a skilled agent of the Inquisition might have spoken, calculating how much longer the power of suffering might be artificially preserved in a body broken on the wheel. . .

"How does she seem to you today?"

"The general conditions are about the same. The heart keeps up wonderfully, but there is a little more oppression of the diaphragm."

"Yes—her breathing is harder. Last night she suffered horribly at times."

"Oh—she'll suffer," Wyant murmured. "Of course the hypodermics can be increased."

"Just what did Dr. Garford say this morning?"

"He is astonished at her strength."

"But there's no hope?—I don't know why I ask!"

"Hope?" Wyant looked at her. "You mean of what's called recovery—of deferring death indefinitely?"

She nodded.

"How can Garford tell—or any one? We all know there have been cases where such injury to the cord has not caused death. This may be one of those cases; but the biggest man couldn't say now."

Justine hid her eyes. "What a fate!"

"Recovery? Yes. Keeping people alive in such cases is one of the refinements of cruelty that it was left for Christianity to invent."

"And yet—?"

"And yet—it's got to be! Science herself says so—not for the patient, of course; but for herself—for unborn generations, rather. Queer, isn't it? The two creeds are at one."

Justine murmured through her clasped hands: "I wish she were not so strong——"

"Yes; it's wonderful what those frail petted bodies can stand. The fight is going to be a hard one."

She rose with a shiver. "I must go to Cicely——"

The rector of Saint Anne's had called again. Justine, in obedience to Mrs. Gaines's suggestion, had summoned him from Clifton the day after the accident; but, supported by the surgeons and Wyant, she had resisted his admission to the sick-room. Bessy's religious practices had been purely mechanical: her faith had never been associated with the graver moments of her life, and the apparition of a clerical figure at her bedside would portend not consolation but calamity. Since it was all-important that her nervous strength should be sustained, and the gravity of the situation kept from her, Mrs. Gaines yielded to the medical commands, consoled by the ready acquiescence of the rector. But before she left she extracted a promise that he would call frequently at Lynbrook, and wait his opportunity to say an uplifting word to Mrs. Amherst.

The Reverend Ernest Lynde, who was a young man, with more zeal than experience, deemed it his duty to obey this injunction to the letter; but hitherto he had had to content himself with a talk with the housekeeper, or a brief word on the doorstep from Wyant. Today, however, he had asked somewhat insistently for Miss Brent; and Justine, who was free at the moment, felt that she could not refuse to go down. She had seen him only in the pulpit, when once or twice, in Bessy's absence, she had taken Cicely to church: he struck her as a grave young man, with a fine voice but halting speech. His sermons were earnest but ineffective.

As he rose to meet her, she felt that she should like him better out of church. His glance was clear and honest, and there was sweetness in his hesitating smile.

"I am sorry to seem persistent—but I heard you had news of Mr. Langhope, and I was anxious to know the particulars," he explained.

Justine replied that her message had overtaken Mr. Langhope at Wady Halfa, and that he hoped to reach Alexandria in time to catch a steamer to Brindisi at the end of the week.

"Not till then? So it will be almost three weeks—?"

"As nearly as I can calculate, a month."

The rector hesitated. "And Mr. Amherst?"

"He is coming back too."

"Ah, you have heard? I'm glad of that. He will be here soon?"

"No. He is in South America—at Buenos Ayres. There will be no steamer for some days, and he may not get here till after Mr. Langhope."

Mr. Lynde looked at her kindly, with grave eyes that proffered help. "This is terrible for you, Miss Brent."

"Yes," Justine answered simply.

"And Mrs. Amherst's condition——?"

"It is about the same."

"The doctors are hopeful?"

"They have not lost hope."

"She seems to keep her strength wonderfully."

"Yes, wonderfully."

Mr. Lynde paused, looking downward, and awkwardly turning his soft clerical hat in his large kind-looking hands. "One might almost see in it a dispensation—*we* should see one, Miss Brent."

"*We?*" She glanced up apologetically, not quite sure that her tired mind had followed his meaning.

"We, I mean, who believe . . . that not one sparrow falls to the ground. . ." He flushed, and went on in a more mundane tone: "I am glad you have the hope of Mr. Langhope's arrival to keep you up. Modern science—thank heaven!—can do such wonders in sustaining and prolonging life that, even if there is little chance of recovery, the faint spark may be nursed until. . ."

He paused again, conscious that the dusky-browed young woman, slenderly erect in her dark blue linen and nurse's cap, was examining him with an intentness which contrasted curiously with the absent-minded glance she had dropped on him in entering.

"In such cases," she said in a low tone, "there is practically no chance of recovery."

"So I understand."

"Even if there were, it would probably be death-in-life: complete paralysis of the lower body."

He shuddered. "A dreadful fate! She was so gay and active——"

"Yes—and the struggle with death, for the next few weeks, must involve incessant suffering. . . frightful suffering. . . perhaps vainly. . ."

"I feared so," he murmured, his kind face paling.

"Then why do you thank heaven that modern science has found such wonderful ways of prolonging life?"

He raised his head with a start and their eyes met. He saw that the nurse's face was pale and calm—almost judicial in its composure—and his self-possession returned to him.

"As a Christian," he answered, with his slow smile, "I can hardly do otherwise."

Justine continued to consider him thoughtfully. "The men of the older generation—clergymen, I mean," she went on in a low controlled voice, "would of course take that view—must take it. But the conditions are so changed—so many undreamed-of means of prolonging life—prolonging suffering—have been discovered and applied in the last few years, that I wondered. . . in my profession one often wonders. . ."

"I understand," he rejoined sympathetically, forgetting his youth and his inexperience in the simple desire to bring solace to a troubled mind. "I understand your feeling—but you need have no doubt. Human life is sacred, and the fact that, even in this materialistic age, science is continually struggling to preserve and prolong it, shows—very beautifully, I think—how all things work together to fulfill the divine will."

"Then you believe that the divine will delights in mere pain—mere meaningless animal suffering—for its own sake?"

"Surely not; but for the sake of the spiritual life that may be mysteriously wrung out of it."

Justine bent her puzzled brows on him. "I could understand that view of moral suffering—or even of physical pain moderate enough to leave the mind clear, and to call forth qualities of endurance and renunciation. But where the body has been crushed to a pulp, and the mind is no more than a machine for the registering of sense-impressions of physical anguish, of what use can such suffering be to its owner—or to the divine will?"

The young rector looked at her sadly, almost severely. "There, Miss Brent, we touch on inscrutable things, and human reason must leave the answer to faith."

Justine pondered. "So that—one may say—Christianity recognizes no exceptions—?"

"None—none," its authorized exponent pronounced emphatically.

"Then Christianity and science are agreed." She rose, and the young rector, with visible reluctance, stood up also.

"That, again, is one of the most striking evidences—" he began; and then, as the necessity of taking leave was forced upon him, he added appealingly: "I understand your uncertainties, your questionings, and I wish I could have made my point clearer——"

"Thank you; it is quite clear. The reasons, of course, are different; but the result is exactly the same."

She held out her hand, smiling sadly on him, and with a sudden return of youth and self-consciousness, he murmured shyly: "I feel for you"—the man in him yearning over her loneliness, though the pastor dared not press his help. . .

XXVIII

THAT evening, when Justine took her place at the bedside, and the other two nurses had gone down to supper, Bessy turned her head slightly, resting her eyes on her friend.

The rose-shaded lamp cast a tint of life on her face, and the dark circles of pain made her eyes look deeper and brighter. Justine was almost deceived by the delusive semblance of vitality, and a hope that was half anguish stirred in her. She sat down by the bed, clasping the hand on the sheet.

"You feel better tonight?"

"I breathe. . . better. . ." The words came brokenly, between long pauses, but without the hard agonized gasps of the previous night.

"That's a good sign." Justine paused, and then, letting her fingers glide once or twice over the back of Bessy's hand—"You know, dear, Mr. Amherst is coming," she leaned down to say.

Bessy's eyes moved again, slowly, inscrutably. She had never asked for her husband.

"Soon?" she whispered.

"He had started on a long journey—to out-of-the-way places—to study something about cotton growing—my message has just overtaken him," Justine explained.

Bessy lay still, her breast straining for breath. She remained so long without speaking that Justine began to think she was falling back into the somnolent state that intervened between her moments of complete consciousness. But at length she lifted her lids again, and her lips stirred.

"He will be. . . long. . . coming?"

"Some days."

"How. . . many?"

"We can't tell yet."

Silence again. Bessy's features seemed to shrink into a kind of waxen quietude—as though her face were seen under clear water, a long way down. And then, as she lay thus, without sound or movement, two tears forced themselves through her lashes and rolled down her cheeks.

Justine, bending close, wiped them away. "Bessy—"

The wet lashes were raised—an anguished look met her gaze.

"I—I can't bear it. . ."

"What, dear?"

"The pain. . . Shan't I die. . . before?"

"You may get well, Bessy."

Justine felt her hand quiver. "Walk again. . ?"

"Perhaps. . . not that."

"*This?* I can't bear it. . ." Her head drooped sideways, turning away toward the wall.

Justine, that night, kept her vigil with an aching heart. The news of Amherst's return had produced no sign of happiness in his wife—the tears had been forced from her merely by the dread of being kept alive during the long days of pain before he came. The medical explanation might have been that repeated crises of intense physical anguish, and the deep lassitude succeeding them, had so overlaid all other feelings, or at least so benumbed their expression, that it was impossible to conjecture how Bessy's little half-smothered spark of soul had really been affected by the news. But Justine did not believe in this argument. Her experience among the sick had convinced her, on the contrary, that the shafts of grief or joy will find a crack in the heaviest armour of physical pain, that the tiniest gleam of hope will light up depths of mental inanition, and somehow send a ray to the surface. . . It was true that Bessy had never known how to bear pain, and that her own sensations had always formed the centre of her universe—yet, for that very reason, if the thought of seeing Amherst had made her happier it would have lifted, at least momentarily, the weight of death from her body.

Justine, at first, had almost feared the contrary effect—feared that the moral depression might show itself in a lowering of physical resistance. But the body kept up its obstinate struggle against death, drawing strength from sources of vitality unsuspected in that frail envelope. The surgeon's report the next day was more favourable, and every day won from death pointed now to a faint chance of recovery.

Such at least was Wyant's view. Dr. Garford and the consulting surgeons had not yet declared themselves; but the young doctor, strung to the highest point of watchfulness, and constantly in attendance on the patient, was tending toward a hopeful prognosis. The growing conviction spurred him to fresh efforts; at Dr. Garford's request, he had temporarily handed over his Clifton practice to a young New York doctor in need of change, and having installed himself at Lynbrook he gave up his days and nights to Mrs. Amherst's case.

"If any one can save her, Wyant will," Dr. Garford had declared to Justine, when, on the tenth day after the accident, the surgeons held their third consultation. Dr. Garford reserved his own judgment. He had seen cases—they had all seen cases. . . but just at present the signs might point either way. . . Meanwhile Wyant's confidence was an invaluable asset toward the patient's chances of recovery. Hopefulness in the physician was almost as necessary as in the patient—contact with such faith had been known to work miracles.

Justine listened in silence, wishing that she too could hope. But whichever way the prognosis pointed, she felt only a dull despair. She believed no more than Dr. Garford in the chance of recovery—that conviction seemed to her a mirage of Wyant's imagination, of his boyish ambition to achieve the impossible—and every hopeful symptom pointed, in her mind, only to a longer period of useless suffering.

Her hours at Bessy's side deepened her revolt against the energy spent in the fight with death. Since Bessy had learned that her husband was returning she had never, by sign or word, reverted to the fact. Except for a gleam of tenderness, now and then, when Cicely was brought to her, she seemed to have sunk back into herself, as though her poor little flicker of consciousness were wholly centred in the contemplation of its pain. It was not that her mind was clouded—only that it was immersed, absorbed, in that dread mystery of disproportionate anguish which a capricious fate had laid on it. . . And what if she recovered, as they called it? If the flood-tide of pain should ebb, leaving her stranded, a helpless wreck on the desert shores of inactivity? What would life be to Bessy without movement? Thought would never set her blood flowing—motion, in her, could only take the form of the physical processes. Her love for Amherst was dead—even if it flickered into life again, it could but put the spark to smouldering discords and resentments; and would her one uncontaminated sentiment—her affection for Cicely—suffice to reconcile her to the desolate half-life which was the utmost that science could hold out?

Here again, Justine's experience answered no. She did not believe in Bessy's powers of moral recuperation—her body seemed less near death than her spirit. Life had been poured out to her in generous measure, and she had spilled the precious draught—the few drops remaining in the cup could no longer renew her strength.

Pity, not condemnation—profound illimitable pity—flowed from this conclusion of Justine's. To a compassionate heart there could be no sadder instance of the wastefulness of life than this struggle of the small half-formed soul with a destiny too heavy for its strength. If Bessy had had any moral hope to fight for, every pang of suffering would have been worth enduring; but it was intolerable to witness the spectacle of her useless pain.

Incessant commerce with such thoughts made Justine, as the days passed, crave any escape from solitude, any contact with other ideas. Even the reappearance of Westy Gaines, bringing a breath of common-place conventional grief into the haunted silence of the house, was a respite from her questionings. If it was hard to talk to him, to answer his enquiries, to assent to his platitudes, it was harder, a thousand times, to go on talking to herself. . .

Mr. Tredegar's coming was a distinct relief. His dryness was like cautery to her wound. Mr. Tredegar undoubtedly grieved for Bessy; but his grief struck inward, exuding only now and then, through the fissures of his hard manner, in a touch of extra solemnity, the more laboured rounding of a period. Yet, on the whole, it was to his feeling that Justine felt her own to be most akin. If his stoic acceptance of the inevitable proceeded from the resolve to spare himself pain, that at least was a form of strength, an indication of character. She had never cared for the fluencies of invertebrate sentiment.

Now, on the evening of the day after her talk with Bessy, it was more than ever a solace to escape from the torment of her thoughts into the rarefied air of Mr. Tredegar's presence. The day had been a bad one for the patient, and Justine's distress had been increased by the receipt of a cable from Mr. Langhope, announcing that, owing to delay in reaching Brindisi, he had missed the fast steamer from Cherbourg, and would not arrive till four or five days later than he had expected. Mr. Tredegar, in response to her report, had announced his intention of coming down by a late train, and now he and Justine and Dr. Wyant, after dining together, were seated before the fire in the smoking-room.

"I take it, then," Mr. Tredegar said, turning to Wyant, "that the chances of her living to see her father are very slight."

The young doctor raised his head eagerly. "Not in my opinion, sir. Unless unforeseen complications arise, I can almost promise to keep her alive for another month—I'm not afraid to call it six weeks!"

"H'm—Garford doesn't say so."

"No; Dr. Garford argues from precedent."

"And you?" Mr. Tredegar's thin lips were visited by the ghost of a smile.

"Oh, I don't argue—I just feel my way," said Wyant imperturbably.

"And yet you don't hesitate to predict——"

"No, I don't, sir; because the case, as I see it, presents certain definite indications." He began to enumerate them, cleverly avoiding the use of technicalities and trying to make his point clear by the use of simple illustration and analogy. It sickened Justine to listen to his passionate exposition—she had heard it so often, she believed in it so little.

Mr. Tredegar turned a probing glance on him as he ended. "Then, today even, you believe not only in the possibility of prolonging life, but of ultimate recovery?"

Wyant hesitated. "I won't call it recovery—today. Say—life indefinitely prolonged."

"And the paralysis?"

"It might disappear—after a few months—or a few years."

"Such an outcome would be unusual?"

"Exceptional. But then there *are* exceptions. And I'm straining every nerve to make this one!"

"And the suffering—such as today's, for instance—is unavoidable?"

"Unhappily."

"And bound to increase?"

"Well—as the anæsthetics lose their effect. . ."

There was a tap on the door, and one of the nurses entered to report to Wyant. He went out with her, and Justine was left with Mr. Tredegar.

He turned to her thoughtfully. "That young fellow seems sure of himself. You believe in him?"

Justine hesitated. "Not in his expectation of recovery—no one does."

"But you think they can keep the poor child alive till Langhope and her husband get back?"

There was a moment's pause; then Justine murmured: "It can be done. . . I think. . ."

"Yes—it's horrible," said Mr. Tredegar suddenly, as if in answer to her thought.

She looked up in surprise, and saw his eye resting on her with what seemed like a mist of sympathy on its vitreous surface. Her lips trembled, parting as if for speech—but she looked away without answering.

"These new devices for keeping people alive," Mr. Tredegar continued; "they increase the suffering besides prolonging it?"

"Yes—in some cases."

"In this case?"

"I am afraid so."

The lawyer drew out his fine cambric handkerchief, and furtively wiped a slight dampness from his forehead. "I wish to God she had been killed!" he said.

Justine lifted her head again, with an answering exclamation. "Oh, yes!"

"It's infernal—the time they can make it last."

"It's useless!" Justine broke out.

"Useless?" He turned his critical glance on her. "Well, that's beside the point—since it's inevitable."

She wavered a moment—but his words had loosened the bonds about her heart, and she could not check herself so suddenly. "Why inevitable?"

Mr. Tredegar looked at her in surprise, as though wondering at so unprofessional an utterance from one who, under ordinary circumstances, showed the absolute self-control and submission of the well-disciplined nurse.

"Human life is sacred," he said sententiously.

"Ah, that must have been decreed by some one who had never suffered!" Justine exclaimed.

Mr. Tredegar smiled compassionately: he evidently knew how to make allowances for the fact that she was overwrought by the sight of her friend's suffering. "Society decreed it—not one person," he corrected.

"Society—science—religion!" she murmured, as if to herself.

"Precisely. It's the universal consensus—the result of the world's accumulated experience. Cruel in individual instances—necessary for the general welfare. Of course your training has taught you all this; but I can understand that at such a time. . ."

"Yes," she said, rising wearily as Wyant came in.

Her worst misery, now, was to have to discuss Bessy's condition with Wyant. To the young physician Bessy was no longer a suffering, agonizing creature: she was a case—a beautiful case. As the problem developed new intricacies, becoming more and more of a challenge to his faculties of observation and inference, Justine saw the abstract scientific passion supersede his personal feeling of pity. Though his professional skill made him exquisitely tender to the patient under his hands, he seemed hardly conscious that she was a woman who had befriended him, and whom he had so lately seen in the brightness of health and enjoyment. This view was normal enough—it was, as Justine knew, the ideal state of mind for the successful physician, in whom sympathy for the patient as an individual must often impede swift choice and unfaltering action. But what she shrank from was his resolve to save Bessy's life—a resolve fortified to the point of exasperation by the scepticism of the consulting surgeons, who saw in it only the youngster's natural desire to distinguish himself by performing a feat which his elders deemed impossible.

As the days dragged on, and Bessy's sufferings increased, Justine longed for a protesting word from Dr. Garford or one of his colleagues. In her hospital experience she had encountered cases where the useless agonies of death were mercifully shortened by the physician: why was not this a case for such treatment? The answer was simply enough—in the first place, it was the duty of the surgeons to keep their patient alive till her husband and her father could reach her; and secondly, there was that faint illusive hope of so-called recovery, in which none of them believed, yet which they could not ignore in their treatment. The evening after Mr. Tredegar's departure Wyant was setting this forth at great length to Justine. Bessy had had a bad morning: the bronchial symptoms which had developed a day or two before had greatly increased her distress, and there had been, at dawn, a moment of weakness when it seemed that some pitiful power was about to defeat the relentless efforts of science. But Wyant had fought off the peril. By the prompt and audacious use of stimulants—by a rapid marshalling of resources, a display of self-reliance and authority, which Justine could not but admire as she mechanically seconded his efforts—the spark of life had been revived, and Bessy won back for fresh suffering.

"Yes—I say it can be done: tonight I say it more than ever," Wyant exclaimed, pushing the disordered hair from his forehead, and leaning toward Justine across the table on which their brief evening meal had been served. "I say the way the heart has rallied proves that we've got more strength to draw on than any of them have been willing to admit. The breathing's better too. If we can fight off the degenerative processes—and, by George, I believe we can!" He looked up suddenly at Justine. "With you to work with, I believe I could do anything. How you do back a man up! You think with your hands—with every individual finger!"

Justine turned her eyes away: she felt a shudder of repulsion steal over her tired body. It was not that she detected any note of personal admiration in his praise—he had commended her as the surgeon might commend a fine instrument fashioned for his use. But that she should be the instrument to serve such a purpose—that her skill, her promptness, her gift of divining and interpreting the will she worked with, should be at the service of this implacable scientific passion! Ah, no—she could be silent no longer. . .

She looked up at Wyant, and their eyes met.

"Why do you do it?" she asked.

He stared, as if thinking that she referred to some special point in his treatment. "Do what?"

"It's so useless. . . you all know she must die."

"I know nothing of the kind. . . and even the others are not so sure today." He began to go over it all again—repeating his arguments, developing new theories, trying to force into her reluctant mind his own faith in the possibility of success.

Justine sat resting her chin on her clasped hands, her

eyes gazing straight before her under dark tormented brows. When he paused she remained silent.

"Well—don't you believe me?" he broke out with sudden asperity.

"I don't know. . . I can't tell. . ."

"But as long as there's a doubt, even—a doubt my way—and I'll show you there is, if you'll give me time——"

"How much time?" she murmured, without shifting her gaze.

"Ah—that depends on ourselves: on you and me chiefly. That's what Garford admits. *They* can't do much now—they've got to leave the game to us. It's a question of incessant vigilance. . . of utilizing every hour, every moment. . . Time's all I ask, and *you* can give it to me, if any one can!"

Under the challenge of his tone Justine rose to her feet with a low murmur of fear. "Ah, don't ask me!"

"Don't ask you——?"

"I can't—I can't."

Wyant stood up also, turning on her an astonished glance.

"You can't what—?"

Their eyes met, and she thought she read in his a sudden divination of her inmost thoughts. The discovery electrified her flagging strength, restoring her to immediate clearness of brain. She saw the gulf of self-betrayal over which she had hung, and the nearness of the peril nerved her to a last effort of dissimulation.

"I can't. . . talk of it. . . any longer," she faltered, letting her tears flow, and turning on him a face of pure womanly weakness.

Wyant looked at her without answering. Did he distrust even these plain physical evidences of exhaustion, or was he merely disappointed in her, as in one whom he had believed to be above the emotional failings of her sex?

"You're over-tired," he said coldly. "Take tonight to rest. Miss Mace can replace you for the next few hours—and I may need you more tomorrow."

XXIX

FOUR more days had passed. Bessy seldom spoke when Justine was with her. She was wrapped in a thickening cloud of opiates—morphia by day, bromides, sulphonal, chloral hydrate at night. When the cloud broke and consciousness emerged, it was centred in the one acute point of bodily anguish. Darting throes of neuralgia, agonized oppression of the breath, the diffused misery of the whole helpless body—these were reducing their victim to a mere instrument on which pain played its incessant deadly variations. Once or twice she turned her dull eyes on Justine, breathing out: "I want to die," as some inevitable lifting or re-adjusting thrilled her body with fresh pangs; but there were no signs of contact with the outer world—she had ceased even to ask for Cicely. . .

And yet, according to the doctors, the patient held her own. Certain alarming symptoms had diminished, and while others persisted, the strength to fight them persisted too. With such strength to call on, what fresh agonies were reserved for the poor body when the narcotics had lost their power?

That was the question always before Justine. She never again betrayed her fears to Wyant—she carried out his orders with morbid precision, trembling lest any failure in efficiency should revive his suspicions. She hardly knew what she feared his suspecting—she only had a confused sense that they were enemies, and that she was the weaker of the two.

And then the anæsthetics began to fail. It was the sixteenth day since the accident, and the resources of alleviation were almost exhausted. It was not sure, even now, that Bessy was going to die—and she was certainly going to suffer a long time. Wyant seemed hardly conscious of the increase of pain—his whole mind was fixed on the prognosis. What matter if the patient suffered, as long as he proved his case? That, of course, was not his way of putting it. In reality, he did all he could to allay the pain, surpassed himself in new devices and experiments. But death confronted him implacably, claiming his due: so many hours robbed from him, so much tribute to pay; and Wyant, setting his teeth, fought on—and Bessy paid.

Justine had begun to notice that it was hard for her to get a word alone with Dr. Garford. The other nurses were not in the way—it was Wyant who always contrived to be there. Perhaps she was unreasonable in seeing a special intention in his presence: it was natural enough that the two persons in charge of the case should confer together with their chief. But his persistence annoyed her, and she was glad when, one afternoon, the surgeon asked him to telephone an important message to town.

As soon as the door had closed, Justine said to Dr. Garford: "She is beginning to suffer terribly."

He answered with the large impersonal gesture of the man to whom physical suffering has become a painful general fact of life, no longer divisible into individual cases. "We are doing all we can."

"Yes." She paused, and then raised her eyes to his dry kind face. "Is there any hope?"

Another gesture—the fatalistic sweep of the lifted palms. "The next ten days will tell—the fight is on, as Wyant says. And if any one can do it, that young fellow can. There's stuff in him—and infernal ambition."

"Yes: but do *you* believe she can live—?"

Dr. Garford smiled indulgently on such unprofessional insistence; but she was past wondering what they must all think of her.

"My dear Miss Brent," he said, "I have reached the age when one always leaves a door open to the unexpected."

As he spoke, a slight sound at her back made her turn. Wyant was behind her—he must have entered as she put her question. And he certainly could not have had time to descend the stairs, walk the length of the house, ring up New York, and deliver Dr Garford's message. . . The same thought seemed to strike the surgeon. "Hello, Wyant?" he said.

"Line busy," said Wyant curtly.

About this time, Justine gave up her night vigils. She could no longer face the struggle of the dawn hour, when life ebbs lowest; and since her duties extended beyond the sick-room she could fairly plead that she was more needed about the house by day. But Wyant protested: he wanted her most at the difficult hour.

"You know you're taking a chance from her," he said, almost sternly.

"Oh, no——"

He looked at her searchingly. "You don't feel up to it?"

"No."

He turned away with a slight shrug; but she knew he resented her defection.

The day watches were miserable enough. It was the nineteenth day now; and Justine lay on the sofa in Amherst's sitting-room, trying to nerve herself for the nurse's summons. A page torn out of the calendar lay before her—she had been calculating again how many days must elapse before Mr. Langhope could arrive. Ten days—ten days and ten nights! And the length of the nights was double. . . As for Amherst, it was impossible to set a date for his coming, for his steamer from Buenos Ayres called at various ports on the way northward, and the length of her stay at each was dependent on the delivery of freight, and on the dilatoriness of the South American official.

She threw down the calendar and leaned back, pressing her hands to her temples. Oh, for a word with Amherst—he alone would have understood what she was undergoing! Mr. Langhope's coming would make no difference—or rather, it would only increase the difficulty of the situation. Instinctively Justine felt that, though his heart would be wrung by the sight of Bessy's pain, his cry would be the familiar one, the traditional one: *Keep her alive!* Under his surface originality, his verbal audacities and ironies, Mr. Langhope was the creature of accepted forms, inherited opinions: he had never really thought for himself on any of the pressing problems of life.

But Amherst was different. Close contact with many forms of wretchedness had freed him from the bondage of accepted opinion. He looked at life through no eyes but his own; and what he saw, he confessed to seeing. He never tried to evade the consequences of his discoveries.

Justine's remembrance flew back to their first meeting at Hanaford, when his confidence in his own powers was still unshaken, his trust in others unimpaired. And, gradually, she began to relive each detail of their talk at Dillon's bedside—her first impression of him, as he walked down the ward; the first sound of his voice; her surprised sense of his authority; her almost involuntary submission to his will. . . Then her thoughts passed on to their walk home from the hospital—she recalled his sober yet unsparing summary of the situation at Westmore, and the note of insight with which he touched on the hardships of the workers. . . Then, word by word, their talk about Dillon came back. . . Amherst's indignation and pity. . . his shudder of revolt at the man's doom.

"*In your work, don't you ever feel tempted to set a poor devil free?*" And then, after her conventional murmur of protest: "*To save what, when all the good of life is gone?*"

To distract her thoughts she stretched her hand toward the book-case, taking out the first volume in reach—the little copy of Bacon. She leaned back, fluttering its pages aimlessly—so wrapped in her own misery that the meaning of the words could not reach her. It was useless to try to read: every perception of the outer world was lost in the hum of inner activity that made her mind like a forge throbbing with heat and noise. But suddenly her glance fell on some pencilled sentences on the fly-leaf. They were in Amherst's hand, and the sight arrested her as though she had heard him speak.

La vraie morale se moque de la morale...

We perish because we follow other men's examples...

Socrates used to call the opinions of the many by the name of Lamiæ—bugbears to frighten children...

A rush of air seemed to have been let into her stifled mind. Were they his own thoughts? No—her memory recalled some confused association with great names. But at least they must represent his beliefs—must embody deeply-felt convictions—or he would scarcely have taken the trouble to record them.

She murmured over the last sentence once or twice: *The opinions of the many—bugbears to frighten children...* Yes, she had often heard him speak of current judgments in that way... she had never known a mind so free from the spell of the Lamiæ.

Some one knocked, and she put aside the book and rose to her feet. It was a maid bringing a note from Wyant.

"There has been a motor accident beyond Clifton, and I have been sent for. I think I can safely be away for two or three hours, but ring me up at Clifton if you want me. Miss Mace has instructions, and Garford's assistant will be down at seven."

She looked at the clock: it was just three, the hour at which she was to relieve Miss Mace. She smoothed the hair from her forehead, straightened her cap, tied on the apron she had laid aside...

As she entered Bessy's sitting-room the nurse came out, memoranda in hand. The two moved to the window for a moment's conference, and as the wintry light fell on Miss Mace's face, Justine saw that it was white with fatigue.

"You're ill!" she exclaimed.

The nurse shook her head. "No—but it's awful... this afternoon..." Her glance turned to the sick-room.

"Go and rest—I'll stay till bedtime," Justine said.

"Miss Safford's down with another headache."

"I know: it doesn't matter. I'm quite fresh."

"You *do* look rested!" the other exclaimed, her eyes lingering enviously on Justine's face.

She stole away, and Justine entered the room. It was true that she felt fresh—a new spring of hope had welled up in her. She had her nerves in hand again, she had regained her steady vision of life...

But in the room, as the nurse had said, it was awful. The time had come when the effect of the anæsthetics must be carefully husbanded, when long intervals of pain must purchase the diminishing moments of relief. Yet from Wyant's standpoint it was a good day—things were looking well, as he would have phrased it. And each day now was a fresh victory.

Justine went through her task mechanically. The glow of strength and courage remained, steeling her to bear what had broken down Miss Mace's professional fortitude. But when she sat down by the bed Bessy's moaning began to wear on her. It was no longer the utterance of human pain, but the monotonous whimper of an animal—the kind of sound that a compassionate hand would instinctively crush into silence. But her hand had other duties; she must keep watch on pulse and heart, must reinforce their action with the tremendous stimulants which Wyant was now using, and, having revived fresh sensibility to pain, must presently try to allay it by the cautious use of narcotics.

It was all simple enough—but suppose she should

not do it? Suppose she left the stimulants untouched? Wyant was absent, one nurse exhausted with fatigue, the other laid low by headache. Justine had the field to herself. For three hours at least no one was likely to cross the threshold of the sick-room... Ah, if no more time were needed! But there was too much life in Bessy—her youth was fighting too hard for her! She would not sink out of life in three hours... and Justine could not count on more than that.

She looked at the little travelling-clock on the dressing-table, and saw that its hands marked four. An hour had passed already... She rose and administered the prescribed restorative; then she took the pulse, and listened to the beat of the heart. Strong still—too strong!

As she lifted her head, the vague animal wailing ceased, and she heard her name: "Justine——"

She bent down eagerly. "Yes?"

No answer: the wailing had begun again. But the one word showed her that the mind still lived in its torture-house, that the poor powerless body before her was not yet a mere bundle of senseless reflexes, but her friend Bessy Amherst, dying, and feeling herself die...

Justine reseated herself, and the vigil began again. The second hour ebbed slowly—ah, no, it was flying now! Her eyes were on the hands of the clock and they seemed leagued against her to devour the precious minutes. And now she could see by certain spasmodic symptoms that another crisis of pain was approaching —one of the struggles that Wyant, at times, had almost seemed to court and exult in.

Bessy's eyes turned on her again. "*Justine*——"

She knew what that meant: it was an appeal for the hypodermic needle. The little instrument lay at hand, beside a newly-filled bottle of morphia. But she must wait—must let the pain grow more severe. Yet she could not turn her gaze from Bessy, and Bessy's eyes entreated her again—*Justine!* There was really no word now—the whimperings were uninterrupted. But Justine heard an inner voice, and its pleading shook her heart. She rose and filled the syringe—and returning with it, bent above the bed. . .

She lifted her head and looked at the clock. The second hour had passed. As she looked, she heard a step in the sitting-room. Who could it be? Not Dr. Garford's assistant—he was not due till seven. She listened again. . . One of the nurses? No, not a woman's step——

The door opened, and Wyant came in. Justine stood by the bed without moving toward him. He paused also, as if surprised to see her there motionless. In the intense silence she fancied for a moment that she heard Bessy's violent agonized breathing. She tried to speak, to drown the sound of the breathing; but her lips trembled too much, and she remained silent.

Wyant seemed to hear nothing. He stood so still that she felt she must move forward. As she did so, she picked up from the table by the bed the memoranda that it was her duty to submit to him.

"Well?" he said, in the familiar sick-room whisper.

"She is dead."

He fell back a step, glaring at her, white and incredulous.

"*Dead?*— When——?"

"A few minutes ago. . ."

"*Dead—?* It's not possible!"

He swept past her, shouldering her aside, pushing in an electric button as he sprang to the bed. She perceived then that the room had been almost in darkness. She recovered command of herself, and followed him. He was going through the usual rapid examination—pulse, heart, breath—hanging over the bed like some angry animal balked of its prey. Then he lifted the lids and bent close above the eyes.

"Take the shade off that lamp!" he commanded.

Justine obeyed him.

He stooped down again to examine the eyes. . . he remained stooping a long time. Suddenly he stood up and faced her.

"Had she been in great pain?"

"Yes."

"Worse than usual?"

"Yes."

"What had you done?"

"Nothing—there was no time."

"No time?" He broke off to sweep the room again with his excited incredulous glance. "Where are the others? Why were you here alone?" he demanded.

"It came suddenly. I was going to call——"

Their eyes met for a moment. Her face was perfectly calm—she could feel that her lips no longer trembled. She was not in the least afraid of Wyant's scrutiny.

As he continued to look at her, his expression slowly passed from incredulous wrath to something softer—more human—she could not tell what. . .

"This has been too much for you—go and send one of the others. . . It's all over," he said.

BOOK IV

XXX

ON a September day, somewhat more than a year and a half after Bessy Amherst's death, her husband and his mother sat at luncheon in the dining-room of the Westmore house at Hanaford.

The house was John Amherst's now, and shortly after the loss of his wife he had established himself there with his mother. By a will made some six months before her death, Bessy had divided her estate between her husband and daughter, placing Cicely's share in trust, and appointing Mr. Langhope and Amherst as her guardians. As the latter was also her trustee, the whole management of the estate devolved on him, while his control of the Westmore mills was ensured by his receiving a slightly larger proportion of the stock than his step-daughter.

The will had come as a surprise, not only to Amherst himself, but to his wife's family, and more especially to her legal adviser. Mr. Tredegar had in fact had nothing to do with the drawing of the instrument; but as it had been drawn in due form, and by a firm of excellent standing, he was obliged, in spite of his private views, and Mr. Langhope's open adjurations that he should "do something," to declare that there was no pretext for questioning the validity of the document.

To Amherst the will was something more than a proof of his wife's confidence: it came as a reconciling word from her grave. For the date showed that it had been made at a moment when he supposed himself to have lost all influence over her—on the morrow of the day when she had stipulated that he should give up the management of the Westmore mills, and yield the care of her property to Mr. Tredegar.

While she smote him with one hand, she sued for pardon with the other; and the contradiction was so characteristic, it explained and excused in so touching a way the inconsistencies of her impulsive heart and hesitating mind, that he was filled with that tender compunction, that searching sense of his own shortcomings, which generous natures feel when they find they have underrated the generosity of others. But Amherst's was not an introspective mind, and his sound moral sense told him, when the first pang of self-reproach had subsided, that he had done his best by his wife, and was in no way to blame if her recognition of the fact had come too late. The self-reproach subsided; and, instead of the bitterness of the past, it left a softened memory which made him take up his task with the sense that he was now working with Bessy and not against her.

Yet perhaps, after all, it was chiefly the work itself which had healed old wounds, and quelled the tendency to vain regrets. Amherst was only thirty-four; and in the prime of his energies the task he was made for had been given back to him. To a sound nature, which finds its outlet in fruitful action, nothing so simplifies the complexities of life, so tends to a large acceptance of its vicissitudes and mysteries, as the sense of doing something each day toward clearing one's own bit of the wilderness. And this was the joy at last conceded to Amherst. The mills were virtually his; and the fact that he ruled them not only in his own right but as Cicely's representative, made him doubly eager to justify his wife's trust in him.

Mrs. Amherst, looking up from a telegram which the parlour-maid had handed her, smiled across the table at her son.

"From Maria Ansell—they are all coming tomorrow."

"Ah—that's good," Amherst rejoined. "I should have been sorry if Cicely had not been here."

"Mr. Langhope is coming too," his mother continued. "I'm glad of that, John."

"Yes," Amherst again assented.

The morrow was to be a great day at Westmore.

The Emergency Hospital, planned in the first months of his marriage, and abandoned in the general reduction of expenditure at the mills, had now been completed on a larger and more elaborate scale, as a memorial to Bessy. The strict retrenchment of all personal expenses, and the leasing of Lynbrook and the town house, had enabled Amherst, in eighteen months, to lay by enough income to carry out this plan, which he was impatient to see executed as a visible commemoration of his wife's generosity to Westmore. For Amherst persisted in regarding the gift of her fortune as a gift not to himself but to the mills: he looked on himself merely as the agent of her beneficent intentions. He was anxious that Westmore and Hanaford should take the same view; and the opening of the Westmore Memorial Hospital was therefore to be performed with an unwonted degree of ceremony.

"I am glad Mr. Langhope is coming," Mrs. Amherst repeated, as they rose from the table. "It shows, dear—doesn't it?—that he's really gratified—that he appreciates your motive. . ."

She raised a proud glance to her tall son, whose head seemed to tower higher than ever above her small proportions. Renewed self-confidence, and the habit of command, had in fact restored the erectness to Amherst's shoulders and the clearness to his eyes. The cleft between the brows was gone, and his veiled inward gaze had given place to a glance almost as outward-looking and unspeculative as his mother's.

"It shows—well, yes—what you say!" he rejoined with a slight laugh, and a tap on her shoulder as she passed.

He was under no illusions as to his father-in-law's attitude: he knew that Mr. Langhope would willingly have broken the will which deprived his grand-daughter of half her inheritance, and that his subsequent show of friendliness was merely a concession to expediency. But in his present mood Amherst almost believed that time and closer relations might turn such sentiments into honest liking. He was very fond of his little step-daughter, and deeply sensible of his obligations toward her; and he hoped that, as Mr. Langhope came to recognize this, it might bring about a better understanding between them.

His mother detained him. "You're going back to the mills at once? I wanted to consult you about the rooms. Miss Brent had better be next to Cicely?"

"I suppose so—yes. I'll see you before I go." He nodded affectionately and passed on, his hands full of papers, into the Oriental smoking-room, now dedicated to the unexpected uses of an office and study.

Mrs. Amherst, as she turned away, found the parlour-maid in the act of opening the front door to the highly-tinted and well-dressed figure of Mrs. Harry Dressel.

"I'm so delighted to hear that you're expecting Justine," began Mrs. Dressel as the two ladies passed into the drawing-room.

"Ah, you've heard too?" Mrs. Amherst rejoined, enthroning her visitor in one of the monumental plush armchairs beneath the threatening weight of the Bay of Naples.

"I hadn't till this moment; in fact I flew in to ask for news, and on the door-step there was such a striking-looking young man enquiring for her, and I heard the parlour-maid say she was arriving tomorrow."

"A young man? Some one you didn't know?" Striking apparitions of the male sex were of infrequent occurrence at Hanaford, and Mrs. Amherst's unabated interest in the movement of life caused her to dwell on this statement.

"Oh, no—I'm sure he was a stranger. Extremely slight and pale, with remarkable eyes. He was so disappointed—he seemed sure of finding her."

"Well, no doubt he'll come back tomorrow.—You know we're expecting the whole party," added Mrs. Amherst, to whom the imparting of good news was always an irresistible temptation.

Mrs. Dressel's interest deepened at once. "Really? Mr. Langhope too?"

"Yes. It's a great pleasure to my son."

"It must be! I'm so glad. I suppose in a way it

will be rather sad for Mr. Langhope—seeing everything here so unchanged——"

Mrs. Amherst straightened herself a little. "I think he will prefer to find it so," she said, with a barely perceptible change of tone.

"Oh, I don't know. They were never very fond of this house."

There was an added note of authority in Mrs. Dressel's accent. In the last few months she had been to Europe and had had nervous prostration, and these incontestable evidences of growing prosperity could not always be kept out of her voice and bearing. At any rate, they justified her in thinking that her opinion on almost any subject within the range of human experience was a valuable addition to the sum-total of wisdom; and unabashed by the silence with which her comment was received, she continued her critical survey of the drawing-room.

"Dear Mrs. Amherst—you know I can't help saying what I think—and I've so often wondered why you don't do this room over. With these high ceilings you could do something lovely in Louis Seize."

A faint pink rose to Mrs. Amherst's cheeks. "I don't think my son would ever care to make any changes here," she said.

"Oh, I understand his feeling; but when he begins

to entertain—and you know poor Bessy always *hated* this furniture."

Mrs. Amherst smiled slightly. "Perhaps if he marries again—" she said, seizing at random on a pretext for changing the subject.

Mrs. Dressel dropped the hands with which she was absent-mindedly assuring herself of the continuance of unbroken relations between her hat and her hair.

"*Marries again?* Why—you don't mean—? He doesn't think of it?"

"Not in the least—I spoke figuratively," her hostess rejoined with a laugh.

"Oh, of course—I see. He really *couldn't* marry, could he? I mean, it would be so wrong to Cicely—under the circumstances."

Mrs. Amherst's black eye-brows gathered in a slight frown. She had already noticed, on the part of the Hanaford clan, a disposition to regard Amherst as imprisoned in the conditions of his trust, and committed to the obligation of handing on unimpaired to Cicely the fortune his wife's caprice had bestowed on him; and this open expression of the family view was singularly displeasing to her.

"I had not thought of it in that light—but it's really of no consequence how one looks at a thing that is not going to happen," she said carelessly.

"No—naturally; I see you were only joking. He's

so devoted to Cicely, isn't he?" Mrs. Dressel rejoined, with her bright obtuseness.

A step on the threshold announced Amherst's approach.

"I'm afraid I must be off, mother—" he began, halting in the doorway with the instinctive masculine recoil from the afternoon caller.

"Oh, Mr. Amherst, how d'you do? I suppose you're very busy about tomorrow? I just flew in to find out if Justine was really coming," Mrs. Dressel explained, a little fluttered by the effort of recalling what she had been saying when he entered.

"I believe my mother expects the whole party," Amherst replied, shaking hands with the false *bonhomie* of the man entrapped.

"How delightful! And it's so nice to think that Mr. Langhope's arrangement with Justine still works so well," Mrs. Dressel hastened on, nervously hoping that her volubility would smother any recollection of what he had chanced to overhear.

"Mr. Langhope is lucky in having persuaded Miss Brent to take charge of Cicely," Mrs. Amherst quietly interposed.

"Yes—and it was so lucky for Justine too! When she came back from Europe with us last autumn, I could see she simply hated the idea of taking up her nursing again."

Amherst's face darkened at the allusion, and his mother said hurriedly: "Ah, she was tired, poor child; but I'm only afraid that, after the summer's rest, she may want some more active occupation than looking after a little girl."

"Oh, I think not—she's so fond of Cicely. And of course it's everything to her to have a comfortable home."

Mrs. Amherst smiled. "At her age, it's not always everything."

Mrs. Dressel stared slightly. "Oh, Justine's twenty-seven, you know; she's not likely to marry now," she said, with the mild finality of the early-wedded.

She rose as she spoke, extending cordial hands of farewell. "You must be so busy preparing for the great day... if only it doesn't rain! . . No, *please*, Mr. Amherst! . . It's a mere step—I'm walking. . ."

That afternoon, as Amherst walked out toward Westmore for a survey of the final preparations, he found that, among the pleasant thoughts accompanying him, one of the pleasantest was the anticipation of seeing Justine Brent.

Among the little group who were to surround him on the morrow, she was the only one discerning enough to understand what the day meant to him, or with sufficient knowledge to judge of the use he had made of his great opportunity. Even now that the opportunity had come, and all obstacles were levelled, sympathy with his work was as much lacking as ever; and only Duplain, at length reinstated as manager, really understood and shared in his aims. But Justine Brent's sympathy was of a different kind from the manager's. If less logical, it was warmer, more penetrating—like some fine imponderable fluid, so subtle that it could always find a way through the clumsy processes of human intercourse. Amherst had thought very often of this quality in her during the weeks which followed his abrupt departure for Georgia; and in trying to define it he had said to himself that she felt with her brain.

And now, aside from the instinctive understanding between them, she was set apart in his thoughts by her association with his wife's last days. On his arrival from the south he had gathered on all sides evidences of her tender devotion to Bessy: even Mr. Tredegar's chary praise swelled the general commendation. From the surgeons he heard how her unwearied skill had helped them in their fruitless efforts; poor Cicely, awed by her loss, clung to her mother's friend with childish tenacity; and the young rector of Saint Anne's, shyly acquitting himself of his visit of condolence, dwelt chiefly on the consolatory thought of Miss Brent's presence at the death-bed.

The knowledge that Justine had been with his wife till the end had, in fact, done more than anything else to soften Amherst's regrets; and he had tried to express something of this in the course of his first talk with her. Justine had given him a clear and self-possessed report of the dreadful weeks at Lynbrook; but at his first allusion to her own part in them, she shrank into a state of distress which seemed to plead with him to refrain from even the tenderest touch on her feelings. It was a peculiarity of their friendship that silence and absence had always mysteriously fostered its growth; and he now felt that her reticence deepened the understanding between them as the freest confidences might not have done.

Soon afterward, an opportune attack of nervous prostration had sent Mrs. Harry Dressel abroad; and Justine was selected as her companion. They remained in Europe for six months; and on their return Amherst learned with pleasure that Mr. Langhope had asked Miss Brent to take charge of Cicely.

Mr. Langhope's sorrow for his daughter had been aggravated by futile wrath at her unaccountable will; and the mixed sentiment thus engendered had found expression in a jealous outpouring of affection toward Cicely. He took immediate possession of the child, and in the first stages of his affliction her companionship had been really consoling. But as time passed, and the pleasant habits of years reasserted themselves, her presence became, in small unacknowledged ways, a source of domestic irritation. Nursery hours disturbed the easy routine of his household; the elderly parlour-maid who had long ruled it resented the intervention of Cicely's nurse; the little governess, involved in the dispute, broke down and had to be shipped home to Germany; a successor was hard to find, and in the interval Mr. Langhope's privacy was invaded by a stream of visiting teachers, who were always wanting to consult him about Cicely's lessons, and lay before him their tiresome complaints and perplexities. Poor Mr. Langhope found himself in the position of the mourner who, in the first fervour of bereavement, has undertaken the construction of an imposing monument without having counted the cost. He had meant that his devotion to Cicely should be a monument to his paternal grief; but the foundations were scarcely laid when he found that the funds of time and patience were almost exhausted.

Pride forbade his consigning Cicely to her step-father, though Mrs. Amherst would gladly have undertaken her care; Mrs. Ansell's migratory habits made it impossible for her to do more than intermittently hover and advise; and a new hope rose before Mr. Langhope when it occurred to him to appeal to Miss Brent.

The experiment had proved a success, and when

Amherst met Justine again she had been for some months in charge of the little girl, and change and congenial occupation had restored her to a normal view of life. There was no trace in her now of the dumb misery which had haunted him at their parting; she was again the vivid creature who seemed more charged with life than any one he had ever known. The crisis through which she had passed showed itself only in a smoothing of the brow and deepening of the eyes, as though a bloom of experience had veiled without deadening the first brilliancy of youth.

As he lingered on the image thus evoked, he recalled Mrs. Dressel's words: "Justine is twenty-seven—she's not likely to marry now."

Oddly enough, he had never thought of her marrying—but now that he heard the possibility questioned, he felt a disagreeable conviction of its inevitableness. Mrs. Dressel's view was of course absurd. In spite of Justine's feminine graces, he had formerly felt in her a kind of elfin immaturity, as of a flitting Ariel with untouched heart and senses: it was only of late that she had developed the subtle quality which calls up thoughts of love. Not marry? Why, the vagrant fire had just lighted on her—and the fact that she was poor and unattached, with her own way to make, and no setting of pleasure and elegance to embellish her—these disadvantages seemed as nothing to Amherst against the warmth of personality in which she moved. And besides, she would never be drawn to the kind of man who needed fine clothes and luxury to point him to the charm of sex. She was always finished and graceful in appearance, with the pretty woman's art of wearing her few plain dresses as if they were many and varied; yet no one could think of her as attaching much importance to the upholstery of life. . . No, the man who won her would be of a different type, have other inducements to offer. . . and Amherst found himself wondering just what those inducements would be.

Suddenly he remembered something his mother had said as he left the house—something about a distinguished-looking young man who had called to ask for Miss Brent. Mrs. Amherst, innocently inquisitive in small matters, had followed her son into the hall to ask the parlour-maid if the gentleman had left his name; and the parlour-maid had answered in the negative. The young man was evidently not indigenous: all the social units of Hanaford were intimately known to each other. He was a stranger, therefore, presumably drawn there by the hope of seeing Miss Brent. But if he knew that she was coming he must be intimately acquainted with her movements. . . The thought came to Amherst as an unpleasant surprise. It showed him for the first time how little he knew of Justine's personal life, of the ties she might have formed outside the Lynbrook circle. After all, he had seen her chiefly not among her own friends but among his wife's. Was it reasonable to suppose that a creature of her keen individuality would be content to subsist on the fringe of other existences? Somewhere, of course, she must have a centre of her own, must be subject to influences of which he was wholly ignorant. And since her departure from Lynbrook he had known even less of her life. She had spent the previous winter with Mr. Langhope in New York, where Amherst had seen her only on his rare visits to Cicely; and Mr. Langhope, on going abroad for the summer, had established his grand-daughter in a Bar Harbour cottage, where, save for two flying visits from Mrs. Ansell, Miss Brent had reigned alone till his return in September.

Very likely, Amherst reflected, the mysterious visitor was a Bar Harbour acquaintance—no, more than an acquaintance: a friend. And as Mr. Langhope's party had left Mount Desert but three days previously, the arrival of the unknown at Hanaford showed a singular impatience to rejoin Miss Brent.

As he reached this point in his meditations, Amherst found himself at the street-corner where it was his habit to pick up the Westmore trolley. Just as it bore down on him, and he sprang to the platform, another car, coming in from the mills, stopped to discharge its passengers. Among them Amherst noticed a slender undersized man in shabby clothes, about whose retreating back, as he crossed the street to signal a Station Avenue car, there was something dimly familiar, and suggestive of troubled memories. Amherst leaned out and looked again: yes, the back was certainly like Dr. Wyant's—but what could Wyant be doing at Hanaford, and in a Westmore car?

Amherst's first impulse was to spring out and overtake him. He knew how admirably the young physician had borne himself at Lynbrook; he even recalled Dr. Garford's saying, with his kindly sceptical smile: "Poor Wyant believed to the end that we could save her"—and felt again his own inward movement of thankfulness that the cruel miracle had not been worked.

He owed a great deal to Wyant, and had tried to express his sense of the fact by warm words and a liberal fee; but since Bessy's death he had never returned to Lynbrook, and had consequently lost sight of the young doctor.

Now he felt that he ought to try to rejoin him, to find out why he was at Hanaford, and make some proffer of hospitality; but if the stranger were really Wyant, his choice of the Station Avenue car made it appear that he was on his way to catch the New York express; and in any case Amherst's engagements at Westmore made immediate pursuit impossible.

He consoled himself with the thought that if the physician was not leaving Hanaford he would be certain to call at the house; and then his mind flew back to Justine Brent. But the pleasure of looking forward to her arrival was disturbed by new feelings. A sense of reserve and embarrassment had sprung up in his mind, checking that free mental communion which, as he now perceived, had been one of the unconscious promoters of their friendship. It was as though his thoughts faced a stranger instead of the familiar presence which had so long dwelt in them; and he began to see that the feeling of intelligence existing between Justine and himself was not the result of actual intimacy, but merely of the charm she knew how to throw over casual intercourse.

When he had left his house, his mind was like a summer sky, all open blue and sunlit rolling clouds; but gradually the clouds had darkened and massed themselves, till they drew an impenetrable veil over the upper light and stretched threateningly across his whole horizon.

XXXI

THE celebrations at Westmore were over. Hanaford society, mustering for the event, had streamed through the hospital, inspected the clinic, complimented Amherst, recalled itself to Mr. Langhope and Mrs.

Ansell, and streamed out again to regain its carriages and motors.

The chief actors in the ceremony were also taking leave. Mr. Langhope, somewhat pale and nervous after the ordeal, had been helped into the Gaines landau with Mrs. Ansell and Cicely; Mrs. Amherst had accepted a seat in the Dressel victoria; and Westy Gaines, with an *empressement* slightly tinged by condescension, was in the act of placing his electric phaeton at Miss Brent's disposal.

She stood in the pretty white porch of the hospital, looking out across its squares of flower-edged turf at the long street of Westmore. In the warm gold-powdered light of September the factory town still seemed a blot on the face of nature; yet here and there, on all sides, Justine's eye saw signs of humanizing change. The rough banks along the street had been levelled and sodded; young maples, set in rows, already made a long festoon of gold against the dingy house-fronts; and the houses themselves—once so irreclaimably outlawed and degraded—showed, in their white-curtained windows, their flowery white-railed yards, a growing approach to civilized human dwellings.

Glancing the other way, one still met the grim pile of factories cutting the sky with their harsh roof-lines and blackened chimneys; but here also were signs of improvement. One of the mills had already been enlarged, another was scaffolded for the same purpose, and young trees and neatly-fenced turf replaced the surrounding desert of trampled earth.

As Amherst came out of the hospital, he heard Miss Brent declining a seat in Westy's phaeton.

"Thank you so much; but there's some one here I want to see first—one of the operatives—and I can easily take a Hanaford car." She held out her hand with the smile that ran like colour over her whole face; and Westy, nettled by this unaccountable disregard of her privileges, mounted his chariot alone.

As he glided mournfully away, Amherst turned to Justine. "You wanted to see the Dillons?" he asked.

Their eyes met, and she smiled again. He had never seen her so sunned-over, so luminous, since the distant November day when they had picnicked with Cicely beside the swamp. He wondered vaguely if she were more elaborately dressed than usual, or if the festal impression she produced were simply a reflection of her mood.

"I do want to see the Dillons—how did you guess?" she rejoined; and Amherst felt a sudden impulse to reply: "For the same reason that made you think of them."

The fact of her remembering the Dillons made him absurdly happy; it re-established between them the mental communion that had been checked by his thoughts of the previous day.

"I suppose I'm rather self-conscious about the Dillons, because they're one of my object lessons—they illustrate the text," he said laughing, as they went down the steps.

Westmore had been given a half-holiday for the opening of the hospital, and as Amherst and Justine turned into the street, parties of workers were dispersing toward their houses. They were still a dull-eyed stunted throng, to whom air and movement seemed to have been too long denied; but there was more animation in the groups, more light in individual faces; many of the younger men returned Amherst's good-day with a look of friendliness, and the women to whom he spoke met him with a volubility that showed the habit of frequent intercourse.

"How much you have done!" Justine exclaimed, as he rejoined her after one of these asides; but the next moment he saw a shade of embarrassment cross her face, as though she feared to have suggested comparisons she had meant to avoid.

He answered quite naturally: "Yes—I'm beginning to see my way now; and it's wonderful how they respond—" and they walked on without a shadow of constraint between them, while he described to her what was already done, and what direction his projected experiments were taking.

The Dillons had been placed in charge of one of the old factory tenements, now transformed into a lodging-house for unmarried operatives. Even its harsh brick exterior, hung with creepers and brightened by flower-borders, had taken on a friendly air; and indoors it had a clean sunny kitchen, a big dining-room with cheerful-coloured walls, and a room where the men could lounge and smoke about a table covered with papers.

The creation of these model lodging-houses had always been a favourite scheme of Amherst's, and the Dillons, incapacitated for factory work, had shown themselves admirably adapted to their new duties. In Mrs. Dillon's small hot sitting-room, among the starched sofa-tidies and pink shells that testified to the family prosperity, Justine shone with enjoyment and sympathy. She had always taken an interest in the lives and thoughts of working-people: not so much the constructive interest of the sociological mind as the vivid imaginative concern of a heart open to every human appeal. She liked to hear about their hard struggles and small pathetic successes: the children's sicknesses, the father's lucky job, the little sum they had been able to put by, the plans they had formed for Tommy's advancement, and how Sue's good marks at school were still ahead of Mrs. Hagan's Mary's.

"What I really like is to gossip with them, and give them advice about the baby's cough, and the cheapest way to do their marketing," she said laughing, as she and Amherst emerged once more into the street. "It's the same kind of interest I used to feel in my dolls and guinea pigs—a managing, interfering old maid's interest. I don't believe I should care a straw for them if I couldn't dose them and order them about."

Amherst laughed too: he recalled the time when he had dreamed that just such warm personal sympathy was her sex's destined contribution to the broad work of human beneficence. Well, it had not been a dream: here was a woman whose deeds spoke for her. And suddenly the thought came to him: what might they not do at Westmore together! The brightness of it was blinding—like the dazzle of sunlight which faced them as they walked toward the mills. But it left him speechless, confused—glad to have a pretext for routing Duplain out of the office, introducing him to Miss Brent, and asking him for the keys of the buildings. . .

It was wonderful, again, how she grasped what he was doing in the mills, and saw how his whole scheme hung together, harmonizing the work and leisure of the operatives, instead of treating them as half machine, half man, and neglecting the man for the machine. Nor was she content with Utopian generalities: she wanted to know the how and why of each case, to hear what conclusions he drew from his results, to what solutions his experiments pointed.

In explaining the mill work he forgot his constraint and returned to the free comradery of mind that had always marked their relation. He turned the key reluctantly in the last door, and paused a moment on the threshold.

"Anything more?" he said, with a laugh meant to hide his desire to prolong their tour.

She glanced up at the sun, which still swung free of the tall factory roofs.

"As much as you've time for. Cicely doesn't need me this afternoon, and I can't tell when I shall see Westmore again."

Her words fell on him with a chill. His smile faded, and he looked away for a moment.

"But I hope Cicely will be here often," he said.

"Oh, I hope so too," she rejoined, with seeming unconsciousness of any connection between the wish and her previous words.

Amherst hesitated. He had meant to propose a visit to the old Eldorado building, which now at last housed the long-desired night-schools and nursery; but since she had spoken he felt a sudden indifference to showing her anything more. What was the use, if she meant to leave Cicely, and drift out of his reach? He could get on well enough without sympathy and comprehension, but his momentary indulgence in them made the ordinary taste of life a little flat.

"There must be more to see?" she continued, as they turned back toward the village; and he answered absently: "Oh, yes—if you like."

He heard the change in his own voice, and knew by her quick side-glance that she had heard it too.

"Please let me see everything that is compatible with my getting a car to Hanaford by six."

"Well, then—the night-school next," he said with an effort at lightness; and to shake off the importunity of his own thoughts he added carelessly, as they walked on: "By the way—it seems improbable—but I think I saw Dr. Wyant yesterday in a Westmore car."

She echoed the name in surprise. "Dr. Wyant? Really! Are you sure?"

"Not quite; but if it wasn't he it was his ghost. You haven't heard of his being at Hanaford?"

"No. I've heard nothing of him for ages."

Something in her tone made him return her side-glance; but her voice, on closer analysis, denoted only indifference, and her profile seemed to express the same negative sentiment. He remembered a vague Lynbrook rumour to the effect that the young doctor had been attracted to Miss Brent. Such floating seeds of gossip seldom rooted themselves in his mind, but now the fact acquired a new significance, and he wondered how he could have thought so little of it at the time. Probably her somewhat exaggerated air of indifference simply meant that she had been bored by Wyant's attentions, and that the reminder of them still roused a slight self-consciousness.

Amherst was relieved by this conclusion, and murmuring: "Oh, I suppose it can't have been he," led her rapidly on to the Eldorado. But the old sense of free communion was again obstructed, and her interest in the details of the schools and nursery now seemed to him only a part of her wonderful art of absorbing herself in other people's affairs. He was a fool to have been duped by it—to have fancied it was anything more personal than a grace of manner.

As she turned away from inspecting the blackboards in one of the empty school-rooms he paused before her and said suddenly: "You spoke of not seeing Westmore again. Are you thinking of leaving Cicely?"

The words were almost the opposite of those he had intended to speak; it was as if some irrepressible inner conviction flung defiance at his surface distrust of her.

She stood still also, and he saw a thought move across her face. "Not immediately—but perhaps when Mr. Langhope can make some other arrangement——"

Owing to the half-holiday they had the school-building to themselves, and the fact of being alone with her, without fear of interruption, woke in Amherst an uncontrollable longing to taste for once the joy of unguarded utterance.

"Why do you go?" he asked, moving close to the platform on which she stood.

She hesitated, resting her hand on the teacher's desk. Her eyes were kind, but he thought her tone was cold.

"This easy life is rather out of my line," she said at length, with a smile that draped her words in vagueness.

Amherst looked at her again—she seemed to be growing remote and inaccessible. "You mean that you don't want to stay?"

His tone was so abrupt that it called forth one of her rare blushes. "No—not that. I have been very happy with Cicely—but soon I shall have to be doing something else."

Why was she blushing? And what did her last phrase mean? "Something else—?" The blood hummed in his ears—he began to hope she would not answer too quickly.

She had sunk into the seat behind the desk, propping her elbows on its lid, and letting her interlaced hands support her chin. A little bunch of violets which had been thrust into the folds of her dress detached itself and fell to the floor.

"What I mean is," she said in a low voice, raising her eyes to Amherst's, "that I've had a great desire lately to get back to real work—my special work. . . I've been too idle for the last year—I want to do some hard nursing; I want to help people who are miserable."

She spoke earnestly, almost passionately, and as he listened his undefined fear was lifted. He had never before seen her in this mood, with brooding brows, and the darkness of the world's pain in her eyes. All her glow had faded—she was a dun thrush-like creature, clothed in semi-tints; yet she seemed much nearer than when her smile shot light on him.

He stood motionless, his eyes absently fixed on the bunch of violets at her feet. Suddenly he raised his head, and broke out with a boyish blush: "Could it have been Wyant who was trying to see you?"

"Dr. Wyant—trying to see me?" She lowered her hands to the desk, and sat looking at him with open wonder.

He saw the irrelevance of his question, and burst, in spite of himself, into youthful laughter.

"I mean— It's only that an unknown visitor called at the house yesterday, and insisted that you must have arrived. He seemed so annoyed at not finding you, that I thought. . . I imagined. . . it must be some one who knew you very well. . . and who had followed you here. . . for some special reason. . ."

Her colour rose again, as if caught from his; but her eyes still declared her ignorance. "Some special reason——?"

"And just now," he blurted out, "when you said you might not stay much longer with Cicely—I thought of the visit—and wondered if there was some one you meant to marry. . ."

A silence fell between them. Justine rose slowly, her eyes screened under the veil she had lowered. "No—I don't mean to marry," she said, half-smiling, as she came down from the platform.

Restored to his level, her small shadowy head just in a line with his eyes, she seemed closer, more approachable and feminine—yet Amherst did not dare to speak.

She took a few steps toward the window, looking out into the deserted street. "It's growing dark—I must go home," she said.

"Yes," he assented absently as he followed her. He had no idea what she was saying. The inner voices in which they habitually spoke were growing louder than outward words. Or was it only the voice of his own desires that he heard—the cry of new hopes and unguessed capacities of living? All within him was flood-tide: this was the top of life, surely—to feel her alike in his brain and his pulses, to steep sight and hearing in the joy of her nearness, while all the while thought spoke clear: "This is the mate of my mind."

He began again abruptly. "Wouldn't you marry, if it gave you the chance to do what you say—if it offered you hard work, and the opportunity to make things better. . . for a great many people. . . as no one but yourself could do it?"

It was a strange way of putting his case: he was aware of it before he ended. But it had not occurred to him to tell her that she was lovely and desirable—in his humility he thought that what he had to give would plead for him better than what he was.

The effect produced on her by his question, though undecipherable, was extraordinary. She stiffened a little, remaining quite motionless, her eyes on the street.

"*You!*" she just breathed; and he saw that she was beginning to tremble.

His wooing had been harsh and clumsy—he was afraid it had offended her, and his hand trembled too as it sought hers.

"I only thought—it would be a dull business to most women—and I'm tied to it for life. . . but I thought . . . I've seen so often how you pity suffering. . . how you long to relieve it. . ."

She turned away from him with a shuddering sigh. "Oh, I *hate* suffering!" she broke out, raising her hands to her face.

Amherst was frightened. How senseless of him to go on reiterating the old plea! He ought to have pleaded for himself—to have let the man in him seek her and take his defeat, instead of beating about the flimsy bush of philanthropy.

"I only meant—I was trying to make my work recommend me. . ." he said with a half-laugh, as she remained silent, her eyes still turned away.

The silence continued for a long time—it stretched between them like a narrowing interminable road, down which, with a leaden heart, he seemed to watch her gradually disappearing. And then, unexpectedly, as she shrank to a tiny speck at the dip of the road, the perspective was mysteriously reversed, and he felt her growing nearer again, felt her close to him—felt her hand in his.

"I'm really just like other women, you know—I shall like it because it's your work," she said.

XXXII

EVERY one agreed that, on the whole, Mr. Langhope had behaved extremely well.

He was just beginning to regain his equanimity in the matter of the will—to perceive that, in the eyes of the public, something important and distinguished was being done at Westmore, and that the venture, while reducing Cicely's income during her minority, might, in some incredible way, actually make for its ultimate increase. So much Mr. Langhope, always eager to take the easiest view of the inevitable, had begun to let fall in his confidential comments on Amherst; when his newly-regained balance was rudely shaken by the news of his son-in-law's marriage.

The free expression of his anger was baffled by the fact that, even by the farthest stretch of self-extenuating logic, he could find no one to blame for the event but himself.

"Why on earth don't you say so—don't you call me a triple-dyed fool for bringing them together?" he challenged Mrs. Ansell, as they had the matter out together in the small intimate drawing-room of her New York apartment.

Mrs. Ansell, stirring her tea with a pensive hand, met the challenge composedly.

"At present you're doing it for me," she reminded him; "and after all, I'm not so disposed to agree with you."

"Not agree with me? But you told me not to engage Miss Brent! Didn't you tell me not to engage her?"

She made a hesitating motion of assent.

"But, good Lord, how was I to help myself? No man was ever in such a quandary!" he broke off, leaping back to the other side of the argument.

"No," she said, looking up at him suddenly. "I believe that, for the only time in your life, you were sorry then that you hadn't married me."

She held his eyes for a moment with a look of gentle malice; then he laughed, and drew forth his cigarette-case

"Oh, come—you've inverted the formula," he said, reaching out for the enamelled match-box at his elbow. She let the pleasantry pass with a slight smile, and he went on reverting to his grievance: "Why *didn't* you want me to engage Miss Brent?"

"Oh, I don't know. . . some instinct."

"You won't tell me?"

"I couldn't if I tried; and now, after all——"

"After all—what?"

She reflected. "You'll have Cicely off your mind, I mean."

"Cicely off my mind?" Mr. Langhope was beginning to find his charming friend less consolatory than usual. After all, the most magnanimous woman has her circuitous way of saying *I told you so*. "As if any good governess couldn't have done that for me!" he grumbled.

"Ah—the present care for her. But I was looking ahead," she rejoined.

"To what—if I may ask?"

"The next few years—when Mrs. Amherst may have children of her own."

"Children of her own?" He bounded up, furious at the suggestion.

"Had it never occurred to you?"

"Hardly as a source of consolation!"

"I think a philosophic mind might find it so."

"I should really be interested to know how!"

Mrs. Ansell put down her cup, and again turned her gentle tolerant eyes upon him.

"Mr. Amherst, as a father, will take a more conservative view of his duties. Every one agrees that, in spite of his theories, he has a good head for business; and whatever he does at Westmore for the advantage of his children will naturally be for Cicely's advantage too."

Mr. Langhope returned her gaze thoughtfully. "There's something in what you say," he admitted after a pause. "But it doesn't alter the fact that, with Amherst unmarried, the whole of the Westmore fortune would have gone back to Cicely—where it belongs."

"Possibly. But it was so unlikely that he would remain unmarried."

"I don't see why! A man of honour would have felt bound to keep the money for Cicely."

"But you must remember that, from Mr. Amherst's standpoint, the money belongs rather to Westmore than to Cicely."

"He's no better than a socialist, then!"

"Well—supposing he isn't: the birth of a son and heir will cure that."

Mr. Langhope winced, but she persisted gently: "It's really safer for Cicely as it is—" and before the end of the conference he found himself confessing, half against his will: "Well, since he hadn't the decency to remain single, I'm thankful he hasn't inflicted a stranger on us; and I shall never forget what Miss Brent did for my poor Bessy. . ."

It was the view she had wished to bring him to, and the view which, in due course, with all his accustomed grace and adaptability, he presented to the searching gaze of a society profoundly moved by the incident of Amherst's marriage. "Of course, if Mr. Langhope approves—" society reluctantly murmured; and that Mr. Langhope did approve was presently made manifest by every outward show of consideration toward the newly-wedded couple.

Amherst and Justine had been married in September; and after a holiday in Canada and the Adirondacks they returned to Hanaford for the winter. Amherst had proposed a short flight to Europe; but his wife preferred to settle down at once to her new duties.

The announcement of her marriage had been met by Mrs. Dressel with a comment which often afterward returned to her memory. "It's splendid for you, of course, dear, *in one way*," her friend had murmured, between disparagement and envy—"that is, if you can stand talking about the Westmore mill-hands all the rest of your life."

"Oh, but I couldn't—I should hate it!" Justine had

energetically rejoined; meeting Mrs. Dressel's admonitory "Well, then?" with the laughing assurance that *she* meant to lead the conversation.

She knew well enough what the admonition meant. To Amherst, so long thwarted in his chosen work, the subject of Westmore was becoming an *idée fixe;* and it was natural that Hanaford should class him as a man of one topic. But Justine had guessed at his other side; a side as long thwarted, and far less articulate, which she intended to wake into life. She had felt it in him from the first, though their talks had so uniformly turned on the subject which palled on Hanaford; and it had been revealed to her during the silent hours among his books, when she had grown into such close intimacy with his mind.

She did not, assuredly, mean to spend the rest of her days talking about the Westmore mill-hands; but in the arrogance of her joy she wished to begin her married life in the setting of its habitual duties, and to achieve the victory of evoking the secret unsuspected Amherst out of the preoccupied business man chained to his task. Dull lovers might have to call on romantic scenes to wake romantic feelings; but Justine's glancing imagination leapt to the challenge of extracting poetry from the prose of routine.

And this was precisely the triumph that the first months brought her. To mortal eye, Amherst and

Justine seemed to be living at Hanaford: in reality they were voyaging on unmapped seas of adventure. The seas were limitless, and studded with happy islands: every fresh discovery they made about each other, every new agreement of ideas and feelings, offered itself to these intrepid explorers as a friendly coast where they might beach their keel and take their bearings. Thus, in the thronging hum of metaphor, Justine sometimes pictured their relation; seeing it, again, as a journey through crowded populous cities, where every face she met was Amherst's; or, contrarily, as a multiplication of points of perception, so that one became, for the world's contact, a surface so multitudinously alive that the old myth of hearing the grass grow and walking the rainbow explained itself as the heightening of personality to the utmost pitch of sympathy.

In reality, the work at Westmore became an almost necessary sedative after these flights into the blue. She felt sometimes that they would have been bankrupted of sensations if daily hours of drudgery had not provided a reservoir in which fresh powers of enjoyment could slowly gather. And their duties had the rarer quality of constituting, precisely, the deepest, finest bond between them, the clarifying element which saved their happiness from stagnation, and kept it in the strong mid-current of human feeling.

It was this element in their affection which, in the last days of November, was unexpectedly put on trial. Mr. Langhope, since his return from his annual visit to Europe, showed signs of diminishing strength and elasticity. He had had to give up his nightly dinner parties, to desert his stall at the Opera: to take, in short, as he plaintively put it, his social pleasures homœopathically. Certain of his friends explained the change by saying that he had never been "quite the same" since his daughter's death; while others found its determining cause in the shock of Amherst's second marriage. But this insinuation Mr. Langhope in due time discredited by writing to ask the Amhersts if they would not pity his loneliness and spend the winter in town with him. The proposal came in a letter to Justine, which she handed to her husband one afternoon on his return from the mills.

She sat behind the tea-table in the Westmore drawing-room, now at last transformed, not into Mrs. Dressel's vision of "something lovely in Louis Seize," but into a warm yet sober setting for books, for scattered flowers, for deep chairs and shaded lamps in pleasant nearness to each other.

Amherst raised his eyes from the letter, thinking as he did so how well her bright head, with its flame-like play of meanings, fitted into the background she had made for it. Still unobservant of external details, he was begininng to feel a vague well-being of the eye wherever her touch had passed.

"Well, we must do it," he said simply.

"Oh, must we?" she murmured, holding out his cup.

He smiled at her note of dejection. "Unnatural woman! New York *versus* Hanaford—do you really dislike it so much?"

She tried to bring a tone of consent into her voice. "I shall be very glad to be with Cicely again—and that, of course," she reflected, "is the reason why Mr. Langhope wants us."

"Well—if it is, it's a good reason."

"Yes. But how much shall you be with us?"

"If you say so, I'll arrange to get away for a month or two."

"Oh, no: I don't want that!" she said, with a smile that triumphed a little. "But why should not Cicely come here?"

"If Mr. Langhope is cut off from his usual amusements, I'm afraid that would only make him more lonely."

"Yes, I suppose so." She put aside her untasted cup, resting her elbows on her knees, and her chin on her clasped hands, in the attitude habitual to her in moments of inward debate.

Amherst rose and seated himself on the sofa beside

her. "Dear! What is it?" he said, drawing her hands down, so that she had to turn her face to his.

"Nothing... I don't know... a superstition. I've been so happy here!"

"Is our happiness too perishable to be transplanted?"

She smiled and answered by another question. "You don't mind doing it, then?"

Amherst hesitated. "Shall I tell you? I feel that it's a sort of ring of Polycrates. It may buy off the jealous gods."

A faint shrinking from some importunate suggestion seemed to press her closer to him. "Then you feel they *are* jealous?" she breathed, in a half-laugh.

"I pity them if they're not!"

"Yes," she agreed, rallying to his tone. "I only had a fancy that they might overlook such a dull place as Hanaford."

Amherst drew her to him. "Isn't it, on the contrary, in the ash-heaps that the rag-pickers prowl?"

There was no disguising it: she was growing afraid of her happiness. Her husband's analogy of the ring expressed her fear. She seemed to herself to carry a blazing jewel on her breast—something that singled her out for human envy and divine pursuit. She had a preposterous longing to dress plainly and shabbily, to subdue her voice and gestures, to try to slip through life unnoticed; yet all the while she knew that her jewel would shoot its rays through every disguise. And from the depths of ancient atavistic instincts came the hope that Amherst was right—that by sacrificing their precious solitude to Mr. Langhope's convenience they might still deceive the gods.

Once pledged to her new task, Justine, as usual, espoused it with ardour. It was pleasant, even among greater joys, to see her husband again frankly welcomed by Mr. Langhope; to see Cicely bloom into happiness at their coming; and to overhear Mr. Langhope exclaim, in a confidential aside to his son-in-law: "It's wonderful, the *bien-être* that wife of yours diffuses about her!"

The element of *bien-être* was the only one in which Mr. Langhope could draw breath; and to those who kept him immersed in it he was prodigal of delicate attentions. The experiment, in short, was a complete success; and even Amherst's necessary weeks at Hanaford had the merit of giving a finer flavour to his brief appearances.

Of all this Justine was thinking as she drove down Fifth Avenue one January afternoon to meet her husband at the Grand Central station. She had tamed her happiness at last: the quality of fear had left it, and it nestled in her heart like some wild creature subdued to human ways. And, as her inward bliss became more and more a quiet habit of the mind, the longing to help and minister returned, absorbing her more deeply in her husband's work.

She dismissed the carriage at the station, and when his train had arrived they emerged together into the cold winter twilight and turned up Madison Avenue. These walks home from the station gave them a little more time to themselves than if they had driven; and there was always so much to tell on both sides. This time the news was all good: the work at Westmore was prospering, and on Justine's side there was a more cheerful report of Mr. Langhope's health, and—best of all—his promise to give them Cicely for the summer. Amherst and Justine were both anxious that the child should spend more time at Hanaford, that her young associations should begin to gather about Westmore; and Justine exulted in the fact that the suggestion had come from Mr. Langhope himself, while she and Amherst were still planning how to lead him up to it.

They reached the house while this triumph was still engaging them; and in the doorway Amherst turned to her with a smile.

"And of course—dear man!—he believes the idea is all his. There's nothing you can't make people believe, you little Jesuit!"

"I don't think there is!" she boasted, falling gaily

into his tone; and then, as the door opened, and she entered the hall, her eyes fell on a blotted envelope which lay among the letters on the table.

The parlour-maid proffered it with a word of explanation. "A gentleman left it for you, madam; he asked to see you, and said he'd call for the answer in a day or two."

"Another begging letter, I suppose," said Amherst, turning into the drawing-room, where Mr. Langhope and Cicely awaited them; and Justine, carelessly pushing the envelope into her muff, murmured "I suppose so" as she followed him.

XXXIII

OVER the tea-table Justine forgot the note in her muff; but when she went upstairs to dress it fell to the floor, and she picked it up and laid it on her dressing-table.

She had already recognized the hand as Wyant's, for it was not the first letter she had received from him.

Three times since her marriage he had appealed to her for help, excusing himself on the plea of difficulties and ill-health. The first time he wrote, he alluded vaguely to having married, and to being compelled, through illness, to give up his practice at Clifton. On receiving this letter she made enquiries, and learned that, a month or two after her departure from Lynbrook, Wyant had married a Clifton girl—a pretty piece of flaunting innocence, whom she remembered about the lanes, generally with a young man in a buggy. There had evidently been something obscure and precipitate about the marriage, which was a strange one for the ambitious young doctor. Justine conjectured that it might have been the cause of his leaving Cilfton—or perhaps he had already succumbed to the fatal habit she had suspected in him. At any rate he seemed, in some mysterious way, to have dropped in two years from promise to failure; yet she could not believe that, with his talents, and the name he had begun to make, such a lapse could be more than temporary. She had often heard Dr. Garford prophesy great things for him; but Dr. Garford had died suddenly during the previous summer, and the loss of this powerful friend was mentioned by Wyant among his misfortunes.

Justine was anxious to help him, but her marriage to a rich man had not given her the command of much money. She and Amherst, choosing to regard themselves as pensioners on the Westmore fortune, were scrupulous in restricting their personal expenditure; and her work among the mill-hands brought many demands on the modest allowance which her husband had insisted on her accepting. In reply to Wyant's first appeal, which reached her soon after her marriage, she had sent him a hundred dollars; but when the second came, some two months later—with a fresh tale of ill-luck and ill-health—she had not been able to muster more than half the amount. Finally a third letter had arrived, a short time before their leaving for New York. It told the same story ot persistent misfortune, but on this occasion Wyant, instead of making a direct appeal for money, suggested that, through her hospital connections, she should help him to establish a New York practice. His tone was half-whining, half-peremptory, his once precise writing smeared and illegible; and these indications, combined with her former suspicions, convinced her that, for the moment, he was unfit for medical work. At any rate, she could not assume the responsibility of recommending him; and in answering she advised him to apply to some of the physicians he had worked with at Lynbrook, softening her refusal by the enclosure of a small sum of money. To this letter she received no answer. Wyant doubtless found the money insufficient, and resented her unwillingness to help him by the use of her influence; and she felt sure that the note before her contained a renewal of his former request.

An obscure reluctance made her begin to undress before opening it. She felt slightly tired and indolently happy, and she did not wish any jarring impression to break in on the sense of completeness which her husband's coming always put into her life. Her happiness was making her timid and luxurious: she was beginning to shrink from even trivial annoyances.

But when at length, in her dressing-gown, her loosened hair about her shoulders, she seated herself before the toilet-mirror, Wyant's note once more confronted her. It was absurd to put off reading it—if he asked for money again, she would simply confide the whole business to Amherst.

She had never spoken to her husband of her correspondence with Wyant. The mere fact that the latter had appealed to her, instead of addressing himself to Amherst, made her suspect that he had a weakness to hide, and counted on her professional discretion. But his continued importunities would certainly release her from any such supposed obligation; and she thought with relief of casting the weight of her difficulty on her husband's shoulders.

She opened the note and read.

"I did not acknowledge your last letter because I was ashamed to tell you that the money was not enough to be of any use. But I am past shame now. My wife was confined three weeks ago, and has been desperately ill ever since. She is in no state to move, but we shall be put out of these rooms unless I can get money or work at once. A word from you would have given me a start in New York—and I'd be willing to begin again as an interne or a doctor's assistant.

"I have never reminded you of what you owe me, and I should not do so now if I hadn't been to hell and back since I saw you. But I suppose you would rather have me remind you than apply to Mr. Amherst. You can tell me when to call for my answer."

Justine laid down the letter and looked up. Her eyes rested on her own reflection in the glass, and it frightened her. She sat motionless, with a thickly-beating heart, one hand clenched on the letter.

"*I suppose you would rather have me remind you than apply to Mr. Amherst.*"

That was what his importunity meant, then! She had been paying blackmail all this time... Somewhere, from the first, in an obscure fold of consciousness, she had felt the stir of an unnamed, unacknowledged fear; and now the fear raised its head and looked at her. Well! She would look back at it, then: look it straight in the malignant eye. What was it, after all, but a "bugbear to scare children"—the ghost of the opinion of the many? She had suspected from the first that Wyant knew of her having shortened the term of Bessy Amherst's sufferings—returning to the room when he did, it was almost impossible that he should not have guessed what had happened; and his silence had made her believe that he understood her motive and approved it. But, supposing she had been mistaken, she still had nothing to fear, since she had done nothing that her own conscience condemned. If the act were to do again she would do it—she had never known a moment's regret!

Suddenly she heard Amherst's step in the passage—heard him laughing and talking as he chased Cicely up the stairs to the nursery.

If she was not afraid, why had she never told Amherst?

Why, the answer to that was simple enough! She had not told him *because she was not afraid.* From the first she had retained sufficient detachment to view her act impartially, to find it completely justified by circumstances, and to decide that, since those circumstances could be but partly and indirectly known to her husband, she not only had the right to keep her own counsel, but was actually under a kind of obligation not to force on him the knowledge of a fact that he could not alter and could not completely judge. . . Was there any flaw in this line of reasoning? Did it not show a deliberate weighing of conditions, a perfect rectitude of intention? And, after all, she had had Amherst's virtual consent to her act! She knew his feelings on such matters—his independence of traditional judgments, his horror of inflicting needless pain—she was as sure of his intellectual assent as of her own.

She was even sure that, when she told him, he would appreciate her reasons for not telling him before. . .

For now of course he must know everything—this horrible letter made it inevitable. She regretted that she had decided, though for the best of reasons, not to speak to him of her own accord; for it was intolerable that he should think of any external pressure as having brought her to avowal. But no! he would not think that. The understanding between them was so complete that no deceptive array of circumstances could ever make her motives obscure to him. She let herself rest a moment in the thought. . .

Presently she heard him moving in the next room—he had come back to dress for dinner. She would go to him now, at once—she could not bear this weight on her mind the whole evening. She pushed back her chair, crumpling the letter in her hand; but as she did so, her eyes again fell on her reflection. She could not go to her husband with such a face! If she was not afraid, why did she look like that?

Well—she was afraid! It would be easier and simpler to admit it. She was afraid—afraid for the first time—afraid for her own happiness! She had had just eight months of happiness—it was horrible to think of losing it so soon. . . Losing it? But why should she lose it? The letter must have affected her brain. . . all her thoughts were in a blur of fear. . . Fear of what? Of the man who understood her as no one else understood her? The man to whose wisdom and mercy she trusted as the believer trusts in God? This was a kind of abominable nightmare—even Amherst's image had been distorted in her mind! The only way to clear her brain, to recover the normal sense of things, was to go to him now, at once, to feel his arms about her, to let his kiss dispel her fears... She rose with a long breath of relief.

She had to cross the length of the room to reach his door, and when she had gone half-way she heard him knock.

"May I come in?"

She was close to the fire-place, and a bright fire burned on the hearth.

"Come in!" she answered; and as she did so, she turned and dropped Wyant's letter into the fire. Her hand had crushed it into a little ball, and she saw the flames spring up and swallow it before her husband entered.

It was not that she had changed her mind—she still meant to tell him everything. But to hold the letter was like holding a venomous snake—she wanted to exterminate it, to forget that she had ever seen the blotted repulsive characters. And she could not bear to have Amherst's eyes rest on it, to have him know that any man had dared to write to her in that tone.

What vile meanings might not be read between Wyant's phrases? She had a right to tell the story in her own way—the true way. . .

As Amherst approached, in his evening clothes, the heavy locks smoothed from his forehead, a flower of Cicely's giving in his button-hole, she thought she had never seen him look so kind and handsome.

"Not dressed? Do you know that it's ten minutes to eight?" he said, coming up to her with a smile.

She roused herself, putting her hands to her hair. "Yes, I know—I forgot," she murmured, longing to feel his arms about her, but standing rooted to the ground, unable to move an inch nearer.

It was he who came close, drawing her lifted hands into his. "You look worried—I hope it was nothing troublesome that made you forget?"

The divine kindness in his voice, his eyes! Yes—it would be easy, quite easy, to tell him. . .

"No—yes—I was a little troubled. . ." she said, feeling the warmth of his touch flow through her hands reassuringly.

"Dear! What about?"

She drew a deep breath. "The letter——"

He looked puzzled. "What letter?"

"Downstairs. . . when we came in. . . it was not an ordinary begging-letter."

"No? What then?" he asked, his face clouding.

She noticed the change, and it frightened her. Was he angry? Was he going to be angry? But how absurd! He was only distressed at her distress.

"What then?" he repeated, more gently.

She looked up into his eyes for an instant. "It was a horrible letter——" she whispered, as she pressed her clasped hands against him.

His grasp tightened on her wrists, and again the stern look crossed his face. "Horrible? What do you mean?"

She had never seen him angry—but she felt suddenly that, to the guilty creature, his anger would be terrible. He would crush Wyant—she must be careful how she spoke.

"I didn't mean that—only painful. . ."

"Where is the letter? Let me see it."

"Oh, no" she exclaimed, shrinking away.

"Justine, what has happened? What ails you?"

On a blind impulse she had backed toward the hearth, propping her arms against the mantel-piece while she stole a secret glance at the embers. Nothing remained of it—no, nothing.

But suppose it was against herself that his anger turned? The idea was preposterous, yet she trembled at it. It was clear that she must say *something* at once—must somehow account for her agitation. But the sense that she was unnerved—no longer in control of her face, her voice—made her feel that she would tell her story badly if she told it now. . . Had she not the right to gain a respite, to choose her own hour? Weakness—weakness again! Every delay would only increase the phantom terror. Now, *now*—with her head on his breast!

She turned toward him and began to speak impulsively.

"I can't show you the letter, because it's not—not my secret——"

"Ah?" he murmured, perceptibly relieved.

"It's from some one—unlucky—whom I've known about. . ."

"And whose troubles have been troubling you? But can't we help?"

She shone on him through gleaming lashes. "Some one poor and ill—who needs money, I mean——" She tried to laugh away her tears. "And I haven't any! That's *my* trouble!"

"Foolish child! And to beg you are ashamed? And so you're letting your tears cool Mr. Langhope's soup?" He had her in his arms now, his kisses drying her cheek; and she turned her head so that their lips met in a long pressure.

"Will a hundred dollars do?" he asked with a smile as he released her.

A hundred dollars! No—she was almost sure they would not. But she tried to shape a murmur of gratitude. "Thank you—thank you! I hated to ask. . ."

"I'll write the cheque at once."

"No—no," she protested, "there's no hurry."

But he went back to his room, and she turned again to the toilet-table. Her face was painful to look at still—but a light was breaking through its fear. She felt the touch of a narcotic in her veins. How calm and peaceful the room was—and how delicious to think that her life would go on in it, safely and peacefully, in the old familiar way!

As she swept up her hair, passing the comb through it, and flinging it dexterously over her lifted wrist, she heard Amherst cross the floor behind her, and pause to lay something on her writing-table.

"Thank you," she murmured again, lowering her head as he passed.

When the door had closed on him she thrust the last pin into her hair, dashed some drops of Cologne on her face, and went over to the writing-table. As she picked up the cheque she saw it was for three hundred dollars.

XXXIV

ONCE or twice, in the days that followed, Justine found herself thinking that she had never known happiness before. The old state of secure well-being seemed now like a dreamless sleep; but this new bliss, on its sharp pinnacle ringed with fire—this thrilling conscious joy, daily and hourly snatched from fear —this was living, not sleeping!

Wyant acknowledged her gift with profuse, almost servile thanks. She had sent it without a word—saying to herself that pity for his situation made it possible to ignore his baseness. And the days went on as before. She was not conscious of any change, save in the heightened, almost artificial quality of her happiness, till one day in March, when Mr. Langhope announced that he was going for two or three weeks to a friend's shooting-box in the south. The anniversary of Bessy's death was approaching, and Justine knew that at that time he always absented himself.

"Supposing you and Amherst were to carry off Cicely till I come back? Perhaps you could persuade him to break away from work for once—or, if that's impossible, you could take her with you to Hanaford. She looks a little pale, and the change would be good for her."

This was a great concession on Mr. Langhope's part, and Justine saw the pleasure in her husband's face. It was the first time that his father-in-law had suggested Cicely's going to Hanaford.

"I'm afraid I can't break away just now, sir," Amherst said, "but it will be delightful for Justine if you'll give us Cicely while you're away."

"Take her by all means, my dear fellow: I always sleep on both ears when she's with your wife."

It was nearly three months since Justine had left Hanaford—and now she was to return there alone with her husband! There would be hours, of course, when the child's presence was between them—or when, again, his work would keep him at the mills. But in the evenings, when Cicely was in bed—when he and she sat alone together in the Westmore drawing-room—in Bessy's drawing-room! . . . No—she must find some excuse for remaining away till she had again grown used to the idea of being alone with Amherst. Every day she was growing a little more used to it; but it would take time—time, and the full assurance that Wyant was silenced. Till then she could not go back to Hanaford.

She found a pretext in her own health. She pleaded that she was a little tired, below par. . . and to return to Hanaford meant returning to hard work; with the best will in the world she could not be idle there. Might she not, she suggested, take Cicely to Tuxedo or Lakewood, and thus get quite away from household cares and good works? The pretext rang hollow—it was so unlike her! She saw Amherst's eyes rest anxiously on her as Mr. Langhope uttered his prompt assent. Certainly she did look tired—Mr. Langhope himself had noticed it. Had he perhaps over-taxed her energies, left the household too entirely on her shoulders? Oh, no—it was only the New York air. . .

like Cicely, she pined for a breath of the woods. . . And so, the day Mr. Langhope left, she and Cicely were packed off to Lakewood.

They stayed there a week: then a fit of restlessness drove Justine back to town. She found an excuse in the constant rain—it was really useless, as she wrote Mr. Langhope, to keep the child imprisoned in an over-heated hotel while they could get no benefit from the outdoor life. In reality, she found the long lonely hours unendurable. She pined for a sight of her husband, and thought of committing Cicely to Mrs. Ansell's care, and making a sudden dash for Hanaford. But the vision of the long evenings in the Westmore drawing-room again restrained her. No—she would simply go back to New York, dine out occasionally, go to a concert or two, trust to the usual demands of town life to crowd her hours with small activities. . . And in another week Mr. Langhope would be back and the days would resume their normal course.

On arriving, she looked feverishly through the letters in the hall. None from Wyant—that fear was allayed! Every day added to her reassurance. By this time, no doubt, he was on his feet again, and ashamed—unutterably ashamed—of the threat that despair had wrung from him. She felt almost sure that his shame would keep him from ever attempting to see her, or even from writing again.

"A gentleman called to see you yesterday, madam—he would give no name," the parlour-maid said. And there was the sick fear back on her again! She could hardly control the trembling of her lips as she asked: "Did he leave no message?"

"No, madam: he only wanted to know when you'd be back."

She longed to return: "And did you tell him?" but restrained herself, and passed into the drawing-room. After all, the parlour-maid had not described the caller—why jump to the conclusion that it was Wyant?

Three days passed, and no letter came—no sign. She struggled with the temptation to describe Wyant to the servants, and to forbid his admission. But it would not do. They were nearly all old servants, in whose eyes she was still the intruder, the upstart sick-nurse—she could not wholly trust them. And each day she felt a little easier, a little more convinced that the unknown visitor had not been Wyant.

On the fourth day she received a letter from Amherst. He hoped to be back on the morrow, but as his plans were still uncertain he would telegraph in the morning—and meanwhile she must keep well, and rest, and amuse herself. . .

Amuse herself! That evening, as it happened, she was going to the theatre with Mrs. Ansell. She and

Mrs. Ansell, though outwardly on perfect terms, had not greatly advanced in intimacy. The agitated, decentralized life of the older woman seemed futile and trivial to Justine; but on Mr. Langhope's account she wished to keep up an appearance of friendship with his friend, and the same motive doubtless inspired Mrs. Ansell. Just now, at any rate, Justine was grateful for her attentions, and glad to go about with her. Anything—anything to get away from her own thoughts! That was the pass she had come to.

At the theatre, in a proscenium box, the publicity, the light and movement, the action of the play, all helped to distract and quiet her. At such moments she grew ashamed of her fears. Why was she tormenting herself? If anything happened she had only to ask her husband for more money. She never spoke to him of her good works, and there would be nothing to excite suspicion in her asking help again for the friend whose secret she was pledged to keep... But nothing was going to happen. As the play progressed, and the stimulus of talk and laughter flowed through her veins, she felt a complete return of confidence. And then suddenly she glanced across the house, and saw Wyant looking at her.

He sat rather far back, in one of the side rows just beneath the balcony, so that his face was partly shaded. But even in the shadow it frightened her. She had been prepared for a change, but not for this ghastly deterioration. And he continued to look at her.

She began to be afraid that he would do something conspicuous—point at her, or stand up in his seat. She thought he looked half-mad—or was it her own hallucination that made him appear so? She and Mrs. Ansell were alone in the box for the moment, and she started up, pushing back her chair. . .

Mrs. Ansell leaned forward. "What is it?"

"Nothing—the heat—I'll sit back for a moment."

But as she withdrew into the back of the box, she was seized by a new fear. If he was still watching, might he not come to the door and try to speak to her? Her only safety lay in remaining in full view of the audience; and she returned to Mrs. Ansell's side.

The other members of the party came back—the bell rang, the foot-lights blazed, the curtain rose. She lost herself in the mazes of the play. She sat so motionless, her face so intently turned toward the stage, that the muscles at the back of her neck began to stiffen. And then, quite suddenly, toward the middle of the act, she felt an undefinable sense of relief. She could not tell what caused it—but slowly, cautiously, while the eyes of the others were intent upon the stage, she turned her head and looked toward Wyant's seat. It was empty.

Her first thought was that he had gone to wait for

her outside. But no—there were two more acts: why should he stand at the door for half the evening?

At last the act ended; the entr'acte elapsed; the play went on again—and still the seat was empty. Gradually she persuaded herself that she had been mistaken in thinking that the man who had occupied it was Wyant. Her self-command returned, she began to think and talk naturally, to follow the dialogue on the stage—and when the evening was over, and Mrs. Ansell set her down at her door, she had almost forgotten her fears.

The next morning she felt calmer than for many days. She was sure now that if Wyant had wished to speak to her he would have waited at the door of the theatre; and the recollection of his miserable face made apprehension yield to pity. She began to feel that she had treated him coldly, uncharitably. They had been friends once, as well as fellow-workers; but she had been false even to the comradeship of the hospital. She should have sought him out and given him sympathy as well as money; had she shown some sign of human kindness his last letter might never have been written.

In the course of the morning Amherst telegraphed that he hoped to settle his business in time to catch the two o'clock express, but that his plans were still uncertain. Justine and Cicely lunched alone, and after luncheon the little girl was despatched to her dancing-class. Justine herself meant to go out when the brougham returned. She went up to her room to dress, planning to drive in the park, and to drop in on Mrs. Ansell before she called for Cicely; but on the way downstairs she saw the servant opening the door to a visitor. It was too late to draw back; and descending the last steps she found herself face to face with Wyant.

They looked at each other a moment in silence; then Justine murmured a word of greeting and led the way to the drawing-room.

It was a snowy afternoon, and in the raw ash-coloured light she thought he looked more changed than at the theatre. She remarked, too, that his clothes were worn and untidy, his gloveless hands soiled and tremulous. None of the degrading signs of his infirmity were lacking; and she saw at once that, while in the early days of the habit he had probably mixed his drugs, so that the conflicting symptoms neutralized each other, he had now sunk into open morphia-taking. She felt profoundly sorry for him; yet as he followed her into the room physical repulsion again mastered the sense of pity.

But where action was possible she was always self-controlled, and she turned to him quietly as they seated themselves.

"I have been wishing to see you," she said, looking at him. "I have felt that I ought to have done so sooner—to have told you how sorry I am for your bad luck."

He returned her glance with surprise: they were evidently the last words he had expected.

"You're very kind," he said in a low embarrassed voice. He had kept on his shabby over-coat, and he twirled his hat in his hands as he spoke.

"I have felt," Justine continued, "that perhaps a talk with you might be of more use——"

He raised his head, fixing her with bright narrowed eyes. "I have felt so too: that's my reason for coming. You sent me a generous present some weeks ago—but I don't want to go on living on charity."

"I understand that," she answered. "But why have you had to do so? Won't you tell me just what has happened?"

She felt the words to be almost a mockery; yet she could not say "I read your history at a glance"; and she hoped that her question might draw out his wretched secret, and thus give her the chance to speak frankly.

He gave a nervous laugh. "Just what has happened? It's a long story—and some of the details are not particularly pretty." He broke off, moving his hat more rapidly through his trembling hands.

"Never mind: tell me."

"Well—after you all left Lynbrook I had rather a bad break-down—the strain of Mrs. Amherst's case, I suppose. You remember Bramble, the Clifton grocer? Miss Bramble nursed me—I daresay you remember her too. When I recovered I married her—and after that things didn't go well."

He paused, breathing quickly, and looking about the room with odd, furtive glances. "I was only half-well, anyhow—I couldn't attend to my patients properly—and after a few months we decided to leave Clifton, and I bought a practice in New Jersey. But my wife was ill there, and things went wrong again—damnably. I suppose you've guessed that my marriage was a mistake. She had an idea that we should do better in New York—so we came here a few months ago, and we've done decidedly worse."

Justine listened with a sense of discouragement. She saw now that he did not mean to acknowledge his failing, and knowing the secretiveness of the drug-taker she decided that he was deluded enough to think he could still deceive her.

"Well," he began again, with an attempt at jauntiness, "I've found out that in my profession it's a hard struggle to get on your feet again, after illness or—or any bad set-back. That's the reason I asked you to say a word for me. It's not only the money, though I need that badly—I want to get back my self-respect. With my record I oughtn't to be where I am—and you can speak for me better than any one."

"Why better than the doctors you've worked with?" Justine put the question abruptly, looking him straight in the eyes.

His glance dropped, and an unpleasant flush rose to his thin cheeks.

"Well—as it happens, you're better situated than any one to help me to the particular thing I want."

"The particular thing——?"

"Yes. I understand that Mr. Langhope and Mrs. Ansell are both interested in the new wing for paying patients at Saint Christopher's. I want the position of house-physician there, and I know you can get it for me."

His tone changed as he spoke, till with the last words it became rough and almost menacing.

Justine felt her colour rise, and her heart began to beat confusedly. Here was the truth, then: she could no longer be the dupe of her own compassion. The man knew his power and meant to use it. But at the thought her courage was in arms.

"I'm sorry—but it's impossible," she said.

"Impossible—why?"

She continued to look at him steadily. "You said just now that you wished to regain your self-respect.

Well, you must regain it before you can ask me—or any one else—to recommend you to a position of trust."

Wyant half-rose, with an angry murmur. "My self-respect? What do you mean? *I* meant that I'd lost courage—through ill-luck——"

"Yes; and your ill-luck has come through your own fault. Till you cure yourself you're not fit to cure others."

He sank back into his seat, glowering at her under sullen brows; then his expression gradually changed to half-sneering admiration. "You're a plucky one!" he said.

Justine repressed a movement of disgust. "I am very sorry for you," she said gravely. "I saw this trouble coming on you long ago—and if there is any other way in which I can help you——"

"Thanks," he returned, still sneering. "Your sympathy is very precious—there was a time when I would have given my soul for it. But that's over, and I'm here to talk business. You say you saw my trouble coming on—did it ever occur to you that you were the cause of it?"

Justine glanced at him with frank contempt. "No—for I was not," she replied.

"That's an easy way out of it. But you took everything from me—first my hope of marrying you; then my chance of a big success in my career; and I was desperate—weak, if you like—and tried to deaden my feelings in order to keep up my pluck."

Justine rose to her feet with a movement of impatience. "Every word you say proves how unfit you are to assume any responsibility—to do anything but try to recover your health. If I can help you to that, I am still willing to do so."

Wyant rose also, moving a step nearer. "Well, get me that place, then—I'll see to the rest: I'll keep straight."

"No—it's impossible."

"You won't?"

"I can't," she repeated firmly.

"And you expect to put me off with that answer?"

She hesitated. "Yes—if there's no other help you'll accept."

He laughed again—his feeble sneering laugh was disgusting. "Oh, I don't say that. I'd like to earn my living honestly—funny preference—but if you cut me off from that, I suppose it's only fair to let you make up for it. My wife and child have got to live."

"You choose a strange way of helping them; but I will do what I can if you will go for a while to some institution——"

He broke in furiously. "Institution be damned! You can't shuffle me out of the way like that. I'm all right—good food is what I need. You think I've got morphia in me—why, it's hunger!"

Justine heard him with a renewal of pity. "Oh, I'm sorry for you—very sorry! Why do you try to deceive me?"

"Why do you deceive *me?* You know what I want and you know you've got to let me have it. If you won't give me a line to one of your friends at Saint Christopher's you'll have to give me another cheque—that's the size of it."

As they faced each other in silence Justine's pity gave way to a sudden hatred for the poor creature who stood shivering and sneering before her.

"You choose the wrong tone—and I think our talk has lasted long enough," she said, stretching her hand to the bell.

Wyant did not move. "Don't ring—unless you want me to write to your husband," he rejoined.

A sick feeling of helplessness overcame her; but she turned on him firmly. "I pardoned you once for that threat!"

"Yes—and you sent me some money the next day."

"I was mistaken enough to think that, in your distress, you had not realized what you wrote. But if you're a systematic blackmailer——"

"Gently—gently. Bad names don't frighten me—it's hunger and debt I'm afraid of."

Justine felt a last tremor of compassion. He was abominable—but he was pitiable too.

"I will really help you—I will see your wife and do what I can—but I can give you no money today."

"Why not?"

"Because I have none. I am not as rich as you think."

He smiled incredulously. "Give me a line to Mr. Langhope, then "

"No."

He sat down once more, leaning back with a weak assumption of ease. "Perhaps Mr. Amherst will think differently."

She whitened, but said steadily: "Mr. Amherst is away."

"Very well—I can write."

For the last five minutes Justine had foreseen this threat, and had tried to force her mind to face dispassionately the chances it involved. After all, why not let him write to Amherst? The very vileness of the deed must rouse an indignation which would be all in her favour, would inevitably dispose her husband to readier sympathy with the motive of her act, as contrasted with the base insinuations of her slanderer. It seemed impossible that Amherst should condemn her when his condemnation involved the fulfilling of Wyant's calculations: a reaction of scorn would throw him into unhesitating championship of her conduct. All this was so clear that, had she been advising any one else, her confidence in the course to be taken might have strengthened the feeblest will; but with the question lying between herself and Amherst—with the vision of those soiled hands literally laid on the spotless fabric of her happiness, judgment wavered, foresight was obscured—she felt tremulously unable to face the steps between exposure and vindication. Her final conclusion was that she must, at any rate, gain time: buy off Wyant till she had been able to tell her story in her own way, and at her own hour, and then defy him when he returned to the assault. The idea that whatever concession she made would be only provisional, helped to excuse the weakness of making it, and enabled her at last, without too painful a sense of falling below her own standards, to reply in a low voice: "If you'll go now, I will send you something next week."

But Wyant did not respond as readily as she had expected. He merely asked, without altering his insolently easy attitude: "How much? Unless it's a good deal, I prefer the letter."

Oh, why could she not cry out: "Leave the house at once—your vulgar threats are nothing to me"— Why could she not even say in her own heart: *I will tell my husband tonight?*

"You're afraid," said Wyant, as if answering her

thought. "What's the use of being afraid when you can make yourself comfortable so easily? You called me a systematic blackmailer—well, I'm not that yet. Give me a thousand and you'll see the last of me—on what used to be my honour."

Justine's heart sank. She had reached the point of being ready to appeal again to Amherst—but on what pretext could she ask for such a sum?

In a lifeless voice she said: "I could not possibly get more than one or two hundred."

Wyant scrutinized her a moment: her despair must have rung true to him. "Well, you must have something of your own—I saw your jewelry last night at the theatre," he said.

So it had been he—and he had sat there appraising her value like a murderer!

"Jewelry—?" she faltered.

"You had a thumping big sapphire—wasn't it?—with diamonds round it."

It was her only jewel—Amherst's marriage gift. She would have preferred a less valuable present, but his mother had persuaded her to accept it, saying that it was the bride's duty to adorn herself for the bridegroom.

"I will give you nothing—" she was about to exclaim; when suddenly her eyes fell on the clock. If Amherst had caught the two o'clock express he would be at the house within the hour; and the only thing that seemed of consequence now, was that he should not meet Wyant. Supposing she still found courage to refuse—there was no knowing how long the humiliating scene might be prolonged: and she must be rid of the creature at any cost. After all, she seldom wore the sapphire—months might pass without its absence being noted by Amherst's careless eye; and if Wyant should pawn it, she might somehow save money to buy it back before it was missed. She went through these calculations with feverish rapidity; then she turned again to Wyant.

"You won't come back—ever?"

"I swear I won't," he said.

He moved away toward the window, as if to spare her; and she turned and slowly left the room.

She never forgot the moments that followed. Once outside the door she was in such haste that she stumbled on the stairs, and had to pause on the landing to regain her breath. In her room she found one of the housemaids busy, and at first could think of no pretext for dismissing her. Then she bade the woman go down and send the brougham away, telling the coachman to call for Miss Cicely at six.

Left alone, she bolted the door, and as if with a thief's hand, opened her wardrobe, unlocked her jewel-box, and drew out the sapphire in its flat morocco case.

She restored the box to its place, the key to its ring—then she opened the case and looked at the sapphire. As she did so, a little tremor ran over her neck and throat, and closing her eyes she felt her husband's kiss, and the touch of his hands as he fastened on the jewel.

She unbolted the door, listened intently on the landing, and then went slowly down the stairs. None of the servants were in sight, yet as she reached the lower hall she was conscious that the air had grown suddenly colder, as though the outer door had just been opened. She paused, and listened again. There was a sound of talking in the drawing-room. Could it be that in her absence a visitor had been admitted? The possibility frightened her at first—then she welcomed it as an unexpected means of ridding herself of her tormentor.

She opened the drawing-room door, and saw her husband talking with Wyant.

XXXV

AMHERST, his back to the threshold, sat at a table writing: Wyant stood a few feet away, staring down at the fire.

Neither had heard the door open; and before they were aware of her entrance Justine had calculated that she must have been away for at least five minutes, and that in that space of time almost anything might have passed between them.

For a moment the power of connected thought left her; then her heart gave a bound of relief. She said to herself that Wyant had doubtless made some allusion to his situation, and that her husband, conscious only of a great debt of gratitude, had at once sat down to draw a cheque for him. The idea was so reassuring that it restored all her clearness of thought.

Wyant was the first to see her. He made an abrupt movement, and Amherst, rising, turned and put an envelope in his hand.

"There, my dear fellow——"

As he turned he caught sight of his wife.

"I caught the twelve o'clock train after all—you got my second wire?" he asked.

"No," she faltered, pressing her left hand, with the little case in it, close to the folds of her dress.

"I was afraid not. There was a bad storm at Hanaford, and they said there might be a delay."

At the same moment she found Wyant advancing with extended hand, and understood that he had concealed the fact of having already seen her. She accepted the cue, and shook his hand, murmuring: "How do you do?"

Amherst looked at her, perhaps struck by her manner. "You have not seen Dr. Wyant since Lynbrook?"

"No," she answered, thankful to have this pretext for her emotion.

"I have been telling him that he should not have left us so long without news—especially as he has been ill, and things have gone rather badly with him. But I hope we can help now. He has heard that Saint Christopher's is looking for a house-physician for the paying patients' wing, and as Mr. Langhope is away I have given him a line to Mrs. Ansell."

"Extremely kind of you," Wyant murmured, passing his hand over his forehead.

Justine stood silent. She wondered that her husband had not noticed that tremulous degraded hand. But he was always so blind to externals—and he had no medical experience to sharpen his perceptions.

Suddenly she felt impelled to speak "I am sorry Dr. Wyant has been—unfortunate. Of course you will want to do everything to help him; but would it not be better to wait till Mr. Langhope comes back?"

"Wyant thinks the delay might make him lose the place. It seems the board meets tomorrow. And Mrs. Ansell really knows much more about it. Isn't she the secretary of the ladies' committee?"

"I'm not sure—I believe so. But surely Mr. Langhope should be consulted."

She felt Wyant's face change: his eyes settled on her in a threatening stare.

Amherst looked at her also, and there was surprise in his glance. "I think I can answer for my father-in-law. He feels as strongly as I do how much we all owe to Dr. Wyant."

He seldom spoke of Mr. Langhope as his father-in-law, and the chance designation seemed to mark a closer tie between them, to exclude Justine from what was after all a family affair. For a moment she felt tempted to accept the suggestion, and let the responsibility fall where it would. But it would fall on Amherst—and that was intolerable.

"I think you ought to wait," she insisted.

An embarrassed silence settled on the three.

Wyant broke it by advancing toward Amherst. "I shall never forget your kindness," he said; "and I hope to prove to Mrs. Amherst that it's not misplaced."

The words were well chosen, and well spoken; Justine saw that they produced a good effect. Amherst grasped the physician's hand with a smile. "My dear fellow, I wish I could do more. Be sure to call on me again if you want help."

"Oh, you've put me on my feet," said Wyant gratefully.

He bowed slightly to Justine and turned to go; but as he reached the threshold she moved after him.

"Dr. Wyant—you must give back that letter."

He stopped short with a whitening face.

She felt Amherst's eyes on her again; and she said desperately, addressing him: "Dr. Wyant understands my reasons."

Her husband's glance turned abruptly to Wyant. "Do you?" he asked after a pause.

Wyant looked from one to the other. The moisture came out on his forehead, and he passed his hand over it again. "Yes," he said in a dry voice. "Mrs. Amherst wants me farther off—out of New York."

"Out of New York? What do you mean?"

Justine interposed hastily, before the answer could come. "It is because Dr. Wyant is not in condition—for such a place—just at present."

"But he assures me he is quite well."

There was another silence; and again Wyant broke in, this time with a slight laugh. "I can explain what Mrs. Amherst means; she intends to accuse me of the morphine habit. And I can explain her reason for doing so—she wants me out of the way."

Amherst turned on the speaker; and, as she had foreseen, his look was terrible. "You haven't explained that yet," he said.

"Well—I can." Wyant waited another moment. "I know too much about her," he declared.

There was a low exclamation from Justine, and Amherst strode toward Wyant. "You infernal blackguard!" he cried.

"Oh, gently——" Wyant muttered, flinching back from his outstretched arm.

"My wife's wish is sufficient. Give me back that letter."

Wyant straightened himself. "No, by God, I won't!" he retorted furiously. "I didn't ask you for it till you offered to help me; but I won't let it be taken back without a word, like a thief that you'd caught with your umbrella. If your wife won't explain I will. She's afraid I'll talk about what happened at Lynbrook."

Amherst's arm fell to his side. "At Lynbrook?"

Behind him there was a sound of inarticulate appeal—but he took no notice.

"Yes. It's she who used morphia—but not on herself. She gives it to other people. She gave an overdose to Mrs. Amherst."

Amherst looked at him confusedly. "An overdose?"

"Yes—purposely, I mean. And I came into the room at the wrong time. I can prove that Mrs. Amherst died of morphia-poisoning."

"John!" Justine gasped out, pressing between them.

Amherst gently put aside the hand with which she had caught his arm. "Wait a moment: this can't rest here. You can't want it to," he said to her in an undertone.

"Why do you care. . . for what he says. . . when I don't?" she breathed back with trembling lips.

"You can see I am not wanted here," Wyant threw in with a sneer.

Amherst remained silent for a brief space; then he turned his eyes once more to his wife.

Justine lifted her face: it looked small and spent, like an extinguished taper.

"It's true," she said.

"True?"

"I *did* give. . . an overdose. . . intentionally, when I knew there was no hope, and when the surgeons said she might go on suffering. She was very strong. . . and I couldn't bear it. . . you couldn't have borne it. . ."

There was another silence; then she went on in a stronger voice, looking straight at her husband: "And now will you send this man away?"

Amherst glanced at Wyant without moving. "Go," he said curtly.

Wyant, instead, moved a step nearer. "Just a minute, please. It's only fair to hear my side. Your wife says there was no hope; yet the day before she. . . gave the dose, Dr. Garford told her in my presence that Mrs. Amherst might live."

Again Amherst's eyes addressed themselves slowly to Justine; and she forced her lips to articulate an answer.

"Dr. Garford said. . . one could never tell. . . but

I know he didn't believe in the chance of recovery. . . no one did."

"Dr. Garford is dead," said Wyant grimly.

Amherst strode up to him again. "You scoundrel —leave the house!" he commanded.

But still Wyant sneeringly stood his ground. "Not till I've finished, I can't afford to let myself be kicked out like a dog because I happen to be in the way. Every doctor knows that in cases of spinal lesion recovery is becoming more and more frequent—if the patient survives the third week there's every reason to hope. Those are the facts as they would appear to any surgeon. If they're not true, why is Mrs. Amherst afraid of having them stated? Why has she been paying me for nearly a year to keep them quiet?"

"Oh——" Justine moaned.

"I never thought of talking till luck went against me. Then I asked her for help—and reminded her of certain things. After that she kept me supplied pretty regularly." He thrust his shaking hand into an inner pocket. "Here are her envelopes. . . Quebec. . . Montreal. . . Saranac. . . I know just where you went on your honeymoon. She had to write often, because the sums were small. Why did she do it, if she wasn't afraid? And why did she go upstairs just now to fetch me something? If you don't believe me, ask her what she's got in her hand."

Amherst did not heed this injunction. He stood motionless, gripping the back of a chair, as if his next gesture might be to lift and hurl it at the speaker.

"Ask her——" Wyant repeated.

Amherst turned his head slowly, and his dull gaze rested on his wife. His face looked years older—lips and eyes moved as heavily as an old man's.

As he looked at her, Justine came forward without speaking, and laid the little morocco case in his hand. He held it there a moment, as if hardly understanding her action—then he tossed it on the table at his elbow, and walked up to Wyant.

"You hound," he said—"now go!"

XXXVI

WHEN Wyant had left the room, and the house-door had closed on him, Amherst spoke to his wife.

"Come upstairs," he said.

Justine followed him, scarcely conscious where she went, but moving already with a lighter tread. Part of her weight of misery had been lifted with Wyant's going. She had suffered less from the fear of what her husband might think than from the shame of making her avowal in her defamer's presence. And her faith in Amherst's comprehension had begun to revive. He had dismissed Wyant with scorn and horror—did not that show that he was on her side already? And how many more arguments she had at her call! Her brain hummed with them as she followed him up the stairs.

In her bedroom he closed the door and stood motionless, the same heavy half-paralyzed look on his face. It frightened her and she went up to him.

"John!" she said timidly.

He put his hand to his head. "Wait a moment——" he returned; and she waited, her heart slowly sinking again.

The moment over, he seemed to recover his power of movement. He crossed the room and threw himself into the armchair near the hearth.

"Now tell me everything."

He sat thrown back, his eyes fixed on the fire, and the vertical lines between his brows forming a deep scar in his white face.

Justine moved nearer, and touched his arm beseechingly. "Won't you look at me?"

He turned his head slowly, as if with an effort, and his eyes rested reluctantly on hers.

"Oh, not like that!" she exclaimed.

He seemed to make a stronger effort at self-control. "Please don't heed me—but say what there is to say," he said in a level voice, his gaze on the fire.

She stood before him, her arms hanging down, her clasped fingers twisting restlessly.

"I don't know that there is much to say—beyond what I've told you."

There was a slight sound in Amherst's throat, like the ghost of a derisive laugh. After another interval he said: "I wish to hear exactly what happened."

She seated herself on the edge of a chair near by, bending forward, with hands interlocked and arms extended on her knees—every line reaching out to him, as though her whole slight body were an arrow winged with pleadings. It was a relief to speak at last, even face to face with the stony image that sat in her husband's place; and she told her story, detail by detail, omitting nothing, exaggerating nothing, speaking slowly, clearly, with precision, aware that the bare facts were her strongest argument.

Amherst, as he listened, shifted his position once, raising his hand so that it screened his face; and in that attitude he remained when she had ended.

As she waited for him to speak, Justine realized that her heart had been alive with tremulous hopes. All through her narrative she had counted on a murmur of perception, an exclamation of pity: she had felt sure of melting the stony image. But Amherst said no word.

At length he spoke, still without turning his head. "You have not told me why you kept this from me."

A sob formed in her throat, and she had to wait to steady her voice.

"No—that was my wrong—my weakness. When I did it I never thought of being afraid to tell you—I had talked it over with you in my own mind. . . so often . . . before. . ."

"Well?"

"Then—when you came back it was harder. . . though I was still sure you would approve me."

"Why harder?"

"Because at first—at Lynbrook—I *could not* tell it all over, in detail, as I have now. . . it was beyond human power. . . and without doing so, I couldn't make it all clear to you. . . and so should only have added to your pain. If you had been there you would have done as I did. . . I felt sure of that from the first. But coming afterward, you couldn't judge. . . no one who was not there could judge. . . and I wanted to spare you. . ."

"And afterward?"

She had shrunk in advance from this question, and she could not answer it at once. To gain time she echoed it. "Afterward?"

"Did it never occur to you, when we met later—when you first went to Mr. Langhope——"?

"To tell you then? No—because by that time I had come to see that I could never be quite sure of making you understand. No one who was not there at the time could know what it was to see her suffer."

"You thought it all over, then—decided definitely against telling me?"

"I did not have to think long. I felt I had done right —I still feel so—and I was sure you would feel so, if you were in the same circumstances."

There was another pause. Then Amherst said: "And last September—at Hanaford?"

It was the word for which she had waited—the word of her inmost fears. She felt the blood mount to her face.

"Did you see no difference—no special reason for telling me then?"

"Yes——" she faltered.

"Yet you said nothing."

"No."

Silence again. Her eyes strayed to the clock, and some dim association of ideas told her that Cicely would soon be coming in.

"Why did you say nothing?"

He lowered his hand and turned toward her as he spoke; and she looked up and faced him.

"Because I regarded the question as settled. I had decided it in my own mind months before, and had never regretted my decision. I should have thought it morbid. . . unnatural. . . to go over the whole subject again. . . to let it affect a situation that had come about . . . so much later. . . so unexpectedly."

"Did you never feel that, later, if I came to know—if others came to know—it might be difficult——?"

"No; for I didn't care for the others—and I believed that, whatever your own feelings were, you would know I had done what I thought right."

She spoke the words proudly, strongly, and for the first time the hard lines of his face relaxed, and a slight tremor crossed it.

"If you believed this, why have you been letting that cur blackmail you?"

"Because when he began I saw for the first time that what I had done might be turned against me by—by those who disliked our marriage. And I was afraid for my happiness. That was my weakness. . . it is what I am suffering for now."

"*Suffering!*" he echoed ironically, as though she had presumed to apply to herself a word of which he had the grim monopoly. He rose and took a few aimless steps; then he halted before her.

"That day—last month—when you asked me for money. . . was it. . . ?"

"Yes——" she said, her head sinking.

He laughed. "You couldn't tell me—but you could use my money to bribe that fellow to conspire with you!"

"I had none of my own."

"No—nor I either! You used *her* money.—God!" he groaned, turning away with clenched hands.

Justine had risen also, and she stood motionless, her hands clasped against her breast, in the drawn shrinking attitude of a fugitive overtaken by a blinding storm. He moved back to her with an appealing gesture.

"And you didn't see—it didn't occur to you—that your doing. . . as you did. . . was an obstacle—an insurmountable obstacle—to our ever. . . ?"

She cut him short with an indignant cry. "No! No! for it was *not*. How could it have anything to do with what. . . came after. . . with you or me? I did it only for Bessy—it concerned only Bessy!"

"Ah, don't name her!" broke from him harshly, and she drew back, cut to the heart.

There was another pause, during which he seemed to fall into a kind of dazed irresolution, his head on his breast, as though unconscious of her presence. Then he roused himself and went to the door.

As he passed her she sprang after him. "John—John! Is that all you have to say?"

"What more is there?"

"What more? Everything!—What right have you to turn from me as if I were a murderess? I did nothing but what your own reason, your own arguments, have justified a hundred times! I made a mistake in not telling you at once—but a mistake is not a crime. It can't be your real feeling that turns you from me—it must be the dread of what other people would think! But when have you cared for what other people thought? When have your own actions been governed by it?"

He moved another step without speaking, and she caught him by the arm. "No! you sha'n't go—not like that!—Wait!"

She turned and crossed the room. On the lower shelf of the little table by her bed a few books were ranged: she stooped and drew one hurriedly forth, opening it at the fly-leaf as she went back to Amherst.

"There—read that. The book was at Lynbrook—in your room—and I came across it by chance the very day. . ."

It was the little volume of Bacon which she was thrusting at him. He took it with a bewildered look, as if scarcely following what she said.

"Read it—read it!" she commanded; and mechanically he read out the words he had written.

"*La vraie morale se moque de la morale. . . We perish because we follow other men's examples. . . Socrates called the opinions of the many Lamiæ.*—Good God!" he exclaimed, flinging the book from him with a gesture of abhorrence.

Justine watched him with panting lips, her knees

trembling under her. "But you wrote it—you wrote it! I thought you meant it!" she cried, as the book spun across a table and dropped to the floor.

He looked at her coldly, almost apprehensively, as if she had grown suddenly dangerous and remote; then he turned and walked out of the room.

The striking of the clock roused her. She rose to her feet, rang the bell, and told the maid, through the door, that she had a headache, and was unable to see Miss Cicely. Then she turned back into the room, and darkness closed on her. She was not the kind to take grief passively—it drove her in anguished pacings up and down the floor. She walked and walked till her legs flagged under her; then she dropped stupidly into the chair where Amherst had sat. . .

All her world had crumbled about her. It was as if some law of mental gravity had been mysteriouly suspended, and every firmly-anchored conviction, every accepted process of reasoning, spun disconnectedly through space. Amherst had not understood her—worse still, he had judged her as the world might judge her! The core of her misery was there. With terrible clearness she saw the suspicion that had crossed his mind—the suspicion that she had kept silence in the beginning because she loved him, and feared to lose him if she spoke.

And what if it were true? What if her unconscious guilt went back even farther than his thought dared to track it? She could not now recall a time when she had not loved him. Every chance meeting with him, from their first brief talk at Hanaford, stood out embossed and glowing against the blur of lesser memories. Was it possible that she had loved him during Bessy's life—that she had even, sub-consciously, blindly, been urged by her feeling for him to perform the act?

But she shook herself free from this morbid horror—the rebound of health was always prompt in her, and her mind instinctively rejected every form of moral poison. No! Her motive had been normal, sane and justifiable—completely justifiable. Her fault lay in having dared to rise above conventional restrictions, her mistake in believing that her husband could rise with her. These reflections steadied her but they did not bring much comfort. For her whole life was centred in Amherst, and she saw that he would never be able to free himself from the traditional view of her act. In looking back, and correcting her survey of his character in the revealing light of the last hours, she perceived that, like many men of emancipated thought, he had remained subject to the old conventions of feeling. And he had probably never given much thought to women till he met her—had always been content to deal with them in the accepted currency of sentiment.

After all, it was the currency they liked best, and for which they offered their prettiest wares!

But what of the intellectual accord between himself and her? She had not been deceived in that! He and she had really been wedded in mind as well as in heart. But until now there had not arisen in their lives one of those searching questions which call into play emotions rooted far below reason and judgment, in the dark primal depths of inherited feeling. It is easy to judge impersonal problems intellectually, turning on them the full light of acquired knowledge; but too often one must still grope one's way through the personal difficulty by the dim taper carried in long-dead hands. . .

But was there then no hope of lifting one's individual life to a clearer height of conduct? Must one be content to think for the race, and to feel only—feel blindly and incoherently—for one's self? And was it not from such natures as Amherst's—natures in which independence of judgment was blent with strong human sympathy—that the liberating impulse should come?

Her mind grew weary of revolving in this vain circle of questions. The fact was that, in their particular case, Amherst had not risen above prejudice and emotion; that, though her act was one to which his intellectual sanction was given, he had turned from her with instinctive repugnance, had dishonoured her by the most wounding suspicions. The tie between them was forever stained and debased.

Justine's long hospital-discipline made it impossible for her to lose consciousness of the lapse of time, or to let her misery thicken into mental stupor. She could not help thinking and moving; and she presently lifted herself to her feet, turned on the light, and began to prepare for dinner. It would be terrible to face her husband across Mr. Langhope's pretty dinner-table, and afterward in the charming drawing-room, with its delicate old ornaments and intimate luxurious furniture; but she could not continue to sit motionless in the dark: it was her innermost instinct to pick herself up and go on.

While she dressed she listened anxiously for Amherst's step in the next room; but there was no sound, and when she dragged herself downstairs the drawing-room was empty, and the parlour-maid, after a decent delay, came to ask if dinner should be postponed.

She said no, murmuring some vague pretext for her husband's absence, and sitting alone through the succession of courses which composed the brief but carefully-studied *menu.* When this ordeal was over she returned to the drawing-room and took up a book. It chanced to be a new volume on labour problems, which Amherst must have brought back with him from Westmore; and it carried her thoughts instantly to the mills. Would this disaster poison their work there as well as their personal relation? Would he think of her as carrying contamination even into the task their love had illumined?

The hours went on without his returning, and at length it occurred to her that he might have taken the night train to Hanaford. Her heart contracted at the thought: she remembered—though every nerve shrank from the analogy—his sudden flight at another crisis in his life, and she felt obscurely that if he escaped from her now she would never recover her hold on him. But could he be so cruel—could he wish any one to suffer as she was suffering?

At ten o'clock she could endure the drawing-room no longer, and went up to her room again. She undressed slowly, trying to prolong the process as much as possible, to put off the period of silence and inaction which would close in on her when she lay down on her bed. But at length the dreaded moment came—there was nothing more between her and the night. She crept into bed and put out the light; but as she slipped between the cold sheets a trembling seized her, and after a moment she drew on her dressing-gown again and groped her way to the lounge by the fire.

She pushed the lounge closer to the hearth and lay down, still shivering, though she had drawn the quilted coverlet up to her chin. She lay there a long time, with closed eyes, in a mental darkness torn by sudden flashes of memory. In one of these flashes a phrase of Amherst's stood out—a word spoken at Westmore, on the day of the opening of the Emergency Hospital, about a good-looking young man who had called to see her. She remembered Amherst's boyish burst of jealousy, his sudden relief at the thought that the visitor might have been Wyant. And no doubt it *was* Wyant—Wyant who had come to Hanaford to threaten her, and who, baffled by her non-arrival, or for some other unexplained reason, had left again without carrying out his purpose.

It was dreadful to think by how slight a chance her first draught of happiness had escaped that drop of poison; yet, when she understood, her inward cry was: "If it had happened, my dearest need not have suffered!"... Already she was feeling Amherst's pain more than her own, understanding that it was harder to bear than hers because it was at war with all the reflective part of his nature.

As she lay there, her face pressed into the cushions, she heard a sound through the silent house—the opening and closing of the outer door. She turned cold, and lay listening with strained ears... Yes; now there was a step on the stairs—her husband's step! She heard him turn into his own room. The throbs of her heart almost deafened her—she only distinguished confusedly that he was moving about within, so close that it was as if she felt his touch. Then her door opened and he entered.

He stumbled slightly in the darkness before he found the switch of the lamp; and as he bent over it she saw that his face was flushed, and that his eyes had an excited light which, in any one less abstemious, might almost have seemed like the effect of wine.

"Are you awake?" he asked.

She started up against the cushions, her black hair streaming about her small ghostly face.

"Yes."

He walked over to the lounge and dropped into the low chair beside it.

"I've given that cur a lesson he won't forget," he exclaimed, breathing hard, the redness deepening in his face.

She turned on him in joy and trembling. "John! —Oh, John! You didn't follow him? Oh, what happened? What have you done?"

"No. I didn't follow him. But there are some things that even the powers above can't stand. And so they managed to let me run across him—by the merest accident—and I gave him something to remember."

He spoke in a strong clear voice that had a brightness like the brightness in his eyes. She felt its heat in her veins—the primitive woman in her glowed at contact with the primitive man. But reflection chilled her the next moment.

"But why—why? Oh, how could you? Where did it happen—oh, not in the street?"

As she questioned him, there rose before her the terrified vision of a crowd gathering—the police, newspapers, a hideous publicity. He must have been mad to do it—and yet he must have done it because he loved her!

"No—no. Don't be afraid. The powers looked after that too. There was no one about—and I don't think he'll talk much about it."

She trembled, fearing yet adoring him. Nothing could have been more unlike the Amherst she fancied she knew than this act of irrational anger which had magically lifted the darkness from his spirit; yet, magically also, it gave him back to her, made them one flesh once more. And suddenly the pressure of opposed emotions became too strong, and she burst into tears.

She wept painfully, violently, with the resistance of strong natures unused to emotional expression; till at length, through the tumult of her tears, she felt her husband's reassuring touch.

"Justine," he said, speaking once more in his natural voice.

She raised her face from her hands, and they looked at each other.

"Justine—this afternoon—I said things I didn't mean to say."

Her lips parted, but her throat was still full of sobs, and she could only look at him while the tears ran down.

"I believe I understand now," he continued, in the same quiet tone.

Her hand shrank from his clasp, and she began to tremble again. "Oh, if you only *believe*. . . if you're not sure. . . don't pretend to be!"

He sat down beside her and drew her into his arms. "I am sure," he whispered, holding her close, and pressing his lips against her face and hair.

"Oh, my husband—my husband! You've come back to me?"

He answered her with more kisses, murmuring through them: "Poor child—poor child—poor Justine. . ." while he held her fast.

With her face against him she yielded to the childish luxury of murmuring out unjustified fears. "I was afraid you had gone back to Hanaford—— "

"Tonight? To Hanaford?"

"To tell your mother."

She felt a contraction of the arm embracing her, as though a throb of pain had stiffened it.

"I shall never tell any one," he said abruptly; but as he felt in her a responsive shrinking he gathered her close again, whispering through the hair that fell about her cheek: "Don't talk, dear. . . let us never talk of it again. . ." And in the clasp of his arms her terror and anguish subsided, giving way, not to the deep peace of tranquillized thought, but to a confused well-being that lulled all thought to sleep.

XXXVII

BUT thought could never be long silent between them; and Justine's triumph lasted but a day. With its end she saw what it had been made of: the ascendency of youth and sex over his subjugated judgment. Her first impulse was to try and maintain it—why not use the protective arts with which love inspired her? She who lived so keenly in the brain could live as intensely in her feelings; her quick imagination tutored her looks and words, taught her the spells to weave about shorn giants. And for a few days she and Amherst lost themselves in this self-evoked cloud of passion, both clinging fast to the visible, the palpable in their relation, as if conscious already that its finer essence had fled.

Amherst made no allusion to what had passed, asked for no details, offered no reassurances—behaved as if the whole episode had been effaced from his mind. And from Wyant there came no sound: he seemed to have disappeared from life as he had from their talk.

Toward the end of the week Amherst announced that he must return to Hanaford; and Justine at once declared her intention of going with him.

He seemed surprised, disconcerted almost; and for the first time the shadow of what had happened fell visibly between them.

"But ought you to leave Cicely before Mr. Langhope comes back?" he suggested.

"He will be here in two days."

"But he will expect to find you."

"It is almost the first of April. We are to have Cicely with us for the summer. There is no reason why I should not go back to my work at Westmore."

There was in fact no reason that he could produce; and the next day they returned to Hanaford together.

With her perceptions strung to the last pitch of sensitiveness, she felt a change in Amherst as soon as they re-entered Bessy's house. He was still scrupulously considerate, almost too scrupulously tender; but with a tinge of lassitude, like a man who tries to keep up under the stupefying approach of illness. And she began to hate the power by which she held him. It was not thus they had once walked together, free in mind though so linked in habit and feeling; when their love was not a deadening drug but a vivifying element that cleared thought instead of stifling it. There were moments when she felt that open alienation would be easier, because it would be nearer the truth. And at such moments she longed to speak, to beg him to utter his mind, to go with her once for all into the depths of the subject they continued to avoid. But at the last her heart always failed her: she could not face the thought of losing him, of hearing him speak estranging words to her.

They had been at Hanaford for about ten days when, one morning at breakfast, Amherst uttered a sudden exclamation over a letter he was reading.

"What is it?" she asked in a tremor.

He had grown very pale, and was pushing the hair from his forehead with the gesture habitual to him in moments of painful indecision.

"What is it?" Justine repeated, her fear growing.

"Nothing——" he began, thrusting the letter under the pile of envelopes by his plate; but she continued to look at him anxiously, till she drew his eyes to hers.

"Mr. Langhope writes that they've appointed Wyant to Saint Christopher's," he said abruptly.

"Oh, the letter—we forgot the letter!" she cried.

"Yes—we forgot the letter."

"But how dare he——?"

Amherst said nothing, but the long silence between them seemed full of ironic answers, till she brought out, hardly above her breath: "What shall you do?"

"Write at once—tell Mr. Langhope he's not fit for the place."

"Of course——" she murmured

He went on tearing open his other letters, and glancing at their contents. She leaned back in her chair, her cup of coffee untasted, listening to the recurrent crackle of torn paper as he tossed aside one letter after another.

Presently he rose from his seat, and as she followed him from the dining-room she noticed that his breakfast had also remained untasted. He gathered up his letters and walked toward the smoking-room; and after a moment's hesitation she joined him.

"John," she said from the threshold.

He was just seating himself at his desk, but he turned to her with an obvious effort at kindness which made the set look of his face the more marked.

She closed the door and went up to him.

"If you write that to Mr. Langhope—Dr. Wyant will—will tell him," she said.

"Yes—we must be prepared for that."

She was silent, and Amherst flung himself down on the leather ottoman against the wall. She stood before him, clasping and unclasping her hands in speechless distress.

"What would you have me do?" he asked at length, almost irritably.

"I only thought. . . he told me he would keep straight. . . if he only had a chance," she faltered out.

Amherst lifted his head slowly, and looked at her. "You mean—I am to do nothing? Is that it?"

She moved nearer to him with beseeching eyes. "I can't bear it. . . I can't bear that others should come between us," she broke out passionately.

He made no answer, but she could see a look of suffering cross his face, and coming still closer, she sank down on the ottoman, laying her hand on his. "John . . . oh, John, spare me," she whispered.

For a moment his hand lay quiet under hers; then he drew it out, and enclosed her trembling fingers.

"Very well—I'll give him a chance—I'll do nothing," he said, suddenly putting his other arm about her.

The reaction caught her by the throat, forcing out a dry sob or two; and as she pressed her face against him he raised it up and gently kissed her.

But even as their lips met she felt that they were sealing a treaty with dishonour. That his kiss should come to mean that to her! It was unbearable—worse than any personal pain—the thought of dragging him down to falsehood through her weakness.

She drew back and rose to her feet, putting aside his detaining hand.

"No—no! What am I saying? It can't be—you

must tell the truth." Her voice gathered strength as she spoke. "Oh, forget what I said—I didn't mean it!"

But again he seemed sunk in inaction, like a man over whom some baneful lethargy is stealing.

"John—John—forget!" she repeated urgently.

He looked up at her. "You realize what it will mean?"

"Yes—I realize. . . But it must be. . . And it will make no difference between us. . . will it?"

"No—no. Why should it?" he answered apathetically.

"Then write—tell Mr. Langhope not to give him the place. I want it over."

He rose slowly to his feet, without looking at her again, and walked over to the desk. She sank down on the ottoman and watched him with burning eyes while he drew forth a sheet of note-paper and began to write.

But after he had written a few words he laid down his pen, and swung his chair about so that he faced her.

"I can't do it in this way," he exclaimed.

"How then? What do you mean?" she said, starting up.

He looked at her. "Do you want the story to come from Wyant?"

"Oh——" She looked back at him with sudden

insight. "You mean to tell Mr. Langhope yourself?"

"Yes. I mean to take the next train to town and tell him."

Her trembling increased so much that she had to rest her hands against the edge of the ottoman to steady herself. "But if. . . if after all. . . Wyant should not speak?"

"Well—if he shouldn't? Could you bear to owe our safety to *him?*"

"Safety!"

"It comes to that, doesn't it, if *we're* afraid to speak?"

She sat silent, letting the bitter truth of this sink into her till it poured courage into her veins.

"Yes—it comes to that," she confessed.

"Then you feel as I do?"

"That you must go——?"

"That this is intolerable!"

The words struck down her last illusion, and she rose and went over to the writing-table. "Yes—go," she said.

He stood up also, and took both her hands, not in a caress, but gravely, almost severely.

"Listen, Justine. You must understand exactly what this means—may mean. I am willing to go on as we are now. . . as long as we can. . . because I love you. . . because I would do anything to spare you pain. But if I speak I must say everything—I must follow this thing up to its uttermost consequences. That's what I want to make clear to you."

Her heart sank with a foreboding of new peril. "What consequences?"

"Can't you see for yourself—when you look about this house?"

"This house——?"

He dropped her hands and took an abrupt turn across the room.

"I owe everything to her," he broke out, "all I am, all I have, all I have been able to give you—and I must go and tell her father that you. . ."

"Stop—stop!" she cried, lifting her hands as if to keep off a blow.

"No—don't make me stop. We must face it," he said doggedly.

"But this—this isn't the truth! You put it as if—almost as if——"

"Yes—don't finish.—Has it occurred to you that *he* may think that?" Amherst asked with a terrible laugh. But at that she recovered her courage, as she always did when an extreme call was made on it.

"No—I don't believe it! If he *does*, it will be because you think it yourself. . ." Her voice sank, and she lifted her hands and pressed them to her temples. "And if you think it, nothing matters. . . one way or the other. . ." She paused, and her voice regained its strength. "That is what I must face before you go: what *you* think, what *you* believe of me. You've never told me that."

Amherst, at the challenge, remained silent, while a slow red crept to his cheek-bones.

"Haven't I told you by—by what I've done?" he said slowly.

"No—what you've done has covered up what you thought; and I've helped you cover it—I'm to blame too! But it was not for this that we. . . that we had that half-year together. . . not to sink into connivance and evasion! I don't want another hour of sham happiness. I want the truth from you, whatever it is."

He stood motionless, staring moodily at the floor. "Don't you see that's my misery—that I don't know myself?"

"You don't know. . . what you think of me?"

"Good God, Justine, why do you try to strip life naked? I don't know what's been going on in me these last weeks——"

"You must know what you think of my motive. . . for doing what I did."

She saw in his face how he shrank from the least allusion to the act about which their torment revolved. But he forced himself to raise his head and look at her. "I have never—for one moment—questioned your motive—or failed to see that it was justified. . . under the circumstances. . ."

"Oh, John—John!" she broke out in the wild joy of hearing herself absolved; but the next instant her subtle perceptions felt the unconscious reserve behind his admission.

"Your mind justifies me—not your heart; isn't *that* your misery?" she said.

He looked at her almost piteously, as if, in the last resort, it was from her that light must come to him. "On my soul, I don't know. . . I can't tell. . . it's all dark in me. I know you did what you thought best. . . if I had been there, I believe I should have asked you to do it. . . but I wish to God——"

She interrupted him sobbingly. "Oh, I ought never to have let you love me! I ought to have seen that I was cut off from you forever. I have brought you wretchedness when I would have given my life for you! I don't deserve that you should forgive me for that."

Her sudden outbreak seemed to restore his self-possession. He went up to her and took her hand with a quieting touch.

"There is no question of forgiveness, Justine. Don't let us torture each other with vain repinings. Our business is to face the thing, and we shall be better for having talked it out. I shall be better, for my part, for having told Mr. Langhope. But before I go I want to be sure that you understand the view he may take. . . and the effect it will probably have on our future."

"Our future?" She started. "No, I don't understand."

Amherst paused a moment, as if trying to choose the words least likely to pain her. "Mr. Langhope knows that my marriage was. . . unhappy; through my fault, he no doubt thinks. And if he chooses to infer that. . . that you and I may have cared for each other. . . before. . . and that it was *because* there was a chance of recovery that you——"

"Oh——"

"We must face it," he repeated inflexibly. "And you must understand that, if there is the faintest hint of this kind, I shall give up everything here, as soon as it can be settled legally—God, how Tredegar will like the job!—and you and I will have to go and begin life over again. . . somewhere else."

For an instant a mad hope swelled in her—the vision of escaping with him into new scenes, a new life, away from the coil of memories that bound them down as in a net. But the reaction of reason came at once—she saw him cut off from his chosen work, his career destroyed, his honour clouded, above all—ah, this was what wrung them both!—his task undone, his people flung back into the depths from which he had lifted them. And all through her doing—all because she had clutched at happiness with too rash a hand! The thought stung her to passionate activity of mind—made her resolve to risk anything, dare anything, before she involved him farther in her own ruin. She felt her brain clear gradually, and the thickness dissolve in her throat.

"I understand," she said in a low voice, raising her eyes to his.

"And you're ready to accept the consequences? Think again before it's too late."

She paused. "That is what I should like. . . what I wanted to ask you. . . the time to think."

She saw a slight shade cross his face, as if he had not expected this failure of courage in her; but he said quietly: "You don't want me to go today?"

"Not today—give me one more day."

"Very well."

She laid a timid hand on his arm. "Please go out to Westmore as usual—as if nothing had happened. And tonight. . . when you come back. . . I shall have decided."

"Very well," he repeated.

"You'll be gone all day?"

He glanced at his watch. "Yes—I had meant to be; unless——"

"No; I would rather be alone. Good-bye," she said, letting her hand slip softly along his coat-sleeve as he turned to the door

XXXVIII

AT half-past six that afternoon, just as Amherst, on his return from the mills, put the key into his door at Hanaford, Mrs. Ansell, in New York, was being shown into Mr. Langhope's library.

As she entered, her friend rose from his chair by the fire, and turned on her a face so disordered by emotion that she stopped short with an exclamation of alarm.

"Henry—what has happened? Why did you send for me?"

"Because I couldn't go to you. I couldn't trust myself in the streets—in the light of day."

"But why? What is it?—Not Cicely——?"

He struck both hands upward with a comprehensive gesture. "Cicely—every one—the whole world!" His clenched fist came down on the table against which he was leaning. "Maria, my girl might have been saved!"

Mrs. Ansell looked at him with growing perturbation. "Saved—Bessy's life? But how? By whom?"

"She might have been allowed to live, I mean—to recover. She was killed, Maria; that woman killed her!"

Mrs. Ansell, with another cry of bewilderment, let herself drop helplessly into the nearest chair. "In heaven's name, Henry—what woman?"

He seated himself opposite to her, clutching at his stick, and leaning his weight heavily on it—a white dishevelled old man. "I wonder why you ask—just to spare me?"

Their eyes met in a piercing exchange of question and answer, and Mrs. Ansell tried to bring out reasonably: "I ask in order to understand what you are saying."

"Well, then, if you insist on keeping up appearances—my daughter-in-law killed my daughter. There you have it." He laughed silently, with a tear on his reddened eye-lids.

Mrs. Ansell groaned. "Henry, you are raving—I understand less and less."

"I don't see how I can speak more plainly. She told me so herself, in this room, not an hour ago."

"She told you? Who told you?"

"John Amherst's wife. Told me she'd killed my child. It's as easy as breathing—if you know how to use a morphia-needle."

Light seemed at last to break on his hearer. "Oh, my poor Henry—you mean—she gave too much? There was some dreadful accident?"

"There was no accident. She killed my child—

killed her deliberately. Don't look at me as if I were a madman. She sat in that chair you're in when she told me."

"Justine? Has she been here today?" Mrs. Ansell paused in a painful effort to readjust her thoughts. "But *why* did she tell you?"

"That's simple enough. To prevent Wyant's doing it."

"Oh——" broke from his hearer, in a long sigh of fear and intelligence. Mr. Langhope looked at her with a smile of miserable exultation.

"You knew—you suspected all along?—But now you must speak out!" he exclaimed with a sudden note of command.

She sat motionless, as if trying to collect herself. "I know nothing—I only meant—why was this never known before?"

He was upon her at once. "You think—because they understood each other? And now there's been a break between them? He wanted too big a share of the spoils? Oh, it's all so abysmally vile!"

He covered his face with a shaking hand, and Mrs. Ansell remained silent, plunged in a speechless misery of conjecture. At length she regained some measure of her habitual composure, and leaning forward, with her eyes on his face, said in a quiet tone: "If I am to help you, you must try to tell me just what has happened."

He made an impatient gesture. "Haven't I told you? She found that her accomplice meant to speak, and rushed to town to forestall him."

Mrs. Ansell reflected. "But why—with his place at Saint Christopher's secured—did Dr. Wyant choose this time to threaten her—if, as you imagine, he's an accomplice?"

"Because he's a drug-taker, and she didn't wish him to have the place."

"She didn't wish it? But that does not look as if she were afraid. She had only to hold her tongue!"

Mr. Langhope laughed sardonically. "It's not quite so simple. Amherst was coming to town to tell me."

"Ah—*he* knows?"

"Yes—and she preferred that I should have her version first."

"And what is her version?"

The furrows of misery deepened in Mr. Langhope's face. "Maria—don't ask too much of me! I can't go over it again. She says she wanted to spare my child—she says the doctors were keeping her alive, torturing her uselessly, as a. . . a sort of scientific experiment. . . She forced on me the hideous details. . ."

Mrs. Ansell waited a moment.

"Well! May it not be true?"

"Wyant's version is different. *He* says Bessy would have recovered—he says Garford thought so too."

"And what does she answer? She denies it?"

"No. She admits that Garford was in doubt. But she says the chance was too remote—the pain too bad . . . that's her cue, naturally!"

Mrs. Ansell, leaning back in her chair, with hands meditatively stretched along its arms, gave herself up to silent consideration of the fragmentary statements cast before her. The long habit of ministering to her friends in moments of perplexity and distress had given her an almost judicial keenness in disentangling and coordinating facts incoherently presented, and in seizing on the thread of motive that connected them; but she had never before been confronted with a situation so poignant in itself, and bearing so intimately on her personal feelings; and she needed time to free her thoughts from the impending rush of emotion.

At last she raised her head and said: "Why did Mr. Amherst let her come to you, instead of coming himself?"

"He knows nothing of her being here. She persuaded him to wait a day, and as soon as he had gone to the mills this morning she took the first train to town."

"Ah——" Mrs. Ansell murmured thoughtfully; and Mr. Langhope rejoined, with a conclusive gesture: "Do you want more proofs of panic-stricken guilt?"

"Oh, guilt—" His friend revolved her large soft

muff about a drooping hand. "There's so much still to understand."

"Your mind does not, as a rule, work so slowly!" he said with some asperity; but she paid no heed to his tone.

"Amherst, for instance—how long has he known of this?" she continued.

"A week or two only—she made that clear."

"And what is his attitude?"

"Ah—that, I conjecture, is just what she means to keep us from knowing!"

"You mean she's afraid——?"

Mr. Langhope gathered his haggard brows in a frown. "She's afraid, of course—mortally—I never saw a woman more afraid. I only wonder she had the courage to face me."

"Ah—that's it! Why *did* she face you? To extenuate her act—to give you her version, because she feared his might be worse? Do you gather that that was her motive?"

It was Mr. Langhope's turn to hesitate. He furrowed the thick Turkey rug with the point of his ebony stick, pausing once or twice to revolve it gimlet-like in a gap of the pile.

"Not her avowed motive, naturally."

"Well—at least, then, let me have that."

"Her avowed motive? Oh, she'd prepared one, of

course—trust her to have a dozen ready! The one she produced was—simply the desire to protect her husband."

"Her husband? Does *he* too need protection?"

"My God, if he takes her side——! At any rate, her fear seemed to be that what she had done might ruin him; might cause him to feel—as well he may!—that the mere fact of being her husband makes his situation as Cicely's step-father, as my son-in-law, intolerable. And she came to clear him, as it were—to find out, in short, on what terms I should be willing to continue my present relations with him as though this hideous thing had not been known to me."

Mrs. Ansell raised her head quickly. "Well—and what were your terms?"

He hesitated. "She spared me the pain of proposing any—I had only to accept hers."

"Hers?"

"That she should disappear altogether from my sight—and from the child's, naturally. Good heaven, I should like to include Amherst in that! But I'm tied hand and foot, as you see, by Cicely's interests; and I'm bound to say she exonerated him completely—completely!"

Mrs. Ansell was again silent, but a swift flight of thoughts traversed her drooping face. "But if you are to remain on the old terms with her husband, how is she to disappear out of your life without also disappearing out of his?"

Mr. Langhope gave a slight laugh. "I leave her to work out that problem."

"And you think Amherst will consent to such conditions?"

"He's not to know of them."

The unexpectedness of the reply reduced Mrs. Ansell to a sound of inarticulate interrogation; and Mr. Langhope continued: "Not at first, that is. She had thought it all out—foreseen everything; and she wrung from me—I don't yet know how!—a promise that when I saw him I would make it appear that I cleared him completely, not only of any possible complicity, or whatever you choose to call it, but of any sort of connection with the matter in my thoughts of him. I am, in short, to let him feel that he and I are to continue on the old footing—and I agreed, on the condition of her effacing herself somehow—of course on some other pretext."

"Some other pretext? But what conceivable pretext? My poor friend, he adores her!"

Mr. Langhope raised his eyebrows slightly. "We haven't seen him since this became known to him. *She* has; and she let slip that he was horror-struck."

Mrs. Ansell looked up with a quick exclamation.

"Let slip? Isn't it much more likely that she forced it on you—emphasized it to the last limit of credulity?" She sank her hands to the arms of the chair, and exclaimed, looking him straight in the eyes: "You say she was frightened? It strikes me she was dauntless!"

Mr. Langhope stared a moment; then he said, with an ironic shrug: "No doubt, then, she counted on its striking me too."

Mrs. Ansell breathed a shuddering sigh. "Oh, I understand your feeling as you do—I'm deep in the horror of it myself. But I can't help seeing that this woman might have saved herself—and that she's chosen to save her husband instead. What I don't see, from what I know of him," she musingly proceeded, "is how, on any imaginable pretext, she will induce him to accept the sacrifice."

Mr. Langhope made a resentful movement. "If that's the only point your mind dwells on——!"

Mrs. Ansell looked up. "It doesn't dwell anywhere as yet—except, my poor Henry," she murmured, rising to move toward him, and softly laying her hand on his bent shoulder—"except on your distress and misery—on the very part I can't yet talk of, can't question you about. . ."

He let her hand rest there a moment; then he turned, and drawing it into his own tremulous fingers, pressed it silently, with a clinging helpless grasp that drew the tears to her eyes.

Justine Brent, in her earliest girlhood, had gone through one of those emotional experiences that are the infantile diseases of the heart. She had fancied herself beloved of a youth of her own age; had secretly returned his devotion, and had seen it reft from her by another. Such an incident, as inevitable as the measles, sometimes, like that mild malady, leaves traces out of all proportion to its actual virulence. The blow fell on Justine with tragic suddenness, and she reeled under it, thinking darkly of death, and renouncing all hopes of future happiness. Her ready pen often beguiled her into recording her impressions, and she now found an escape from despair in writing the history of a damsel similarly wronged. In her tale, the heroine killed herself; but the author, saved by this vicarious sacrifice, lived, and in time even smiled over her manuscript.

It was many years since Justine Amherst had recalled this youthful incident; but the memory of it recurred to her as she turned from Mr. Langhope's door. For a moment death seemed the easiest escape from what confronted her; but though she could no longer medicine her despair by turning it into fiction, she knew at once that she must somehow transpose it into terms of action, that she must always escape from life into more life, and not into its negation.

She had been carried into Mr. Langhope's presence by that expiatory passion which still burns so high, and draws its sustenance from so deep down, in the unsleeping hearts of women. Though she had never wavered in her conviction that her act had been justified her ideas staggered under the sudden comprehension of its consequences. Not till that morning had she seen those consequences in their terrible, unsuspected extent, had she understood how one stone rashly loosened from the laboriously erected structure of human society may produce remote fissures in that clumsy fabric. She saw that, having hazarded the loosening of the stone, she should have held herself apart from ordinary human ties, like some priestess set apart for the service of the temple. And instead, she had seized happiness with both hands, taken it as the gift of the very fate she had herself precipitated! She remembered some old Greek saying to the effect that the gods never forgive the mortal who presumes to love and suffer like a god. She had dared to do both, and the gods were bringing ruin on that deeper self which had its life in those about her.

So much had become clear to her when she heard Amherst declare his intention of laying the facts before Mr. Langhope. His few broken words lit up the farthest verge of their lives. She saw that his retrospective reverence for his wife's memory, which was far as possible removed from the strong passion of the mind and senses that bound him to herself, was indelibly stained and desecrated by the discovery that all he had received from the one woman had been won for him by the deliberate act of the other. This was what no reasoning, no appeal to the calmer judgment, could ever, in his inmost thoughts, undo or extenuate. It could find appeasement only in the renunciation of all that had come to him from Bessy; and this renunciation, so different from the mere sacrifice of material well-being, was bound up with consequences so far-reaching, so destructive to the cause which had inspired his whole life, that Justine felt the helpless terror of the mortal who has launched one of the heavenly bolts.

She could think of no way of diverting it but the way she had chosen. She must see Mr. Langhope first, must clear Amherst of the least faint association with her act or her intention. And to do this she must exaggerate, not her own compunction—for she could not depart from the exact truth in reporting her feelings and convictions—but her husband's first instinctive movement of horror, the revulsion of feeling her confession had really produced in him. This was the most painful part of her task, and for this reason her excited imagination clothed it with a special expiatory value.

If she could purchase Amherst's peace of mind, and the security of his future, by confessing, and even over-emphasizing, the momentary estrangement between them there would be a bitter joy in such payment!

Her hour with Mr. Langhope proved the correctness of her intuition. She could save Amherst only by effacing herself from his life: those about him would be only too ready to let her bear the full burden of obloquy. She could see that, for a dozen reasons, Mr. Langhope, even in the first shock of his dismay, unconsciously craved a way of exonerating Amherst, of preserving intact the relation on which so much of his comfort had come to depend. And she had the courage to make the most of his desire, to fortify it by isolating Amherst's point of view from hers; so that, when the hour was over, she had the solace of feeling that she had completely freed him from any conceivable consequence of her act.

So far, the impetus of self-sacrifice had carried her straight to her goal; but, as frequently happens with such atoning impulses, it left her stranded just short of any subsequent plan of conduct. Her next step, indeed, was clear enough: she must return to Hanaford, explain to her husband that she had felt impelled to tell her own story to Mr. Langhope, and then take up her ordinary life till chance offered her a pretext for fulfilling her promise. But what pretext was likely to present itself? No symbolic horn would sound the hour of fulfillment; she must be her own judge, and hear the call in the depths of her own conscience.

XXXIX

WHEN Amherst, returning late that afternoon from Westmore, learned of his wife's departure, and read the note she had left, he found it, for a time, impossible to bring order out of the confusion of feeling produced in him.

His mind had been disturbed enough before. All day, through the routine of work at the mills, he had laboured inwardly with the difficulties confronting him; and his unrest had been increased by the fact that his situation bore an ironic likeness to that in which, from a far different cause, he had found himself at the other crisis of his life. Once more he was threatened with the possibility of having to give up Westmore, at a moment when concentration of purpose and persistency of will were at last beginning to declare themselves in tangible results. Before, he had only given up dreams; now it was their fruition that he was asked to surrender. And he was fixed in his resolve to withdraw absolutely from Westmore if the statement he had to make to Mr. Langhope was received with the least hint of an offensive mental reservation. All forms of moral compromise had always been difficult to Amherst, and like many men absorbed in large and complicated questions he craved above all clearness and peace in his household relation. The first months of his second marriage had brought him, as a part of richer and deeper joys, this enveloping sense of a clear moral medium, in which no subterfuge or equivocation could draw breath. He had felt that henceforth he could pour into his work all the combative energy, the powers of endurance, resistance, renovation, which had once been unprofitably dissipated in the vain attempt to bring some sort of harmony into life with Bessy. Between himself and Justine, apart from their love for each other, there was the wider passion for their kind, which gave back to them an enlarged and deepened reflection of their personal feeling. In such an air it had seemed that no petty egotism could hamper their growth, no misintelligence obscure their love; yet all the while this pure happiness had been unfolding against a sordid background of falsehood and intrigue from which his soul turned with loathing.

Justine was right in assuming that Amherst had never thought much about women. He had vaguely regarded them as meant to people that hazy domain of feeling designed to offer the busy man an escape from thought. His second marriage, leading him to the blissful discovery that woman can think as well as feel, that there are beings of the ornamental sex in whom brain and heart have so enlarged each other that their emotions are as clear as thought, their thoughts as warm as emotions—this discovery had had the effect of making him discard his former summary conception of woman as a bundle of inconsequent impulses, and admit her at a stroke to full mental equality with her lord. The result of this act of manumission was, that in judging Justine he could no longer allow for what was purely feminine in her conduct. It was incomprehensible to him that she, to whom truth had seemed the essential element of life, should have been able to draw breath, and find happiness, in an atmosphere of falsehood and dissimulation. His mind could assent—at least in the abstract—to the reasonableness of her act; but he was still unable to understand her having concealed it from him. He could enter far enough into her feelings to allow for her having kept silence on his first return to Lynbrook, when she was still under the strain of a prolonged and terrible trial; but that she should have continued to do so when he and she had discovered and confessed their love for each other, threw an intolerable doubt on her whole course.

He stayed late at the mills, finding one pretext after another for delaying his return to Hanaford, and trying, while he gave one part of his mind to the methodical performance of his task, to adjust the other to some definite view of the future. But all was darkened and confused by the sense that, between himself and Justine, complete communion of thought was no longer possible. It had, in fact, never existed; there had always been a locked chamber in her mind, and he knew not yet what other secrets might inhabit it.

The shock of finding her gone when he reached home gave a new turn to his feelings. She had made no mystery of her destination, leaving word with the servants that she had gone to town to see Mr. Langhope; and Amherst found a note from her on his study table.

"I feel," she wrote, "that I ought to see Mr. Langhope myself, and be the first to tell him what must be told. It was like you, dearest, to wish to spare me this, but it would have made me more unhappy; and Mr. Langhope might wish to hear the facts in my own words. I shall come back tomorrow, and after that it will be for you to decide what must be done."

The brevity and simplicity of the note were characteristic; in moments of high tension Justine was always calm and direct. And it was like her, too, not to make any covert appeal to his sympathy, not to seek to entrap his judgment by caressing words and plaintive allusions. The quiet tone in which she stated her purpose matched the firmness and courage of the act, and for a moment Amherst was shaken by a revulsion of feeling. Her heart was level with his, after all—if she had done wrong she would bear the brunt of it alone. It was so exactly what he himself would have felt and done in such a situation that faith in her flowed back through all the dried channels of his heart. But an instant later the current set the other way. The wretched years of his first marriage had left in him a residue of distrust, a tendency to dissociate every act from its ostensible motive. He had been too profoundly the dupe of his own enthusiasm not to retain this streak of scepticism, and it now moved him to ask if Justine's sudden departure had not been prompted by some other cause than the one she avowed. Had that alone actuated her, why not have told it to him, and asked his consent to her plan? Why let him leave the house without a hint of her purpose, and slip off by the first train as soon as he was safe at Westmore? Might it not be that she had special reasons for wishing Mr. Langhope to *hear her own version first*—that there were questions she wished to parry herself, explanations she could trust no one to make for her? The thought plunged Amherst into deeper misery. He knew not how to defend himself against these disintegrating suspicions—he felt only that, once the accord between two minds is broken, it is less easy to restore than the passion between two hearts. He dragged heavily through his solitary evening, and awaited with dread and yet impatience a message announcing his wife's return.

It would have been easier—far easier—when she left Mr. Langhope's door, to go straight out into the darkness and let it close in on her for good.

Justine felt herself yielding to the spell of that suggestion as she walked along the lamplit pavement, hardly conscious of the turn her steps were taking. The door of the house which a few weeks before had been virtually hers had closed on her without a question. She had been suffered to go out into the darkness without being asked whither she was going, or under what roof her night would be spent. The contrast between her past and present sounded through the tumult of her thoughts like the evil laughter of temptation. The house at Hanaford, to which she was returning, would look at her with the same alien face—nowhere on earth, at that moment, was a door which would open to her like the door of home.

In her painful self-absorption she followed the side street toward Madison Avenue, and struck southward down that tranquil thoroughfare. There was a physical relief in rapid motion, and she walked on, still hardly aware of her direction, toward the clustered lights of Madison Square. Should she return to Hanaford, she had still several hours to dispose of before the departure of the midnight train; and if she did not return, hours and dates no longer existed for her.

It would be easier—infinitely easier—not to go back. To take up her life with Amherst would, under any circumstances, be painful enough; to take it up under the tacit restriction of her pledge to Mr. Langhope seemed more than human courage could face. As she approached the square she had almost reached the conclusion that such a temporary renewal was beyond her strength—beyond what any standard of duty exacted. The question of an alternative hardly troubled her. She would simply go on living, and find an escape in work and material hardship. It would not be hard for so inconspicuous a person to slip back into the obscure mass of humanity.

She paused a moment on the edge of the square, vaguely seeking a direction for her feet that might permit the working of her thoughts to go on uninterrupted; and as she stood there, her eyes fell on the bench near the corner of Twenty-sixth Street, where she had sat with Amherst on the day of his flight from Lynbrook. He too had dreamed of escaping from insoluble problems into the clear air of hard work and simple duties; and she remembered the words with which she had turned him back. The cases, of course, were not identical, since he had been flying in anger and wounded pride from a situation for which he was in no wise to blame;

yet, if even at such a moment she had insisted on charity and forbearance, how could she now show less self-denial than she had exacted of him?

"If you go away for a time, surely it ought to be in such a way that your going does not seem to cast any reflection on Bessy..." That was how she had put it to him, and how, with the mere change of a name, she must now, for reasons as cogent, put it to herself. It was just as much a part of the course she had planned to return to her husband now, and take up their daily life together, as it would, later on, be her duty to drop out of that life, when her doing so could no longer involve him in the penalty to be paid.

She stood a little while looking at the bench on which they had sat, and giving thanks in her heart for the past strength which was now helping to build up her failing courage: such a patchwork business are our best endeavours, yet so faithfully does each weak upward impulse reach back a hand to the next.

Justine's explanation of her visit to Mr. Langhope was not wholly satisfying to her husband. She did not conceal from him that the scene had been painful, but she gave him to understand, as briefly as possible, that Mr. Langhope, after his first movement of uncontrollable distress, had seemed able to make allowances for the pressure under which she had acted, and that he had, at any rate, given no sign of intending to let her confession make any change in the relation between the households. If she did not—as Amherst afterward recalled—put all this specifically into words, she contrived to convey it in her manner, in her allusions, above all in her recovered composure. She had the demeanour of one who has gone through a severe test of strength, but come out of it in complete control of the situation. There was something slightly unnatural in this prompt solution of so complicated a difficulty, and it had the effect of making Amherst ask himself what, to produce such a result, must have been the gist of her communication to Mr. Langhope. If the latter had shown any disposition to be cruel, or even unjust, Amherst's sympathies would have rushed instantly to his wife's defence; but the fact that there was apparently to be no call on them left his reason free to compare and discriminate, with the final result that the more he pondered on his father-in-law's attitude the less intelligible it became.

A few days after Justine's return he was called to New York on business; and before leaving he told her that he should of course take the opportunity of having a talk with Mr. Langhope.

She received the statement with the gentle composure from which she had not departed since her return from town; and he added tentatively, as if to provoke her to a clearer expression of feeling: "I shall not be satisfied, of course, till I see for myself just how he feels—just how much, at bottom, this has affected him—since my own future relation to him will, as I have already told you, depend entirely on his treatment of you."

She met this without any sign of disturbance. "His treatment of me was very kind," she said. "But would it not, on your part," she continued hesitatingly, "be kinder not to touch on the subject so soon again?"

The line deepened between his brows. "Touch on it? I sha'n't rest till I've gone to the bottom of it! Till then, you must understand," he summed up with decision, "I feel myself only on sufferance here at Westmore."

"Yes—I understand," she assented; and as he bent over to kiss her for goodbye a tenuous impenetrable barrier seemed to lie between their lips.

It was Justine's turn to await with a passionate anxiety her husband's home-coming; and when, on the third day, he reappeared, her dearly acquired self-control gave way to a tremulous eagerness. This was, after all, the turning-point in their lives: everything depended on how Mr. Langhope had "played up" to his cue, had kept to his side of their bond.

Amherst's face showed signs of emotional havoc: when feeling once broke out in him it had full play, and she could see that his hour with Mr. Langhope had struck to the roots of life. But the resultant expression was one of invigoration, not defeat; and she gathered at a glance that her partner had not betrayed her. She drew a tragic solace from the success of her achievement; yet it flung her into her husband's arms with a passion of longing to which, as she instantly felt, he did not as completely respond.

There was still, then, something "between" them: somewhere the mechanism of her scheme had failed, or its action had not produced the result she had counted on.

As soon as they were alone in the study she said, as quietly as she could: "You saw your father-in-law? You talked with him?"

"Yes—I spent the afternoon with him. Cicely sent you her love."

She coloured at the mention of the child's name and murmured: "And Mr. Langhope?"

"He is perfectly calm now—perfectly impartial.—This business has made me feel," Amherst added abruptly, "that I have never been quite fair to him. I never thought him a magnanimous man."

"He has proved himself so," Justine murmured, her head bent low over a bit of needlework; and Amherst affirmed energetically: "He has been more than that—generous!"

She looked up at him with a smile. "I am so glad, dear; so glad there is not to be the least shadow between you. . ."

"No," Amherst said, his voice flagging slightly. There was a pause, and then he went on with renewed emphasis: "Of course I made my point clear to him."

"Your point?"

"That I stand or fall by his judgment of you."

Oh, if he had but said it more tenderly! But he delivered it with the quiet resolution of a man who contends for an abstract principle of justice, and not for a passion grown into the fibres of his heart!

"You are generous too," she faltered, her voice trembling a little.

Amherst frowned; and she perceived that any hint, on her part, of recognizing the slightest change in their relations was still like pressure on a painful bruise.

"There is no need for such words between us," he said impatiently; "and Mr. Langhope's attitude," he added, with an effort at a lighter tone, "has made it unnecessary, thank heaven, that we should ever revert to the subject again."

He turned to his desk as he spoke, and plunged into perusal of the letters that had accumulated in his absence.

There was a temporary excess of work at Westmore, and during the days that followed he threw himself into it with a zeal that showed Justine how eagerly he sought any pretext for avoiding confidential moments. The perception was painful enough, yet not as painful as another discovery that awaited her. She too had her tasks at Westmore: the supervision of the hospital, the day nursery, the mothers' club, and the various other organizations whereby she and Amherst were trying to put some sort of social unity into the lives of the mill-hands; and when, on the day after his return from New York, she presented herself, as usual, at the Westmore office, where she was in the habit of holding a brief consultation with him before starting on her rounds, she was at once aware of a new tinge of constraint in his manner. It hurt him, then, to see her at Westmore—hurt him more than to live with her, at Hanaford, under Bessy's roof! For it was there, at the mills, that his real life was led, the life with which Justine had been most identified, the life that had been made possible for both by the magnanimity of that other woman whose presence was now forever between them.

Justine made no sign. She resumed her work as though unconscious of any change; but whereas in the past they had always found pretexts for seeking each other out, to discuss the order of the day's work, or merely to warm their hearts by a rapid word or two, now each went a separate way, sometimes not meeting till they regained the house at night-fall.

And as the weeks passed she began to understand that, by a strange inversion of probability, the relation between Amherst and herself was to be the means of holding her to her compact with Mr. Langhope—if indeed it were not nearer the truth to say that it had made such a compact unnecessary. Amherst had done his best to take up their life together as though there had been no break in it; but slowly the fact was being forced on her that by remaining with him she was subjecting him to intolerable suffering—was coming to be the personification of the very thoughts and associations from which he struggled to escape. Happily her promptness of action had preserved Westmore to him, and in Westmore she believed that he would in time find a refuge from even the memory of what he was now enduring. But meanwhile her presence kept the thought alive; and, had every other incentive lost its power, this would have been enough to sustain her. Fate had, ironically enough, furnished her with an unanswerable reason for leaving Amherst; the impossibility of their keeping up such a relation as now existed between them would soon become too patent to be denied.

Meanwhile, as summer approached, she knew that external conditions would also call upon her to act. The visible signal for her withdrawal would be Cicely's next visit to Westmore. The child's birthday fell in early June; and Amherst, some months previously, had asked that she should be permitted to spend it at Hanaford, and that it should be chosen as the date for the opening of the first model cottages at Hopewood.

It was Justine who had originated the idea of associating Cicely's anniversaries with some significant moment in the annals of the mill colony; and struck by the happy suggestion, he had at once applied himself to hastening on the work at Hopewood. The eagerness of both Amherst and Justine that Cicely should be identified with the developing life of Westmore had been one of the chief influences in reconciling Mr. Langhope to his son-in-law's second marriage. Husband and wife had always made it clear that they regarded themselves as the mere trustees of the Westmore revenues, and that Cicely's name should, as early as possible, be associated with every measure taken for the welfare of the people. But now, as Justine knew, the situation was changed; and Cicely would not be allowed to come to Hanaford until she herself had left it. The manifold threads of divination that she was perpetually throwing out in Amherst's presence told her, without word or sign on his part, that he also awaited Cicely's birthday as a determining date in their lives. He spoke confidently, and as a matter of course, of Mr. Langhope's bringing his grand-daughter at the promised time; but Justine could hear a note of challenge in his voice, as though he felt that Mr. Langhope's sincerity had not yet been put to the test.

As the time drew nearer it became more difficult for her to decide just how she should take the step she had determined on. She had no material anxiety for the future, for although she did not mean to accept a penny from her husband after she had left him, she knew it would be easy for her to take up her nursing again; and she knew also that her hospital connections would enable her to find work in a part of the country far enough distant to remove her entirely from his life. But she had not yet been able to invent a reason for leaving that should be convincing enough to satisfy him, without directing his suspicions to the truth. As she revolved the question she suddenly recalled an exclamation of Amherst's—a word spoken as they entered Mr. Langhope's door, on the fatal afternoon when she had found Wyant's letter awaiting her.

"There's nothing you can't make people believe, you little Jesuit!"

She had laughed in pure joy at his praise of her; for every bantering phrase had then been a caress. But now the words returned with a sinister meaning. She knew they were true as far as Amherst was concerned: in the arts of casuistry and equivocation a child could have outmatched him, and she had only to exert her will to dupe him as deeply as she pleased. Well!

the task was odious, but it was needful: it was the bitterest part of her expiation that she must deceive him once more to save him from the results of her former deception. This decision once reached, every nerve in her became alert for an opportunity to do the thing and have it over; so that, whenever they were alone together, she was in an attitude of perpetual tension, her whole mind drawn up for its final spring.

The decisive word came, one evening toward the end of May, in the form of an allusion on Amherst's part to Cicely's approaching visit. Husband and wife were seated in the drawing-room after dinner, he with a book in hand, she bending, as usual, over the needlework which served at once as a pretext for lowered eyes, and as a means of disguising her fixed preoccupation.

"Have you worked out a plan?" he asked, laying down his book. "It occurred to me that it would be rather a good idea if we began with a sort of festivity for the kids at the day nursery. You could take Cicely there early, and I could bring out Mr. Langhope after luncheon. The whole performance would probably tire him too much."

Justine listened with suspended thread. "Yes—that seems a good plan."

"Will you see about the details, then? You know it's only a week off."

"Yes, I know." She hesitated, and then took the

spring. "I ought to tell you John—that I—I think I may not be here. . ."

He raised his head abruptly, and she saw the blood mount under his fair skin. "Not be here?" he exclaimed.

She met his look as steadily as she could. "I think of going away for awhile."

"Going away? Where? What is the matter—are you not well?"

There was her pretext—he had found it for her! Why should she not simply plead ill-health? Afterward she would find a way of elaborating the details and making them plausible. But suddenly, as she was about to speak, there came to her the feeling which, up to one fatal moment in their lives, had always ruled their intercourse—the feeling that there must be truth, and absolute truth, between them. Absolute, indeed, it could never be again, since he must never know of the condition exacted by Mr. Langhope; but that, at the moment, seemed almost a secondary motive compared to the deeper influences that were inexorably forcing them apart. At any rate, she would trump up no trivial excuse for the step she had resolved on; there should be truth, if not the whole truth, in this last decisive hour between them.

"Yes; I am quite well—at least my body is," she said quietly. "But I am tired, perhaps; my mind has been going round too long in the same circle." She paused for a brief space, and then, raising her head, and looking him straight in the eyes: "Has it not been so with you?" she asked.

The question seemed to startle Amherst. He rose from his chair and took a few steps toward the hearth, where a small fire was crumbling into embers. He turned his back to it, resting an arm on the mantel-shelf; then he said, in a somewhat unsteady tone: "I thought we had agreed not to speak of all that again."

Justine shook her head with a fugitive half-smile. "I made no such agreement, And besides, what is the use, when we can always hear each other's thoughts speak, and they speak of nothing else?"

Amherst's brows darkened. "It is not so with mine," he began; but she raised her hand with a silencing gesture.

"I know you have tried your best that it should not be so; and perhaps you have succeeded better than I. But I am tired, horribly tired—I want to get away from everything!"

She saw a look of pain in his eyes. He continued to lean against the mantel-shelf, his head slightly lowered, his unseeing gaze fixed on a remote scroll in the pattern of the carpet; then he said in a low tone: "I can only repeat again what I have said before—that I understand why you did what you did."

"Thank you," she answered, in the same tone.

There was another pause, for she could not trust herself to go on speaking; and presently he asked, with a tinge of bitterness in his voice: "That does not satisfy you?"

She hesitated. "It satisfies me as much as it does you—and no more," she replied at length.

He looked up hastily. "What do you mean?"

"Just what I say. We can neither of us go on living on that understanding just at present." She rose as she spoke, and crossed over to the hearth. "I want to go back to my nursing—to go out to Michigan, to a town where I spent a few months the year before I first came to Hanaford. I have friends there, and can get work easily. And you can tell people that I was ill and needed a change."

It had been easier to say than she had imagined, and her voice held its clear note till the end; but when she had ceased, the whole room began to reverberate with her words, and through the clashing they made in her brain she felt a sudden uncontrollable longing that they should provoke in him a cry of protest, of resistance. Oh, if he refused to let her go—if he caught her to him, and defied the world to part them—what then of her pledge to Mr. Langhope, what then of her resolve to pay the penalty alone?

But in the space of a heart-beat she knew that peril

—that longed-for peril!—was past. Her husband had remained silent—he neither moved toward her nor looked at her; and she felt in every slackening nerve that in the end he would let her go.

XL

MR. LANGHOPE, tossing down a note on Mrs. Ansell's drawing-room table, commanded imperiously: "Read that!"

She set aside her tea-cup, and looked up, not at the note, but into his face, which was crossed by one of the waves of heat and tremulousness that she was beginning to fear for him. Mr. Langhope had changed greatly in the last three months; and as he stood there in the clear light of the June afternoon it came to her that he had at last suffered the sudden collapse which is the penalty of youth preserved beyond its time.

"What is it?" she asked, still watching him as she put out her hand for the letter.

"Amherst writes to remind me of my promise to take Cicely to Hanaford next week, for her birthday."

"Well—it was a promise, wasn't it?" she rejoined, running her eyes over the page.

"A promise—yes; but made before. . . Read the note—you'll see there's no reference to his wife. For all I know, she'll be there to receive us."

"But that was a promise too."

"That neither Cicely nor I should ever set eyes on her? Yes. But why should she keep it? I was a fool that day—she fooled me as she's fooled us all! But you saw through it from the beginning—you said at once that she'd never leave him."

Mrs. Ansell reflected. "I said that before I knew all the circumstances. Now I think differently."

"You think she still means to go?"

She handed the letter back to him. "I think this is to tell you so."

"This?" He groped for his glasses, dubiously scanning the letter again.

"Yes. And what's more, if you refuse to go she'll have every right to break her side of the agreement."

Mr. Langhope sank into a chair, steadying himself painfully with his stick. "Upon my soul, I sometimes think you're on her side!" he ejaculated.

"No—but I like fair play," she returned, measuring his tea carefully into his favourite little porcelain teapot.

"Fair play?"

"She's offering to do her part. It's for you to do yours now—to take Cicely to Hanaford."

"If I find her there, I never cross Amherst's threshold again!"

Mrs. Ansell, without answering, rose and put his teacup on the slender-legged table at his elbow; then, before returning to her seat, she found the enamelled match-box and laid it by the cup. It was becoming difficult for Mr. Langhope to guide his movements about her small encumbered room; and he had always liked being waited on

Mrs. Ansell's prognostication proved correct. When Mr. Langhope and Cicely arrived at Hanaford they found Amherst alone to receive them. He explained briefly that his wife had been unwell, and had gone to seek rest and change at the house of an old friend in the west. Mr. Langhope expressed a decent amount of regret, and the subject was dropped as if by common consent. Cicely, however, was not so easily silenced. Poor Bessy's uncertain fits of tenderness had produced more bewilderment than pleasure in her sober-minded child; but the little girl's feelings and perceptions had developed rapidly in the equable atmosphere of her step-mother's affection. Cicely had reached the age when children put their questions with as much ingenuity as persistence, and both Mr. Langhope and Amherst longed for Mrs. Ansell's aid in parrying her incessant interrogations as to the cause and length of Justine's absence, what she had said before going, and what promise she had made about coming back. But Mrs. Ansell had not come to Hanaford. Though it had become a matter of habit to include her in the family pilgrimages to the mills she had firmly maintained the plea of more urgent engagements; and the two men, with only Cicely between them, had spent the long days and longer evenings in unaccustomed and unmitigated propinquity.

Mr. Langhope, before leaving, thought it proper to touch tentatively on his promise of giving Cicely to Amherst for the summer; but to his surprise the latter, after a moment of hesitation, replied that he should probably go to Europe for two or three months.

"To Europe? Alone?" escaped from Mr. Langhope before he had time to weigh his words.

Amherst frowned slightly. "I have been made a delegate to the Berne conference on the housing of factory operatives," he said at length, without making a direct reply to the question; "and if there is nothing to keep me at Westmore, I shall probably go out in July.' He waited a moment, and then added: "My wife has decided to spend the summer in Michigan."

Mr. Langhope's answer was a vague murmur of assent, and Amherst turned the talk to other matters.

Mr. Langhope returned to town with distinct views on the situation at Hanaford.

"Poor devil—I'm sorry for him: he can hardly speak

of her," he broke out at once to Mrs. Ansell, in the course of their first confidential hour together.

"Because he cares too much—he's too unhappy?"

"Because he loathes her!" Mr. Langhope brought out with emphasis.

Mrs. Ansell drew a deep sigh which made him add accusingly: "I believe you're actually sorry!"

"Sorry?" She raised her eye-brows with a slight smile. "Should one not always be sorry to know there's a little less love and a little more hate in the world?"

"You'll be asking *me* not to hate her next!"

She still continued to smile on him. "It's the haters, not the hated, I'm sorry for," she said at length; and he flung back impatiently: "Oh, don't let's talk of her. I sometimes feel she takes up more place in our lives than when she was with us!"

Amherst went to the Berne conference in July, and spent six weeks afterward in rapid visits to various industrial centres and model factory villages. During his previous European pilgrimages his interest had by no means been restricted to sociological questions: the appeal of an old civilization, reaching him through its innumerable forms of tradition and beauty, had roused that side of his imagination which his work at home left untouched. But upon his present state of deep moral commotion the spells of art and history were powerless to work. The foundations of his life had been shaken, and the fair exterior of the world was as vacant as a maniac's face. He could only take refuge in his special task, barricading himself against every expression of beauty and poetry as so many poignant reminders of a phase of life that he was vainly trying to cast off and forget.

Even his work had been embittered to him, thrust out of its place in the ordered scheme of things. It had cost him a hard struggle to hold fast to his main purpose, to convince himself that his real duty lay, not in renouncing the Westmore money and its obligations, but in carrying out his projected task as if nothing had occurred to affect his personal relation to it. The mere fact that such a renunciation would have been a deliberate moral suicide, a severing once for all of every artery of action, made it take on, at first, the semblance of an obligation, a sort of higher duty to the abstract conception of what he owed himself. But Justine had not erred in her forecast. Once she had passed out of his life, it was easier for him to return to a dispassionate view of his situation, to see, and boldly confess to himself that he saw, the still higher duty of sticking to his task, instead of sacrificing it to any ideal of personal disinterestedness. It was this gradual process of adjustment that saved him from the desolating scepticism which falls on the active man when the sources of his activity are tainted. Having accepted his fate, having consented to see in himself merely the necessary agent of a good to be done, he could escape from self-questioning only by shutting himself up in the practical exigencies of his work, closing his eyes and his thoughts to everything which had formerly related it to a wider world, had given meaning and beauty to life as a whole.

The return from Europe, and the taking up of the daily routine at Hanaford, were the most difficult phases in this process of moral adaptation.

Justine's departure had at first brought relief. He had been too sincere with himself to oppose her wish to leave Hanaford for a time, since he believed that, for her as well as for himself, a temporary separation would be less painful than a continuance of their actual relation. But as the weeks passed into months he found he was no nearer to a clear view of his own case: the future was still dark and enigmatic. Justine's desire to leave him had revived his unformulated distrust of her. What could it mean but that there were thoughts within her which could not be at rest in his presence? He had given her every proof of his wish to forget the past, and Mr. Langhope had behaved with unequalled magnanimity. Yet Justine's unhappiness was evident: she could not conceal her longing to escape from the conditions her act had created. Was it because, in reality, she was conscious of other motives than the one she acknowledged? She had insisted, almost unfeelingly as it might have seemed, on the abstract rightness of what she had done, on the fact that, ideally speaking, her act could not be made less right, less justifiable, by the special accidental consequences that had flowed from it. Because these consequences had caught her in a web of tragic fatality she would not be guilty of the weakness of tracing back the disaster to any intrinsic error in her original motive. Why, then, if this was her real, her proud attitude toward the past—and since those about her believed in her sincerity, and accepted her justification as valid from her point of view if not from theirs—why had she not been able to maintain her posture, to carry on life on the terms she had exacted from others?

A special circumstance contributed to this feeling of distrust; the fact, namely, that Justine, a week after her departure from Hanaford, had written to say that she could not, from that moment till her return, consent to accept any money from Amherst. As her manner was, she put her reasons clearly and soberly, without evasion or ambiguity.

"Since you and I," she wrote, "have always agreed in regarding the Westmore money as a kind of wage for our services at the mills, I cannot be satisfied to go on drawing that wage while I am unable to do any work in return. I am sure you must feel as I do about this; and you need have no anxiety as to the practical side of the question, since I have enough to live on in some savings from my hospital days, which were invested for me two years ago by Harry Dressel, and are beginning to bring in a small return. This being the case, I feel I can afford to interpret in any way I choose the terms of the bargain between myself and Westmore."

On reading this, Amherst's mind had gone through the strange dual process which now marked all his judgments of his wife. At first he had fancied he understood her, and had felt that he should have done as she did; then the usual reaction of distrust set in, and he asked himself why she, who had so little of the conventional attitude toward money, should now develop this unexpected susceptibility. And so the old question presented itself in another shape: if she had nothing to reproach herself for, why was it intolerable to her to live on Bessy's money? The fact that she was doing no actual service at Westmore did not account for her scruples—she would have been the last person to think that a sick servant should be docked of his pay. Her reluctance could come only from that hidden cause of compunction which had prompted her departure, and which now forced her to sever even the merely material links between herself and her past.

Amherst, on his return to Hanaford, had tried to find in these considerations a reason for his deep unrest. It was his wife's course which still cast a torturing doubt on what he had braced his will to accept and put behind him. And he now told himself that the perpetual galling sense of her absence was due to this uneasy consciousness of what it meant, of the dark secrets it enveloped and held back from him. In actual truth, every particle of his being missed her, he lacked her at every turn. She had been at once the partner of his task, and the *pays bleu* into which he escaped from it; the vivifying thought which gave meaning to the life he had chosen, yet never let him forget that there was a larger richer life outside, to which he was rooted by deeper and more intrinsic things than any abstract ideal of altruism. His love had preserved his identity, saved him from shrinking into the mere nameless unit which the social enthusiast is in danger of becoming unless the humanitarian passion is balanced, and a little overweighed, by a merely human one. And now this equilibrium was lost forever, and his deepest pain lay in realizing that he could not regain it, even by casting off Westmore and choosing the narrower but richer individual existence that her love might once have offered. His life was in truth one indivisible organism, not two halves artificially united. Self and other-self were ingrown from the roots—whichever portion fate restricted him to would be but a mutilated half-live fragment of the whole.

Happily for him, chance made this crisis of his life coincide with a strike at Westmore. Soon after his return to Hanaford he found himself compelled to grapple with the hardest problem of his industrial career, and he was carried through the ensuing three months on that tide of swift obligatory action that sweeps the ship-wrecked spirit over so many sunken reefs of fear and despair. The knowledge that he was better able to deal with the question than any one who might conceivably have taken his place—this conviction, which was presently confirmed by the peaceable adjustment of the strike, helped to make the sense of his immediate usefulness outbalance that other, disintegrating doubt as to the final value of such efforts. And so he tried to settle down into a kind of mechanical altruism, in which the reflexes of habit should take the place of that daily renewal of faith and enthusiasm which had been fed from the springs of his own joy.

The autumn came and passed into winter; and after Mr. Langhope's re-establishment in town Amherst began to resume his usual visits to his step-daughter.

His natural affection for the little girl had been deepened by the unforeseen manner in which her fate had been entrusted to him. The thought of Bessy, softened to compunction by the discovery that her love had persisted under their apparently hopeless estrangement—this feeling, intensified to the verge of morbidness by the circumstances attending her death, now sought expression in a passionate devotion to her child. Accident had, in short, created between Bessy and himself a retrospective sympathy which the resumption of life together would have dispelled in a week—one of the exhalations from the past that depress the vitality of those who linger too near the grave of dead experiences.

Since Justine's departure Amherst had felt himself still more drawn to Cicely; but his relation to the child was complicated by the fact that she would not be satisfied as to the cause of her step-mother's absence. Whenever Amherst came to town, her first question was for Justine; and her memory had the precocious persistence sometimes developed in children too early deprived of their natural atmosphere of affection. Cicely had always been petted and adored, at odd times and by divers people; but some instinct seemed to tell her that, of all the tenderness bestowed on her, Justine's most resembled the all-pervading motherly element in which the child's heart expands without ever being conscious of its needs.

If it had been embarrassing to evade Cicely's questions in June it became doubly so as the months passed, and the pretext of Justine's ill-health grew more and more difficult to sustain. And in the following March Amherst was suddenly called from Hanaford by the news that the little girl herself was ill. Serious complications had developed from a protracted case of scarlet fever, and for two weeks the child's fate was uncertain. Then she began to recover, and in the joy of seeing life come back to her, Mr. Langhope and Amherst felt as though they must not only gratify every wish she expressed, but try to guess at those they saw floating below the surface of her clear vague eyes.

It was noticeable to Mrs. Ansell, if not to the others, that one of these unexpressed wishes was the desire to see her stepmother. Cicely no longer asked for Justine; but something in her silence, or in the gesture with which she gently put from her other offers of diversion and companionship, suddenly struck Mrs. Ansell as more poignant than speech.

"What is it the child wants?" she asked the governess, in the course of one of their whispered consultations; and the governess, after a moment's hesitation, replied: "She said something about a letter she wrote to Mrs. Amherst just before she was taken ill—about having had no answer, I think."

"Ah—she writes to Mrs. Amherst, does she?"

The governess, evidently aware that she trod on delicate ground, tried at once to defend herself and her pupil.

"It was my fault, perhaps. I suggested once that her little compositions should take the form of letters —it usually interests a child more—and she asked if they might be written to Mrs. Amherst."

"Your fault? Why should not the child write to her step-mother?" Mrs. Ansell rejoined with studied surprise; and on the other's murmuring: "Of course —of course——" she added haughtily: "I trust the letters were sent?"

The governess floundered. "I couldn't say—but perhaps the nurse. . ."

That evening Cicely was less well. There was a slight return of fever, and the doctor, hastily summoned, hinted at the possibility of too much excitement in the sick-room.

"Excitement? There has been no excitement," Mr. Langhope protested, quivering with the sudden renewal of fear.

"No? The child seemed nervous, uneasy. It's hard to say why, because she is unusually reserved for her age."

The medical man took his departure, and Mr. Langhope and Mrs. Ansell faced each other in the disarray produced by a call to arms when all has seemed at peace.

"I shall lose her—I shall lose her!" the grandfather broke out, sinking into his chair with a groan.

Mrs. Ansell, gathering up her furs for departure, turned on him abruptly from the threshold.

"It's stupid, what you're doing—stupid!" she exclaimed with unwonted vehemence.

He raised his head with a startled look. "What do you mean—what I'm doing?"

"The child misses Justine. You ought to send for her."

Mr. Langhope's hands dropped to the arms of his chair, and he straightened himself up with a pale flash of indignation. "You've had moments lately——!"

"I've had moments, yes; and so have you—when the child came back to us, and we stood there and wondered how we could keep her, tie her fast. . . and in those moments I saw. . . saw what she wanted. . . and so did you!"

Mr. Langhope turned away his head. "You're a sentimentalist!" he flung scornfully back.

"Oh, call me any bad names you please!"

"I won't send for that woman!"

"No." She fastened her furs slowly, with the gentle deliberate movements that no emotion ever hastened or disturbed.

"Why do you say no?" he challenged her.

"To make you contradict me, perhaps," she ventured, after looking at him again.

"Ah——" He shifted his position, one elbow supporting his bowed head, his eyes fixed on the ground. Presently he brought out: "Could one ask her to come—and see the child—and go away again—for good?"

"To break the compact at your pleasure, and enter into it again for the same reason?"

"No—no—I see." He paused, and then looked up at her suddenly. "But what if Amherst won't have her back himself?"

"Shall I ask him?"

"I tell you he can't bear to hear her name!"

"But he doesn't know why she has left him."

Mr. Langhope gathered his brows in a frown. "Why—what on earth—what possible difference would that make?"

Mrs. Ansell, from the doorway, shed a pitying glance on him. "Ah—if you don't see!" she murmured.

He sank back into his seat with a groan. "Good heavens, Maria, how you torture me! I see enough as it is—I see too much of the cursed business!"

She paused again, and then slowly moved a step or two nearer, laying her hand on his shoulder.

"There's one thing you've never seen yet, Henry:

what Bessy herself would do now—for the child—if she could."

He sat motionless under her light touch, his eyes on hers, till their inmost thoughts felt for and found each other, as they still sometimes could, through the fog of years and selfishness and worldly habit; then he dropped his face into his hands, hiding it from her with the instinctive shrinking of an aged grief.

XLI

AMHERST, Cicely's convalescence once assured, had been obliged to go back to Hanaford; but some ten days later, on hearing from Mrs. Ansell that the little girl's progress was less rapid than had been hoped, he returned to his father-in-law's for a Sunday.

He came two days after the talk recorded in the last chapter—a talk of which Mrs. Ansell's letter to him had been the direct result. She had promised Mr. Langhope that, in writing to Amherst, she would not go beyond the briefest statement of fact; and she had kept her word, trusting to circumstances to speak for her.

Mrs. Ansell, during Cicely's illness, had formed the habit of dropping in on Mr. Langhope at the tea hour instead of awaiting him in her own drawing-room; and on the Sunday in question she found him alone. Beneath his pleasure in seeing her, which had grown more marked as his dependence on her increased, she at once discerned traces of recent disturbance; and her first question was for Cicely.

He met it with a discouraged gesture. "No great change—Amherst finds her less well than when he was here before."

"He's upstairs with her?"

"Yes—she seems to want him."

Mrs. Ansell seated herself in silence behind the tea-tray, of which she was now recognized as the officiating priestess. As she drew off her long gloves, and mechanically straightened the row of delicate old cups, Mr. Langhope added with an effort: "I've spoken to him—told him what you said."

She looked up quickly.

"About the child's wish," he continued. "About her having written to his wife. It seems her last letters have not been answered."

He paused, and Mrs. Ansell, with her usual calm precision, proceeded to measure the tea into the fluted Georgian tea-pot. She could be as reticent in approval as in reprehension, and not for the world would she have seemed to claim any share in the turn that events appeared to be taking. She even preferred the risk of leaving her old friend to add half-reproachfully: "I told Amherst what you and the nurse thought.'

"Yes?"

"That Cicely pines for his wife. I put it to him in black and white." The words came out on a deep strained breath, and Mrs. Ansell faltered: "Well?"

"Well—he doesn't know where she is himself."

"Doesn't *know?*"

"They're separated—utterly separated. It's as I told you: he could hardly name her."

Mrs. Ansell had unconsciously ceased her ministrations, letting her hands fall on her knee while she brooded in blank wonder on her companion's face.

"I wonder what reason she could have given him?" she murmured at length.

"For going? He loathes her, I tell you!"

"Yes—but *how did she make him?*"

He struck his hand violently on the arm of his chair. "Upon my soul, you seem to forget!"

"No." She shook her head with a half smile. "I simply remember more than you do."

"What more?" he began with a flush of anger; but she raised a quieting hand.

"What does all that matter—if, now that we need her, we can't get her?"

He made no answer, and she returned to the dispensing of his tea; but as she rose to put the cup in his hand he asked, half querulously: "You think it's going to be very bad for the child, then?"

Mrs. Ansell smiled with the thin edge of her lips. "One can hardly set the police after her——!"

"No; we're powerless," he groaned in assent.

As the cup passed between them she dropped her eyes to his with a quick flash of interrogation; but he sat staring moodily before him, and she moved back to the sofa without a word.

On the way downstairs she met Amherst descending from Cicely's room.

Since the early days of his first marriage there had always been, on Amherst's side, a sense of obscure antagonism toward Mrs. Ansell. She was almost the embodied spirit of the world he dreaded and disliked: her serenity, her tolerance, her adaptability, seemed to smile away and disintegrate all the high enthusiasms, the stubborn convictions, that he had tried to plant in the shifting sands of his married life. And now that Bessy's death had given her back the attributes with which his fancy had originally invested her, he had come to regard Mrs. Ansell as embodying the evil influences that had come between himself and his wife.

Mrs. Ansell was probably not unaware of the successive transitions of feeling which had led up to this unflattering view; but her life had been passed among petty rivalries and animosities, and she had the patience and adroitness of the spy in a hostile camp.

She and Amherst exchanged a few words about Cicely; then she exclaimed, with a glance through the panes of the hall door: "But I must be off—I'm on foot, and the crossings appal me after dark."

He could do no less, at that, than offer to guide her across the perils of Fifth Avenue; and still talking of Cicely, she led him down the thronged thoroughfare till her own corner was reached, and then her own door; turning there to ask, as if by an afterthought: "Won't you come up? There's one thing more I want to say."

A shade of reluctance crossed his face, which, as the vestibule light fell on it, looked hard and tired, like a face set obstinately against a winter gale; but he murmured a word of assent, and followed her into the shining steel cage of the lift.

In her little drawing-room, among the shaded lamps and bowls of spring flowers, she pushed a chair forward, settled herself in her usual corner of the sofa, and said with a directness that seemed an echo of his own tone: "I asked you to come up because I want to talk to you about Mr. Langhope."

Amherst looked at her in surprise. Though his father-in-law's health had been more or less unsatisfactory for the last year, all their concern, of late, had been for Cicely.

"You think him less well?" he enquired.

She waited to draw off and smooth her gloves, with

one of the deliberate gestures that served to shade and supplement her speech.

"I think him extremely unhappy."

Amherst moved uneasily in his seat. He did not know where she meant the talk to lead them, but he guessed that it would be over painful places, and he saw no reason why he should be forced to follow her.

"You mean that he's still anxious about Cicely?"

"Partly that—yes." She paused. "The child will get well, no doubt; but she is very lonely. She needs youth, heat, light. Mr. Langhope can't give her those, or even a semblance of them; and it's an art I've lost the secret of," she added with her shadowy smile.

Amherst's brows darkened. "I realize all she has lost——"

Mrs. Ansell glanced up at him quickly. "She is twice motherless," she said.

The blood rose to his neck and temples, and he tightened his hand on the arm of his chair. But it was a part of Mrs. Ansell's expertness to know when such danger signals must be heeded and when they might be ignored, and she went on quietly: "It's the question of the future that is troubling Mr. Langhope. After such an illness, the next months of Cicely's life should be all happiness. And money won't buy the kind she needs: one can't pick out the right companion for such a child as one can match a ribbon. What she wants is spontaneous affection, not the most superlative manufactured article. She wants the sort of love that Justine gave her."

It was the first time in months that Amherst had heard his wife's name spoken outside of his own house. No one but his mother mentioned Justine to him now; and of late even his mother had dropped her enquiries and allusions, prudently acquiescing in the habit of silence which his own silence had created about him. To hear the name again—the two little syllables which had been the key of life to him, and now shook him as the turning of a rusted lock shakes a long-closed door—to hear her name spoken familiarly, affectionately, as one speaks of some one who may come into the room the next moment—gave him a shock that was half pain, and half furtive unacknowledged joy. Men whose conscious thoughts are mostly projected outward, on the world of external activities, may be more moved by such a touch on the feelings than those who are perpetually testing and tuning their emotional chords. Amherst had foreseen from the first that Mrs. Ansell might mean to speak of his wife; but though he had intended, if she did so, to cut their talk short, he now felt himself irresistibly constrained to hear her out.

Mrs. Ansell, having sped her shaft, followed its flight through lowered lashes, and saw that it had struck a vulnerable point; but she was far from assuming that the day was won.

"I believe," she continued, "that Mr. Langhope has said something of this to you already, and my only excuse for speaking is that I understood he had not been successful in his appeal."

No one but Mrs. Ansell—and perhaps she knew it—could have pushed so far beyond the conventional limits of discretion without seeming to overstep them by a hair; and she had often said, when pressed for the secret of her art, that it consisted simply in knowing the pass-word. That word once spoken, she might have added, the next secret was to give the enemy no time for resistance; and though she saw the frown reappear between Amherst's eyes, she went on, without heeding it: "I entreat you, Mr. Amherst, to let Cicely see your wife."

He reddened again, and pushed back his chair, as if to rise.

"No—don't break off like that! Let me say a word more. I know your answer to Mr. Langhope—that you and Justine are no longer together. But I thought of you as a man to sink your personal relations at such a moment as this."

"To sink them?" he repeated vaguely: and she went on: "After all, what difference does it make?"

"What difference?" He stared in unmitigated wonder, and then answered, with a touch of irony: "It might at least make the difference of my being unwilling to ask a favour of her."

Mrs. Ansell, at this, raised her eyes and let them rest full on his. "Because she has done you so great a one already?"

He stared again, sinking back automatically into his chair. "I don't understand you."

"No." She smiled a little, as if to give herself time. "But I mean that you shall. If I were a man I suppose I couldn't, because a man's code of honour is such a clumsy cast-iron thing. But a woman's, luckily, can be cut over—if she's clever—to fit any new occasion; and in this case I should be willing to reduce mine to tatters if necessary."

Amherst's look of bewilderment deepened. "What is it that I don't understand?" he asked at length, in a low voice.

"Well—first of all, why Mr. Langhope had the right to ask you to send for your wife."

"The right?"

"You don't recognize such a right on his part?"

"No—why should I?"

"Supposing she had left you by his wish?"

"His wish? *His*——?"

He was on his feet now, gazing at her blindly, while the solid world seemed to grow thin about him. Her next words reduced it to a mist.

"My poor Amherst—why else, on earth, should she have left you?"

She brought it out clearly, in her small chiming tones; and as the sound travelled toward him it seemed to gather momentum, till her words rang through his brain as if every incomprehensible incident in the past had suddenly boomed forth the question. Why else, indeed, should she have left him? He stood motionless for a while; then he approached Mrs. Ansell and said: "Tell me."

She drew farther back into her corner of the sofa, waving him to a seat beside her, as though to bring his inquisitory eyes on a level where her own could command them; but he stood where he was, unconscious of her gesture, and merely repeating: "Tell me."

She may have said to herself that a woman would have needed no farther telling; but to him she only replied, slanting her head up to his: "To spare you and himself pain—to keep everything, between himself and you, as it had been before you married her."

He dropped down beside her at that, grasping the back of the sofa as if he wanted something to clutch and throttle. The veins swelled in his temples, and as he pushed back his tossed hair Mrs. Ansell noticed for the first time how gray it had grown on the under side.

"And he asked this of my wife—he accepted it?'"

"Haven't *you* accepted it?"

"I? How could I guess her reasons—how could I imagine——?"

Mrs. Ansell raised her brows a hair's breadth at that. "I don't know. But as a fact, he didn't ask—it was she who offered, who forced it on him, even!"

"Forced her going on him?"

"In a sense, yes; by making it appear that *you* felt as he did about—about poor Bessy's death: that the thought of what had happened at that time was as abhorrent to you as to him—that *she* was as abhorrent to you. No doubt she foresaw that, had she permitted the least doubt on that point, there would have been no need of her leaving you, since the relation between yourself and Mr. Langhope would have been altered—destroyed. . ."

"Yes. I expected that—I warned her of it. But how did she make him think——?"

"How can I tell? To begin with, I don't know your real feeling. For all I know she was telling the truth—and Mr. Langhope of course thought she was."

"That I abhorred her? Oh——" he broke out, on his feet in an instant.

"Then why——?"

"Why did I let her leave me?" He strode across the room, as his habit was in moments of agitation, turning back to her again before he answered. "Because I *didn't* know—didn't know anything! And because her insisting on going away like that, without any explanation, made me feel. . . imagine there was. . . something she didn't *want* me to know. . . something she was afraid of not being able to hide from me if we stayed together any longer."

"Well—there was: the extent to which she loved you."

Mrs. Ansell, her hands clasped on her knee, her gaze holding his with a kind of visionary fixity, seemed to reconstruct the history of his past, bit by bit, with the words she was dragging out of him.

"I see it—I see it all now," she went on, with a repressed fervour that he had never divined in her. "It was the only solution for her, as well as for the rest of you. The more she showed her love, the more it would have cast a doubt on her motive. . . the greater distance she would have put between herself and you. And so she showed it in the only way that was safe for both of you, by taking herself away and hiding it in her heart; and before going, she secured your peace of mind, your future. If she ruined anything, she rebuilt the ruin. Oh, she paid—she paid in full!"

Justine had paid, yes—paid to the utmost limit of whatever debt toward society she had contracted by overstepping its laws. And her resolve to discharge the debt had been taken in a flash, as soon as she had seen that man can commit no act alone, whether for good or evil. The extent to which Amherst's fate was involved in hers had become clear to her with his first word of reassurance, of faith in her motive. And instantly a plan for releasing him had leapt full-formed into her mind, and had been carried out with swift unflinching resolution. As he forced himself, now, to look down the suddenly illuminated past to the weeks which had elapsed between her visit to Mr. Langhope and her departure from Hanaford, he wondered not so much at her swiftness of resolve as at her firmness in carrying out her plan—and he saw, with a blinding flash of insight, that it was in her love for him that she had found her strength.

In all moments of strong mental tension he became totally unconscious of time and place, and he now remained silent so long, his hands clasped behind him, his eyes fixed on an indeterminate point in space, that Mrs. Ansell at length rose and laid a questioning touch on his arm.

"It's not true that you don't know where she is?"

His face contracted. "At this moment I don't. Lately she has preferred. . . not to write. . ."

"But surely you must know how to find her?"

He tossed back his hair with an energetic movement. "I should find her if I didn't know how!"

They stood confronted in a gaze of silent intensity, each penetrating farther into the mind of the other than would once have seemed possible to either one; then Amherst held out his hand abruptly. "Good-bye —and thank you," he said.

She detained him a moment. "We shall see you soon again—see you both?"

His face grew stern. "It's not to oblige Mr. Langhope that I am going to find my wife."

"Ah, now you are unjust to him!" she exclaimed.

"Don't let us speak of him!" he broke in.

"Why not? When it is from him the request comes —the entreaty—that everything in the past should be forgotten?"

"Yes—when it suits his convenience!"

"Do you imagine that—even judging him in that way—it has not cost him a struggle?"

"I can only think of what it has cost her!"

Mrs. Ansell drew a deep sighing breath. "Ah— but don't you see that she has gained her point, and that nothing else matters to her?"

"Gained her point? Not if, by that, you mean that things here can ever go back to the old state —that she and I can remain at Westmore after this!"

Mrs. Ansell dropped her eyes for a moment; then she lifted to his her sweet impenetrable face.

"Do you know what you have to do—both you and he? Exactly what she decides," she affirmed

XLII

JUSTINE'S answer to her husband's letter bore a New York address; and the surprise of finding her in the same town with himself, and not half an hour's walk from the room in which he sat, was so great that it seemed to demand some sudden and violent outlet of physical movement.

He thrust the letter in his pocket, took up his hat, and leaving the house, strode up Fifth Avenue toward the Park in the early spring sunlight.

The news had taken five days to reach him, for in order to reestablish communication with his wife he had been obliged to write to Michigan, with the request that his letter should be forwarded. He had never supposed that Justine would be hard to find, or that she had purposely enveloped her movements in mystery. When she ceased to write he had simply concluded that, like himself, she felt the mockery of trying to keep up a sort of distant, semi-fraternal relation, marked by the occasional interchange of inexpressive letters. The inextricable mingling of thought and sensation which made the peculiar closeness of their union could never, to such direct and passionate natures, be replaced by the pretense of a temperate friendship. Feeling thus himself, and instinctively assuming the same feeling in his wife, Amherst had respected her silence, her wish to break definitely with their former life. She had written him, in the autumn, that she intended to leave Michigan for a few months, but that, in any emergency, a letter addressed to her friend's house would reach her; and he had taken this as meaning that, unless the emergency arose, she preferred that their correspondence should cease. Acquiescence was all the easier because it accorded with his own desire. It seemed to him, as he looked back, that the love he and Justine had felt for each other was like some rare organism which could maintain life only in its special element; and that element was neither passion nor sentiment, but truth. It was only on the heights that they could breathe.

Some men, in his place, even while accepting the inevitableness of the moral rupture, would have felt concerned for the material side of the case. But it was characteristic of Amherst that this did not trouble him. He took it for granted that his wife would return to her nursing. From the first he had felt certain that it would be intolerable to her to accept aid from him, and that she would choose rather to support herself by the exercise of her regular profession; and, aside from such motives, he, who had always turned to hard work as the surest refuge from personal misery, thought it natural that she should seek the same means of escape.

He had therefore not been surprised, on opening her

letter that morning, to learn that she had taken up her hospital work; but in the amazement of finding her so near he hardly grasped her explanation of the coincidence. There was something about a Buffalo patient suddenly ordered to New York for special treatment, and refusing to go in with a new nurse—but these details made no impression on his mind, which had only room for the fact that chance had brought his wife back at the very moment when his whole being yearned for her.

She wrote that, owing to her duties, she would be unable to see him till three that afternoon; and he had still six hours to consume before their meeting. But in spirit they had met already—they were one in an intensity of communion which, as he strode northward along the bright crowded thoroughfare, seemed to gather up the whole world into one throbbing point of life.

He had a boyish wish to keep the secret of his happiness to himself, not to let Mr. Langhope or Mrs. Ansell know of his meeting with Justine till it was over; and after twice measuring the length of the Park he turned in at one of the little wooden restaurants which were beginning to unshutter themselves in anticipation of spring custom. If only he could have seen Justine that morning! If he could have brought her there, and they could have sat opposite each other, in the bare empty room, with sparrows bustling and twittering in the lilacs against the open window! The room was ugly enough—but how she would have delighted in the delicate green of the near slopes, and the purplish haze of the woods beyond! She took a childish pleasure in such small adventures, and had the knack of giving a touch of magic to their most commonplace details. Amherst, as he finished his cold beef and indifferent eggs, found himself boyishly planning to bring her back there the next day. . .

Then, over the coffee, he re-read her letter.

The address she gave was that of a small private hospital, and she explained that she would have to receive him in the public parlour, which at that hour was open to other visitors. As the time approached, the thought that they might not be alone when they met became insufferable; and he determined, if he found any one else in possession of the parlour, to wait in the hall, and meet her as she came down the stairs.

He continued to elaborate this plan as he walked back slowly through the Park, He had timed himself to reach the hospital a little before three; but though it lacked five minutes to the hour when he entered the parlour, two women were already seated in one of its windows. They looked around as he came in, evidently as much annoyed by his appearance as he had been to find them there. The older of the two showed a sallow middle-aged face beneath her limp crape veil; the other was a slight tawdry creature, with nodding feathers, and innumerable chains and bracelets which she fingered ceaselessly as she talked.

They eyed Amherst with resentment, and then turned away, continuing their talk in low murmurs, while he seated himself at the marble-topped table littered with torn magazines. Now and then the younger woman's voice rose in a shrill staccato, and a phrase or two floated over to him. "She'd simply worked herself to death—the nurse told me so. . . She expects to go home in another week, though how she's going to stand the *fatigue*——" and then, after an inaudible answer: "It's all *his* fault, and if I was her I wouldn't go back to him for anything!"

"Oh, Cora, he's real sorry now," the older woman protestingly murmured; but the other, unappeased, rejoined with ominously nodding plumes: "*You* see—if they do make it up, it'll never be the same between them!"

Amherst started up nervously, and as he did so the clock struck three, and he opened the door and passed out into the hall. It was paved with black and white marble; the walls were washed in a dull yellowish tint, and the prevalent odour of antiseptics was mingled with a stale smell of cooking. At the back rose a straight staircase carpeted with brass-bound India-rubber, like a ship's companion-way; and down that staircase she would come in a moment—he fancied he heard her step now. . .

But the step was that of an elderly black-gowned woman in a cap—the matron probably.

She glanced at Amherst in surprise, and asked: "Are you waiting for some one?"

He made a motion of assent, and she opened the parlour door, saying: "Please walk in."

"May I not wait out here?" he urged.

She looked at him more attentively. "Why, no, I'm afraid not. You'll find the papers and magazines in here."

Mildly but firmly she drove him in before her, and closing the door, advanced to the two women in the window. Amherst's hopes leapt up: perhaps she had come to fetch the visitors upstairs! He strained his ears to catch what was being said, and while he was thus absorbed the door opened, and turning at the sound he found himself face to face with his wife.

He had not reflected that Justine would be in her nurse's dress; and the sight of the dark blue uniform and small white cap, in which he had never seen her since their first meeting in the Hope Hospital, obliterated all bitter and unhappy memories, and gave him the illusion of passing back at once into the clear air of their early friendship. Then he looked at her and remembered.

He noticed that she had grown thinner than ever or rather that her thinness, which had formerly had a healthy reed-like strength, now suggested fatigue and languor. And her face was spent, extinguished—the very eyes were lifeless. All her vitality seemed to have withdrawn itself into the arch of dense black hair which still clasped her forehead like the noble metal of some antique bust.

The sight stirred him with a deeper pity, a more vehement compunction; but the impulse to snatch her to him, and seek his pardon on her lips, was paralyzed by the sense that the three women in the window had stopped talking and turned their heads toward the door.

He held his hand out, and Justine's touched it for a moment; then he said in a low voice: "Is there no other place where I can see you?"

She made a negative gesture. "I am afraid not to-day."

Ah, her deep sweet voice—how completely his ear had lost the sound of it!

She looked doubtfully about the room, and pointed to a sofa at the end farthest from the windows.

"Shall we sit there?" she said.

He followed her in silence, and they sat down side by side. The matron had drawn up a chair and resumed her whispered conference with the women in the window. Between the two groups stretched the bare length of the room, broken only by a few arm-chairs of stained wood, and the marble-topped table covered with magazines.

The impossibility of giving free rein to his feelings developed in Amherst an unwonted intensity of perception, as though a sixth sense had suddenly emerged to take the place of those he could not use. And with this new-made faculty he seemed to gather up, and absorb into himself, as he had never done in their hours of closest communion, every detail of his wife's person, of her face and hands and gestures. He noticed how her full upper lids, of the tint of yellowish ivory, had a slight bluish discolouration, and how little thread-like blue veins ran across her temples to the roots of her hair. The emaciation of her face, and the hollow shades beneath her cheek-bones, made her mouth seem redder and fuller, though a little line on each side, where it joined the cheek, gave it a tragic droop. And her hands! When her fingers met his he recalled having once picked up, in the winter woods, the little feather-light skeleton of a frozen bird—and that was what her touch was like.

And it was he who had brought her to this by his cruelty, his obtuseness, his base readiness to believe the worst of her! He did not want to pour himself out in self-accusation—that seemed too easy a way of escape. He wanted simply to take her in his arms, to ask her to give him one more chance—and then to show her! And all the while he was paralyzed by the group in the window.

"Can't we go out? I must speak to you," he began again nervously.

"Not this afternoon—the doctor is coming. To-morrow——"

"I can't wait for tomorrow!"

She made a faint, imperceptible gesture, which read to his eyes: "You've waited a whole year."

"Yes, I know," he returned, still constrained by the necessity of muffling his voice, of perpetually measuring the distance between themselves and the window. "I know what you might say—don't you suppose I've said it to myself a million times? But I didn't know—I couldn't imagine——"

She interrupted him with a rapid movement. "What do you know now?"

"What you promised Langhope——"

She turned her startled eyes on him, and he saw the blood run flame-like under her skin. "But *he* promised not to speak!" she cried.

"He hasn't—to me. But such things make themselves known. Should you have been content to go on in that way forever?"

She raised her head and her eyes rested in his. "If you were," she answered simply.

"Justine!"

Again she checked him with a silencing motion. "Please tell me just what has happened."

"Not now—there's too much else to say. And nothing matters except that I'm with you."

"But Mr. Langhope——"

"He asks you to come. You're to see Cicely to-morrow."

Her lower lip trembled a little, and a tear flowed over and hung on her lashes.

"But what does all that matter now? We're together after this horrible year," he insisted.

She looked at him again. "But what is really changed?"

"Everything—everything! Not changed, I mean—just gone back."

"To where. . . we were. . . before?" she whispered; and he whispered back: "To where we were before."

There was a scraping of chairs on the floor, and with a sense of release Amherst saw that the colloquy in the window was over.

The two visitors, gathering their wraps about them, moved slowly across the room, still talking to the matron in excited undertones, through which, as they neared the threshold, the younger woman's staccato again broke out.

"I tell you, if she does go back to him, it'll never be the same between them!"

"Oh, Cora, I wouldn't say that," the other ineffectually wailed; then they moved toward the door, and a moment later it had closed on them.

Amherst turned to his wife with outstretched arms. "Say you forgive me, Justine!"

She held back a little from his entreating hands, not reproachfully, but as if with a last scruple for himself.

"There's nothing left. . . of the horror?" she asked below her breath.

"To be without you—that's the only horror!"

"You're *sure*——?"

"Sure!"

"It's just the same to you. . . just as it was. . . before?"

"Just the same, Justine!"

"It's not for myself, but you."

"Then, for me—never speak of it!" he implored.

"Because it's *not* the same, then?" leapt from her.

"Because it's wiped out—because it's never been!"

"Never?"

"Never!"

He felt her yield to him at that, and under his eyes, close under his lips, was her face at last. But as they kissed they heard the handle of the door turn, and drew apart quickly, her hand lingering in his under the fold of her dress.

A nurse looked in, dressed in the white uniform and pointed cap of the hospital. Amherst fancied that she smiled a little as she saw them.

"Miss Brent—the doctor wants you to come right up and give the morphine."

The door shut again as Justine rose to her feet. Amherst remained seated—he had made no motion to retain her hand as it slipped from him.

"I'm coming," she called out to the retreating nurse; then she turned slowly and saw her husband's face.

"I must go," she said in a low tone.

Her eyes met his for a moment; but he looked away again as he stood up and reached for his hat.

"Tomorrow, then——" he said, without attempting to detain her.

"Tomorrow?"

"You must come away from here—you must come home," he repeated mechanically.

She made no answer, and he held his hand out and took hers. "Tomorrow," he said, drawing her toward him; and their lips met again, but not in the same kiss.

XLIII

JUNE again at Hanaford—and Cicely's birthday.

The anniversary was to coincide, this year, with the opening of the old house at Hopewood, as a kind of pleasure-palace—gymnasium, concert-hall and museum —for the recreation of the mill-hands.

The idea had first come to Amherst on the winter afternoon when Bessy Westmore had confessed her love for him under the snow-laden trees of Hopewood. Even then the sense that his personal happiness was enlarged and secured by its promise of happiness to others had made him wish that the scene associated with the opening of his new life should be made to commemorate a corresponding change in the fortunes of Westmore. But when the control of the mills passed into his hands other and more necessary improvements pressed upon him; and it was not till now that the financial condition of the company had permitted the execution of his plan.

Justine, on her return to Hanaford, had found the work already in progress, and had been told by her husband that he was carrying out a projected scheme of Bessy's. She had felt a certain surprise, but had concluded that the plan in question dated back to the early days of his first marriage, when, in his wife's eyes, his connection with the mills still invested them with interest.

Since Justine had come back to her husband, both had tacitly avoided all allusions to the past, and the recreation-house at Hopewood being, as she divined, in some sort an expiatory offering to Bessy's plaintive shade, she had purposely refrained from questioning Amherst about its progress, and had simply approved the plans he submitted to her.

Fourteen months had passed since her return, and now, as she sat beside her husband in the carriage which was conveying them to Hopewood, she said to herself that her life had at last fallen into what promised to be its final shape—that as things now were they would probably be to the end. And outwardly at least they were what she and Amherst had always dreamed of their being. Westmore prospered under the new rule. The seeds of life they had sown there were springing up in a promising growth of bodily health and mental activity, and above all in a dawning social consciousness. The mill-hands were beginning to understand the meaning of their work, in its relation to their own lives and to the larger economy. And outwardly, also, the new growth was showing itself in the humanized aspect of the place. Amherst's young maples were tall enough now to cast a shade on the grass-bordered streets; and the well-kept turf, the bright cottage gardens, the new central group of library, hospital and club-house, gave to the mill-village the hopeful air of a "rising" residential suburb.

In the bright June light, behind their fresh green mantle of trees and creepers, even the factory buildings looked less stern and prison-like than formerly; and the turfing and planting of the adjoining river-banks had transformed a waste of foul mud and refuse into a little park where the operatives might refresh themselves at midday.

Yes—Westmore was alive at last: the dead city of which Justine had once spoken had risen from its grave, and its blank face had taken on a meaning. As Justine glanced at her husband she saw that the same thought was in his mind. However achieved, at whatever cost of personal misery and error, the work of awakening and freeing Westmore was done, and that work had justified itself.

She looked from Amherst to Cicely, who sat opposite, eager and rosy in her mourning frock—for Mr. Langhope had died some two months previously—and as intent as her step-parents on the scene before her. Cicely was old enough now to regard her connection with Westmore as something more than a nursery game. She was beginning to learn a great deal about the mills, and to understand, in simple, friendly ways, something of her own relation to them. The work and play of the children, the interests and relaxations provided for their elders, had been gradually explained to her by Justine, and she knew that this shining tenth birthday of hers was to throw its light as far as the clouds of factory-smoke extended.

As they mounted the slope to Hopewood, the spacious

white building, with its enfolding colonnades, its broad terraces and tennis-courts, shone through the trees like some bright country-house adorned for its master's home-coming; and Amherst and his wife might have been driving up to the house which had been built to shelter their wedded happiness. The thought flashed across Justine as their carriage climbed the hill. She was as much absorbed as Amherst in the welfare of Westmore, it had become more and more, to both, the refuge in which their lives still met and mingled; but for a moment, as they paused before the flower-decked porch, and he turned to help her from the carriage, it occurred to her to wonder what her sensations would have been if he had been bringing her home—to a real home of their own—instead of accompanying her to another philanthropic celebration. But what need had they of a real home, when they no longer had any real life of their own? Nothing was left of that secret inner union which had so enriched and beautified their outward lives. Since Justine's return to Hanaford they had entered, tacitly, almost unconsciously, into a new relation to each other: a relation in which their personalities were more and more merged in their common work, so that, as it were, they met only by avoiding each other.

From the first, Justine had accepted this as inevitable; just as she had understood, when Amherst had sought her out in New York, that his remaining at Westmore, which had once been contingent on her leaving him, now depended on her willingness to return and take up their former life.

She accepted the last condition as she had accepted the other, pledged to the perpetual expiation of an act for which, in the abstract, she still refused to hold herself to blame. But life is not a matter of abstract principles, but a succession of pitiful compromises with fate, of concessions to old tradition, old beliefs, old charities and frailties. That was what her act had taught her—that was the word of the gods to the mortal who had laid a hand on their bolts. And she had humbled herself to accept the lesson, seeing human relations at last as a tangled and deep-rooted growth, a dark forest through which the idealist cannot cut his straight path without hearing at each stroke the cry of the severed branch: "*Why woundest thou me?*"

The lawns leading up to the house were already sprinkled with holiday-makers, while along the avenue came the rolling of wheels, the throb of motor-cars; and Justine, with Cicely beside her, stood in the wide hall to receive the incoming throng, in which Hanaford society was indiscriminately mingled with the operatives in their Sunday best.

While his wife welcomed the new arrivals, Amherst,

supported by some young Westmore cousins, was guid ing them into the concert-hall, where he was to say a word on the uses of the building before declaring it open for inspection. And presently Justine and Cicely, summoned by Westy Gaines, made their way through the rows of seats to a corner near the platform. Her husband was there already, with Halford Gaines and a group of Hanaford dignitaries, and just below them sat Mrs. Gaines and her daughters, the Harry Dressels, and Amherst's radiant mother.

As Justine passed between them, she wondered how much they knew of the events which had wrought so profound and permanent change in her life. She had never known how Hanaford explained her absence or what comments it had made on her return. But she saw to-day more clearly than ever that Amherst had become a power among his townsmen, and that if they were still blind to the inner meaning of his work, its practical results were beginning to impress them profoundly. Hanaford's sociological creed was largely based on commercial considerations, and Amherst had won Hanaford's esteem by the novel feat of defying its economic principles and snatching success out of his defiance.

And now he had advanced a step or two in front of the "representative" semi-circle on the platform, and was beginning to speak.

Justine did not hear his first words. She was looking up at him, trying to see him with the eyes of the crowd, and wondering what manner of man he would have seemed to her if she had known as little as they did of his inner history.

He held himself straight, the heavy locks thrown back from his forehead, one hand resting on the table beside him, the other grasping a folded blue-print which the architect of the building had just advanced to give him. As he stood there, Justine recalled her first sight of him in the Hope Hospital, five years earlier—was it only five years? They had dealt deep strokes to his face, hollowing the eye-sockets, accentuating the strong modelling of nose and chin, fixing the lines between the brows; but every touch had a meaning—it was not the languid hand of time which had remade his features, but the sharp chisel of thought and action.

She roused herself suddenly to the consciousness of what he was saying.

"For the idea of this building—of a building dedicated to the recreation of Westmore—is not new in my mind; but while it remained there as a mere idea, it had already, without my knowledge, taken definite shape in the thoughts of the owner of Westmore."

There was a slight drop in his voice as he designated Bessy, and he waited a moment before continuing: "It was not till after the death of my first wife that I learned of her intention—that I found by accident, among her papers, this carefully-studied plan for a pleasure-house at Hopewood."

He paused again, and unrolling the blue-print, held it up before his audience.

"You cannot, at this distance," he went on, "see all the admirable details of her plan; see how beautifully they were imagined, how carefully and intelligently elaborated. She who conceived them longed to see beauty everywhere—it was her dearest wish to bestow it on her people here. And her ardent imagination outran the bounds of practical possibility. We cannot give you, in its completeness, the beautiful thing she had imagined—the great terraces, the marble porches, the fountains, lily-tanks, and cloisters. But you will see that, wherever it was possible—though in humbler materials, and on a smaller scale—we have faithfully followed her design; and when presently you go through this building, and when, hereafter, you find health and refreshment and diversion here, I ask you to remember the beauty she dreamed of giving you, and to let the thought of it make her memory beautiful among you and among your children. . ."

Justine had listened with deepening amazement. She was seated so close to her husband that she had recognized the blue-print the moment he unrolled it. There was no mistaking its origin—it was simply the plan of the gymnasium which Bessy had intended to build at Lynbrook, and which she had been constrained to abandon owing to her husband's increased expenditure at the mills. But how was it possible that Amherst knew nothing of the original purpose of the plans, and by what mocking turn of events had a project devised in deliberate defiance of his wishes, and intended to declare his wife's open contempt for them, been transformed into a Utopian vision for the betterment of the Westmore operatives?

A wave of anger swept over Justine at this last derisive stroke of fate. It was grotesque and pitiable that a man like Amherst should create out of his regrets a being who had never existed, and then ascribe to her feelings and actions of which the real woman had again and again proved herself incapable!

Ah, no, Justine had suffered enough—but to have this imaginary Bessy called from the grave, dressed in a semblance of self-devotion and idealism, to see her petty impulses of vindictiveness disguised as the motions of a lofty spirit—it was as though her small malicious ghost had devised this way of punishing the wife who had taken her place!

Justine had suffered enough—suffered deliberately and unstintingly, paying the full price of her error, not seeking to evade its least consequence. But no sane judgment could ask her to sit quiet under this last hallucination. What! This unreal woman, this phantom that Amherst's uneasy imagination had evoked, was to come between himself and her, to supplant her first as his wife, and then as his fellow-worker? Why should she not cry out the truth to him, defend herself against the dead who came back to rob her of such wedded peace as was hers? She had only to tell the true story of the plans to lay poor Bessy's ghost forever!

The confused throbbing impulses within her were stifled under a long burst of applause—then she saw Westy Gaines at her side again, and understood that he had come to lead Cicely to the platform. For a moment she clung jealously to the child's hand, hardly aware of what she did, feeling only that she was being thrust farther and farther into the background of the life she had helped to call out of chaos. Then a contrary impulse moved her. She gently freed Cicely's hand, and a moment later, as she sat with bent head and throbbing breast, she heard the child's treble piping out above her:

"In my mother's name, I give this house to Westmore."

Applause again—and then Justine found herself enveloped in a general murmur of compliment and congratulation. Mr. Amherst had spoken admirably—a "beautiful tribute—" ah, he had done poor Bessy justice! And to think that till now Hanaford had never fully known how she had the welfare of the mills at heart—how it was really only *her* work that he was carrying on there! Well, he had made that perfectly clear—and no doubt Cicely was being taught to follow in her mother's footsteps: everyone had noticed how her step-father was associating her with the work at the mills. And his little speech would, as it were, consecrate the child's relation to that work, make it appear to her as the continuance of a beautiful, a sacred tradition. . .

And now it was over. The building had been inspected, the operatives had dispersed, the Hanaford company had rolled off down the avenue, Cicely, among them, driving away tired and happy in Mrs. Dressel's victoria, and Amherst and his wife were alone.

Amherst, after bidding good-bye to his last guests, had gone back to the empty concert-room to fetch the blue-print lying on the platform. He came back with it, between the uneven rows of empty chairs, and joined Justine, who stood waiting in the hall. His face was slightly flushed, and his eyes had the light which in happy moments burned through their veil of thought.

He laid his hand on his wife's arm, and drawing her toward a table spread out the blueprint before her.

"You haven't seen this, have you?" he said.

She looked down at the plan without answering, reading in the left-hand corner the architect's conventional inscription: "Swimming-tank and gymnasium designed for Mrs. John Amherst."

Amherst looked up, perhaps struck by her silence.

"But perhaps you *have* seen it—at Lynbrook? It must have been done while you were there."

The quickened throb of her blood rushed to her brain like a signal. "Speak—speak now!" the signal commanded.

Justine continued to look fixedly at the plan. "Yes, I have seen it," she said at length.

"At Lynbrook?"

"At Lynbrook."

"*She* showed it to you, I suppose—while I was away?"

Justine hesitated again. "Yes, while you were away."

"And did she tell you anything about it, go into details about her wishes, her intentions?"

Now was the moment—now! As her lips parted she looked up at her husband. The illumination still lingered on his face—and it was the face she loved. He was waiting eagerly for her next word.

"No, I heard no details. I merely saw the plan lying there."

She saw his look of disappointment. "She never told you about it?"

"No—she never told me."

It was best so, after all. She understood that now. It was now at last that she was paying her full price.

Amherst rolled up the plan with a sigh and pushed it into the drawer of the table. It struck her that he too had the look of one who has laid a ghost. He turned to her and drew her hand through his arm.

"You're tired, dear. You ought to have driven back with the others," he said.

"No, I would rather stay with you."

"You want to drain this good day to the dregs, as I do?"

"Yes," she murmured, drawing her hand away.

"It *is* a good day, isn't it?" he continued, looking about him at the white-panelled walls, the vista of large bright rooms seen through the folding doors. "I feel as if we had reached a height, somehow—a height where one might pause and draw breath for the next climb. Don't you feel that too, Justine?"

"Yes—I feel it."

"Do you remember once, long ago—one day when you and I and Cicely went on a picnic to hunt orchids—how we got talking of the one best moment in life—the moment when one wanted most to stop the clock?"

The colour rose in her face while he spoke. It was a long time since he had referred to the early days of their friendship—the days *before*. . .

"Yes, I remember," she said.

"And do you remember how we said that it was with most of us as it was with Faust? That the moment one wanted to hold fast to was not, in most lives, the moment of keenest personal happiness, but the other kind—the kind that would have seemed grey and colourless at first: the moment when the meaning of life began to come out from the mists—when one could look out at last over the marsh one had drained?"

A tremor ran through Justine. "It was you who said that," she said, half-smiling.

"But didn't you feel it with me? Don't you now?"

"Yes—I do now," she murmured.

He came close to her, and taking her hands in his, kissed them one after the other.

"Dear," he said, "let us go out and look at the marsh we have drained."

He turned and led her through the open doorway to the terrace above the river. The sun was setting behind the wooded slopes of Hopewood, and the trees about the house stretched long blue shadows across the lawn. Beyond them rose the smoke of Westmore.